stepdog

stepdog

NICOLE GALLAND

WM
WILLIAM MORROW
An Imprint of HarperCollins*Publishers*

P.S.™ is a trademark of HarperCollins Publishers.

STEPDOG. Copyright © 2015 by Nicole Galland. All rights reserved. Printed in the United States of America. No part of this book may be used or reproduced in any manner whatsoever without written permission except in the case of brief quotations embodied in critical articles and reviews. For information address HarperCollins Publishers, 195 Broadway, New York, NY 10007.

HarperCollins books may be purchased for educational, business, or sales promotional use. For information please e-mail the Special Markets Department at SPsales@harpercollins.com.

FIRST EDITION

Designed by Diahann Sturge

Photograph on title page and part openers by © greg801 via iStock.com
Golden Retriever Dog Photograph on title page and part openers by © Mikkel Bigandt via Shutterstock, Inc.

Library of Congress Cataloging-in-Publication Data has been applied for.

ISBN 978-0-06-236947-5

15 16 17 18 19 OV/RRD 10 9 8 7 6 5 4 3 2 1

For "blended families" everywhere

stepdog

Part One

Chapter 1

So there I was in peril of my life because, at the end of the work-day eight months earlier, my lovely brunette boss sacked me (not my fault, I'm great at what I do—it was the funding) and I'd panicked, same as that. I read in the *Boston Globe* horoscopes that Aries people are supposed to be impulsive and maybe there is something to that, because before I knew it, sitting across Sara's little cubicle from her on that stupid little plastic chair with hollow metal legs, I'd grabbed her and was kissing that beautiful face, rather than just saying something reasonable like, "But, Sara, if you sack me, I'll miss seeing you every day."

It was an *amazing* kiss—she had *gorgeous* lips—but then it was over, and I pulled away and saw her startled green eyes and realized what I'd just done, and I was mortified. "Jesus, I'm sorry, Sara," I said. "I'm so sorry, I don't know what got into me."

Her eyes were practically popping out of her head, and for a moment I thought she would slap me. But she burst out laughing. Took it really well. Especially because then she rolled her chair closer, moved her face in close to mine, and her gaze moved back and forth between my eyes and my mouth, and then fuck me if *she* didn't kiss *me*. So then I kissed her and then she kissed me and then I kissed her and then we slid right off our chairs onto the industrial carpet.

"Goodness." She grinned. "I didn't see *this* coming. I should have fired you sooner."

"I wish you had," I said heartily. "I'd much rather be snogging the prettiest bird in Boston than fiddling Ravel for a bunch of tossers looking at oil paintings." She burst out laughing again, charmed by my Irish eloquence.

So on the heels of *that*—which honestly took me by surprise no less than her—we obviously had to leave the museum together and figure out what the hell had just happened. I'm not sure which of us even suggested it.

Well, I suppose, it must have been me, as I'm usually the one does all the talking.

It was about the last thing I ever would have expected an hour earlier, but there I was nearly skipping up the employees' exit ramp, next to a gorgeous short-haired brunette with teasing green eyes. I knew those eyes so well. They were my friend Sara's eyes, my boss's eyes. I'd always loved their beauty, but somehow now all of a sudden I was *mesmerized* by them. I was so giddy and in that kind of humor that I left my fiddle behind in her cubicle and didn't even notice. She slipped off her suit jacket and tucked it under her arm—and suddenly her outfit was no more than a green linen sundress. Sacking aside, the day just kept getting better.

We strolled through a warm evening breeze past the grand façade of the museum down Huntington Avenue, unspeaking in our mutual delighted shock. We should have been talking about *why* the funding ran out for the Guest Artist program, or was it possible to find *another* funding source, or *something* related to why I had just been let go, but I was too giddy—all I could focus on was that I'd just kissed the most fantastically gorgeous woman who had been hiding in plain sight right in front of me for months, and—far more amazing—she'd kissed me back. What had been a warm, playful friendship shifted, all of a sudden, without explanation, to . . . something else. Like a door had suddenly opened and—*bang!*—we got to invent whatever was waiting on the other side. I felt tickling in my lower ribs, and under my feet, and down the back of my neck. Like a starting pistol was about to go off for a race I knew I could win. Where had this even *come* from?

Oh Jesus, had I just been saying all of that out loud? Or had I maybe not been saying anything at all? Better say something normal and mundane, I decided, just to make sure this isn't a dream.

"I'm starving," I said.

"Let's eat," she said quickly. Decisive. I liked that about her.

"Italian?"

"Twist my arm," she said.

I was going out to dinner with Sara Renault! I couldn't wait to tell my mate Danny, he'd met her once and said all kinds of improper things about her sexy backside—he wouldn't be saying them anymore. Not to my face, anyway.

We realized that we had floated down Huntington halfway to Copley Square, before we thought to actually stop in front of a restaurant, which happened to be a little Italian bistro called Napoli. Despite being named after (my *favorite*) Italian football team, it looked romantic—amber walls, candlelight, intimate tables, the atmospheric clacking of the Green Line trains through the open window.

"Here?" I said, peeling my eyes off her. She nodded, looking as dazed as I felt.

"Just give me a sec," she said, suddenly reaching into her purse for her phone. I tried not to stare as she thumb-typed a message with amazing speed and sent it off.

"Pretty good text-erity you've got there," I said.

She rolled her eyes. "At least you won't be underfoot making those awful puns anymore," she said, and added, "I just had to ask my neighbor to feed the dog."

If I'd been paying more attention, that moment would have held portents for me. But I was never one for portents. Leave portents to the Hamlets of the world; I was more of a Laertes, quick on the draw, slow to reflect, and if you think that's foolish, even Samuel Beckett said dancing first and thinking later is the natural order. So there. But back to our story.

Everything about the place—about existence, in that moment—was magical, perfect. The late-afternoon amber light at that perfectly photographable angle, the soft summer breeze, the scents of Mediterranean spices wafting out from the kitchen. A host, dark-haired and sharp-looking, was standing at attention at the door, and seeing us linger, he welcomed us, gestured us in. He looked so pleased to see us I wondered if he owned the place. (I noticed he gave Sara the eye—subtly. Naturally he had to, since he was Italian and she was beautiful.)

He escorted us to a little table by the window, and then sent over the waiter, also pretty sharp-looking, who introduced himself as Mario and pulled out his pad.

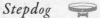

"And would you like something to drink on this lovely evening?" he asked with a whisper of an Italian accent.

"I'd like a burgundy, if you have one," said Sara.

"We have only Italian wines, but if you like burgundy, I recommend a Barbaresco." She nodded, and he jotted it down. "And you, sir?"

I supposed if he was Italian, he knew his football. "Are you a Napoli fan?" I asked him.

He froze, pen on pad, grinned briefly as he realized what kind of bloke he was serving, and then frowned to cover it. Sara glanced between us, uncertainly. "No, no," he said firmly. "That's the owner's team. I'm for A.C. Milan. Of course."

"A.C. Milan? Ah, yeah. Pickin' the club with all the money?"

He focused intently on his pad, but a twitch in his lip let me know he could handle the slagging. "I suppose *you,* sir," he replied, "are for Liverpool?"

Even Sara knew to cringe at that one.

"Would you like to take this outside?" I slapped the table. "I'll tell you, Mario, your tip's getting smaller by the minute."

"What is this cultured and beautiful lady doing with such a man?" Mario asked the ceiling, then winked at Sara, who beamed, and looked even more beautiful for it. Thank Jesus for Aries impulsiveness, I thought—that kiss was the best move I have ever made.

Off Mario went to get Sara the Barbaresco, and myself a cranberry soda with a twist of lime. It's not what you're thinking—I'm not an alcoholic, I just have a cultural predisposition toward overindulgence in social settings. I never drank alone, or to cure my sorrows. It was purely for sport, and when I drank I was a live wire; you should've seen me when I had a skinful. I was everyone's friend, the life of the party, the fella literally dancing on the tables at the pub . . . but it was a horrible feeling waking up in the morning with no memory at all, hoping I hadn't hurt anyone's feelings or said anything stupid, then getting a phone call from someone I hardly knew: "So when can you come over to read my play?" So about a year earlier I'd decided to back off. Funny how quickly my phone stopped ringing, but I didn't miss those days.

Sara's phone binged. She glanced at the screen, and smiled. "Oh, good, she can do it." Off my questioning look: "Feed the dog. That means I can stay a while." Again, there was the portent I should have picked up on, but I didn't, because she went on to say, "Let's split some dishes, what do you say?"

That made it feel like a *date*. (And did I mention it was a *gorgeous* evening?) At Mario's recommendation, we chose a *calamari fritti* app with aioli, followed by something called Seafood Brodetto, with a house speciality, on the side, of asparagus cooked with cracked pepper and Parmesan. The food was all succulent, a mouthwatering orgy of Italian secret ingredients.

But even better was Sara's company, the energy between us . . . *Fantastico*. Perfectly simpatico. You never know how people are going to eat, do you, if they're going to be the sort to pick the food out of their molars right in front of you, or be fussy about how to hold a fork. Sara and I were on the same page—tastefully relaxed and prone to treat asparagus as finger food. Although she didn't especially go for my using two asparagi as antennae to demonstrate I was an alien.

"I'm aware of your immigration status," she said drily. "But those things don't match your eyes."

All the exposition and confessions that must usu
on first dates—family background, professional life,
relationships, hopes, dreams, hobbies, select idiosyncrasies you're
willing to cop to—these things, we'd already shared with each
other over the past months, between school groups, summer
camp groups, and tours, under the chaperoning eyes of George
Washington, Paul Revere, Madame Cézanne, van Gogh's *Ber-
ceuse.* I knew she used to be a landscape painter. She knew my ma
had died when I was young. I knew she adored her dog (don't all
Americans?). She knew I was having immigration issues, and I
was *pretty* sure she knew what I was planning to do about it, but
I didn't think it worth reminding her at the moment. It might
interrupt the flow.

So our evening's conversation was just a continuation of our
friendly workday chats, only with my dizzying new acute appreciation of how luscious her lips and fingers were, how striking was
her dark spiky hair against her pale skin—and how badly I hoped
she was noticing equally favorable things about me. As usual, she
continued to "educate" me on American politics (Irish political
corruption had rendered me a cynic); for my part, I continued to
vainly expound the merits of football (the real kind). We considered the virtues of Debussy versus Ravel, neither of whom actually deserved our endorsement, especially with Joplin around. I'm
wired to associate people with certain music, and Sara's sound
track was, to me, the "Maple Leaf Rag"—precise yet playful, con-
trolled yet offbeat, just like her. I always banged out a fair version
of it on the guitar for the turn-of-the-century part of the Americas
wing. Or always did until today, I suppose.

We had a very earnest discussion about crunchy chocolate biscuits versus chewy ones, debated who was the second best *New York Times* crossword puzzle editor, and there was a cracker of a punning contest, which I won, although her refusal to play may have given me a leg up. Mario was the soundest waiter in the history of Italian bistros, even though he did mention to Sara he thought she "could do better than this," meaning me.

"Mario, she's not the one tipping you tonight," I said.

"Liverpool fans can't add up to anything." Again he winked at Sara.

"He's kind of cute," she said to me slyly, when he'd gone.

I don't know what kind of special high you have to be on to enjoy watching somebody else flirt with the girl you've just realized you might want to spend the rest of your life kissing, but I was delighted by the whole thing. "See, what's going on here is that you are so dizzy with your newfound appreciation for me that it's coloring how you look at everything else," I explained to her. "*Everyone* is going to look cute to you now, because that's how much *I've* charmed you."

She laughed again. God, I loved her laugh, it was one of the first things I'd ever liked about her. Sara called herself a reformed watercolorist—she'd spent a few years painting and teaching before her long-term boyfriend (clearly a wanker) pressured her to be a grown-up, which, long story short, had eventually led to her job at the Museum of Fine Arts. She was a funny mix of sassy, offbeat Greenwich Village (she spent her childhood in her great-grandparents' brownstone, long since sold off) and practical, straitlaced midwestern (post-brownstone, she'd come of age outside Chicago). You had to really *earn* a laugh from her, but once you'd earned it, you could come back for seconds pretty easily. I earned my first laugh the second week there. I found out she had a soft spot for van Gogh, so I came to the museum the next day with my head bandaged, and left on her desk, in a lovely gift box, a mutilated-ear-shaped sculpture made of Spam and Tabasco sauce. She'd almost wept with the laughing.

We savored the evening. We were one of the first tables in, we dined slowly through happy hour and the evening rush, and we nearly closed the place down, with mostaccioli for dessert and then a delicious espresso from a true barista. In all that time our bar tab was just two glasses of wine for Sara, but I tipped Mario as if we'd been boozing it up all night.

By the end of the evening it was clear that we were getting on even better than we did at work—and *everyone* at work was aware of how well we got on. But despite the buzzing I felt, from my ears all the way down to my Achilles tendons, I wanted to be gentlemanly. And—to be honest—even when you're certain the attraction is reciprocal, it's something else completely to *act* on that certainty. I'm pretty shy beneath all the bluster. So I decided to delicately query her about What Might Come Next, in her estimation. "When Mario finally kicks us out of here," I said, by way of delicate query, "would you like to be escorted home like the virtuous lady that you are, or would you prefer to sell your body on the streets for bus fare?"

"I'd hardly be virtuous to invite a man home after a first kiss," she said.

"You'd be even less virtuous if you sold your body for bus fare."

"Well, yes," she said, considering. "And you were so well behaved in my office, I'm sure I've got nothing to worry about if I let you insinuate your way into my home."

"Right, you were a blushing virgin there yourself."

"I have no idea what you're talking about," she said, so po-faced that I actually worried for a moment I'd misjudged the whole evening. Till she grinned slyly.

"Well, just so you know, it was my favorite sacking ever," I said as I tucked away my wallet. "You sack most excellently."

"Do I?" she asked, biting her lower lip so adorably it made me want to nibble on it with her. And in a suggestive tone: "You want me to sack you some more?"

She said that! *She said it!*

I can't even remember what I said in response, but she didn't slap me, so it couldn't have been too crass. I do remember that I pulled her chair out for her, letting my hand brush along her bare upper arm as she rose. I felt the electricity and saw her shiver a bit; she smiled over her shoulder at me and I was the happiest unemployed man on earth.

We waved to Mario as we left. "Ciao!"

He beamed a big smile to Sara and, with a grin, gave me the finger . . . Wanker. Sara cracked up. Then he said, gesturing us closer, "*Slán leat.*"

I stopped short, amazed. "How the fuck do you know Irish?"

Mario smiled nostalgically. "Ah, it's a long story," he said. "I met a beautiful redhead once . . . but not so beautiful as your lady. Signora, if he doesn't behave himself, remember I'm here, yes?" And, of course, he winked at her.

I could have kissed the bastard, because that was a fantastic excuse to put a protective arm around her and pull her toward me. She did not resist, and she fit under my shoulder as if we'd been carved from the same block of wood. I'd never been so happily aware of every atom on the whole left side of me as at that moment.

THERE WAS A bench at the bus stop; we sat there and let a bus or two go by first, just sitting in happy silence side by side, our shoulders and upper arms pressing against each other in the swampy August night.

"I'm so glad I fired you," she said. "If you were around the museum now, I'd get in so much trouble."

"I'd sue you for sexual harassment," I said.

We finally got on a 39 bus, still shoulder-jostling all the way out to Jamaica Plain, where we hopped off by the Monument. We strolled down Centre Street, toward the roundabout. Anticipation made me silent; she looked at me adoringly but had not yet officially invited me in, and this was all happening so fast. As we approached her building, I made a mental note to myself not to be presumptuous about what would happen once we were inside, but I knew, even as I made the note, I would misplace it. I wondered briefly, again, if I should tell her about getting married, but shelved the idea at once; it had nothing to do with what was going on between us here, and I didn't want to ruin the mood. I'd tell her tomorrow, if it seemed relevant.

She opened the outer door, then pivoted left in the hallway to open the inner one. The dulcet tones of an NPR commentator droned from within.

"That's a feeble deterrent for burglars," I told her. "I put right-wing talk radio on *really loud* when I go out—that stuff would scare anyone off, even the most zealous vandal."

She gave me a skeptical look.

"Not really," I admitted immediately. "I don't even lock my door, to be honest. I believe what's meant to be mine will remain mine according to karmic law, and whatever I'm meant to lose, I'll lose with or without locks on my door."

"That's a bit fatalistic," Sara said, fishing in her purse for her keys.

"Of course it is, I'm *Irish*," I said.

"I hadn't noticed," she said.

As Sara opened the door inward, she made a cooing noise and stooped down to greet the dog I had forgotten about.

I'd have taken Sara for a rescue-dog type, but this mutt held itself with the grace of a pedigreed champion. It was typical dog size, I s'pose, with a warm golden coat, and intelligent, bright brown eyes. Its entire torso was wiggling with excitement, but it hardly made a noise beyond an urgent, suppressed whimper of joy. It spun gleefully in rapid, tight little circles anticlockwise, keeping its eyes peeled on Sara as it circled, its backside wagging as much as its tail.

Sara bent down like Diana Spencer talking to a kindergartner; the dog stopped circling so it could meet her nose to nose, its arse still shimmying a Motown beat. Sara cooed and spoke as if it were a kid, like most Yanks do with dogs: "Halloooo, puppeee, I'm home! Were you a *good* girl? I bet you were a *good* girl"—all that bollocks. Suddenly I could see her both as a little girl and as a mother—both lovely aspects of her personality but neither one fitting the moment's mood. She scratched the dog's face. The happy whimper deepened and the body slightly stilled. Then Sara rose, stepped away, and said formally, as if the dog could really understand English, "Cody, I want you to meet Rory."

"Hiya, Cody," I said in greeting, and squatted down to be closer to eye level. In fairness, it was a lovely dog. It sprang to me, tail and backside wagging, damp nose raised hopefully toward me. I held up a hand to cover my mouth. "No kisses," I said, "but aren't you a lovely little fella."

"Cody's a girl," Sara said sweetly.

"Lovely girl," I said. I brushed her head with my fingertips. Beautiful coat. I scratched her ears. Her hair was silky as a baby's. I started to massage behind her ears.

Cody's mouth moved into an actual grin. She collapsed submissively onto her back on the floor as if her bones had suddenly gone all jelly, her legs splayed—a very tarty position, even for a dog. She gave me an expectant look and her tail thumped the floor like a metronome.

"Aw, she wants you to pet her belly," said Sara approvingly. "She likes you."

So the dog and I had a grand time bonding right inside the door. I rubbed her chest, which made her eyes roll back ecstatically. She suddenly leapt up and began spinning around in the tiny circles again (the dog, not Sara), stretched into a perfect Downward-Facing Dog, then flopped on her back again into the tarty-dog pose, all the while her hopeful dark gaze glued to my face, her tail flinging itself side to side. She was hilarious. This would be easy. I liked that pooch right away.

But I liked Sara more. So after those few minutes, I rose up, and looked around the place. It was small but chic, with Sara's organic-fair-trade/art-school-grad aesthetic. Sara was doing her coming-home routine: turning off the radio, checking the dog's water bowl, bolting the front door.

"Oooo . . . boss lady's taken me captive," I said, pleased. "Even after she fires me, she's still got me under lock and key. Bet you've got a lash hidden around here, too?"

"And a gang of tenth graders ready to leap out and make fun of your fiddle playing. There's a secret escape hatch," she said over her shoulder, smiling as she pulled a batik silk curtain closed against the light from the street. "But you'll have to torture me to learn where it is."

We stood there, at opposite corners of her coffee table, taking in the moment. I was starting to believe that this was, *really was,* A Moment. It truly was nothing either of us had seen coming, and yet here it was, so fast and so natural.

It's easy enough to describe a first kiss, because it's a specific action. It's harder to describe those few moments of chitchat, of tentative body language and bits of touching and little noises, that let two people tell each other: right, we're going to bed together. Not to "get laid," but because you seem fantastic and it would be such an honor—not just a pleasure but an *honor*—to be intimate with you. I looked her all over. She was curvy, with a graceful neck, and how could I ever have looked at those legs and not thought about wanting to run my hand down them? She gave me a drowsy contented look and took the lead, moving around the table like flowing caramel, leaned against me, and slipped her hand into my back pocket, casually, naturally, as if we were a couple. She tipped her chin up toward me with an inviting smile.

Snogging aside, I was dizzy by the time we reached the bedroom, and we hadn't even got our clothes off yet.

We didn't bother with the lamp; streetlight streamed through a window, leaving her in silhouette. She stepped out of her sandals. Her arms began to reach behind her to unzip her dress.

"Let me do that," I said quietly.

I stepped toward her, rested one hand on her cool shoulder, tugged the zipper, the green fabric falling away from itself, revealing a smooth, pale back. Then I stepped away so I could watch her silhouette as the dress slid to the floor. What a gorgeous silhouette she made. She stepped closer to me, reached for my waist, and shyly began to lift my shirt. I raised my arms to help her.

"Over here," she whispered. Tossing my shirt aside, she settled onto the bed, and with a gentle tug on my belt loops, invited me to join her.

Wow, this was *happening*. Almost fainting with pleasure, I began to unzip my jeans, then remembered my boots were still on. I leaned down to take one off, and dizzy as I was, began to lose my balance; I toppled to the side and stumbled, my still-booted foot landing hard on a hairy rope—

—that YELPED—

Sara sat bolt upright. "Cody?" she cried, just as I said, hopping around for balance, "Fucking dog! *Jesus*—"

Sara hurriedly turned on the bedside lamp. It threw a warm fuzzy light on her gorgeous naked body—which I was seeing for the first time under not-ideal conditions.

The dog was standing wide-eyed by the open door. Its tail thumped the doorjamb cautiously and it looked back and forth between us, unhurt but wildly alert, looking almost as if it were expecting praise for having survived getting its tail stepped on.

"I forgot about you," Sara said with affectionate apology to the dog, who used this as an excuse to move farther into the room.

"The dog's going, right?" I said.

Sara gave me a sheepish smile. *God,* she was gorgeous. "She normally sleeps on the bed with me."

I know Americans do that. I know Londoners do that. I know back in the Middle Ages, everyone did that, for warmth. But I couldn't make the algebra work out here. Either the dog was on the bed, or I was on the bed, but not both. I did not want to ruin the moment but I'm not into being watched (unless I'm onstage, getting paid for it—and dressed).

"Can we negotiate this?" I asked.

All of the air got sucked out of the room and there was a giant, bedroom-shaped vacuum that kept either of us from speaking for a moment.

"She's a lovely dog," I added, in case that made it easier. "Just having her here in the room with us—"

"Right, yes, I've never had to think about it before, that's all," Sara said awkwardly. "I haven't had anyone over since I left my ex."

That news made me very happy, especially being delivered by such a beautiful and very undressed woman who had just peeled my shirt off me. "Well, there's a first time for everything," I said. "Her bed in the living room looked comfortable, she can sleep out there."

"She'll be confused," Sara said, looking a little confused herself.

"She's a dog," I said, in a tone clearly implying that a dog was a fantastic thing to be. Which I'm sure it is if you're a dog. "She'll figure it out."

Sara had grown a little furrow between her eyes. I was surprised how much it changed the shape of her face, although the rest of that lovely naked body was unaffected, as was my interest in it.

"All right, then," she said. "Come on, pup." She got up off the bed and patted her bare knee.

The dog looked at her, cocked its head in confusion, then checked me out and wagged its tail. It gave me an imploring, hopeful look, as if I could maybe save it from Sara's inexplicable deviation from routine.

"Puppy, let's go," she said, and grabbed a robe from the back of the door. Throwing it over her shoulders, she backed out of the room, gesturing the dog to follow her.

The dog looked up at me. Up at the bed. Up at Sara. Its tail wagged harder—and then it turned and leapt joyfully, gracefully, onto the bed, and having landed, glanced between us as if expecting praise.

"Come on, now," I said, "Get off the bed."

"Come on, Cody," Sara said firmly. The dog cocked its head again for a moment, then jumped up as if on a trampoline, and landed bowing, as if starting a game, then renewed its industrious tail wagging. It was so cheerful that I felt a bit of a prat for wanting it to leave.

"Go on," I insisted. More wagging. I steeled myself against the dog's gleefulness, scooped it into my arms, bent down, and plopped it gently on the floor. I wasn't rough, but I was firm. The dog yelped and so did Sara, who was still distractingly naked: "Rory!"

I straightened. "Doesn't she listen to you?" I asked, more huffily than I wanted to.

On the floor, the dog swooned into her tarty-dog pose, dark eyes beseeching, tail still wagging. Even in submission, she fucking radiated joy.

"Stop that," I ordered. "Or we'll sell you to the North Koreans."

I slid my foot under one hind leg so I could lift it and scoot her over onto her side, but before I could—

"Rory!" Sara shouted. "Stop! Don't *kick* her!"

I stared at her, shocked. "I wasn't going to kick her!"

"You were! Your foot—"

"I was only—"

"Come here, puppy," she said desperately. The dog scrambled up and leapt toward her, and she knelt to cradle it protectively against her nude paleness. "Good girl, it's okay, it's okay."

"I wasn't going to kick her," I said again. "Even *she* knows I wasn't going to kick her, that's just in your head. What kind of prick do you take me for?"

She gave me a wary look. "I'm going to go settle her in," she said. She led the dog back to the living room, closing the door behind herself.

I threw myself supine onto the bed, shirtless, jeans half unzipped, boots still on, libido fading. "I can't *believe* this is how the evening ends," I growled to the ceiling.

Chapter 2

Sara came back into the bedroom looking distressed, and I thought, *Bollocks.* The mood was probably ruined for good now.

"Look, I'm sorry," I said. "I *really* wasn't going to kick—"

Her rushed nod silently interrupted me. I sat up. Without looking at me, she clutched her robe tighter at the throat, covered her face with her hand as if suddenly self-conscious, and said, "This was just all so unexpected—"

"I know," I said in a conciliatory tone.

After a moment, she moved her hand away from her face to untie her robe, and let it slip down to the ground so that she stood there naked before me again.

That meant she really liked me. Thank God. Maybe the mood wasn't ruined. But just to make sure, before the mood got moody again, rather than just jumping up to grab her . . .

"The whole thing is a surprise to us both and there's no rule about what happens," I went on. (I do go on.) "Twelve hours ago—six, even!—if you'd told me I'd be sitting on Sara Renault's bed right now, I'd have said bollocks, or at least I'd say, well, that must be due to there's something wrong with her ceiling and I'm helping her fix it like a friend would do. If you *need* your dog sleeping on your bed—"

"Rory—"

"I mean, sure, I kissed you, and it was a gorgeous evening and I could so easily fall in love with you, but I wasn't *planning* on it—to be honest, if you hadn't sacked me, I'd be home in my own bed right now watching footy highlights, and the dog—"

"Rory—" She tried again.

"And I don't want to pressure you into anything and you don't owe me a thing 'cept my final pay—"

"Rory, shut up!" she said, almost laughing with frustration.

"It's not like we've got to work out a living arrangement here or anything. It's just a kiss that ran amok, it shouldn't cause any upset—"

She actually threw herself on top of me on the bed.

That felt *amazing*.

So at least we had an understanding. Enough that we could complete the removal of clothes with the kind of shy intensity that's full of mischief, not insecurity or worry.

She was gorgeous. I don't even mean physical beauty, although she had that, too . . . but she had a *glow* to her, it surrounded her, like an egg, like an aura, and I wanted to be inside of it with her. She let me in. I've never felt that with anyone before. When we made love I felt my entire body climax. She was luscious. And unselfconscious for a woman who had not been naked in front of anyone else lately.

And in the morning, everything was fine. Even with the dog,

who was sleeping on the floor right outside the bedroom, and was just as happy to see us as when we'd come home last night. No sulking, no timidity. As if sleeping outside the door was the most comfortable thing in the world, and greeting Rory in the morning was an established part of the routine of Being Sara's Dog.

Still, Sara bent over and spoke in a coddling, cooing way, which wasn't really necessary for anyone but Sara, because the dog was *fine*. But Cody was no idiot—her lot dines out on affection, so when it's offered, of course she's going to take it. Her tail whacked the wall steadily, she gave Sara an adoring look with those pretty dark eyes, and made a feint of licking Sara's cheek without actually touching it. There was something Little Match Girl–ish about the meekness of that incomplete kiss—it was absurdly endearing, so I made a mental note to try it myself sometime. Sara kissed the dog between the eyes and then straightened up.

Then Cody, suddenly more Tom Sawyer than Little Match Girl, approached me, her mouth a lolling grin, tail wagging; I patted her head and said, "Hey, pup," and that was that. The interspecies equivalent of a casual high five. Sara looked mollified.

So it was all good. We moved into the kitchen, where Sara sat me down at the small table, and tied on an MFA apron with Japanese irises on it.

"Scrambled eggs okay?" she asked.

"Deadly," I said approvingly.

After sitting there a few moments trying to ignore the dog's quizzical gaze, I caught another aroma, and for a brief shudder thought I was back in my family's dismal flat in Dublin.

"Are you . . . frying a tomato?" I asked, incredulous.

She pressed down the handle of the toaster. "Yep," she said, pleased with herself. "I would have made you black pudding but I didn't have any congealed pig's blood handy."

"You don't have rashers by any chance? Not that crap American bacon."

"Sorry. Next time."

It took all my self-control not to punch the air with a great cry of triumph: Yes! *Next time!* There would be a next time!

Instead I stood and moved around the counter to embrace her. "Actually I don't eat Irish breakfast," I confided. "Fried tomato is like an acid flashback to my da making us breakfast after the nightshift at Cadbury's."

"Your father was a chocolatier? I thought—"

"Factory job. After Ma died he had to do everything. He was a shite cook."

She was still a moment. "No fried tomato, then."

I kissed her forehead, and then hugging her tighter, nuzzled the nape of her neck. "You're a darling anyhow," I said.

So we skipped the tomato, but Sara scrambled perfect eggs, and she had Lyons tea—*and* Kerrygold butter for the toast—what are the odds of *that*? So it was a gorgeous breakfast. "I think I'll keep her," I said to the dog as I set down my fork.

"I think you'd better let me keep you," Sara corrected. "You're the one without a job. Sorry about that," she said again, as she'd said five times or more yesterday.

I shrugged. "You don't control the funding," I said. "Anyhow, my visa is for acting, not music. I'm surprised no one from Immigration ever showed up to snap my fiddle strings. And my sponsor went under, so I've no way to renew the visa. I'll be undocumented again, and you'd have to sack me anyhow. This tea is deadly."

She frowned thoughtfully. "I bet the museum could renew your visa, if we could just find the money to keep you on."

I laughed and set down my mug. "I'm not a bad fiddler but I'm a crap violinist, Sara, and you know it. If Jefferson heard *my* version of the Corelli, it would *never* be his favorite. Unless you were planning to have a special exhibit on the Folk Art of the Potato Famine or something, you'd do better going to Boston Conservatory for a guest musician. I'll go back to what I did before."

"What, working under the table? In construction?" Sara said, mildly appalled. "What a waste of your talent!"

"If I'd a shilling for every time I've heard that," I said with a rueful smile. "It's grand. I had a good run at the museum, and I learned loads of stuff I wouldn't have otherwise, and I met some cool people, and anyhow I was getting tired of looking at Washington's horse's arse." I shrugged. "And I'm sure to get a play soon, something always comes along. Meanwhile, back I go under the table. Keeps my biceps manly. You're going to be late for work."

She started slightly, then reached for my plate.

"I'll do that," I said, in the hopes this gesture assured I would find myself breakfasting here at this fine establishment soon again.

She smiled. "What a lovely houseguest. Stay here for a while if you like, take a shower, watch TV. Cody always likes company, and you got canned yesterday, so I know you're free."

I declined. But I enjoyed watching her go through her morning routine; the domesticity felt almost as intimate as helping her undress. She opened the dog door to the boxy little yard, changed

Cody's water, left little treats hidden round the flat, "to give her something to do, " and turned on the radio to NPR, "so she feels less lonely."

"So that's not to deter burglars," I said.

"I have a fierce guard dog for that," Sara said.

"Nuzzles them to death, does she?"

We left the house together, both saying good-bye to the dog, who looked at Sara with a bereft expression. Sara cheerily promised to return, but Cody turned away and heaved a disbelieving sigh as I pulled the door closed.

I walked Sara to her bus stop and promised to call later. We still had not really defined what this Thing was going on between us. But it was definitely a Thing, with a capital *T,* and that was *fantastic*. We almost ate each other's lips off saying good-bye to each other as the bus drove up, and I could see her waving through the back-end window for two whole blocks.

It was a gorgeous late-August morning, and being unemployed— so with plenty of time free—I decided to walk part of the way home to Somerville. I needed time to soak all of this in. So many changes in so little time.

I headed off along the Emerald Necklace toward Jamaica Pond, the warm moist air already curling my locks against the back of my neck. I hazarded jaywalking across the Jamaicaway when the lights were in my favor, reached the far sidewalk, and stepped onto the plush green grass that led down to the pond. I took off my boots and socks, then my shirt, and just lay under the trees for a while, pretending to be on holiday. It was heavenly, if I ignored how the grass tickled my back. Later on I'd have to call Danny's uncle about getting my old construction job back, but for now, I drifted off into a lovely dreamscape full of Sara. That ended when my pocket buzzed.

Lazily, without sitting up, I reached for my phone. I saw a California number that I recognized but (for superstitious reasons) had never saved into my contacts. It was Dougie Martin.

Dougie was an L.A. talent agent. He was not *my* agent; I didn't have an agent, since my arts visa didn't let me join the unions. But he was a friend. He'd actually started out years ago as an actor in Boston, where he was my understudy in the *H.M.S. Pinafore* (so, unsurprisingly, my sound track for him was "A British Tar," although Dougie himself was a Vermonter). It had been a long run, and we all started to improvise a bit. I upgraded Ralph Rackstraw's brief lament about "misery" to a longish soliloquy on "Dostoyevskian darkness," and Dougie, watching from the wings, was transported; he had been my biggest fan ever since. He wasn't half bad himself—we went on to be dead together as Stoppard's Rosencrantz and Guildenstern—and a year later, he'd gone to New York to give it a go there, but decided the competition and the crap money wasn't worth it. So he'd started working as an agent's assistant, and seeing there was money to be made, he got into *that* game. Then the agency opened offices in L.A., and voilà, now he was out there. He was always on me about getting a green card so I could move out to Hollywood and make us both a load of money. He was gas. He talked as boisterously while sober as I once did while drunk.

"Morning, Dougie," I said into the phone, with the mellow cheer of somebody thoroughly and lovingly shagged after a long celibacy. "What's the crack?"

"Morning, Rory!" His voice was tight with excitement. "I just learned about a project coming down the pike and I wanted to see where you were with your immigration status."

I sat up abruptly.

"I've got a performance visa," I said. "But it's up soon. Still no green card."

"Weren't you talking with your cousin's widow or someone about getting married?"

"Sure, we're still talking about it, but everyone thinks it's so easy—it's a nightmare, and nowadays you need authenticity to prove it's a legit marriage, you know, they're all seasoned pros in the JFK Building . . . and why are you asking anyhow?"

"There's a cable pilot in development, a series about an Irish detective whose cover story is he's a rock musician and master of disguises." ("Sounds ridiculous," I said, plainly audible, but he didn't pause to hear me.) "They haven't cast it 'cuz it's still in development but they need someone Irish, sort of Colin Farrell Black Irish type, midthirties, who acts and sings and plays guitar and can do lots of accents. And it's shooting in the Boston area! It's like, *you*, man. Like they were creating it just for *you*."

Jesus, yes! "Ah," I said, feeling my pulse quicken. "But I'm not SAG, I don't—"

"I'll take care of all that once you're legal," he said. "I know the producers. Just get yourself the green card, Rory, and I'll get you the audition."

As I listened, eyes wide, he said he expected it to take a year before shooting began, and even auditions were probably still months away—assuming the whole thing didn't fall apart first anyhow. Cold lava progresses more swiftly than a project in development in the entertainment business. If I started the paperwork right off, I could probably get documented in time for an audition. Which was important, since before I was even allowed to audition for the studio, I'd have to sign something called a test-option contract, which from Dougie's description would require more paperwork than adopting a child from Kazakhstan.

My heart was fluttering, my palms were sweaty, my mouth was dry. I managed to thank him and promised I'd get married right away. We hung up.

I was so agitated and excited, I couldn't focus on the pond and the buzzing insects and the gentle heat and the lush trees and all that I thought would be the highlight of my morning. Now, with adrenaline coursing through me, all I could think about was . . . well, really I could hardly think at all, except I knew I had to call Laura, widow of my favorite cousin, Martin. When he got cancer I'd been there to help with the boys, so we were all close (in a Gordon Lightfoot sound-track sort of way), and she'd offered to give me a green-card marriage if I ever needed it. I'd deflected for a few years, because what a pain in the arse it is for someone to extend themselves that way, and I'd been managing with performance visas all right. But I'd recently been in a premiere that was supposed to transfer to New York—a great role, a drunken Dublin thief, supporting part but I stole the show . . . only the New York producers got nervous that I hadn't a green card, just a visa . . . so it had fallen through.

For bureaucratic reasons, the usual avenues of getting a green card failed me—I was actually born in England, so I was excluded from any amnesty, Morrison visas, and so on, that were intended to help people with Irish birth certificates. And statistically I had virtually no chance to get a work visa from the UK. So there was just the one route left. Time to go through with it.

Which meant now I had to think about blood tests, birth certificates, wedding arrangements, endless immigration forms, updated head shots, auditions, Emmy Award speeches. Yesterday, I'd been a fiddler on an 0-1 visa, playing in an art museum. Five minutes ago, I'd been unemployed and hoping I could get my under-the-table construction job back. Now I had to marry my cousin so I could become a television star. There's America for you.

With a tremor in my fingertips, I scrolled through the contacts on my phone to find Laura's number. Then I froze.

Sara. I wanted to tell Sara first. I wanted to share my excitement. I didn't need her blessing because it wasn't a real marriage—she knew all about my immigration headaches, she'd know I simply had to have that piece of paper. And anyhow it's not as if we had decided we were Anything In Particular yet. She might even tell me last night had just been an apology for sacking me.

Not really.

I started to dial Sara's number.

Then I stopped, agitated. That was crazy. This had nothing to do with Sara, and Sara was fantastically distracting, but I had to stay on target with this first. I checked my watch (yes, I'm one of those who still wears an actual watch). Laura's kids would be in school now, she herself would be on lunch break—she owned a shop—so this was a good time to call.

It was a short, simple, warm conversation, strangely tepid for the intensity of the subject matter: Laura was glad to hear from me, glad I was well, she was well, too, yes, she was still up for it, she was so pleased with me for having a reason to pursue it. She invited me over for dinner the next night to talk about details. She caught me up on what her boys were doing—I'd helped coach their soccer team when they were little, now they were too old for anything but girls, she laughed.

"I know that feeling," I said.

We sent each other love and hung up. I had been walking while talking—not ambling along blissfully as I had down toward Jamaica Pond, this was more of a forced march, and I found myself in Brookline Village. I stopped at a café, ordered an espresso, and claimed a table on the sidewalk, out of the sun.

Now I could call Sara.

"Hi, sexy," she said on answering, and I swear my knees almost buckled even though I was sitting. For a moment I couldn't remember why I'd called her—and then when I did, I did not want to say anything.

"Um . . . I left my fiddle in your office," I said, feeling stupid. "Can I . . . come by and get it?"

"You can," she said agreeably. "Or I could bring it home with me and you could collect it from me there. Feeling lucky?"

"Wow," I said, but for more reasons than she realized. "I would love to do that, but I've got some stuff I have to deal with, something, um, interesting has come up and . . . actually I do want to talk to you about it"—that was a lie, I suddenly realized, I didn't really, not at all, I just wanted to kiss her neck—"but let me maybe get myself organized here . . ." I let it trail off.

"Rory?"

"I'll come by end of day, how's that sound?" I said. "To get the fiddle. And we can go out? Maybe your neighbor can feed the dog again for you?"

I could hear the smile in her voice. "I'd love that," she said. "As long as I get home in time to take her for a run, she didn't get much exercise yesterday. But do you want to tell me what's up?"

"It's nothing, I'll tell you later." It was nothing. It really was nothing.

Five hours, three lattes, hours of walking about, and millions of frantic thoughts later, I met her right downstairs by her cubicle at the MFA. I still had my ID badge, so Wanda, who manned the desk (sound track: ABBA) let me through. I was pretty dazed.

"Hey," Sara said, smiling. With a careful glance down the hallway, she nodded me into the cubicle. There was nobody else around in the hallway. I felt a wave of nostalgia for the simplicity and innocence of the impulsive kiss, in this exact same spot, a very distant twenty-four hours earlier.

She was grinning at me. "It's good to see you," she whispered. "I've been smiling all day just thinking about you." She looked adorably, and unusually, vulnerable. "I've had a spring in my step." She glanced back up at me. "Do you have a spring in your step? Maybe a little one?"

"Oh, darlin', you've no idea," I said. Forgetting for a moment about all the rest of it, I grabbed her and enjoyed the warmth of her against me, the suddenly familiar scent of her hair. I kissed the side of her head.

"Your fiddle's in the corner," she said, glancing down the hall lest anybody see us snogging. "I'm just wrapping up if you want to wait a few moments. You okay? You sounded strange on the phone earlier."

"Actually I've got some interesting news," I said. "I'll tell you when you're finished."

She drew back a little to stare at me. She gestured to her extra chair, the one I slid out of yesterday while I was kissing her. "Tell me now," she said.

So I sat just where I'd sat for the sack/kiss moment, on the same industrial plastic chair with the hollow metal legs, took her hands, and looked into her eyes. I told her about the possible audition. She was thrilled for me.

"Although that means you'd be moving to L.A.?" she said, pushing her lower lip out.

"No, it's shooting right here in Boston. And not for a year. And only if I can get the green card in time."

"How do you do that?" she asked.

"Right. So here's the thing about it," I said.

And then I paused.

I had never until that moment thought about my marrying Laura as anything other than a technical necessity. In the Irish expat community, this kind of thing was pretty common. It generally meant creating the appearance of cohabitation—some clothes planted in a dresser, your name on their outgoing phone message, photos and notes creating a fictional paper trail of intimacy. Friends did it to help out friends. It had no emotional meaning at all, not at all. Until I had to explain it to the woman I was falling precipitously in love with.

"I've got this cousin," I began. Suddenly I felt like my mouth was a cubist painting and I couldn't figure out how to form words naturally. "Actually she's the widow of my cousin, she's a friend, there's nothing between us, never was, never will be, but we've been talking about it for a while and we've made arrangements to get married so I can get a green card, and this opportunity means I have to do that right away."

I saw something in her recoil in self-protection.

"And I just hope that whatever's going on between us here," I continued, feeling myself starting to sweat, "not that we have to define it, but whatever it is, you know, I just hope it's not made weird by my marrying Laura, because *really* it's just for the piece of paper. There's *nothing* between us. Her husband was my favorite cousin. She's like a sister. Trust me," I added, seeing how the startled look on her face wasn't getting any less startled.

I watched her take a moment to collect herself, which was probably no small enterprise given her experience of the last day: a bloke throws himself at her, makes love to her all night, and then tells her he's marrying someone else. Even if it's just for a green card, that can't have been easy to digest. She was a champ.

"I'm not sure, Rory," she said. "You kissed your boss for firing you, who knows what you're capable of with somebody who marries you." I could not tell if she was joking.

"It's not like that! It's just a piece of paper," I repeated, tightening my grip on her hand as she reflexively pulled away. "We wouldn't even be living together or anything, we'd just have to make it look like we were. She's just helping out a friend."

"But how can you date *me* if the government is keeping tabs on you to check how genuine your marriage is to *her*?" she asked.

I felt my entire face light up. I could not hide it even from myself. "Are we dating, then? Would you like that? Because I know I would," I promised her.

"Of course I would," she said.

For a moment that was the most important thing in the world, more important than the marriage or the green card or the audition. "Really?" I beamed.

"Rory," she said in her Diana Spencer–with–kindergartner voice. "I don't sleep with men I'm not dating."

"So we're dating?" I just wanted to make sure. "Official like?"

"I'd like us to, but I don't see how we can if you're supposed to be demonstrating to the government that you're married to somebody else."

"I'll marry her but you can be my mistress," I offered gallantly.

"If your being a husband is what gets you the green card, they'll be watching to make sure you're at least a decent husband."

"It's not like that," I said reassuringly. "They'll just call us in for an interview and ask us some questions, but we know what kind of questions to expect, so we'll be fine."

"And that's it? That's really all there is to it?" she asked, looking skeptical. "That simple? Don't bullshit me on this, Rory."

"Language!" I admonished her. Sara almost never cursed, so it was very charming when she did. I sobered. "All right, not quite that simple. First I'll get a conditional green card. That's good for two years, so they can make sure it's a real marriage. I'll keep some clothes in Laura's closet, and we'll take photos of ourselves at parties—"

"So you'd be going to parties with her," Sara said very quickly. "Not with me. Not with the person you're dating."

I gave her a smile I intended to be comforting, and she gave me a scowl informing me I'd failed. "They're parties we'd both be attending anyhow," I said. "We're good mates, and extended family, and we know all the same people."

"And all those people are going to play along with this?" she asked. "They don't have a problem with it?"

"It's a good ol' laugh," I said, trying to sound cheerful. "Most of my mates are expats, they know what I'm going through, they're fine with it. Really."

"And this goes on for, what did you say, two years? Then what?"

"Then they'll interview us again, to make sure we're still a couple. Then I'll get the *unconditional* green card, and then we'll just get divorced. We won't have lived together, slept together, anything. The whole thing is a fiction."

Sara took a moment to consider this, grimacing. It really was unnerving how much her face changed when she frowned. "So it's just a piece of paper, some staged photos, and an interview about your relationship?"

"About our fake relationship, yes."

She frowned some more.

"That's ridiculous," she said definitively. "If you're getting married just for a piece of paper, you might as well marry the woman you're dating."

"The woman I'm . . . *You?*" I said in disbelief.

"Me," she said, as if it were a done deal. To be clear: It was a demand. It was not a proposal.

I was gobsmacked. "But . . . I *like* you. Romantically. Didn't we just agree to date?"

"That should make it easier to convince them we're a real couple," she said.

"But it'll confuse what's going on between us," I said. "Don't you think?" I was having a reflux of precisely the same fluttery symptoms from when Dougie called.

She shrugged, and took a sip of water from a white ceramic mug on her desk. She picked up a pen and wiggled it between lean fingers—a transparently false act of casualness. "Why? It's just a piece of paper and an interview. We don't even have to tell anyone. Except your *mates,* who will, y'know, think it's a *good ol' laugh.*"

"What if we break up? I mean, I can't imagine breaking up with you, unless you insist on keeping the dog on the bed, but I can easily imagine the reverse, because to be honest, I am one of the most aggravating people I know. My own mother, rest her soul, wouldn't blame you . . ." I drifted into silence as she set down the pen and gave me the Princess Diana look.

"I'm still your friend, Rory. I've worked beside you for months now, I've seen you act, you've told me all about your past. I'm aware you're not a Boy Scout, but I *know* you. I will still help you, even if we stop seeing each other. I know you're talented. You deserve a break." She grinned, unsuccessfully hiding her own case of nerves. "If I can't help you as a boss, at least let me help you as a green-card bride."

I felt dizzy. The word "bride" coming out of her mouth made it seem like, you know, *marriage.* To someone I'd slept with only once. But was already kind of more in love with than anyone ever in my life. Although maybe that was just sex talking . . .

"It would be simpler for me to marry Laura. Really, it doesn't mean any—"

"That will be a lot more complicated in the long run. For one thing, you'll have to stay married for years by the sound of it, soup to nuts, and what if you and I want to get more serious in the meantime?" We both blushed deeply, which in other circumstances would have been almost enjoyable. "I wouldn't have a conversation about this after a normal first date. But there's nothing about any of this that's normal."

I felt both horrified and thrilled by the direction the conversation was taking. "But let's say we keep seeing each other. It's not like we'd be ready to get married *now*, or even *soon*. I don't know that I'm the marrying sort *at all*. So being married might make things, you know . . . weird."

"For me it wouldn't be as weird as dating a married man, even—"

"It's just a piece of paper!"

"Then get that piece of paper with *me*!" she said with exasperation.

"If it's with you, it's not just a piece of paper!" On top of the dry mouth and sweaty palms, I thought I might be having heart palpitations. I had a strong urge to run out of the room and come back a few hours later already married to my cousin and then somehow convince my new girlfriend it was no big deal.

"Can't we *agree* it's just a piece of paper?" she asked. "It could be a team sport: getting Rory O'Connor's green card."

"It's not a game," I said, suddenly sharp. "I've been struggling with my immigration status for a *decade* now, which is *mad* given I am an able-bodied English speaker from the island that spawned half the white population of America. There's a lot of weight here, a lot of history. You're being impulsive in a way that's not like you, Sara. Impulsive is *my* gig."

She looked a little taken aback. "I'm not being impulsive," she argued. "Because I *know* it's just a piece of paper. I think helping you with your green card is a worthy cause no matter our relationship. I'd be jealous to be left out of the effort, in fact. And if things gets weird, at least it's a weirdness I'm actively a part of, not a weirdness I have to watch from the sidelines. I'd have some sense of *agency* in all this. After my last relationship, I need that."

I looked at her. She looked at me. I looked at her some more, knowing eventually I'd have to say something, because it was my turn. She was gorgeous. Those green eyes. Dark lashes. Almond-shaped eyes, almost Persian, a shape you don't often see with green eyes.

"Rory? What do you say?"

I looked down at the industrial carpeting, and her neat, un-manicured feet in their strappy sandals. I wanted to take her dancing in those sandals. Ideally at this very moment, so we wouldn't have to have this conversation. I looked back up at her. "As long as we're *really* clear that it is *only* about a piece of paper," I said.

"Agreed."

"And it doesn't mean *anything* about our *actual* relationship."

"Agreed."

"And if one of us forgets that and starts acting, you know, *spouse*like, the other one gets to dump 'em in the Charles till they smarten up."

"Agreed," she said, with one very serious nod of her head. She held out her right hand.

"Because I'd be very grateful, but I don't want to feel *be-holden*—"

"Shut up," she said, affectionately, and so adorably offhand that—damn the torpedoes!—I had to marry her before anyone else could.

Chapter 3

Sara's strategizing started immediately. Even before we'd gotten up from our chairs, having shaken hands on the purely-pragmatic-no-weird-emotions-involved agreement to get married, she declared we should have friends over for dinner, to tell them we were dating. "That way, whenever we finally decide to reveal that we got married, it won't be too much information for them to digest all at once," she explained.

"All right," I said, still a little dizzy. Her nerves, which had been frayed moments earlier, were steadied by the drive to Be Organized About Things.

She was a great little organizer. She'd sacked me on Monday, and by Wednesday evening she'd arranged a dinner party at her place for Friday.

"Invite Danny," she said over the phone.

"I thought it would just be the museum crowd," I said. I was home at last, lying on my canvas couch, staring up at the cottage-cheese-textured ceiling of my otherwise-tasteful Somerville pad, wondering what *else* could gobsmack me this week.

"We met because of Danny," she said. "He should be part of the mix."

This was indulgence on her part. None of my mates belonged in her world—I myself did not belong in her world, except that between us we were clever enough to slot me into it. Her museum friends (whom she now called "our museum friends," suddenly making us a collective noun) had initials after their names in the MFA brochures; Danny worked for his uncle who was a building contractor, and counted himself lucky for the steady job. When I started at the museum, I hadn't known oil from tempura, or a Homer from a Sargent, or a Chinese Whatever from a Japanese Whatever. And I hadn't known shite about American history, not that I was expert now. If I wasn't known as such a charmer, with the vocabulary of a crossword-puzzle addict, they'd have sussed me out soon enough and given me the deaf ear, I'm sure. I definitely didn't want them giving Danny the deaf ear, he's a sound bloke (sound track: Van Morrison, of course) and an absolute smashing drummer, really top shelf. But a shy type around strangers.

"So call him, okay?" she was saying. "And since you've bragged about your Indian cooking for so long, now's a great time to prove yourself. I think sag paneer and chicken tikka."

"Marriage is bringing out the boss in you. I'm afraid I'll get fired again."

"I'll be your sous-chef," she offered, "then *you* can boss *me*. If you can pull off a full meal in my kitchen, maybe we can convince them we've been at this secret romance thing for a while."

"And what if I make a bollocks of it?"

"The Irish aren't known for their cooking anyhow," she said cheerfully. In my mind's eye I could see the shape of her mouth as she grinned. "Really, spend the next few nights at my place," she insisted. "Get to know the kitchen."

I thought about her kitchen as I glanced about my sorry excuse for one. I loved to cook, but this place was brutal for it. Many of my friendships, especially since I'd stopped drinking, had been cemented by my inviting myself to make dinner for other people in their homes. I even had a backpack full of spices from a store in Central Square that I could throw on my shoulder and take with me on short notice. My superhero identity was Garam-Masala Man.

But of course, just for the fun of it, I had to play hard-to-get first.

"From dinner date to indentured servitude in what, forty-eight hours, is it? Very generous of you. May I make myself familiar with the sous-chef, too? Check out your pantry? Learn how to turn your oven on?"

"Sure, you can even play with my appliances," she purred, in total violation of the rule that Rory Gets All The Good Lines.

"All right, then," I said, domesticated.

By the end of the week, I knew the intricacies of Sara's oven and a lot of other things. I'm thrilled to say these included details I am too much the gentlemen to reveal, but they also included how much to feed the dog, how loud to leave the radio on in the morning for the dog, and how to stop the dog from begging: one pointed finger and a hiss of *"Naughty!"* Which still strikes me as a tragic waste of an excellent word.

Sara's kitchen was laid out smartly. Except for when the dog got underfoot in her quest to show me how well she tracked my every move, I could reach anything by taking a step or two, and it was very well equipped. By half-six Friday, I was in great shape—I'd made Indian rice salad, samosas and pakoras were ready for the deep fry, basmati was on the lowest simmer, and, not to brag, but the chicken tikka smelled *divine*. And I looked the business in Sara's MFA apron, now smeared with turmeric and clove.

"No," I said to the dog for the 347th time, when she tried to hoover up the detritus of my industry. "Lie down."

She wagged her tail and gave me her quizzical look, like she had no idea what "lie down" meant unless it came with a treat or a head scratch. She got neither.

As I stood there barefoot in the kitchen, I opened the windows as wide as they went, partly to cool off the room and let the steam escape, but also to allow the aromatic spices of my little feast to waft down the artsy sidewalks of Jamaica Plain, teasing the neighbors so they could drown in their own salivation. I was quite chuffed with myself. Now all I had to do was wait for everyone to arrive. And tell the dog, for the 348th time, not to hoover the crumbs off the kitchen floor.

Sara's—sorry, *our*—best friend from work, Lena, was a spark plug of a Filipino woman (sound track: salsa) with long, sleek hair who helped curate the Asian art collections. We'd not always hit it off so well, Lena and I—two competitive hotheads in the same building, even a huge museum, is a bit much. Finally we'd made a game of forever treading on each other's ego, and slagging her became a true joy. We'd also invited a superstylish gay couple, Elliot and Steve, who adored Sara. They both did things I never really understood on the more business side of things, if an art museum even has a business side. (Sound track: cool jazz, a sort of Brubeck-Basie mix tape.)

They all three arrived together with Sara, straight from work and dressed accordingly, unselfconscious in their day-job sleekness. Sara managed to look both professional yet not too conventional—she had a tailored but slightly offbeat chicness I just loved.

I hate shaving. I always cut myself, and over the years have lost, to be honest, gallons of blood. I prefer having a beard but it's just not practical in theatre. If you've grown it for the Shakespeare you've immediately got to shave it for the Coward, and then roles like McMurphy in *Cuckoo's Nest* or half the roles in Synge—you just never know what the director expects. So clean-shaven, sadly, is simplest. I couldn't recall if I'd shaved that morning, so as Sara was letting everyone in, I brushed the back of my hand across my chin to check how sandpapery I was. Wasn't bad. When the guests' attentions turned to me, I grinned widely and held out my arms to give all three of them my signature bear hug, turmeric stains be damned.

"You know, we *all* saw this coming, this little thing between you two," Lena said approvingly, in the bustle of Sara accepting gifts of wine and flowers and attaching little whatsits to the stems of the wineglasses and pouring the first round.

"And you didn't put her in protective custody?" I said in mock surprise.

Elliot and Steve were making synchronized agreeing sounds in response to Lena's approval. Then they immediately turned their full attention to the dog, who had been whimpering and spinning hysterically in anticlockwise circles since they had arrived.

As I watched surreptitiously, these two blokes in fastidious nearly matching navy suits bent over and began to greet the dog as if all three of them were puppies. She kept shoving her muzzle against their faces, back and forth between them, like a hyperactive Dorothy recognizing all her kin when she returns to Kansas. Lena joined them with a joyful proclamation of Cody's name, which sent the dog collapsing to the floor for a new round of Pat That Tarty Dog's Belly For An Hour. Elliot and Steve cracked me up—watching the pair of them (Elliot tall and stoic, Steve short and jolly, a bit of Bert and Ernie) dote over the dog, almost weeping with the cuteness, and the *cooing* sounds they made . . . it was hilarious.

"Come on, Elliot," Steve said, "we're getting a pooch."

"Only if we can find one like Cody," Elliot said, and made a kissy face at the dog. I was a model of self-restraint and didn't imitate him, but Jesus, you don't know how hard that was.

I glanced at Sara, who was smiling contentedly at them all. "How do they know her so well?" I asked.

"I used to bring her to the museum with me," she said. "When I first came back to work. I had to wean her into being alone." With a pleased gesture, eyes dancing like a proud mother's: "They *really* liked her. Obviously."

"She's so big!" said Lena, as if proud of the dog for growing.

"But she's still just as cute! Aren't you, Cody?" Elliot, who was usually very dignified.

"What a cutie! What a *cutie*!" Steve, who was usually a little dignified.

There was a tentative knock, and a stocky, redheaded Irishman entered carrying a six-pack of home-brewed ale and plunging the socioeconomic median of the room right down the toilet. The Initialed Ones scrambled to their feet sheepishly.

Danny had not come straight from work, but was dressed

almost as if he had—faded jeans, a brand-new Red Sox jersey, work boots. He did not look like he belonged on the same channel, let alone at the same dinner party, as the rest of them.

I hid a grimace, wondering how this would go, but Sara was brilliant: she tendered hearty introductions all around, and coaxed Danny to speak enough words so they could be charmed by his mellifluous Donegal accent.

I killed the flame under the basmati and plated the tikka. By the time I looked up, all the guests had an alcoholic beverage in one hand (white wine for those with initials after their names, home-brewed ale for Danny) and were cooing at the dog. Even Danny, who had never *met* the dog, was cooing at the dog.

"Booze and puppies," said Sara under her breath to me. "The best social lubricants in North America."

"In North Korea, too," I added. "But for different reasons."

She stuck out her tongue and grinned. "Let's get lots of photos tonight, on everyone's phones," she said. Lowering her voice and dropping her cheek so that her face was turned away from the guests, she added, "We need to have visual evidence that predates the wedding."

As had been happening all week, a brief wave of panic splashed over me, and then I nodded, casually, before sucking down the rest of my seltzer.

The evening, in brief, was a great success. In fact, I'd give it highest marks in the annals of Dinner Parties Hosted By Good People Who Are Lying To Their Guests About Their Motives. (If you grew up in a Catholic country, you'll know that a lie of omission is still a lie.) My food was well received and our company all got along better than I'd expected. Danny won them all over with his drum solo of the knives on the condiments. Like I said: top-shelf drummer.

We'd told all of them beforehand that we were dating, and encouraged the impression (sinful liars that we were) that it had been going on for a while but that we'd been hush-hush about it; only in light of my getting sacked, supposedly, did we decide we could finally spill the beans.

"That was our original plan, too"—Steve grinned—"but then they had to go and legalize gay marriage before either of us could get ourselves fired, so we gave up on the hush-hush."

"And got seventeen gift certificates for the museum gift shop at our wedding," Elliot added drily. They subtly cocked their fingers at each other, their little show of affection. With a sudden jolt, I realized I missed these people after just a few days away from them.

"So I hear you're the one who gets credit for our friends meeting," said Elliot to Danny.

"Aye, true enough, I am surely." Danny laughed shyly, raising his bottle as if to toast himself. I envied him that ale—his fourth in sixty minutes, but who's counting. "Didn't I dare him to pull out the ax and bang out a wee tune on the steps up to the museum? Ach, sure, he was cleaning up in no time, I was watching from the horse statue and they were throwing money at him left, right, and center—imagine how much he'd have made if he were any *good*?"

"Fuck off," I said. We laughed.

"Ach, and Sara comes out and tells him he can't play his guitar," Danny continued in his sickeningly sweet accent, "so instead he pulls out his tin whistle from his back pocket, and starts playing that, and wee Sara, she's so nice, she says she loves the sound but if the security comes, you can't play that either, and *he* says, what about a few tunes on the *fiddle*, then? And she says, no, but tell me, do you just play Irish music on that, or what's your repertoire?—and that's when the chancer starts bullshitting, and the rest is history."

Having never before spoken so many consecutive words to strangers, he then downed the rest of his ale and glanced longingly toward the refrigerator. I got up and played barman.

"He didn't say the *fiddle*, he said the *violin*," Sara corrected him. "He knew what he was doing."

"*Violin* is museum-speak for *fiddle*," I said in a stage whisper to Danny, handing him the ale.

"And you really had *no* American or classical repertoire?" Elliot asked. About every six weeks, Elliot asked me afresh to tell him the story of my bluffing my way into a guest lecturer gig at the MFA when I'd left school at fourteen (and according to my arts visa, was officially in the U.S. only to do Beckett plays and new Irish works). In his world, everyone stuck to whatever they'd been trained for, and he was star-struck by my resourcefulness.

"That's right," I said. Danny seemed relieved that I might take over the narrative duties, and gazed deeply into his ale. "She asked if I could play tunes that fit the eras of the paintings, for when they had tours. So of course I said yes I could, even though I couldn't, and then I spent the weekend cramming on YouTube videos of Ravel and all them."

Delighted guffawing around the table at a story they'd all them heard several times before but still found charming, because to be honest, it is a charming story. I opened my mouth to continue with my favorite part, about how I conned Sara into thinking I was expert on Thomas Jefferson's favorite compositions . . . but the mirth of the table had roused the dog.

Abruptly, almost out of her sleep, she leapt straight upright into the air, instantly upstaging me. Upon landing, she rested her chin heavily on my knee, looking up at me adoringly, for all the world as if she were waiting for me to continue. Gales of human amusement encouraged her. I didn't.

"Naughty," I hissed, and pointed my finger.

She lifted her head obediently—and then, as I opened my mouth to resume my tale, she immediately planted her chin even more firmly on my knee, and wagged her backside with defiant affection.

Everyone laughed.

"I'll sell you to the North Koreans," I warned. Immediately she sank to the floor and showed me her submissive tarty-dog belly, as our audience protested gleefully in her defense.

By the end of the evening, the dog appeared in twice as many photos as did I.

"Only an actor would care about that," said Sara, when I voiced my sentiments.

But I have to admit, although they were mostly Sara's friends, it was a great night, with lots of laughs. I really enjoyed them, and not just because they applauded the chef several times and there were no leftovers. Above all, it was mission accomplished: we had supportive friends and a dinner party all on official record before our wedding.

OUR WEDDING. WHICH was not, we re-agreed every day and every night, any kind of declaration of anything between us. It was simply a piece of paper to be filed away under "favor." It meant nothing. It changed nothing. Not that there could be much to change, anyhow: we were getting married after dating for about a week. (We were mad about each other after dating for about a week, too, but that was a coincidence.)

Massachusetts had a three-day waiting period, and Rhode Island didn't. So Sara took a sick day and we drove the forty-five minutes to Providence. She told no one. I told no one. Not even Danny. Lena, Elliot, and Steve might try to treat it as an actual marriage, and give us gifts (or dire warnings), which would be ridiculous since we weren't even living together. And too many of my mates . . . well, I hadn't seen many of my mates in the past few years, since I'd stopped drinking my paychecks. Danny would get a chuckle, but he'd only really met Sara the one time, and he'd spent half the evening playing with the dog.

PROVIDENCE CITY HALL was a great ol' building, like an old-fashioned post office mushroomed out of control. I half expected to see bubble-gum-ball dispensers around each corner. Marble floors and a broad wooden staircase in the center; the upper corridors were all open, balcony-like, down to the lobby, so everything echoed in a muffled, serious way, like you imagine a sepia photograph would sound. There was something old-school-romantic about the idea of getting married there.

We filled out paperwork, which we then presented, along with our birth certificates and other documents, to our Bartleby-ish clerk (sound track: John Cage, *4'33"*), who was tragically immune to all attempts at levity.

"But I bet I can make him crack a smile," I whispered to Sara as we were in line to return our forms to him. She bit back a smile.

"No bet," she whispered.

"No, c'mon, bet me," I insisted. She shook her head. "I'm taking that as a yes," I whispered. "Bet's on." And then we reached the counter. "We're getting married," I said to Bartleby, grinning. (Having established that we were not *really* "getting married," it was great fun to pretend we were.)

"Yes, sir, that's what this form is for," he said in an uninflected voice, referring to whatever form Sara had just given him.

"Am I not the luckiest man in the world?" I beamed, grabbing Sara round the waist and fiercely kissing her cheek. She yelped with pleased surprise.

He blinked uncomfortably. "Congratulations, sir. I hope you'll be happy."

"I'm already happy!" I assured him. "I'm so happy, I could dance. In fact—"

"Oh, no," muttered my bride-to-be.

"—in fact, I think I will." I took a step back from the counter to make sure he could see me, and began a hornpipe—nothing fancy, just my threes and sevens, basic steps they teach us all in school at about the same age American kids are being taught the birds and the bees (something we were never taught because the Church wanted us to think emergent breasts were miraculous gifts from God, which I for one easily believed).

"*Rory,*" Sara said, with a pained grin for the poor bemused clerk. "He's a little excitable," she explained.

For the record, I am actually very shy. I would never have done that hornpipe if I weren't compelled by Sara's insisting we make that daft bet.

The clerk balefully handed us a list of judges and attorneys qualified to marry us. Standing on the outer steps of City Hall, I called each number in turn, getting bland voice-mail greeting after bland voice-mail greeting. Finally, two names from the end, an older-sounding gentleman answered the phone:

"Joseph Brown. May I help you?"

I hesitated, having given up expectation of reaching a human being. "Yes, em, yes . . . that is, yes." I looked at Sara with wide eyes; she mirrored the expression back at me. I pointed to the phone as if this would elucidate something; she nodded as if elucidated. "My, em, fiancée and I would like to get married. We've filled out all the forms and . . . we got your name from—"

"Are you in the city of Providence right now?" he asked in a tired voice.

"Yes, sir," I chirped. "We're right outside City Hall."

"If you come to my office on Dorrance Street, I can marry you now," he said, as if telling me where to catch a cab.

I was a bit disappointed that we weren't going to get married actually *in* City Hall, but I liked his unromantic, just-a-formality attitude. I got the address from him—and the hitherto unmentioned detail that we'd need to pay him a hundred bucks, cash, off the record—and we hurried to a bland office building round the corner.

It was that solid, old-building blandness that smells of dust and papier-mâché, subtle but insidious. My stomach started fluttering, although I told it there was no reason to—hadn't it been along for the ride all week during all our conversations about how this meant absolutely nothing? Because really, even though I was madly in love with this woman I was about to marry, it meant absolutely nothing. That was the agreement. We weren't even dressed up for it; she was wearing the same green sundress from our first date, I was in my usual cotton pants and collarless shirt.

We—Sara, myself, and my stomach—took a rumbly elevator up to the third floor, where we were met by a deserted corridor of industrial carpet, asbestos ceiling tiles, and fluorescent lights. We wandered cautiously while my stomach kept suggesting we go back downstairs and outside for some fresh air.

The office, when we found it, could have been a dentist's waiting room: more fluorescent lighting, asbestos ceiling tiles, industrial carpeting. The aging, bored-looking Mr. Joseph Brown, Esquire—complete with red necktie, otherwise colorless—got up from his comfortable chair behind his suspiciously-bereft-of-paperwork desk. There was nothing else in the office but a couple of file cabinets and his framed diplomas. It all looked like a stage set for an amateur theatrical.

"You must be Mr. O'Connor and party," he said, with a tired, unenthusiastic smile. I was glad that we weren't getting *married*-married, as this bloke was a buzzkill if ever I met one. I considered another hornpipe, but now that we were *here,* I just wanted to get it *done.* He shook our hands, asked for our paperwork, and said, without expressing the slightest interest in us, "You need two witnesses."

Sara and I exchanged looks. I could see her mentally ticking off the pros and cons of telling Lena, or just Elliot and Steve (Lena had loose lips), or maybe Danny . . .

"There's a jeweler in the next office," Mr. Brown, Esquire, continued in the same dispassionate tone. "He could probably spare a moment to come over here and be a witness for you. His wife spends most of the day with him, so she might be willing to come as well."

"Do we have to bribe them?" I said. As a joke.

He made a noncommittal shrug, and I realized: yes, we have to bribe them.

"They probably wouldn't mind ten dollars for their time," he said impassively.

"Each?"

Again, the noncommittal shrug.

So as Sara stood biting back a nervous grin, I went next door to the equally-dentist's-waiting-room-esque office to invite the nonagenarian jeweler, who sported glasses as thick as the Boston phone book, and his heavily jeweled octogenarian bride, to be our witnesses. They seemed to be expecting me. For a tenner each, they were happy to be witnesses. Not a bad racket, really.

"Is this the deluxe package?" I asked. "Will you be throwing rice at us and playing *Lohengrin* on kazoos and all that?"

They both stared at me uncomprehendingly for a moment. Then the husband—pleased with himself—declared, "Say! You're from Ireland, arntcha?"

"Explains a lot, doesn't it?" I said.

So there we were in a bland room with our bland witnesses and a bland minister administering a bland oath about taking each other to husband and wife, honoring and obeying and having and holding in sickness and health, for better or for worse, for richer, for poorer, to love and to cherish, from this day forward until death do us part, and so on and so forth, none of which I paid attention to because we weren't *really* getting married.

Although we certainly giggled like newlyweds as we said the vows.

Finally we got to the point: we signed a piece of paper—that fateful, magical, elusive *piece of paper* that was going to let me get a green card and therefore join the Screen Actors Guild and therefore finally have a legitimate career, including a touching Oscar acceptance speech in which I gave heartfelt thanks to the beloved and extremely sexy Sara Renault, my soul mate, for making all this possible.

I felt full of bubbles even though this was not personal. We were each going back to our own separate lives, and apartments, and schedules, and social circles. To one side, the jeweler's wife took photos on Sara's smartphone; to the other, the jeweler himself grinned for the camera, to make sure we got our tenners' worth.

" . . . By the power vested in me by the state of Rhode Island, I now pronounce you husband and wife," Mr. Brown, Esquire, was saying. And because he was old-fashioned under all that boredom, he added, with an unexpected wink: "You may now kiss the bride."

Chapter 4

So. We were married, which changed nothing at all, and would continue to change nothing at all, except for certain appearances intended to convince Uncle Sam: I left some clothes in Sara's closet, a few instruments in her living room, a toothbrush in her bathroom. But otherwise, nothing changed.

Well, to be honest, that's not exactly true. I had a mad crush on her, and I was secretly tickled we were married, although I wasn't sure I should admit it, since that seemed a violation of our agreement. I know it was a marriage of convenience, but I had genuinely fallen for her. I had to keep shaking my head and reminding myself: Rory, this is for practical reasons. And then I'd see her looking at me and I'd think, *I'm married to her!*—and I'd get so excited I had to tickle her to have a good excuse to squeeze her. She seemed to like the excuse to squeeze me back.

So it turned out not to be as casual as I'd thought. That's why, in part, I agreed with Sara that we just shouldn't tell anyone, not until we were settled into it ourselves more. My family was mostly back in Ireland now, lured home by the economic boom called the Celtic Tiger and then trapped by the meltdown that followed. Sara's family was mostly in New York or Chicago—as with me, her parents had already passed. She had an older brother lately moved to Milwaukee who would "probably flip out," so there was no family to tell yet.

So we didn't tell anyone. We didn't wear rings. We never considered actually living together. We continued on with our new-romance buoyancy, enchanting and nauseating all our mates by finishing each other's sentences, eating food off each other's plate, practicing our secret handshake in public. We threw lots of little dinner parties in Sara's apartment (the dog loved this, of course), taking photos for reasons we never told anyone, but the parties themselves were such great fun, and it was lovely to be toasted with equal heartiness by everyone from art-history professors to Trad musicians to plumbers. We had the honey-est of honeymoon periods. It really was romance, we agreed once the marriage certificate was stowed away in her bedroom desk. Romance is a glorious thing.

Not at all like being married.

But now what? The "marriage" was just a piece of paper, but a crucial one: the inaugural drop in a cascade of required paperwork. Sara was great with paperwork, from all those years of writing grants and convincing her bosses to hire impertinent fiddlers. A fortnight after the "wedding," she printed out a load of government documents, as well as absurd bits of advice from advisory websites, warning us we'd be asked what color our spouse's toothbrush was at the immigration interview.

That weekend, we huddled together at her coffee table over takeout Chinese. (Weekends I would always stay at Sara's place because her neighbor was away, so there was nobody to feed the dog.)

When I saw all the paperwork I was terrified. I knew to expect it, but my brain just shut down. I couldn't understand bureaucratic lingo. It was a foreign language I couldn't penetrate.

The goal, this first night, was just to get an overview of what was ahead of us. The dog lay stretched out beneath the coffee table on her side. To avoid getting stiff, Sara and I shifted all evening up and down, now sitting on the floor (best for moo shu), now on the sofa (fine for egg rolls). The dog, whose priorities did not match ours, made it clear that when we were on the floor, Sara existed to rub her belly; when we were on the couch, I was nudged into taking over this activity with my foot. I was less compliant than Sara.

Sara read over the forms and commentaries in concentrated quiet, and I pretended to do likewise. The phraseology was a load of mundane shite. Then it occurred to me that maybe some lonely government bureaucrat was an undiscovered poet, and had secretly encoded a complex rhyming scheme into the directions, so obscure and obfuscated that only a close reading of the text would reveal the scansion. I devoted myself to such a process for a good half hour, seeking rhythm where Sara sought meaning.

She had more success than I did.

" . . . ev*a*ding any pro*vi*sion of the *im*migration *laws,*" I tried under my breath, then huffed in disgust and gave up. "This is shite," I said, tossing the form down onto the table.

"Are you reading it closely?" Sara asked.

"Of course," I said, without defining what I considered "close."

"Are you thinking what I'm thinking?"

Every man dreads when a woman asks that.

"I'm thinking this crowd will not be writing for the *New Yorker*."

She gave me a look. Then she said, quite grim, "Rory. I think we might actually have to live together for a while to pull this off."

What? Panic. Slack face. I hadn't lived with anyone, not even a roommate, for years. I talked out loud to myself too much. I didn't want my morning routine of espresso-and-crossword messed with, it was the only thing that kept me from smoking. I didn't like anyone touching my laundry. "Why would we have to do that?" I asked.

"If we're married, we need the same address, for starters," she pointed out.

"We knew that. The plan was to use one address and pretend we both live there."

"And we should have the same health insurance, the same doctors—who's your doctor?"

"I don't have a doctor," I said, feeling defensive. "The Irish don't get sick, we just drop dead from alcoholism or existential melancholy."

"Well, you need a doctor because according to Form . . . hang on . . ." She wiped her left pointer finger on a napkin and poked at the papers. "Form 693 says you have to get a complete physical."

"I am already completely physical."

She rolled her eyes and soldiered on. "We should get on the same car insurance. Open a joint bank account—"

"A *what*?" I coughed, now really choking down panic. "For

what? We don't have any joint expenses. You're taking this too far. My cousin and I weren't bothering to do anything this involved. If we have to move in together, let's at least ease into it."

"The more shared expenses there are, right away, the better. We need a paper trail. That's why we should probably live together—not forever, but until you've gotten the conditional green card. Three or four months at least. Get our mail at the same place, share the utility bills, that kind of thing."

I was horrified. Getting married was one thing—but actually *living* together? We'd only been dating a few weeks. That's not nearly long enough to get over the distraction of another person's scent on the sheets, to become immune to the foreignness of each other's bathroom rituals and daily tics. I *loved* waking up next to her, but then slipping away at dawn to return to a purely Rory-centric world. I loved the frisson that came of not knowing exactly when or where we'd see each other next. Living together would ruin that.

"What do you want, frisson or a green card?" Sara asked, when I said so.

I pursed my lips. Suddenly priorities became clear: okay, so we'd have to live together, temporarily. However, independent of my laundry peccadilloes, and the talking-to-myself, and the espresso at my local café, it would be a bloody pain to pack up and move my LP collection. "You should move to my place," I said decisively, "because it's bigger and closer to the T."

She almost spat from the laughing. "Are you serious?" she asked. "What about Cody?"

As usual, the dog had slipped my mind. "There are plenty of dogs who just stay in all day," I said.

"They don't allow dogs in your building. I saw a sign. So you'll have to move in here or we'll rent a new place together."

Internal alarm bells sounded so loud I got a sudden headache. "You sound terribly casual," I said. Mentally I was trying to guess how many boxes I would need for the LPs.

"I'm just trying to do this thing right," said Sara.

"I have lived in the same place for *ten years,*" I said.

"That's not really true, you sublet it several times to move in ill-advisedly with certain girlfriends," she said. "Remember who you're talking to? I knew your entire romantic history before I was ever close to being a part of it."

"But all my *stuff* was there. I knew I could always come home to my *stuff,*" I said. "Are you telling me to give up the place where all my stuff has lived for ten years, after us dating for a few *weeks?*"

"I said we can move in somewhere new together if that helps. As long as it's dog-friendly."

"It doesn't help, and besides—the *dog* decides where we live?" I said. "It's all about the dog."

"Actually, it's all about the green card," she replied without looking up from the form. "They want to know if you're a communist," she said, reading. "Or a Nazi."

"Don't change the subject, please. This isn't going to work if you keep making me feel like I'm *beholden* to you," I warned.

"I'm not doing that," she said.

"You are."

"I'm not."

"You *are.*"

"I'm *not.*"

"You—" I grabbed a couch cushion, slammed it to my face, and briefly screamed into it with the frustration. God, that felt better. I lowered the cushion. "You are," I said calmly.

"I'm not. But I'm not willing to give up my dog so you can get a green card."

"You should have thought of that before *insisting* that I marry you," I said.

"*You* should have thought of that before marrying a woman with a dog," she retorted.

I moved in with her.

No, let's be clear about this:

I moved in with *them*.

Chapter 5

I sublet my place (month to month). We told all our friends that we were shacking up together; my mates were shocked and stunned, to say the least, knowing me for being single so long, and going on about having my own place—and then moving in with her so fast. Her friends were "concerned but supportive," she reported. Her last live-in relationship had been pretty awful. The museum crowd had seen her through it and now they were all—especially Lena—protective, and so they were a little anxious that it was happening so quickly. (Although for the record, Lena generally liked me, considering me the opposite of the evil ex—she referred to me as "the anti-Jonathan." "That must mean Jonathan has a very small cock," I said, to which Lena replied that that wasn't a very funny joke for me to share with anyone but Sara. Prude.)

Danny lent me his truck to drop off boxes, instruments, and a large suitcase.

And then there I was, moved in with her.

And it was, of course, awkward and weird and yet secretly exciting in its way, because I loved being around her. I digitalized all my music and brought it with me on my iPod, which made me feel very twenty-first-century despite my established history as a Luddite. I kept reminding myself that this was only temporary, for a greater cause, and that we would weather it as friends. And because we were so damn crazy about each other. Who knew, maybe someday we'd think about doing this for real?

Maybe. Probably not, though. Everyone knows romance lasts longer if you don't live together.

Meanwhile, I became preoccupied with earning my keep. I paid for a cleaner to come weekly, after it was made clear that I did not keep the bathroom as neat as I imagined myself keeping it. I pretended to be Colin Farrell on her answering machine. I cooked meals for her, and I gave her foot massages and caressed her in bed. I serenaded her.

And I promised her I would not scratch the very nice paint job in her apartment when I eventually started climbing the walls.

The thing about out-of-work actors and musicians is that, besides being out of work, we can't go job-hunting like normal people do. Between my expired visa and the government checking me out, I wasn't supposed to be working *at all*. I taped an audition for Dougie to send to the producers, to get the ball rolling should the Irish-detective-rock-star series get off the ground. That was exciting, got me downtown to the offices of Boston's best casting director, but took less than an afternoon. Meanwhile I had to turn down *Timon of Athens,* not that I was so excited about it, that character is sort of a prat, but still. I shouldn't've even gone back working for Danny's uncle under the table, but I'd snuck in a few days here and there. I had a bit of a nest egg, so money-wise I was comfortable enough, but I did have a lot of downtime and sometimes got itchy feet.

The first week or so at Sara's I spent getting used to the neighborhood and creating a routine. The ritual became: We got up together, had breakfast, Sara walked the dog around the block while I cleaned up from breakfast. We then deserted the tragically sighing dog, I'd stroll with Sara to the bus stop, then I'd duck in to City Feed to grab a coffee and paper for the crossword. That finished, I loved meandering around Arnold Arboretum. I'd bring a book, headphones, walk for miles, and then treat myself to an afternoon espresso up on Centre Street. I bought a single-speed secondhand bike, and sometimes I'd cycle up to the cemetery, by the overpass, or in the other direction to the village in Brookline, feeding the ducks in Olmstead Park. Sometimes I'd chat with the old folk who sat on the benches along the water, taking time out from their old folks' home across the way. Late afternoon, I'd head back, pick up some groceries at Harvest Co-op, using the pearly-new debit card from our pearly-new joint bank account. Then I'd bring the groceries in, give the dog (half catatonic from her afternoon siesta) a treat, throw on some sounds, and prep the dinner. Sara would come home, and there would be happy hugs and kisses and nuzzles . . . for the dog.

And then some for me.

Sara would head out with Cody for a long off-leash run in the arboretum while I continued getting dinner together. Once I'd indulged her sharing an hour of her limited free time with the dog, the rest of the evening, she was mine. I would entertain her with a few songs, a tickling match, a game of Scrabble using only proper nouns. For a week, our life was a romantic-comedy montage of people-being-playful-in-love scenes. Even though her place never really felt like mine, it was a lovely and manageable limbo. Everything that first week felt like a game, like we were somewhere on vacation, or at worst, we were kids playing house.

But came the day when it was raining torrentially, *and* I was between novels, *and* I'd pulled a thigh muscle, and frankly, after walking Sara to the bus, all I wanted to do was go home and vegetate on my own couch all day while sorting out what to do with my sorry little unemployed arse. I was feeling heavy-duty nostalgia for my own space, for all the familiar energies and colors. But I couldn't go home, as my home was now otherwise occupied. And I couldn't go to my mates', as they were all gainfully employed. And there's only so much time you can sit in a café unless you're writing a novel. But the prospect of lying about all day in someone else's place . . . with someone else's dog . . .

It's for the green card, I reminded myself, waving to Sara as she settled onto her seat on the bus while the rain penetrated my mop of hair all the way to the scalp. I headed back to her apartment.

As I approached, I saw the dog inside, staring dolefully out the window up at the wet treetops. I wondered if I could lock her outside in the yard and have the place truly to myself, without feeling like a right bastard. I realized that probably, I couldn't. She heard the key in the lock, and despite her doleful state, was prepared with her happy-puppy-welcoming-Mum-home routine by the time I'd opened the inner door . . . then she froze, halfway round her first circle, and cocked her head at me in confusion.

"Hey there, Cody!" I said.

At that moment, something clicked in her little canine brain. When I would arrive home before Sara in the early evenings, I was simply a Curiosity . . . but claiming ground in the middle of the morning somehow made me Significant. She leapt at me, joyful, her forelegs grappling against my lower chest, her tongue flicking out snakelike hoping to reach my face. She was frenetic, as if she'd just discovered a long-lost sibling on a passing raft in the Pacific. I pushed her off me and brushed away stray dog hairs; she continued to leap, to prance on her hind legs, to throw herself off balance by the ferocity of her own wagging tail.

"All right, calm down," I said, feeling both flattered and irritated by the attention. She immediately sat, her tail thumping the rug, and stared up at me expectantly.

"Don't stare," I said. I took off my raincoat and hung it on a peg by the door, as she continued to stare at me expectantly.

"Don't stare," I growled. I went into the bathroom to towel off my hair; came back into the living room and settled myself supine on the couch to the natterings of *All Things Considered,* and groped around the coffee table for the remote to the telly, hoping Sara had a sports package (definitely wishful thinking).

The dog, with repressed wiggles, sauntered over to the couch, then sat down right beside me so that she could stare into my face close up, in case I might do something interesting. This made me very squeaky-bummed.

"Sara didn't teach you *don't stare*?" I asked. She moved her head closer to mine and then nudged my shoulder with her nose. Twice. Then a third time, since I was being dense about responding to her and she wasn't used to that.

I pointedly ignored her, simply lay back and stared up at the ceiling listening to NPR since I couldn't find the remote. Eventually she went back to treetop-scouting.

I don't mind an hour or so of NPR, but after a while it all becomes repetitive. I got up and turned off the radio. In the sudden silence, Cody jerked her gaze from the window to me, with joyful expectation, as if I had volunteered to replace Robert Siegel as the day's entertainment.

"Well, now," I said. "It's a bit of a situation here, isn't it? How about I play you some tunes, and in exchange, you promise not to stare at me for the rest of the day?"

She stared at me.

But Cody, to be fair, was a gratifying audience, at least for the guitar (she went under Sara's bed when I tuned the fiddle). In particular, she was fond of the opening riff to "Smoke on the Water," instantly flopping into tarty-dog pose upon hearing it, as if she wanted nothing more than to be ravished by Deep Purple.

It really wasn't a half-bad way to pass the day.

But one day turned into a spate of wretched weather: three days of heavy, torrential downpours followed by another three of driven drizzle. One of those cold damp weeks when the lights have to stay on all day because daylight never got above 60 percent.

So what I thought was a one-off became a new routine. It was good to get back into the habit of daily practice, but that didn't quite fill up the hours either, and being stuck inside with the dog was hard. She watched my every move, she followed me from one room to another, always expectant, always wanting something. Sighing when I didn't provide it. Sliding into tarty-dog pose in a final plea for attention. Sighing *while in* tarty-dog pose when I continued, for my own sanity, to ignore her.

And even as the rain began to clear, the mercury began to drop. I realized with a sinking feeling I'd be earning the green card by spending much of the coming dark New England winter being stalked by a dog in someone else's small apartment.

Sara green-lighted me on adding a sports package to the cable so I could at least catch some footy and watch Manchester United trounce Liverpool. It took the dog a while to get used to my shouting at the telly and dancing a jig when United beat Liverpool. Again. Over the years I'd grown to enjoy American sports, and all the Boston teams, but footy will always be and is my first love. And John Henry, Mr. Owner of the Red Sox, put me in a difficult position when he bought Liverpool F.C.—the playoffs were beginning, and although Sara was not into sports, *everyone* in Boston is into the Red Sox. There's a rule or something. We agreed not to discuss it. But under my guidance, the dog developed a healthy respect for Man United. Not that I talked to her about it; only Americans and Brits discuss sports with their dogs. I talked directly to the television, loudly, and was gratified that she was interested in what I had to say to it.

RAIN FINALLY STOPPED. And after what felt like an eternity, the sun came out. A gorgeous autumn was unfurling in New England. One benefit of being at Sara's was its proximity to Arnold Arboretum. Imagine all the best parks in all the British Isles got dumped together into one place on the outskirts of Boston—and we lived walking distance from the front gate. I went back to walking there every day. The colors were starting, the air was loaded with cool autumn scents and full of thriving birdlife, almost like the rurals in Ireland.

But the days were getting shorter, and that led to a new canine-related tension. Just a little one—we only ever had little tensions, which is mad when you think about it, because what we'd just done was borderline insane. To go from being casual colleagues to living together as a married couple in less than a month. Except for the dog, the only stressor so far was that I was not as clean in the bathroom as I'd given myself credit for all these years. And as I said, I was attending to that. Otherwise, I thought I was doing a brilliant job of waking up in somebody else's bed every morning without going mental, and Sara was doing a brilliant job of waking up with somebody in her bed every morning without going mental either. (The cuddling helped.) Both of us had moments of needing to just get away and have space, but the arboretum, even in the rain, was unfailingly perfect for that.

Speaking of which, our tiny conflict was this: before I came along, Sara would rush home from the museum and take the dog for a brisk long walk each evening. As the days got shorter, the urgency to get home quickly and then out the door right away increased. And once the clocks changed, Sara alerted me, dark simply fell too soon, so she'd have to get up extra early to take Cody for a longer walk than usual before work.

I did not much fancy these scenarios, because they smacked too much of real life, as I was trying to pretend we were still playing house and prolonging our romantic-comedy montages. I fancied a rosy-tinted scenario in which Sara came home and found me cooking dinner, and we had a leisurely chat about the day over a cup of tea. And I also fancied a scenario in which she left for work in the morning at the last possible moment, slightly rumpled and hopefully smelling of me.

So—strategically—I offered to walk the dog every day while Sara was at work. I made this suggestion as I was preparing chicken korma, just to make sure she noticed what a fantastic bloke I was. Her face lit up.

"Do you know how many gold stars you've just earned?" she said, grinning.

"You better believe it," I said.

Cody, staring between us as if she could follow English, joyously collapsed into tarty-dog pose in the middle of the kitchen.

SO THE NEXT morning, as usual, I left Sara at the bus stop, ducked in for a coffee and crossword, finished, and came home. Then I mustered up enthusiasm for the dog, who had taken up a vigilant position by my guitar lest she miss "Smoke on the Water."

"Cody," I said, and she started. "Want to go for a walk? A walk?"

She knew that word. She *loved* that word. She was practically throwing herself at me before I could even grab the retractable leash.

I put the leash on her, and we headed out, the dog dashing ahead like an escaped toddler, and then glancing over her shoulder at me in delighted amazement, as if concerned that I might change my mind about this. Walking Alone With Rory had never happened before, it wasn't part of the routine of Being Sara's Dog, and therefore it was seismic in significance. Each time she realized that yes, we were going to *continue to walk,* she would prance briefly with ecstasy, then return to straining at the leash. She reminded me a bit of myself the one and only time I'd done coke. I had not been on a leash then, but maybe I should have been.

I took her through the main gates of the arboretum, along the paved avenue lined by huge gorgeous trees of stunning crimson and yellow foliage, then off-road, up the slope by the demure lilac bushes, over the crest and down through the yellowing beeches, down by the stream, across Bussey Street to Peters Hill, where everyone let their dog off leash. We jogged happily together up to the top, and looked out over verdant treetops into Boston.

"This is all right, isn't it, Cody?" I said to her, and tousled the top of her head. She stared up at me with the expression she gave Sara right before Sara fed her. Around us, other people and their pets were also taking in the view. A dog walker was getting pulled across the hillside by five mismatched canines, none of them as good-looking as Cody, or as calm. A lanky bloke with a bald head in a dark cashmere coat, sitting on one of the squared-off rocks, gazed out over the vista with a slightly melancholy air, humming what sounded like a Leonard Cohen song (in other words, humming sort of tunelessly in a minor key). A moody-looking, androgynous teenager, skulking on the edge of the viewing area and smoking, was watching all of us more than the view.

"You have a *gawgeous* dog," said a sturdy young mother with a strong Boston accent. She was breathless in her anorak from pushing a strange-looking stroller to the top of the rise. It looked to be a regular stroller, with a regular toddler strapped in . . . but with a sort of skateboard attached to the back of it, and an older boy, maybe four, was standing on this. He had a riot of freckles and red curls, and he gasped with pleasure when he saw the dog, as if there were no others on the hilltop.

The mother held her hand down and the dog trotted to her, tail wagging gently. Cody pushed her soft-haired muzzle into the women's fingers, and was rewarded with a face scratch. She glanced up adoringly at the woman.

"Doggie!" proclaimed the son, already with a thick Boston

accent himself. He toddled off the skateboard to her and sank his fingers with fierce delight into her neck.

"Careful! Gentle!" said his mum, glancing at me whilst grabbing his arm above the elbow as if she might want to tear it off. I shrugged reassuringly. Cody wagged her tail and looked adoringly at the boy even as he strangled her. The mother relaxed her death grip.

"She's so sweet!" said the mum admiringly. "You're lucky. Our dog is a nutcase. Yours is so mellow."

"She's not my dog," I said quickly, on reflex. Then added, in a more measured tone: "She's . . . my . . . wife's dog." I wasn't used to saying "my wife," but this seemed a good time to practice.

The woman looked confused. "Doesn't that make her your dog, too?" she said.

Oh God, that couldn't be right.

"Well, we *just* got married," I said.

"Really? Congratulations!" said the woman, grinning.

"Hey, congratulations!" said the dog walker, over his shoulder as his charges began to nuzzle their way down the hill.

"Cool," said the sulky androgyne, with an approving chin jut. "Congrats."

The tall bald man shifted thoughtfully on the boulder, nodded, and said, "Well done," as if offering a benediction.

"Thanks," I said to all of them, feeling my cheeks burn, but in a good way. "So anyhow, I think of her as my wife's dog."

"She's your *stepdog*," said the bald bloke, quietly pleased with his neologism. Cody, as if also pleased, suddenly ran toward him, almost whining with approval, and threw herself at his feet in tarty-dog pose.

He smiled, with a certain reserve, then reached down and rubbed her belly. "How do you like being a stepdog?" he asked her, without the baby-talk cadence that almost everyone uses to talk to dogs. In response, Cody whacked her tail against his leg.

"Stepdog," I said after a beat. "I suppose that's what she is." The bloke gave me a confiding smile and winked.

That was the beginning of something huge, but I hadn't a clue of that yet, and it took a while to rise to the surface.

Chapter 6

A nd so began our winter routine.

Mornings in the arboretum were great: not only did I stay in shape but I got used to referring to "my wife," as several times a day I was told what a commendable dog I had, and I had to explain she was actually my wife's dog.

Don't get me wrong. I enjoyed bringing Cody out for a walk. We got along. She was the canine version of a top-shelf, graceful teddy bear, and exactly the right height to touch noses with the kids, which was great crack to watch. She was always gentle with them, even when they tugged on her floppy ears and screamed with ecstatic shrillness right into her face. She was the first close encounter of the canine kind for many of them. Occasionally, enamored parents would even take her photo with their kiddies, up there on Peters Hill. She made me appear, by association, the most superlative of dog-dads; any helicopter parent would have envied me for the endless compliments I received about my beautiful, sweet, well-behaved, adorable dog. But I thought of her wholly as Sara's, and felt I'd be lying by omission if I didn't correct people to explain that she was, really, just my wife's dog. My stepdog.

There were regulars, on our walk, I suppose because it was always the same time of day—that dog walker, for instance, was almost always crossing Bussey Street in the opposite direction when we were. In particular, there was a little cadre up on the top of Peters Hill, who always seemed to be planted there, or coming, or going, just as we arrived. I grew friendly with them because first, I'm a friendly bloke, and second, it seemed I was in the company of the park's most popular dog. There were plenty of other dogs on the hill, but I rarely met their people—in general, dog owners introduced their dogs instead of themselves. Anyhow, Cody liked people more than dogs, and so did I, so we were drawn to the small but reliable dogless contingent.

The three I saw most regularly, who I privately referred to in my mind as the Three Musketeers, had all been up on the hill that first morning. I wouldn't call them intimate friends—we didn't trade confidences—but it's nice to have some routine and regularity when you're as rootless as I was then, and they were it.

First was the mother of two, Marie, who was from Dorchester, and who told me with enthusiastic brusqueness she was Irish herself. This is a thing the "Boston Irish" never really understand: if you were born and raised in America, *you're American*. You can be Irish American, but you are not Irish, any more than an African American is actually African. I don't care if your grandparents came from Ireland; I don't even care if your mother did. If you grew up in Southie, you're American, and what we have in common is that we both live in Boston, not that we're both Irish, because we're not. End of story.

Marie was a lovely woman, salt-of-the-earth working class so familiar to me in sensibility, with a brash laugh that made me want to take her to see a football match (and scored her, in my mind, with a Cyndi Lauper sound track). Her little ones got their red hair from her, but she kept her own coif tucked under a hat.

Marie didn't just have two kids, she also had a husband who was on disability from an accident at work, something about driving forklifts. He was getting better, but in the meantime his mother needed more and more help every day because she refused to move into assisted living, so she had instead moved in with them. So Marie had cut way back on her housecleaning schedule to take care of her own household, and she loved her arboretum walks because it was her only chance to have time just for herself (except for the two boys). She talked loud and fast and had a hilarious lack of filter when it came to talking about what was on her mind. That's why I knew so much about her private life without ever asking.

The second Musketeer was Jay, the tall, slightly melancholy man who sat on the boulder in a long cashmere coat. When I say he was bald, I don't mean his hair was thinning or he shaved his head. His head (when he was hatless) looked like it had been *waxed,* as if there weren't even any hair follicles left to grow out of it. His coloring was nondescript, but his face looked like something described in a Victorian novel, both soulful and aloof, both haughty and sad; if he'd a Brit accent he'd've easily passed as a ruined viscount or something. He dressed like he had money, but not like he wanted anyone to notice. Of course, I was fascinated by how a bloke like him could afford to sit on Peters Hill all day, but I didn't want to be a nosey parker. The most I ever got out of him was that he had created something technical that he'd sold to some huge company for a lot of money, and was trying to sort out what to do next with his life. His sound track was Leonard Cohen's "Hallelujah," because he was nearly always singing it under his breath, and he even sounded a bit like Cohen when he did it. Cody really loved him and his grounded, understated alpha-male energy. If dogs have human emotions, I'd almost say she had a crush on him.

The third Musketeer was Alto, the androgynous chain-smoking teen who was obviously playing truant from school. Nobody seemed to have trouble with this, and I certainly didn't. Alto was trans—transgendered, either a boy becoming a girl or a girl becoming a boy; I wasn't sure which at first (I eventually figured it out—the latter) and I would feel like an arsehole for asking, so I just put the gender thing aside (until I figured it out) and got to know Alto as a person. More specifically, as a troubled teen who got a lot of sustenance from seeing the same faces on Peters Hill every day, even for a few short minutes. Alto had dark, wounded eyes that believed they had survived more existential angst than a Beckett character. Nothing was going to get through that armor, even though Alto surely wanted something to penetrate, or else why would he keep coming back to spend time with people who were trying to penetrate it? (His sound track was the Janis Ian song "At Seventeen.")

I realized within a week that there were unspoken connections and confidences among the regulars, whose paths never crossed away from Peters Hill. Little moments, little haiku of connection in the midst of their novel-length lives. So every day, even if it meant waiting around for the opportunity, both Marie and Jay—and now me, too—would say one kind thing to Alto, even if it was just a comment on clothing or weather. I don't know if they even realized they were doing it. Marie had so much on her plate with two kids, and Jay had so little that he often looked lost in space, but they both took time out from their preoccupations to check in with Alto, and that was pretty cool.

It tickled me that these strangers knew I was married to Sara, when none of our actual friends did. They didn't know it was a secret marriage (or for a green card, of course), but still I felt like I was sharing a secret with them, and that probably added to my fondness for them. I could brag on Sara until surely her ears were burning all the way to the museum, and I didn't have to worry they'd try to give me relationship advice, because they all assumed we were just a couple, period, same as that. In fact, they assumed the permanence of our marriage more than we did. And maybe I needed them to.

Because even as the trees grew glorious, the days continued to shorten, the windchill factor grew, and the apartment seemed to shrink. The marriage thing got tricky, took on a weight we should have anticipated but hadn't. Sara and I started pretending we were just lovers who happened to be spending a few days together shacking up, with no long-term plans to cohabitate. This made the in-your-faceness of cohabitation bearable.

We continued to spend time with friends together, eat together, sleep together, shower together, bicker over how much attention the dog was getting together, even contemplate holiday plans together (which was weirdly matrimonial). We trimmed Sara's front steps with jack-o'-lanterns featuring treble clefs and eighth notes, and argued about putting the dog in a costume (I was all for it) and compromised on a Red Sox cap.

And naturally we pursued the immigration process, since that was the only reason we were living together. This meant massive amounts of paperwork, but not all of it was government forms:

Uncle Sam wanted affidavits from our friends stating they knew we had a bona fide marriage.

Which was tricky, as none of our friends knew we had a marriage, period.

"It's TIME," SARA declared, a few days before Halloween. "You talk to Danny, and I'll break the news to the museum crowd."

I tried to imagine those masters of arts and doctors of philosophy learning their beloved little Sara had married an undocumented construction worker.

"Fair enough," I said heavily.

"They'll be delighted," she assured me.

So I gave Danny a ring that Thursday afternoon to see if he could meet up for a chat.

"Ay, surely," he said. "I'll see you in the Plough at half-four. I'm dying for a pint."

"Bit early, isn't it?"

"Ach, sure, it's Little Friday, and sure I've been doing demolition since seven this mornin'. I'd murder a pint."

Fair point, I supposed. I got to the Plough and the Stars bang on half-four, and walked in as Danny was polishing off his pint as another was being set down before him by the barman. He turned to me with a wink and a grin, curled his tongue up, glided it across his top lip, and licked away his Guinness mustache. "Ahhh, lovely. You're a gentleman and a scholar, Dermot," he said to the barman, and then to me: "How's it goin', big man? What's the crack?"

"How's tricks, Dermot?" I asked the barman.

"Great, Rory."

"Can I get—" I began, but Dermot finished my sentence:

"—cranberry and soda," and already had the soda poured. Top barman. "Did you see United?" he asked, sliding it to me.

"Ah, they were brilliant."

And off he went, anticipating another regular's needs.

"C'mon, we'll grab a table, Danny, do you mind?"

"Not at all, man." He swiveled off the stool and planted himself on the bench that ran all the way down the length of the pub.

I threw a tenner on the bar and grabbed a small stool, then sat on the outside facing Danny.

"How's wee Sara?" he asked.

"She's great. She said to give you a big hug, I said no fucking way am I hugging that big sweaty culchie bastard."

"Wanker." We laughed.

"Seriously, though, she sends her best."

"Ah, cheers, man. Be sure to tell her a big hello for me. How's the wee dog of hers?"

"It's grand, y'know," I said, wondering if I should allow myself to wander off topic, "but sometimes it's a bit much."

"What do you mean?"

I grimaced. "Ah, it's just how attached she is to it, way over the top. She talks to it like it's her *kid* or something. When I first met her, the dog was sleeping on the bed!"

Danny chuckled. "Ah, sure, the Yanks are mental that way, aren't they? I remember back on the farm, I had a dog I loved more than my own brothers, but we never let her in the house."

"Is what I'm saying!" I said, relieved to hear somebody else talking sense. "In Dublin we never let the dog inside—sometimes he'd sneak in and it would be like some special holiday for him, just to see what the kitchen looked like!"

"Aye, but they do things different here." Danny sighed.

"But having her in the apartment, you know, it's not a big place, so she's always underfoot, and she's so *needy* all the time. She's always looking at me like she *wants* something. I'm going mental, to be honest."

"Well, you did move in awful quick," said Danny. "Maybe you should move out and sort of ease back into the living arrangement."

"Well, that's the thing I wanted to tell you about, actually—"

"What, you need to crash on my couch, is it? Until your renter leaves?" He shook his head. "Ach, I dunno, man, you'll ruin my chances with the ladies."

"It's nothing like that," I said seriously. He was so surprised I didn't respond with banter or slagging that he frowned a little, and then slid his pint an inch away, a symbolic gesture meaning I had his full attention.

"What is it, then?"

"You remember I was going to marry my cousin's widow for a green card?"

"Laura, aye. Oh, I see it now—wee Sara's upset about it."

"Well . . . she was a bit when I first told her. But then she made a suggestion that would, em, result in her not being upset anymore."

"That being?"

"That I marry her instead."

His eyes bulged for a moment and then he started bellowing with laughter. "Marry your girlfriend? That's a terrible idea!"

"Why do you think we moved in together so fast?"

He stopped laughing, and stared at me. "Ach, come on now, you're not really going to do it, are you?"

I grinned sheepishly. "Already did," I said quietly.

His eyes opened even wider—and so did his mouth. "Come on now, you're full of shite!" he said with an anxious laugh. "You never did."

"We did. A few days after that dinner at Sara's when you met the crew from the museum."

"You're joking me!" he said, eyes still wide.

"I'm telling you, we did."

He laughed and slapped the table hard. "And not tell me!"

"We didn't tell anyone."

"But *me*! You didn't tell *me*! Aren't I your best mate? Ya *fucker*! Rory, that's mad!" He sighed heavily, with a disapproving shake of his head. But then, as I anticipated, he lifted his pint. "Here's a toast to the most devious little wanker I have the pleasure to think of as a friend even if he doesn't tell me he's gone off and got fuckin' *married*!" He drained his pint, licked the froth, and held up the glass. "Dermot!"

Then back to me: "So you're married," he said, and grinned. "So . . . how's it feel?"

"Feels grand," I said. "Except the fuckin' dog."

"Ah, fuck the dog," said Danny.

"No thanks. Not into bestiality. Not that I'm judging you for the suggestion or anything."

He bellowed briefly again. "What's the worst thing about the dog, then?"

"The dog is fine, it's the way Sara *treats* her that sends me round the bend. She talks to it like it can understand her, she's constantly touching it, patting it, scratching its ears, she keeps telling me what's going on inside the dog's head as if she could know, and I want to say to her, 'That's not what the dog is fuckin' thinking, all the dog is thinking is *feed me.*'"

He shrugged. "Sure all girls are like that with dogs."

"And our lives circulate around the dog—we have to be home to feed it and walk it, we never can go away for the weekend, she plans her week around when the dog needs a bath. She doesn't plan her week around when *I* need a bath."

"Well, in fairness, Rory," said Danny. "You're not so dependent on her as the wee dog is."

"She *encourages* the dog to be dependent," I said. "It's maddening to watch, to be honest."

Danny looked confused. "Are you saying that if she convinced the dog to be less dependent, then the dog could somehow give *itself* a bath?" He grinned and raised his glass again. "Now that, I'd pay good money to see."

I GOT HOME before Sara, and of course the dog, as always, greeted me with her usual delirious joy, as if she thought I had been abducted by aliens and my safe return warranted a tribal dance. And maybe a treat. No sooner did I calm her wriggling than she heard Sara's key in the door, glanced at me—checking to see if I wanted to turn in circles with her, I suppose—and then threw herself ecstatically at Sara as she entered. I waited for them to have their moment, which lasted longer than my moment with Sara when finally she gave me a hug and a kiss.

I boiled the kettle for tea and we sat with our mugs at the counter, reporting on how the news had gone over in our respective camps.

"It's fine," she said. "Steve was so excited I think he wants to throw us a party, and Elliot was, you know, cautiously approving. I got a little speech about the meaning of marriage and all that, which I can understand after all they went through for the right to wed."

"Sure," I said. "What about Lena?"

Sara brushed her thick bangs off her forehead with one hand, then nodded with her lower lip protruding a little, a tic of hers when she had tricky news.

"What?" I said. *"What?"*

"No, it's fine. She just wanted me to tell you that she'll lock you into Queen Hatshepsut's sarcophagus if you're taking advantage of my good nature."

"I promise not to take advantage of your good nature," I said solemnly, "as long as I can take advantage of your obvious desire to give yourself to me on the counter. *Right now*." I grabbed her round the waist with one arm suddenly, pushed both mugs out of the way with the other, then reached down to lift her legs up toward the countertop. She shouted with surprised laughter, pretending to fight me off, but I got her fully supine on the counter with little effort, and leaned over her. I reached toward her chest, to slip my hand under her bra, and dove toward her lips for a kiss, which I got, the tart. But before my hand had touched flesh, I realized that the dog was leaping up and down behind me, trying to find purchase on the countertop with a forepaw. Finally she stood upright enough to land a paw on the counter right at Sara's head, and was (barely) able to peer over. She glanced up at me, terribly pleased with herself, tail wagging, and then right at Sara, whose face was only inches from the dog's eyes.

"Hey, puppy." Sara laughed. "Whatcha doing up here? Who's a good dog? Who's a good dog?"

"Oh, well," I said, and pulled away, leaving my wife and her dog grinning at each other like a couple of eejits.

For the record, there was a lot of that kind of thing. Who's a good sport? Who's a good sport? Rory is.

WE FILLED OUT the governmental forms on Halloween while waiting for the kids to collect our homemade cookies. Cody did look comical in her Red Sox cap, which she kept trying to shake off. Sara had sewn herself an eccentric costume that I think was supposed to be an elf (as in Santa's, not Tolkien's). She modeled it for the first time Halloween evening and looked very cute in it.

"That," I declared, taking a bite of a healthy cookie, "admirably reflects both your efficient hands-on midwestern competence and your quirky Greenwich Village quirkiness. Not to mention your sexy legs."

"You said 'quirky' twice."

"Well, it's pretty quirky," I said sympathetically.

"Where's your costume?"

"I don't need a costume," I said, arms wide. "I'm already a real-life alien!"

"I should have seen that coming."

"You'd think so, given how long we've been married and all."

We settled by the coffee table with a plate of biscuits, two biros, and all the forms. I lay on the couch, a territory I had claimed since moving in, as it was the only thing that resembled my place. Sara, as usual, took the armchair, and Cody, as usual, rested her chin heavily on Sara's thigh. Without moving her head, the dog glanced with hopeful eyebrows between the bowl of cookies and Sara.

"No way, puppy," said Sara. "Bad for your tummy."

The dog sighed, tragically.

There were so many bloody forms. There was Biographic Information, there was the Affidavit of Support, with sixteen pages of instructions for Sara, making her financially responsible for me. Then the Petition for Alien Resident, again for Sara, saying Rory O'Connor was her husband so could they please not deport his arse. There was the pivotal Application for Employment Authorization.

Then came the big one: Application to Register Permanent Status. This was only six pages, but Sara commandeered it, partly because she's a little controlling but mostly because she didn't trust me to read it thoroughly. I can't say I blame her—so far my contribution to taming the paperwork had consisted mostly of serenading her with James Taylor songs and spoon-feeding her Ben & Jerry's. Since Sara had cornered the market on Serious Attitude, I suppose it was a kindness—to her—for me to add a little levity. She had been a good sport about it, but I found her reluctance to trust me with the most important form reasonable enough.

"I don't think you really *want* to be trusted," she said sagely, her keen green eyes glancing up from the form. "I think you *like* relying on me to be the grown-up."

"I think *you* like my relying on you to be the grown-up," I corrected. "*And* I think you like my being silly as well. So actually, you're benefiting from this arrangement doubly-o. I'm getting a green card, but you're getting two of your deepest psychological needs met. No, please, you don't have to thank me."

She squelched her smile, and looked back at the form. " 'Have you *ever*'—that's all caps, in bold—'have you **EVER,**'" she read, "'in or outside the United States knowingly committed any crime of moral turpitude—'"

"You're kidding me! Moral *turpitude*? That's not on there."

"'—any crime of moral turpitude, or a drug-related offense for which you have *not* been arrested?'"

I erupted with laughter. "Really? I can't get a green card if I admit I ever got stoned in the privacy of my own flat?"

"Mr. O'Connor," said Sara, wagging a pointy elf shoe at me. "Please take this seriously."

"I've committed a *morally turpitudinous* amount of drug-related offenses, but not in many years."

"I'll mark it no, then," she said.

The other questions I could answer with complete honesty—although Sara, earnest as she was, could not ask many of them with a straight face. No, Uncle Sam, cross my heart, I'd never been a prostitute, hijacker, kidnapper, or assassin, nor had I engaged in any other form of terrorist activity. I'm glad they asked, because the asking of that question would foil all those terrorists and assassins and hijackers and kidnappers applying for green cards.

We were interrupted by a buzz of the bell, and stepped out into the hall together to receive a large trick-or-treating gaggle of zombies, ghouls, and Harry Potter characters. A few protective parents hovered outside on the step pretending to admire our jack-o'-lanterns. When they saw the Red Sox–capped dog, most of the kids squealed and reached toward her.

"Cody!" said one shrill, delighted four-year-old Ron Weasly. It was Marie's son, Nick; I quickly scanned the parent gaggle and saw Marie herself. The dog took a moment to steel herself, and then maneuvered like a veteran celebrity through the group, making sure everyone had a chance to pat her, and delighting Marie's son by pretending to lick his face. He was awfully chuffed with himself for the being the only kid who knew the dog personally; it made him king of the under-fives.

Marie, meanwhile, grinned and waved at me. "'Dat your wife?" she asked, meaning Sara.

"The one and only," I said, feeling strangely exposed. "Sara, Marie, Marie, Sara. I know Marie from the arboretum," I explained to Sara.

"Congratulations!" said Marie. "You're a lucky woman, and he is *so* in love with you."

"Thank you," said Sara. She looked really pleased, which made me feel like a million bucks, as the Americans say.

"And you have the world's best dog," Marie added to Sara. She went on: "And I know you get all the credit, because he's always saying it's not *his* dog, it's his *wife's* dog."

That made me feel even more exposed. "He sure does," Sara said, her smile freezing a wee bit. "Always."

After the gaggle moved down the block, we returned to Sara's living room (sorry, *our* living room) so she could continue to interrogate me on behalf of Homeland Security. No, I did not intend to engage in espionage or overthrow the government. I'd never tortured anyone, denied anyone's ability to practice their religious beliefs, or served in a guerrilla group. "Never too late to start, though," I mused. Sara threw her pen at me.

"Here's that medical form," she said, holding it out. "Report of Medical Examination and Vaccination Record, you have to take it to a government-approved doctor to determine that you do not have . . ."—she pulled it back to read—"tuberculosis, syphilis, malaria, mental illness, or drug addiction." As I began to retort, she said firmly, "No more jokes about moral turpitude, please. You don't get to derail your own immigration process with puerile humor. Also there's another form here you have to take to someplace in Rhode Island, and have them measure your pupils or something."

"That's so *Blade Runner,*" I said approvingly, reaching for the forms.

There was another buzz from outside; Sara dropped the paper to the table and we both rose, which brought the dog dutifully scrambling up again. As we moved to the door, my cell phone rang as well. I glanced at the screen.

There it was again, that Los Angeles number.

"Dougie," I said quietly.

Her eyes widened, and she gestured broadly toward the back of the flat. "Go, take the call! Cody and I can handle the little ninjas."

I changed trajectory toward the bedroom as I answered.

"Rory!" said Dougie. "The Irish-detective-rock-star series got the green light!"

"That's fantastic," I said, suddenly terrified as I stepped into the bedroom and closed the door.

"And guess what, buddy: the producers loved your tape and I got you an audition with the studio!"

I did a triple take in the dark. "A *what*?"

"An audition. For the studio."

" . . . When? Where?" I asked, my stomach turning somersaults.

"It's in New York, at the studio. Date's not set in stone yet. We have to sort out the test-option contract, that'll take a while, I'll get you a good lawyer."

"I . . . I have to have a lawyer to audition?"

"I mentioned it before, Rory. It's a fifty-page contract, it's going to be more of a headache than your immigration paperwork."

"Just to *audition*?"

"You're not just auditioning. You're promising the studio that if they want you, they can have you for as long as they say. I'll e-mail you the details tomorrow, but I wanted to give you a heads-up. Also . . ." He hesitated, but was deliberately trying to keep his voice upbeat. "I don't think it will come up, but don't tell them you don't have the green card yet. If they ask, tell 'em you have it, you just don't have it on you."

Oh, *fuck*. I had been down this road before: three times I'd been cast in major films and then had to excuse myself for lacking the right paperwork. Turned out not even Ben Affleck could make me legal.

"Dougie, tell me, mate: Can I not do this without a green card?"

"Well, they can't *hire* you without a green card, and the contract is essentially a mutual agreement about potentially hiring you, so if you want to get technical, it would be better if you already had the green card, but I think we can fudge it until you actually get it. Just, you know, if you can do anything to expedite the process, that would be great." He was so forcefully chipper I felt exhausted for him.

I found it hard to breathe for a moment as I fumbled for the light. Outside, a little girl shrieked with joy, *"Doggie!"* A cascade of giggles and happy-parent-cooing followed.

Chapter 7

The next day, Dougie sent me an e-mail with a sample test-option contract. He was not exaggerating: that contract was to my immigration application what a Ph.D. thesis is to a primary-school book report. The United States government, for all its fussiness, was readier to give me a work permit than the television studio was to give me an audition slot. Immigration services made fewer demands of my immortal soul than did Redstar Entertainment. After days—weeks, I think, in the end—of faxing (via Sara's office) and tweaking and e-mails, repeat ad nauseam, there was a contract saying that if I took the part, I would be their chattel for up to seven years. When I finally signed it, I felt a rush of exhilaration, as if I'd hit the big time by simply being allowed to audition.

One anxiety-ridden fortnight later I borrowed Sara's MINI Cooper and left at dawn. I drove like a maniac, listening to the scenes Dougie had sent me—I'd recorded them onto my iPod and plugged it into the MINI's sound system. I'm a fast study and I'd already nearly memorized the whole thing. To be fair, the writing was good even if the premise was ridiculous.

I somehow avoided morning rush-hour coming into New York

from Connecticut. Since that is an impossible feat, I decided it was a day for miracles.

In the city, I parked in a painfully overpriced surface lot on the West Side, rushed eastward on foot, with guitar case slung over my back and fiddle case tucked under my left arm. I paused for coffee, and then sauntered in, as if I'd come from just around the corner, to an off-duty soap-opera stage near Lincoln Center. It was sort of like a black-box theater, with the vibe of a rehearsal room or backstage: high-ceilinged, dark, cool, the sound dampened somehow, the peripheries cluttered with lighting equipment and prop tables; marks taped on the floor; the faint smell of makeup and hair spray and gaffer's tape lingering in the air, saturated into the paint or something. Like a theater: an incubator for a fake reality.

There were four or five blokes dressed in casual black, one with a stubbly beard. By the time I got there, I'd convinced myself this was just like any other audition. Two of the blokes were whispering to each other. One then pointed to me as I set down my guitar and fiddle cases.

"Oh, right," said the other one, recognition lighting up his face. "You were what's-his-face."

"I certainly was," I said.

"Yeah," he said happily. "Yeah. In, you know, *Lear*."

Hmm. I'd played Lear's fool once, but it was a shite production.

"The bad guy," he said. "You know, the bastard."

"Edmund!" I said, and now my face lit up, too, because that had been a fantastic production, the best summer of my life—I'd been Edmund the Bastard in *King Lear,* in rep with two other equally great shows in some little barn in Nowheres-ville, upstate New York, only time I'd left Massachusetts as an actor, took the gig to forget about some Boston girl who'd dumped me. The pay was shite but I'd sublet my apartment for the whole summer, and as well as Edmund, I'd been Feste in *Twelfth Night* and Didi in *Godot*. Best summer of my life, creatively.

"I saw you in *everything*," said the bloke who'd been whispering. He had a proprietary glow delivering this announcement, and that was fine with me. "You were *phenomenal*."

"Aw, shucks, I bet you say that to *all* the bastards," I replied, with a flirtatious little swish. "You little motherfucker, you."

Nothing breaks the ice like being adorable and foulmouthed at the same time. I blew him a kiss. He looked very chuffed.

In fact, I sort of flirted with all of them, in the sense I made myself excessively charming and gabby, which comes to me naturally when my adrenaline is pumping and I know I'm on my game.

After I read, they asked me to sing (I'm a tenor but can reach baritone when I need to), and do accents. I did accents from Ireland—north, south, east, and west—then leapt around Europe, America, fumbled terribly on Australia, and steadied myself in England, moving south to north, and played the fiddle and guitar for them (this was a cinch). It was all a little surreal and strangely effortless, and it was gas seeing the delight on all their faces. Is this really all it took to break into prime time? I should have gotten married years ago.

"I love that he's the real deal," said one of the blokes. The others all shook their heads in agreement. Then one of them said, "You have a green card, of course."

"Yeah, of course," I lied, shocked at my own offhandedness. "If I wasn't so nervous I could recite the number off by heart. When you call me back, I'll sing it for you as an aria."

Usually I'm brutal in auditions, but this one I had nailed. I know you can never be certain, but I was more confident about being offered that role than I was of getting legal.

"I knew you'd be great, Rory!" Dougie crowed over the phone afterward as I hustled back to the car. "I'll let you know about callbacks. Get that green card."

When I got home that evening, exhausted but excited, my darling wife had soup and a sandwich waiting for me. After I gulped it down, we put all the paperwork together, threw in affidavits from friends, my last entry visa, certificates from a doctor and a fingerprinter, a copy of our marriage certificate, our birth certificates, passport photos, and filing fees of about $1,400 in a check made payable to the U.S. Department of Homeland Security.

Chucked it in the mail.

And then we waited.

And continued to play house.

With the dog.

Chapter 8

My unemployed status was somewhat ameliorated by getting cast (as I did most years) as Bob Cratchit in New Boston Theater's *Christmas Carol*—a creaky old chestnut I knew by heart, but Sara gave her okay, I loved the cast, especially the kids, it was easy money, a four-week contract (conveniently, they assumed my performance visa was still valid and didn't even ask about it). Best of all, except for a few days right before opening, I was only ever called to rehearsals in the late afternoon, so my arboretum routine with the Three Musketeers was barely interrupted.

Sara and I became increasingly matrimonial as the weeks passed, sometimes truly forgetting the marriage was for a green card. Several times a week I even stopped thinking about my LP collection for hours at a stretch. The Three Musketeers continued to cross my path—and Cody's path—and there was also a constant stream of people seeing the dog for the first time, which allowed me to practice referring to my wife until I could do it without a hesitation.

In fact it became a bit of a running joke. One day, when a new mother told me what a lovely dog I had, Alto immediately declared, sullenly, "It's not his dog," and then Marie said, heartily,

"It's his *wife's* dog," and then Jay concluded, like a tired professor, "It's his *stepdog*." It was as if they'd rehearsed it. We all cracked up, except the woman who had complimented Cody; she looked at us, a little leery, and then headed back down the hill.

"You should take that act on the road," I told them.

Alto looked genuinely tickled, possibly for the first time ever; Marie was cracking up, and even Jay seemed, despite his sad eyes, almost mirthful.

Meanwhile: my wife, my wife's dog, and I had a lovely Thanksgiving dinner with Elliot and Steve, and after my triumphant run as Bob Cratchit (seen by Marie and her son Nick, who thereafter idolized me), we also had a lovely Christmas up in Maine with Danny. Dog in tow, of course. She *loved* the snow. Born for winter, she was. Never seen her so lively. It was great crack taking her out on a frozen lake and watching her try to run without traction.

Mid-January, the United States Citizenship and Immigration Services wrote, summoning us to show up for our green card interview on March 1.

The next six weeks, with one amazing exception, were a fuzzy blur of unexpected normalcy and occasional quibbling about the dog. Because really—to be honest—everything *was really* about the dog. If we ignored her, she moped. If we went out for dinner and a movie, we had to get home straightaway to let her out. If we had a lie-in in the morning, and I was feeling turned on, the dog started to whimper and Sara would scramble to let her out and the mood was ruined, even if she (Sara) returned and crawled under the covers with me.

Otherwise it was all surprisingly cool. Maybe we were still in a honeymoon bubble, maybe we were both buoyed by the reassurance that we would not actually have to keep this up forever . . . but somehow, the six weeks of breakfasts and quotidian chores and private jokes led mysteriously to a sense of our simply being a couple who lived together. Memories of my bachelor life grew as distant as memories of puberty. I still didn't like her doing my laundry; I still wanted to leave my shaving kit in easy reach. I still thought she was getting taken to the cleaners with all her little skin-care products, which she tried to hide from me so I would not expound on the topic of what a rip-off they were. But even when I *tried* to feel panicked or trapped, it seemed increasingly *normal* that I lived with Sara.

And her dog.

The one stellar deviation from normal was the phone call from Dougie telling me I'd made the network callbacks. Fighting heart palpitations, I hopped on the bus to New York. This time some executive types were present, some of whose names I actually recognized from the telly, which made it all suddenly very intimidating and very *real*. I managed to be charming and witty, despite my pounding pulse. One of the blokes said it seemed on the tapes that I played well enough for them to easily overdub a real violinist.

"Excuse me," I said, "my character is not a bloody violinist. I play the fiddle, damn it, and I promise you, nobody in Hollywood will sound as authentic as this here fucker." Then I played "The Wind That Shakes the Barley," and as soon as they exchanged delighted looks, I segued quickly into an acoustic version of the Velvet Underground's "Heroin," just to show my range. At this, they grew quiet and exchanged heavier, more meaningful looks. I had them! It was great crack.

All I needed was the green card.

Then there followed weeks on tenterhooks, waiting for news of the callback as well as waiting for the immigration interview. I heard nothing from Dougie and there was no sense in my calling him because I knew he'd call me as soon as he had news.

There was absolutely no correlation between my irritation with not hearing anything and my irritation with the dog. But in fairness, the dog was getting under foot more than usual, and shedding all over the place, and Sara was spending more time than ever talking gibberish to her and getting distracted by her demands for attention.

THE NIGHT BEFORE the green-card interview, Lena threw a good-luck dinner party for us at her house in Belmont, which was gracious of her—evidence that she was not going to incarcerate me in Queen Hatshepsut's sarcophagus. As we were preparing to head out the door for that, Sara reached for Cody's leash and called her.

"You're bringing the dog?" I asked, in a more appalled voice than I intended.

"Of course I am. She didn't get to see me all day," she said, "and she knows everyone there and they all love her." As I continued to stare at her with rumpled brow, she hooked the leash onto Cody's collar and said patiently, "We do it all the time, Rory. We took her with us to Thanksgiving and for all of Christmas week."

"They were special occasions," I said. "You don't have to take the dog with you on every social outing."

"I do," said Sara offhandedly. "They'll be expecting her."

"Fair enough," I said, not wanting to ruin the mood, so made no more fuss about it . . .

... UNTIL AFTER DINNER.

When we'd arrived in the candlelit foyer, Cody had flung herself toward the guests coming into the foyer to greet us. Happy chaos ensued for a moment around her: as we unbuttoned ourselves from several layers of warmth, Cody dashed to all the guests in turn, whining with urgent happiness, her nails clacking on the polished wooden floor, her backside wagging wildly, her silky ears flopping like the tresses of an unkempt child, making it clear that seeing them again was the best thing that had ever happened in her whole life. Everyone swarmed around her and made high-pitched noises not associated with normal adults. It was a feeding frenzy of mutual affection, but mercifully it was brief, and soon she'd settled in a corner to stare at everyone all night.

The party was lovely, Lena's home was gorgeous and cultured, mostly candlelit, the food was terrific—saffron-scented paella, *suman* (sticky rice!), *lumpiang ubod* (a banana-leaf spring-roll specialty from her hometown, dipped in the most mouthwatering tangy peanut sauce)—the company charming, and lots of photos taken and immediately posted to Facebook per Sara's instructions.

My mate Danny (whose idea of dressing up was to wash his jeans) and, of all people, Elliot (whose idea of dressing down was to loosen his tie) had developed an improbable mutual admiration society over the past couple of months, and our disparate groups of friends were really coming to enjoy one another. I didn't drink, but others did, and there had been a warm, fuzzy, optimistic buzz to the evening. And so, as things were wrapping up, and Elliot and Danny suggested we all head out for a nightcap in a pub in Cambridge, I agreed instantly.

I found Sara helping Lena load the dishwasher. The dog was sitting beside them, helpfully offering to take care of any table scraps, wondering why the loud monster in Lena's sink got to eat them instead.

"The lads want to go for a drink to celebrate," I said cheerily.

Sara wiped her hands on a dishtowel and gave me a questioning look. "What about Cody? It's too far to drive her home and then come all the way back out this way."

" . . . She can stay in the car," I said, trying to make it sound as if I'd already thought this out.

Sara gave me her Princess Diana look. "It's twenty degrees out, Rory."

In this instance, I did not respond well to the Princess Diana look. "Are you saying we can't go out with friends because you insisted on bringing the dog to dinner?"

Lena closed the dishwasher door and then discreetly excused herself to the pantry on some pretext, summoning the dog to follow her. But the pantry was just a step or so away, and so, with an unwonted stiffness between us, Sara and I moved into the candlelit corridor for more privacy. Closer to the front door, in the foyer, the rest of them were sorting out whose coat was whose in the porch light from the transom.

"Look, we've got to be able to go out for a normal evening with friends," I said in a quiet voice. "We shouldn't be prevented because you decide to bring the dog to a dinner party."

"I do it all the time," said Sara, not even bothering to sound defensive. "That's how I live my life, and all my friends know it."

"Well, it's not how I live *my* life," I said. "I shouldn't have to live my life the way you *happen* to live yours."

She shrugged agreeably. "Fine. Go out with the guys and I'll see you when you get home."

"They want to take us *both* out," I said impatiently. "That's sort of the *point*."

She shrugged again. "Then let's take a rain check. We can go out with them tomorrow night, when there's actually something to celebrate. Tomorrow's a workday for some people, you know, so it's getting sort of late for a drink anyhow."

"I would be working if I could!" I said hotly. "*You're* the one not wanting me to work, and now you're telling me I don't get to do what I want because I'm not pulling my weight financially?"

She gave me a strange look. "I wasn't even *thinking* that. I meant Elliot and Steve have to work tomorrow. And doesn't Danny? And we have the interview! It just doesn't make sense to go out now."

"You're making excuses because of the dog."

"I'm explaining what the situation is—"

"Because of the dog!" I nearly shouted. Down the corridor, a hush descended, and demure glances were tossed in our direction. I took a deep breath and sighed it slowly out to calm myself.

She shrugged. "Fine, if you like, because of the dog. The dog is a big part of my life. You know that. I don't need to apologize for how I handle one of my central relationships."

Her smugness incensed me. "It's more *central* than your relationship with *me*?"

"No," she said patiently, "but it's more important than going out for a drink on a worknight, hours before the green-card interview."

I could not abide her self-righteousness. "So you're saying you're fine with making the dog a priority over our friends wanting to do something nice for us?" I could feel the pulse beating in my neck.

"I feel fine about making Cody's well-being a higher priority than hanging out in a bar with my husband who doesn't drink," she said. "If you disagree, go on out with them. Give them my best."

She was calm, and sounded matter-of-fact—in fact she sounded infuriatingly smug—but I could tell that she was seething just as much as I was.

"If you must make that dog the deciding factor in all your priorities," I hissed, now painfully aware of the other guests' interest in our argument, "this is never going to work. After the interview, I'm going to take my apartment back, and I'm going to stop bending over backward trying to accommodate your warped relationship with your fucking dog."

She looked flabbergasted. "That's your reaction to my not going out for a drink? My God, I had no idea you were that *childish*." She said the last word as a fiercely whispered condemnation, and turned on her heels to march back into the kitchen. Where she greeted her dog with her usual cooing affection, which affected me in that moment like fingernails scraping down a chalkboard.

Elliot, Steve, and Danny cautiously approached me in the hallway. All I could manage to do was smile and tell them that of course I was coming out with them, but Sara wasn't feeling well and wanted to head home. I was planning to have a cranberry and soda, of course.

HOURS LATER, RIGHTEOUSLY pissed, I settled clumsily into the bed beside a stone-still Sara. She made an unpleasant sound in her sleep, woke up long enough to say, in a disgusted voice, "My God, you reek," then moved as far to her side of the bed as she could get without falling off, and fell asleep again. It was the first time she'd ever gratuitously insulted me.

AFTER A BRIEF but very deep sleep, consciousness gradually returned, and with it, acute awareness of my first hangover in years. It was brutal. Just horrible. I was sick as a small hospital. My eyes were cemented shut, my lids too dry to slide over the eyeballs; my tongue was stuck to the roof of my mouth, trapping my own sour breath where I could not escape smelling and then swallowing it. My head felt stuffed with wool right off the sheep, complete with all the little twigs and brambles, so that there was a global sense of fogginess pierced by twinges of pain. While trying to get up the courage to force open my eyes, I heard banging outside the bedroom door; each new bang made my head throb. Sara was making a lot of noise to make sure I noticed that I had a hangover.

She was gone by the time I rose. There was a terse note on the counter: *Kennedy Building, Government Center, Room E-160, 11 am.* She thought me too irresponsible to remember when my own fucking green-card interview was.

I looked at the dog, curled up delicately in the bed to which I'd exiled her the very first night, her chin resting on her two crossed paws, the long silk of her ears draping over the side of the dog bed. She looked freakishly human in that pose. We made eye contact, and she raised her head a little as her tail thumped the wall, once.

"Do you have any idea the trouble you have caused me?" I sighed.

Her eyebrows lifted hopefully, and her tail thumped the wall again.

"Of course you don't," I said.

BECAUSE MY HEAD was fuzzy and my eyes refused to focus, buttoning the oxford shirt took ages. I'd planned to iron the suit coat but did not trust myself to manage without burning it. I had shaved before the dinner party last night, thank God; I could not have safely handled any sharp object now. No amount of cold water could make my eyes less bloodshot, my face less puffy, or my brain less clouded. Finally, bundled insufficiently against foul weather, I waddled to Centre Street, bought a large coffee at Fiore's, dragged my sorry arse to the Forest Hills T stop, and rode in to Downtown Crossing. My head was pounding without mercy; the roar of the T made it worse.

It was a grey late-winter morning, spitting down a chilled precipitation too wet to be snow. I had forgotten my hat and the rain felt both cooling and wretched on my ears and neck as I crossed the brick plaza toward the Kennedy Building. I arrived early, but Sara had arrived earlier. She was waiting outside for me: of course, under the circumstances, she would go out of her way to make me appear to be the laggard. Her short dark hair was waving wildly above her pink cheeks in the drizzle, making her look like some deranged pixie, out of place in a concrete jungle. Seeing the cold look she gave me as I approached, I craved a cigarette more than I ever had in my life. We stared at each other for a moment in silence.

"Truce?" I finally said, and held out my hand.

When you are gazed at scornfully by a beautiful woman you're in love with, especially when you deserve some of the scorn but most definitely not all of it . . . that's just rotten. Especially when you also have a headache and your mouth tastes like sour beer and you know you look like shite. And most especially when you are dependent on her immediate cooperation for something you have been striving to attain for fifteen years.

She glanced from my outstretched hand to my eyes and back to my hand. Then back to my eyes. "It's not okay," she said.

"I know that," I said miserably. "But please, can we get through the next hour, don't make me beg."

"I'm not making you beg," she said, affronted. "Who do you think I am?" A pause. With a grimace, she shook my hand. "All right," she said, "let's get this over with."

We reached together grimly for the door.

Chapter 9

As soon as we were inside the lobby, my cell phone rang. Sara looked at me as if I'd just farted in public.

"I'll turn it off," I said, and reached for it.

But out of habit I looked at the screen. "It's Dougie," I said in a stage whisper. "I can't believe the timing."

"We're going to be late," she said. "Call him back."

I stared at the buzzing screen knowing she was right, but still my stomach clenched with each new vibration. Finally it went to voice mail. Sara had already started off down the hall without me, looking washed out, even from the back, under the merciless fluorescent lights. The lights were buzzing at precisely the right pitch to make my swollen brain vibrate painfully within my skull.

Sara was standing inside the waiting room with her back to the door. It was a large room with glazed windows high on one wall and more fluorescent light panels flush in the asbestos-tile ceiling. Rows and rows of moderately comfortable, padded chairs were arranged as if this were a cheap airport lobby. At the far end was a bank of clerks, like hospital admitters or vendors at a train station. Everything was beige—the carpet, the paint on the wall, the clerks' dress, the clerks themselves.

"Let's go," she said as I came near to her, and strode off briskly toward the clerks. I tagged along behind her, longing for water, longing to close my eyes against the fluorescent glare.

We crossed a sea of nationalities, mostly Brazilian. A few Indian families, others Haitian judging by the nearly-Frenchness of their speech. One Asian, some Caucasians. A few Middle Easterners—I silently wished them the most luck, they would need it. Despite the anticipation and multiculturalism one might imagine enlivening such a place, it was tense and depressing. Maybe they had all just estranged themselves from their spouses, too.

We checked in with one of the clerks, then Sara crossed to an empty bank of chairs and sat. I moved as if to sit beside her. She gave me a cold stare, pale skin almost green in the fluorescence, and I moved two chairs away before sitting. Not because I was frightened by her iciness but because my own volcanic irritability was rising in response to it.

I was a white, native English speaker; the system was predisposed to go easy on me as long as I could demonstrate I was in "a bona fide marriage." Suddenly, for the first time ever, I worried about that. Twelve hours earlier I had declared I was moving out because I disapproved of my wife's affection for her dog. Bona fide husbands were probably not quite that reactionary.

"So glad I didn't marry my cousin," I said impulsively. "I mean, I think we'd have done it fine, but this feels so much better."

"Does it," she said, in a damp, uninflected voice.

Oh, fuck.

"Maybe I should just check Dougie's voice mail," I said, desperate for chitchat, and reached into my raincoat pocket for my phone.

She did not bother to argue with me, but released a sigh of fake boredom and looked around the room, making it clear that every stranger in there was worthier of her time than myself. I'd not known she was capable of being so insulting. My hands clenched.

"O'Connor," a male voice called. We looked at each other. I stood up. She didn't move. With nauseating dread, I was sure she wasn't going in to the interview.

"Put away your cell phone," she muttered, finally standing. "For the next half hour this green card is not about your brilliant career, it's about your *marriage*."

Surly but abashed, I put away the phone and grabbed her limp hand as we walked toward the middle-aged official who had called my name. He was tall and gaunt, and grim, like that servant in *The Addams Family*. He introduced himself as Mr. Smith. I bet all the immigration officials called themselves Smith.

He led us along a narrow hall—more industrial carpet, more fluorescent lights—and into his very little office, one of many off the same corridor. It was just large enough for him to slide between his desk and the wall and then sit behind his desk. There were two chairs on the near side and we took these. Sara's hand had remained limp in mine; she pulled it away as soon as we were seated. I tried to give her a reassuring squeeze before she had entirely removed it, but she ignored this and did not look at me. I felt my gut clench. Which made my headache worse. I felt like one of those rubber stress-release dolls, whose eyes bulge out when you squeeze their belly.

Sara, the furrow between her eyebrows misshaping her face,

unclasped a blue plastic accordion file: the most recent tax return, which she'd filed jointly; the records of our joint bank account, including printed statements showing that we both used it regularly. Affidavits from our friends, who all said they saw it coming and that Sara had never seemed so happy. Printed copies of all the photos from the parties and gatherings. She had spent hours preparing this dossier, although I'd like to think I helped some by serenading her and feeding her ice cream while she did so. She looked as if she wanted to simply hand the folder over to the bloke and then close her eyes and hold her breath until he made his decision. She did not want to ruin this for me, but her heart was not in it today.

I sat back in my chair and pretended I did not have a pounding headache or a mouth full of cotton. I wished I was still a smoker, and then I was glad I wasn't because then I'd be craving a smoke even worse than I was now.

The bloke had his own file on us, all the stuff we'd sent in weeks ago. He looked through it, as if for the first time, glancing up at us occasionally. He especially glanced a lot at me, which I'm sure had to do with how miserable I looked. To be fair, his own skin was a sallow pasty color and the bags under his eyes larger than the eyes themselves. I knew I had bags that morning, too, and hoped I did not look as saggy as he did, because that would definitely undermine the charm I needed to ooze, to make up for Sara's lack of spirit. Mr. Smith's expression suggested he was holding a grudge against one of us and hoped to find satisfaction before we left the room. Or maybe that was the hangover talking.

"So," he said at last in a droll voice, looking up. "You're married." He said it as if he already did not buy it. "How did you meet?" His eyes turned to Sara. She fumbled a moment, looking like a deer in headlights. *What a nightmare,* I thought.

Something clicked in Sara and she managed to summarize, succinctly but without enthusiasm, the story of my busking in front of the museum and how I kissed her when she laid me off. This was the story that, if told with her usual twinkly-eyed pleasure, would surely have netted me the green card right away. I could see that she was genuinely trying to look engaged, but what showed most was that she was making an effort. It looked and sounded forced.

Mr. Smith seemed pensive. Then he turned to me. I thought for a moment he was going to ask me what color Sara's toothbrush was. "You moved in together very quickly. Why?" he asked me.

"Because she has a dog," I said in flat, low tones. The pain was shifting from dehydration headache to tension headache.

He blinked. My response didn't exactly answer his question, but he found something useful in it. "What kind of dog?"

"A sort of golden-red silky mutt," I said—too promptly, so that it sounded like something I had memorized. I think that made him suspicious.

"Boy or girl?" he asked.

"Girl," I said more slowly, which again made me sound ragged. "Her name is Sara. I mean Cody." I had to suppress a welling up of the nervous giggles. Sara glared at me like I was mad.

"What kind of food does she eat?" he asked.

"Oh God, I don't know," I said, trying not to groan, the edges of my vision blurring from the pain. I sensed Sara squirm, and Mr. Smith's eyebrows rose a little. A slightly predatory look settled onto his gaunt features; now he looked *interested.* I was about to fuck this up—because of the dog. "The big blue bag with a giant salmon leaping out of a stream," I said.

He continued to gaze at me levelly. He seemed suddenly like a sheriff in a seventies TV show who was nice enough, but about to inform me that he was going to have to take me in. And secretly, he would enjoy it. After all, calling someone out was the only thrill to be had in his job.

"What's her name again?"

"Cody."

"How old is she?"

"She's two," I said.

"Three," Sara corrected. She paled slightly, and gave him a pleading look. "Rory can hardly keep track of his *own* age," she said, a nervous joke. "And he's right about the dog food, it's called Taste of the Wild and you can go online right now and see it. He does most of the shopping because I'm at work. He's bought it plenty of times."

Stop it, I tried to say to her psychically. She was terribly tense, and he was noticing.

He looked at me. "How big is the dog?"

"I'm not sure," I said, fighting off a rising sense of worry, which at least had the benefit of cutting right through the headache and giving me some clarity. This was not going at all the way I'd imagined it. "Maybe sixty-five pounds."

"Where'd she come from?"

"I don't know. She's not my dog. She's my wife's dog." I silently thanked all the young mothers of the arboretum for giving me the chance to learn to say that so offhandedly.

But Mr. Smith frowned. "Doesn't that make her *your* dog?"

"No, and here's why," I said, feeling my Irish temperament well up through the hangover fog and get the better of me. "Sara's mother had just died when Sara and her ex got the puppy, so she was pretty fragile. Her ex was such a wanker that her best friend Lena literally spits when she mentions him. He was very controlling and he decided they were going to have the best dog in the world, so he pressured Sara to take a *leave of absence* from her job at the museum, if you please, so she could be home with the puppy all day and train it. If I were her, I'd hate the dog for all that, but Sara's so affectionate and loving, and she *needs* affection and love, and she used to get it all day long at work, but now she only got it from the dog, plus of course the dog came of age believing that life consisted of spending all day every day with Sara, so they developed a seriously codependent relationship which frankly neither of them has grown out of, and explains why no matter what I do for the dog—and let me tell you, I do a lot, I take her out to the arboretum every weekday and we go to her favorite spots, every single day, rain, hail, sleet, or snow, and I give her treats—I have a whole bag of treats I keep in my anorak that Sara doesn't even know about—"

"You *do*?" said Sara, making nonhostile eye contact with me for the first time since Lena's kitchen.

"And all she wants when Sara comes home is Sara's attention, not mine, so yes, she is my wife's dog, and my stepdog, so I don't know where she came from. That's Sara's business."

I suddenly noticed I was standing up. Somehow in all of that, despite the hangover, I'd risen and started pacing in the tiny office, and didn't even realize it until I stopped.

I sat down. Quickly. "Sorry," I said.

Sara was staring at me. "I didn't know you gave her treats," she said, sotto voce.

"Not nearly as much as you do," I retorted impatiently.

A cough from Mr. Smith silenced us and commanded our complete attention. He grimaced, and looked back and forth between us.

"I think I've seen enough," he said, forebodingly.

I felt my stomach sink into my balls.

"I've been doing this a long time," he went on. "And that was about the most convincing display of matrimony I have ever witnessed in this room. Mr. O'Connor, sir, welcome to the United States of America."

Part Two

Chapter 10

The relief was so huge I almost couldn't feel it, the way your brain can't feel sleep when you're actually asleep.

But I wasn't sure if we were still friends or not. Sara was angry about things that didn't change when my immigration status did. Whatever was roiling around in her kept her from looking at me, so we surged like a harnessed team of horses out to the lobby.

Still . . . this was a *huge* moment, and it was *so* much her doing, and I all wanted was for us to be happy together in it. So I turned to her, grabbed her shoulders, and twisted her suddenly toward me. She stumbled, one ankle tripping against the other, so I grabbed her as she literally fell into my arms. She tensed against the fall and I squeezed her like I hadn't done in nearly twenty-four hours, which is forever when you're newlyweds and madly in love and recently fighting. She was trembling.

She squeezed the bejesus out of me in return, her face buried against my neck. Thank God. Now I really was the happiest man on earth.

"We did it!" I cheered. "*You* did it."

"*You're* the one who convinced him," she said with a relieved laugh. "Congratulations. *Welcome to the United States, Mr. O'Connor.* Wow!"

"Well, thank you, Mrs. O'Connor," I said, beaming. I pulled my head back enough to look her in the eye. "You are still Mrs. O'Connor, aren't you?" I asked carefully.

She gave me the Princess Diana look. "Do you still *want* me to be Mrs. O'Connor?"

I stopped myself from blurting out the obvious answer and pretended I had to muse upon it for a moment. "Oh, I suppose so."

She nodded, pleased. I thought we were over it. But then, of course, she had to point out:

"But Mrs. O'Connor has a dog, okay?"

I took in a larger breath than I meant to, which must have made it seem like I was about to protest because she raised her voice slightly to pre-empt me:

"And your relationship with Mrs. O'Connor's dog is why you just got your green card."

"That's bollocks," I said breezily. "If there were no dog, we wouldn't've had a fight, and I wouldn't've gotten drunk, and there wouldn't've been a problem, and today would have gone totally smoothly."

"There's no way to prove that," she said, and the furrow between her brows was all business.

I desperately wanted this moment to be purely happy and triumphant. "All right," I said, placating. "Cody gets extra treats today, then. But so do we. All right? Let's grab an espresso, 'cuz I fucking need one." I squeezed her hard again, and she squeezed me hard back again, and then we laughed with joy and with relief, and also appreciation at the madness of how it had happened.

She linked her arm with mine, which is always a great feeling with Sara, more than any other bird who's ever linked me. We rushed through the lobby, out the doors, and outside across the damp, raw, windy plaza and down the street to the nearest café, which happily was Bay State Caffeine, a hip Boston café chain of which the hippest was in Jamaica Plain.

It wasn't too crowded, but the elevenses crowd would soon be trickling in, so I gestured at Sara to grab a table by the windows and then I went to order for the both of us.

I'd been so casually confident of this happening (until twelve hours ago) that I really wasn't sure what I was feeling now. It was a shoo-in, and yet it was *huge*. Nothing would change, but everything would change. I heard the barista ask my order. "Double espresso, small chai," I said distractedly. "And one of these." I grabbed a little prewrapped chocolate biscuit and tossed it on the counter. What would change? What would I notice first? Sara would probably tell me it would be that I had to get health insurance, which was silly since I never got sick.

"Rory?" said the barista.

I hate it when people aren't *present* when you're serving them. I worked as a waiter for years when I first got here (under the table, with a fake Social Security number, like many of us). I'd been good enough at charming people to generally get and keep their attention, but it's humiliating to be treated like a robot. And here I was, my first act as a legal resident of the United States, doing it myself. I looked up, guiltily.

The person behind the counter was Alto, my young friend from the arboretum. We smiled tentatively at each other.

"Hey, Alto," I said. "Funny seeing somebody out of their native habitat. What are you doing here? Peters Hill not good enough for you anymore? You getting too full of yourself, is it?"

Alto looked shy but pleased, like a kid called to the front of the class for unexpected praise. "Filling a shift for a friend. I usually work the Centre Street store. What brings you downtown?" And very deadpan: "Where's your wife's dog?"

I grinned. "At home. But my wife is here. Hey, Sara!" I called over to the table, but Sara was in the middle of pulling her scarf off and didn't hear me.

"I'm off in a couple minutes, I'll come over," offered Alto.

I paid, and slipped back toward Sara.

"A friend from the arboretum's here," I said. "He's coming over to say hi. Name's Alto."

She smiled. "You seem to have a whole other secret life at the arboretum."

"Do I?"

"Remember the woman and her kids at Halloween—"

"Oh, Marie, sure," I said. "Her kids are Nick and Ryan."

"See? You could be having an affair and I'd never know."

"Yeah, I meant to tell you, those are actually my kids."

"Ha."

We were both sitting now. Sara adapted her best I-work-in-an-office-so-you-better-take-me-seriously pose, forearms on tabletop, hands clasped with knuckles forward, very schoolmarmish. "All right," she said, "let's talk about it."

"What, Marie's kids? Well, those were my wild days, she

claimed she had a little Irish in her, so I thought I'd take it literally—"

"Rory." Pause. She looked down—generally an adorable gesture on her, but not at this moment—and then back up at me. "I don't ever want a repeat of last night."

"Neither do I," I said quickly. "I'm sorry I got drunk. I really don't get your treatment of the dog, I'm not backing off on that, but getting pissed off is no excuse for getting drunk."

She was already shaking her head. "I trust you, this isn't about your drinking, it's about your temper. You can't blow your top whenever you disapprove of my behavior."

"I almost *never* disapprove of your behavior, Sara. Your behavior is the best thing to happen to me in—"

"That's great, so on the few occasions that I irritate you, could you please try to stay reasonable?"

"Well, I need *you* to be reasonable," I countered. "About the *dog*."

She looked at me with the kind of look that let me know I would disagree with whatever came out of her mouth. "I've been treating the dog the same way for three years. In three years, nobody else has ever had an issue. It's behavior that you might be unfamiliar with but that doesn't make it, objectively, unreasonable."

"Of course it's unreasonable. No dog in Ireland—"

"Rory, we're not in Ireland, we're in America."

"You're all mental when it comes to your dogs."

"We're just different from you. What I do is pretty normal for this culture."

"I know normal," I shot back. "It's not normal."

"Hey there," said a quiet voice over my shoulder. Sara, immediately honey and wildflowers, smiled and looked up.

"Hello," she said, offering her hand to Alto. "Lovely to meet you. I'm Sara, Rory's wife."

"And Cody's owner. It's great to meet you. You have a great dog!"

Sara beamed her satisfaction, like a laser, right into my face, rekindling my hangover headache. "Thank you."

"I'm Alto," said Alto. "Yeah, I know Rory from the arboretum, I'm there most days when he takes Cody for a walk. She's *such* a sweet dog."

These were the most syllables I'd ever heard Alto string together at once without the aid of a cigarette. "How's things, Alto?" I asked. I had no idea what else to ask, since it felt like whatever we talked about at the arboretum should stay at the arboretum. Not that we talked about anything per se at the arboretum.

A slightly nervous nod from Alto. "Okay. They're good. Yeah. How are you?"

Sara and I glanced at each other. She nodded slightly; we both smiled, amnesty accorded. "We're great," I said to Alto. "We're celebrating."

"Rory," called out a voice from the counter.

"I'll get it for you," Alto offered. "Want anything in it?"

"Thanks, mate, no, just as it is."

We watched as Alto retrieved and returned with our drinks, and set them on the tabletop before us. "So, what are you celebrating?"

"A rite of passage, Alto," I said, with a grin. "I just got my green card!" I grabbed Sara's hand. "This beautiful woman made it possible."

Alto looked confused. "You mean you've been, like, illegal?"

"He had a visa," Sara said quickly. "An arts visa. But he couldn't join the Screen Actors Guild or anything, so we got married so he could do that."

Alto gave me a startled expression. "You're an *actor*? I mean, I know you did, like, *Christmas Carol,* but I mean—an *actor*-actor."

"Among other things," I said with a dismissive gesture. "Mostly I walk my wife's dog."

Alto nodded, putting the pieces together, and turned admiringly to Sara. "So, wow, you married him just so he could get a green card?"

"And because she was blown away by how wildly in love with her I was," I said, pulling Sara's wrist to my lips and kissing it. She blushed and grinned, which was, as always, adorable.

"We'd been dating a week when we got married," Sara said in a confessional tone.

"That's so romantic," Alto said, suddenly almost choked up. "And now you're legal or documented or whatever's the correct term?"

"Yep," I grinned.

"Almost," Sara corrected. "It's a conditional card. In two years we have to prove that we're still a couple, and *then* he gets the permanent card. As long as he hasn't broken the law or anything. So—" She grinned at me, teasing. "He's still got plenty of time to get in trouble."

"Wow," said Alto, nodding a little. "Well, congratulations. Funny how we all see each other in the park and never think about, you know, our lives outside the park."

"Tell me about it! You have a secret identity as a barista," I said. "You've been holding out on me, don't you know I need my espressos?"

Alto looked flustered.

"He's joking," Sara said reassuringly. Alto looked reassured. Sara's good that way.

"I'm joking," I said heartily. "Bay State Caffeine is no place to get a decent espresso."

There was a brief moment of silence. I impulsively kissed Sara on the cheek. She kissed me back. The world was my oyster!

"So . . . Are you taking the T back to JP?" asked Alto, and added, when I looked confused, "Jamaica Plain."

"Maybe. What time is it?" Sara asked. In my hungover fog, I'd left my watch at home, so I reached into my raincoat pocket for my phone to check the time. It was turned off. I powered it back up. And remembered:

" . . . Dougie's voice mail," I said. I glanced up at Alto. "My agent left me a message," I said, loving the sound of that, because now it was true. The phone beeped to alert me of the message. I bit my lip excitedly, looking back and forth between them. Sara tensed, with a nervous smile.

"Is it important?" asked Alto.

"Could be," I said, trying to sound breezy, as if I got important voice mails all the time. "Could be life-changing." I winked at Alto as if life-changing voice mails were a matter of course. Alto looked stupefied. Then I tapped in my password, the four-note tune chiming like a TV network jingle.

"You have one new message," my phone told me in an excruciatingly slow female voice. "First message, received at ten fifty-eight A.M." Impulsively, I pressed the speaker button and held the phone out between the three of us. Alto leaned in, thrilled to be part of the crew. He never smiled like this back at the park. I'd have to work on that, I decided.

"Rory!" cheered Dougie's voice. "Call me! Make sure you're sitting down. With a big bottle of champagne."

Sara and I looked at each other, eyes wide, mouths O-ing. I felt shivers all over my body. I could see in my peripheral vision Alto glancing back and forth excitedly between us.

"Good news, then?" Alto asked.

" . . . I think so," I said, nearly hyperventilating. I burst into nervous laughter.

"Rory!" Sara said quietly, eyes shining. It was almost a whine or a whimper—actually, she reminded me a bit of Cody. Maybe Sara was about to slide off the chair into tarty-dog pose. "Oh my *God*, Rory!" And then she was laughing nervously, too.

"Congrats," Alto said. "Whatever it is."

"Thanks," I said. "Not sure, but I think I maybe might have got a television series. Pilot, anyhow." And then I just kept grinning stupidly because I was in Bay State Caffeine and there was no room to dance properly.

Alto's jaw dropped. "Wow! Wow. Rory, that's awesome, *wow*, congratulations!"

"Thanks, man," I said. I suddenly stood up and hugged Alto, which would have been inconceivable in the arboretum. Alto hugged me back—equally inconceivable.

"You've been on a roll," said Alto, admiringly. "When I first met you, remember? You'd just gotten married, and now already you have a green card, and an amazing job. Like, it's all just magically coming together for you."

"I know!" I crowed. "And it's all thanks to this *fantastic* woman!" I threw my arms around Sara's shoulder in an exuberant bear hug and kissed the top of her head. She laughed and reached up to stroke my cheek.

"Congrats," said Alto. There was the tiniest wistfulness in Alto's voice—not self-pity, but a sort of hopeful envy. It caught me up short. I wouldn't have considered our situations parallel at all, but the moment I heard that tone in Alto's voice, I realized that he did. Which made sense, I s'pose. Having an unconventional identity in conventional society, in any sense, is a wee bit like being at sea: you're always looking for lighthouse beacons. Maybe, in the absence of more immediate inspiration, I was suddenly his, same as that.

I released Sara, and tapped Alto's elbow. "I spent years trying to pass under the radar, mate. I know about looking over my shoulder, and not feeling comfortable in my own shoes." It was the first time I'd ever *hinted* acknowledging anything not-conventional about Alto. "Don't let the bastards get you down. You're grand. You'll be grand."

Alto's brown eyes welled up. He nodded slightly. "Thanks, Rory," he said. He looked at Sara. "He's very lucky—and so are you."

She looked slightly choked up, too. "I know," she said. "And now he even has *work*." We grinned at each other and started giggling ridiculously. Nothing on earth like the sound of Sara's laugh.

Chapter 11

When we got home, Cody performed her many "anticlockwise spins of joy" and smacked us with her "happy tail" and of course showed us her "tarty-dog belly." When she had exhausted all possible expressions of gratitude for not being permanently abandoned, I called Dougie while Sara went into the bedroom with her laptop to plan an impromptu weekend getaway.

The first mad thing about calling Dougie—which I had never done, he always called me—was that the call was picked up not by Dougie but by an assistant, who sounded about twelve. He put me on hold. After the longest fifteen seconds of my life, he came back on the line to somberly inform me: "I have Dougie Martin for you."

I wanted to say, *Of course you do, that's why I called,* but that seemed unprofessional, so I settled for, "Thank you."

"Rory! You're the man!"

Suddenly I was almost breathless. "I don't even ... I'm ... What does that mean? Exactly?"

"It means they want you!"

What?! I made spastic-sounding happy noises, and Dougie laughed, and waited for me to calm down, then continued.

"They got the green light for the pilot, that's definitely happening, and they've got a shooting script. They say they're shooting late May. So you've got two and a half months to get out here."

"Get out . . . there?"

"There's been a change, they're shooting it in L.A. But that's great because L.A. is the place you want to be anyhow."

I was dizzy, had to take a breath before I could speak. Jesus, what would Sara say? How would she feel about moving *across the continent*? "And after the pilot?" I asked. "They decide if they want to keep me or not?"

"No, you're attached if they run with it, that's what that monster contract was all about. But now there's one potential hitch . . ."

I didn't like the silence he trailed off to.

"We sort of BS'd them about your immigration status, so I really need you to get that green card pronto."

I burst out laughing. "I just got it this morning. Can you believe the timing?"

"No shit, really?" The relief in his voice was so obvious I could almost smell it. He must have really stretched his neck for me with their legal folks. "Congrats! That's fantastic, Rory, my God, I know how long you've been after that."

"Thanks," I said "I couldn't have done it without—"

"So that means we can move on the SAG status," said Dougie, marching on. "There's a bunch of moving parts here, but it's all really orderly. There won't be any curve balls."

"The move to L.A. is a bit of a curve ball."

"Let me talk to them, they'll pay for that. Let's talk next week and deal with the practical stuff. Just wanted you to have the good news now so you could celebrate over the weekend."

"Thanks, mate," I said. "Wow. And, Dougie, thank you for believing in me and—"

"Yeah, yeah, yeah," he said grandly. "Save it for the wrap party. Love you, man, talk to you next week."

I sat on the couch staring at the coffee table. Cody came over to me and firmly planted her chin on my knee, looking up at me adoringly, tail wagging slowly. Just then, Sara came back into the room, eyebrows raised, face beaming hopefully.

I tried to look cool, just leaned back on the couch and nodded a little. Sara opened her arms wide, shouted with joyful laughter, and nearly threw herself at me.

LENA TOOK CODY for the weekend. Sara and I went away to a B&B in the Berkshires, and hardly got out of bed. Much as I'd love to brag about that, I'm a gentleman, so I'll just resume with my return to earth on Monday morning. That's where the second part of this story begins. Although I was too clueless to realize that until months later.

Chapter 12

Monday morning, I saw Sara off to work as usual, had an espresso and did my crossword puzzle, and then back to the apartment to take Cody for a walk. By that time, Little Miss Organizational Skill Set had already arranged with Lena to have a celebratory lunch for us at the museum later in the week.

I was over the moon and no question, but I can't describe it because . . . it is just hard to describe. I was actually almost in a state of shock.

Anyhow, knowing this lunch was to be held, and feeling (to be honest) a mix of delight and dread at being scrutinized by so many Initialed People, I was truly looking forward to our walk in the arboretum, just me and the dog and the unassuming folks I knew in passing there.

I would never have brought up either the green card or the TV pilot—despite my chatty ways, I am (like most of the Irish race) genetically shy, and bursting out with the news . . . that was never going to happen.

But Alto (although shy) wasn't Irish, and he wasn't me, and he saw no need to keep it a secret. So by the time the dog and I came bounding up Peters Hill in the raw, damp, early-March air, Cody dashing ahead to see if Marie's kids were there (their hands were usually good for a few molecules of junk food) . . .

. . . I had a little cheering section waiting for me. Literally. Alto, Jay, Marie, her little boys, and a few other faces I knew vaguely, all gave me an actual *ovation* as I appeared over the rise. Jay nearly always sat, but he rose to his feet now, his Samuel Beckett–esque eyes pouring into me with knowing approval, as if he sensed my insecurities and had the deepest (if fatalistic) compassion for them.

"Rory O'Connor," he said. "What a journey this life is giving you. Heartiest congratulations, my friend."

Cody, to demonstrate she agreed with him, first leapt on him and then collapsed straight at his feet on the cold, damp grass in a tarty-dog pose.

"It's *so exciting,* almighty God," said Marie, "Is it here in Boston? Hollywood loves Boston."

"Actually, Los Angeles, it turns out," I said, almost dreading the sound of it. Sara had been a little thrown by that development, but then—so like Sara—she was game to go on out.

"*Goodness,*" said Jay, eyebrows raised, while little Nick asked, "Can I watch your TV show, Rory?"

That question made it feel more concrete than anything so far.

" . . . Sure, I suppose, if your mum says it's okay."

"What time will it be on?" he asked, concerned. "I can't watch TV after seven."

"I . . . I don't know." I smiled, tickled, thinking: *It* will *be on. It will be on at* some *time.* What an amazing thing!

I laughed a little, looking down, nervous. I wanted to deck Alto for telling them, but I wanted to hug him, too. He looked chuffed for being the one to deliver the news; it gave him insider status about something pretty cool, and he was preening a little. I far preferred that to the skulking little moper I had first met on this hilltop several months ago. So, as the Yanks like to say, it was all good.

"I believe," said Jay, "that we should have an official celebration. For everyone. If I am not mistaken, this young gentleman"— meaning Marie's son Nick—"has a birthday coming up."

"I am not a *genman*," said Nick defiantly, as if Jay were teasing him. "I am a *boy*."

"A boy who is one year older soon, aren't you?" said Jay, like a pleased pedagogue. "Would you like a party?"

Nick's eyes glowed and he glanced at his mother, his backside wiggling not unlike Cody's when she greeted us each morning. "Mommy?" he asked hopefully, grinning up at her so intensely his eyes were shut.

"That's very nice of Mr. Jay, isn't it, Nick?" said Marie. To Jay, smiling in amazement: "I can't believe you know his birthday!"

Jay shrugged. "I have a knack for those kinds of details. Last year around this time, I think it was even my first visit to the arboretum, I'd just moved to the neighborhood, and you two were having an argument about his party. It is hard to forget a three-year-old demanding chocolate fondue for his birthday dinner."

Marie burst out laughing as Nick said, pleased with himself for his originality, "Hey, guess what! I want chocolate fondue for my birthday dinner!"

"Oh, I don't think so, mister. How about a cake?" said his mother.

"Okay," Nick said, upon reflection.

"Really, though, let's have a little party," said Jay. "I live just there." He pointed vaguely toward one of the triple-deckers on the Roslindale side of the hill, the back decks of their upper floors gazing at us through the leafless trees. "I can bring hot spiced cider right over here in a thermos or two."

"I'll make a cake," said Marie.

"Chocolate," said Nick. "*Dark* chocolate."

"Yes, bossy-man," said his mother.

"As chocolate as chocolate fondue."

"A gentleman who knows what he wants," said Jay approvingly.

"I told you," Nick scolded, "I'm not a genman, I'm a boy."

"I'm not so good at cooking," said Alto, awkward but eager (eager in a repressed sort of way). "But I can bring, like, paper plates and utensils and cups from work."

"Ach, thievery," I said approvingly.

"Very useful, and practical," said Jay.

"What can I bring?" I asked. Garam-Masala Man did not get called upon to serve up many winter picnics.

"You are the guest of honor," declared Jay. "You and Nick. You two don't have to bring anything. Now, what's a good day?"

Wednesday was established. I realized I was looking forward to this gathering considerably more than the MFA luncheon on Thursday that Lena was arranging.

I LOVE BIRTHDAYS and I did not want to show up empty-handed to a four-year-old's. So I went to the toy store on Centre Street and got Nick some cheap pirate gear: hat, eye patch, and of course, shiny plastic cutlass. I modeled it at home for Sara the night before, explaining the context. She responded so well to the look that I went back to get another set for myself.

Late Wednesday morning, we all converged around the top of Peters Hill. It wasn't windy—in fact, it was strangely mild, high forties, nearly sunny—but except for some early bulbs pushing up here and there, it really wasn't springlike yet at all. In Ireland, this weather could nearly be accounted summer, but in America, even in Boston, it was a raw day for a party, and it seemed mildly daft. I mean that in the best way, though, in that all of us would surely look back at our clumsy attempt and feel fond of one another that we were all in it together.

First came my presents, to Nick and myself. We geared up as twin pirates and *yarrrrr'd* at each other, brandishing plastic cutlasses, while Marie, holding her giggling toddler Ryan, took photos on her smartphone (or, as they say in Boston, her smaht-phone). A few folks on the hillside stared, giggled, clustered to watch. When we took a breather, I tried to dress up Cody with the hat and eye patch, but she was having none of it; she elegantly shook the hat off her head, removed the eye patch with one grace-ful swat of her back paw, and then trotted over to lean against Alto, whose languid body language as he smoked promised the least danger of frivolity. She looked up adoringly at him as if he would have treats for her.

Then Jay—seated as usual on his chiseled rock—held the plat-ter with the chocolate cake as Marie set Ryan in the pram and lit the candles. We all sang "Happy Birthday" to Nick, and after the official verse, I kept crooning, so he could be serenaded with the most important verse: "Happy Birthday to *you,* you live in the *zoo,* you look like a *monkey,* and you *smell* like one, too." This was delivered in a grand, *yarrrring Pirates of Penzance* manner, and judging by his cascade of giggles, he was pleased.

I'm going to make a damn fine da one day, I thought. *And the kids will be gorgeous with Sara as their ma.* Although in the good-cop-bad-cop scheme of parenting, she would definitely be the bad cop. That would be fine, though. More playtime for me. Cody could be the nanny.

Nick blew out the candles on the cake, and I sliced pieces for everyone as Jay held the tray—which, by the way, was enormous. Curious regulars who had never had the good taste to bond with our unlikely clique hovered near, watching, whispering, chuckling with appreciation . . . and with anticipation, those chancers. There were maybe ten of them. Marie, no doubt anticipating we'd attract attention (even before she knew what dashing pirates we would make) had baked a cake to feed a small army, so after obligatory Large Pieces for Celebrants, I cut the rest into wee squares, and there was your man Alto with the paper plates and plastic forks, which meant no cigarette for fully half an hour, score one for lung capacity. Soon we were feeding the hilltop, with half the cake still left over.

I have to say, it was pretty cool. I felt, for the first time since I gave up drinking, like I was becoming part of a social scene.

"Good man, Jay," I said. "This was your idea."

"It takes a village," he said with a peaceable shrug, setting the platter down beside himself on the rock so he could have a slice himself.

Nick had inhaled his cake while I was cutting and serving everyone else, and he approached me again, chocolate frosting and dark chocolate crumbs all over his face, even on his eyelashes.

"Yarrr!" he declared, brandishing his cutlass with the blade upside down. "I'm Pirate Nicholas and I'm taking you prisoner! *Yarrr!"*

Cody was on board with this. Her tail was wagging the rest of her body, and she was half bouncing and half bowing beside me, looking up at me earnestly, begging me to engage the enemy. Her eyes were shining and I swear she nearly barked.

"Yarrr!" I answered Nick, at which Cody leapt up like a Lippizaner, or a kangaroo, springing straight into the air, and then took off around the circle of people, making sure they all knew that Great Stuff was about to happen. I pulled my eye patch back down over my eye, and brandished the cake knife. "You are not taking me prisoner without a fight. Let me get my cutlass. Squire!" I handed off the knife to Squire Alto, and received my cutlass and hat, which I tapped firmly onto my head. I hopped backward from Jay's boulder, to give us more sparring room. Nick excitedly hopped after me. I thought Cody might join in the hop-fest but she now hung back beside Marie, watching, although she looked very excited and approving and, may I even say, proud of her dog walker for looking so dashing and fierce.

"En garde!" I commanded, and lunged.

"On God!" Nick thought he echoed, lunging back. I tapped his cutlass blade with mine and stuck my tongue out at him. He gave me a fierce grimace, and growled like a good pirate. He was adorable. I made a mental note to buy a plastic cutlass for Sara—cutlasses were definitely the way to resolve future disputes.

"Take that!" I said, poking my cutlass at him repeatedly as I jumped backward so that he had to chase me in a circle. Our audience was crying with laughter now.

"Wait!" Nick said, very seriously. He stopped chasing me and frowned. "I need my eye patch," he declared.

"Time out for eye patch," I called out, lowering my weapon and glancing expectantly around the circle. "Anyone have an extra eye patch for this little sea—*oh no!*"

I said it at the same moment Marie cried out and even Jay gave a gasp of distress: just beyond the perimeter of the circle, Cody was eagerly licking clean the platter on which Marie had brought the cake.

Moments earlier, there had been half of a very large chocolate cake sitting on that platter. Cody's muzzle was creamy with dark frosting.

I had just poisoned Sara's dog.

Chapter 13

"O h Jesus," I said, and before I could stop myself, added, for clarity: "Fuck!" I dropped the cutlass and sprang toward the dog. "Cody! Cody, *leave it*! *Drop it!*"

Cody didn't mind leaving it, since there was nothing left. She turned to me with a crafty look in her eye, rapidly and energetically licking her chops. Her expression seemed to say: *Everything is going to be different now. I'm never listening to you again unless there's chocolate cake.*

In the background, like a movie sound track, I heard the slow-motion mutterings of concerned voices, with every possible variant of "chocolate is toxic to dogs" uttered in a range of tones— blaming, shaming, fearful, blaming, mournful, angry, sad, resigned, blaming, pedantic, and some blaming, too.

"Cody!" I cried again. It took forever to reach her, like I was running through molasses, and once I actually had my hands on her, I didn't know what to do. My mind went blank with panic. I grabbed her collar and tried to open her jaws with my free hand, as if I could reach down her throat and pull the cake back out.

I felt as if I were surrounded by the entire morning population of the park. Nick wasn't crying, thank God; that relieved the tiny corner of my mind still aware of him and his birthday celebration. But he was definitely mimicking the concern of his mum and all the other grown-ups. All the grown-ups who were responsible enough not to poison their spouse's dog.

From the chaos came one clear, strong, calm voice: Jay's. "Let's get her to my house," he said, a hand on my shoulder. "It's right there."

"What do we do?" I said in a shaken voice. "We have to call a vet. Sara is going to kill me."

"No, it'll be fine," he said. "We have to make her vomit up the cake, and as long as she does it right away, she'll be fine."

"I don't know how to do that," I said, staring at her while her tongue kept working industriously to get every last bit of scrumptious chocolaty poison off her muzzle. "How do you make a dog vomit?"

"Hydrogen peroxide," said Calm Jay. "You force it down their throat and they puke it up immediately along with everything else in their stomach. I promise you, Rory, it's simple and straightforward, we just need to do it quickly."

"He's right," said Alto, looking spooked. "I saw that on the Animal Channel. The chocolate won't kill her, but it could make her pretty sick."

"Oh God," I said. "Sara will never forgive me."

"She doesn't even need to know," said Jay.

"It seems very harsh on the stomach," said Marie.

"Not as harsh as chocolate," I said, hating myself. "Okay, let's go. Thank you, Jay, I'm in your debt, mate." I was shaking. I grabbed for her leash, which I usually tied around my waist. But

I had taken it off to duel with Nick and had no idea where I'd left it.

"Here," said Alto, magically materializing with it.

With an anxious sigh, I clipped the leash onto Cody's collar. She seemed slightly subdued already, but that was probably because her stomach was distended from the amount of cake she'd just swallowed. I don't think I could have eaten that much cake in the course of a whole afternoon.

"This way," said Jay with parental firmness, raising me up and gesturing down the path. He paused, turned around, and addressed the concerned little gathering: "The dog's going to be fine, everyone, please don't worry about it." Then apologized quietly to Marie and Nick for the interruption of the party—taking the blame on himself, in fact, as he was the one who had put the platter down to eat his own slice. Nick ran over to Cody and gave her a huge hug, which she liked because it allowed her to lick the chocolate frosting off his face.

"Cody, don't be such a pig next time," he told her. "You get sick if you eat too much cake, didn't Rory ever tell you that?" He kissed her between the eyes and ran back to his mother to collect his pirate uniform. I wanted to die.

We started walking briskly toward Jay's and I realized Squire Alto was walking with us. "It's okay, man," said Alto, patting my elbow. "Want a cigarette?"

"I am a fuckup," I said irritably.

"I'm the one who set the tray down," said Jay.

"But the dog wasn't your responsibility," I said. "I'm the one who should have noticed and kept her from it. Sara's going to kill me. She's going to say I subconsciously wanted to kill the dog—"

"I'm sure that's nonsense," said Jay, so indulgently that for a moment I thought, in my distress, that he suspected this himself.

"She can never know about this," I said. "If you ever meet her, or"—to Alto—"if you ever see her again. She can never know."

"Whatever you say," said Jay as he removed one glove and reached into his coat pocket. "It's really not a big deal."

We came down onto the main paved walkway and then Jay kept walking—across the blacktop, and straight toward the edge of the park, which here was some eight feet higher than the houses abutting it. There were, I saw now, several locked gates rising from the parapet-like park boundary, with subtle footpaths leading to them.

Jay had been softly humming (as usual) Leonard Cohen's "Hallelujah." "Down here," he said, and led us toward one such path. He pushed the gate, which opened onto a set of wooden stairs down into the yard of the nearest triple-decker. It was a handsome building, painted darkish green with gold and russet trim . . . a staid Victorian look that suited him. If he hadn't an American accent, I really would have suspected he was a down-on-his-luck baron.

"Nice," I said.

"Thank you. I just bought it about a year ago."

"When you sold your thing?" Alto asked.

He nodded. "When I sold my thing."

"What thing?" I asked. I vaguely remembered something about this from an earlier conversation but was too stressed now to recall the details. "I wouldn't mind selling a thing if it meant I could buy a nice house."

Jay huffed self-deprecatingly. "I designed a little program Merck pharmaceuticals bought. Doesn't put me in the one percent, but it bought me a home and a Get Out of Jail Free card from my day job, for a few years anyhow, until I get bored. Here we are. I live in the middle unit. I've got tenants upstairs and down." He pulled out his keys. The fob on his key chain (really, who but a ruined baron would have a *fob*?) was a little metal figure.

"Is that a dog?" I asked.

"Oh," said Jay, glancing down absently at it before inserting the key. "Yes. I like dogs. Part of why I enjoy going to the hill every day."

"Why don't you have one of your own?" Alto asked.

"I lost one recently," he said. "Still recovering. Nothing in the world says contentment like your dog curled up asleep at your feet. You get incredibly attached."

"You have no idea," I said while Alto, who was nicer than I, said, "Sorry for your loss."

Jay's home, unsurprisingly, was classy and somewhat dark and old-world-ish, with overstuffed leather chairs facing a fireplace and several book-lined walls. "Make yourselves comfortable," he said, "over by the fire. I'll collect what I need and be right back." As he vanished down the hall he called back: "It looks real but it's gas. The switch is on the right if you want to turn it on."

Alto looked delighted. "Well, *yeah,*" he said, and began to hunt for the switch.

I looked worriedly at Cody. "Oh, you." I sighed. Her tail thumped the floor, once, languidly. She seemed droopy—I hoped that was from eating so much so fast, and not because she would soon be dead of chocolate toxicity. She rested her chin on my leg hard, pressing down, and looked up at me with those heart-melting dark eyes, asking me to make her feel better. She was so completely dependent upon me and I felt so completely useless.

About a minute later, as the "fire" was starting to warm, Jay came in with a brown bottle of hydrogen peroxide, several towels, and a small stack of *New York Times* under his arm.

"All right, let's set up for triage," he said. "Alto, if you can spread the newspaper on top of the towel, in front of the fire."

"Let me get the rug out of the way," I said, desperate to feel useful. I lifted the heavy leather chair enough to roll back the corner of the very nice, plush, silk Turkish carpet that covered much of this room.

"Thank you," said Jay. "If you're squeamish you might not want to watch this."

"I better force myself," I said, already feeling my gorge rise.

"I think I'll step away," said Alto.

"There's a bowl of water in the kitchen, can you just bring that in first?" Jay asked, with an encouraging smile. Alto did, then stepped outside for a smoke. God, how I wanted to join him.

I don't see the need to go into the details, but in all fairness, on a purely mechanical level, it was pretty amazing. In went a small bottle's worth of hydrogen peroxide, out came large blobs of chocolate cake, deposited obediently on the newspaper, which Jay deftly covered, lifted, and moved out of sight. He held Cody firmly but gently throughout. She was trembling, and gave him a B-movie starlet's look of despair, but did not try to escape from him. She was resigned to her fate, and even seemed to consider him the boss of her now.

He pulled the dish of water closer to her. "Drink," he said. "Cody, drink."

She stared up at him pleadingly.

"Maybe a treat," he said, considering her. Then, to me, "Hamburger okay?"

"Better than chocolate cake," I said.

For about a quarter hour, we all sat hunkered down in front of the (pretty realistic-looking) gas fireplace, waiting for Cody to perk up and drink some water. Jay claimed the towels were headed for the trash heap anyhow, and took them—neatly packed—outside to put them straight into the bin. We chatted about this and that—Alto's applying for a job as a waiter at an upscale restaurant (he actually wanted to be a community activist, but was too shy), Jay's contemplated trip to Peru, my upcoming phone call with my agent to sort out the ensuing move to L.A. I was still too freaked out about Cody to get all that excited about talking shop, but I answered questions the other two politely put to me.

Eventually, Cody got interested in the water dish, and drank a lot of it, all at once. We all three quietly cheered her.

"That calls for a celebration," said Jay. "Is it too early to bring out the scotch?"

"None for me, thanks," I said. "Those days are behind me."

"Duly noted," he said, without judgment.

"I've got a shift starting soon," said Alto, but I could see he marked it as a rite of passage that he'd just been invited to drink with the grown-ups. In Dublin, when I was his age, I was long past such initiations.

"Well, no fun drinking alone," said Jay peaceably. "Perhaps another time."

Within another quarter hour, Cody seemed like a slightly tired version of herself, and was declared entirely fine by Jay. Alto excused himself to work, and I plied Jay with endless gratitude, which he deflected with a certain noblesse oblige.

"Come by for tea sometime," he said as I clipped the leash onto Cody's collar at the door. "I'd hate for your only association of my home to be of your wife's dog vomiting."

We smiled, shook hands, and then because I am an affectionate sort, I gave him a big hug. He really was very tall. I often forgot that because he was usually sitting down, the quiet patriarch on his boulder throne on Peters Hill.

Chapter 14

Back home, with "Hallelujah" stuck in my head, I found myself pacing the apartment anxiously watching Cody as intently as she usually watched me (ironic, as in her subdued state she seemed nearly indifferent to my existence). I couldn't get a thing done. I was afraid to even shop for dinner lest Cody keel over whilst I was at the co-op.

In the end I did something I would normally never, ever have done.

I sat on the couch and said, "Cody." She glanced over as if bored. I patted the space right beside me on the couch. Her expression changed immediately, almost human, unmistakable: *You've got to be kidding me. You never let me near the couch.*

"Cody," I repeated, nodding, and patting the cushion more insistently. "C'mon, girl. Up! Up on the couch, Cody."

She gave me an appraising look, then trotted toward me and sat, politely, her gaze switching between my face and my hand, which was still patting the couch. "Yes! Yes, Cody," I kept promising. "C'mon up!"

She leapt lightly onto the couch and sat, very upright and proper, and looked at me. There was an awkward moment between us, almost like a first date that wasn't going well.

"You can lie down, Cody," I said, patting the cushions again. "Lie down."

She looked down her nose at me as if to say, *What is this* lie down *you are referring to?* But after a moment, she relented, and carefully—staring at me—lowered herself to the sofa cushions, her head near my knee.

"Good girl," I said.

In response she raised her head, shifted her weight forward slightly, and rested her chin on my knee. That's an adorable feeling even if you don't like dogs, really it is, because it feels like you're being claimed, and who doesn't want to be wanted? So I smiled at her.

She raised herself slightly and wiggled forward so that the whole bottom of her jaw was on my leg.

"Oh, it's like that, is it?" I said, grinning. Without moving her head, she glanced up at me. I smiled down at her. God, was I grateful for this moment. If this moment wasn't happening, I'd be so fucked in the Sara Renault department, I couldn't even imagine it.

Suddenly Cody pushed herself up into a sort of crouch and scoot-slithered her way all the way across my lap. Her tail was off to one knee, her head and forepaws lolling off the other side. It was inverted tarty-dog pose. For a moment neither of us moved. Then, when it was clear I wasn't going to push her off, she looked up at me and wagged her tail tentatively. She thought this was just fantastic. I began to stroke the soft hair on her back, and felt a heavy, peaceful calm descend on me.

I stared into space for an hour, contemplating how much worse things could be right now. I fell into a reverie.

The reverie was interrupted by an unexpected phone call. It shouldn't have been unexpected, but due to the reverie, it was.

"Rory O'Connor," said the barely pubescent male voice on the other end of the line. "I have Doug Martin for you, please hold."

"SO HERE'S WHAT it means for us," I said, stirring in exactly the right amount of honey Sara likes because I am an attentive and loving partner that way, even if I do let her dog eat five pounds of chocolate cake.

Sara had come home a little early, remembering (better than I did) about my phone conference with Dougie and the executive producers. I pushed the mug to Sara across the counter. She kicked off her shoes, folded one leg under herself, and settled onto the stool. She cupped her hands around the mug, as that particular smile that comes from a nice cup of tea settled onto her face. "I'm all ears," she said.

"Are you really? That's tragic. How will you eat?"

She stuck her tongue out at me, then said eagerly, "Go on, then."

I took a deep breath to calm myself. It was exciting, but scary. I knew from friends of mine—from Dougie himself, in fact—how quickly even a sure thing could fall apart in television.

"So, they ordered a whole season—"

Sara grinned and very quietly, adorably, squealed with glee.

"But that doesn't mean anything really. First we have to make the pilot, then it gets screened along with a bunch of other pilots, and the studio decides which one they want to make, usually based on all kinds of backroom politics. But if it gets selected, then it gets aired while we're scrambling to shoot the rest of the season."

"So . . . we're going to Los Angeles?" said Sara.

God, how I'd prayed for her to ask exactly that.

I gave her a hopeful look. "Would you really come with me?"

"As long as your stepdog can come, too."

I'd been all over Cody since we got home from the misadventure. It should have made Sara suspicious, but in fairness she was too pleased, I think, to look too hard at it. Cody was in the kitchen area with me, which normally I never allowed. At this moment, she nudged her nose to the back of my knee.

"Oh . . ." I pretended to need to mull it over. As if I had a choice in the matter. "I suppose she can come."

"How was your little picnic today?" Sara asked.

I drew in a sharp breath and then exhaled the tension onto Cody, bending over to give her a very rough head scratch. "It was fun, wasn't it, Cody?" I said. "A gathering is always better when an Irishman's involved, even Henry V knew that, isn't it?" Having calmed myself, I stood upright and looked at Sara. "Marie made a delicious cake and the pirate costumes went over like gangbusters. We looked the business when we were dueling."

She grinned. "Get out. You dueled with a three-year-old."

"He's actually four. And actually, he let me win," I confided.

Her interest, thank God, was sated, and her attention went elsewhere.

"ACH, SO THAT'S the last time I'll ever taste your chicken tikka masala," said Danny poignantly, patting his midriff. "Next time round, sure your personal chef will be making it for us on a patio looking out over Beverly Hills."

"My personal chef wouldn't be stupid enough to compete with me when it comes to tikka masala," I assured him. "I'm Garam-Masala Man. Cheers." I tapped my seltzer to his pint and we both drank.

I'd made Danny dinner as thanks for help moving all my LPs into storage. Those were nearly the only thing from my old apartment that I kept. I'd sold pretty much all the rest to the bloke who had been my subletter, who conveniently had just started dating my landlord (their sound track being something from Aerosmith). We were nearing the end of several weeks of planning and transition, and as much as I loved Sara, it was a bit of a relief that she was working late and that a mate of mine was over.

The dog, though, was still underfoot. It had only taken a few days for my sentimentality about her to fade. It wasn't her fault; it was Sara's behavior pushing my buttons. You don't want to know how many conversations we had about dealing with Cody while moving to L.A. It would have been the simplest of enterprises without the dog—or even with the dog if Sara had just been willing to trust the airlines not to kill Cody in transit. But she didn't trust them, and so our entire move was revolving around what would work for the dog.

"So when are you out of here?" asked Danny, pushing his empty plate, almost literally licked clean, across the counter to me. I put it in the sink with mine.

"We gave May first as our out date, but we're planning to get on the road April twenty-sixth." Chuffed, I added, "I have a meeting in New York on the twenty-eighth with the executive producers, a sort of welcome-to-the-winner's-circle coffee."

Danny's eyes lit up. "Never! Really? I suppose you'll be treatin' them to coffee, then, now you're a star and all."

I gave him a wry look. "I'm not getting rich off this pilot, mate. Although to be fair, the executive producer called me five times to say how thrilled he was we were going to be working together—it was great crack the first two or three times, but after that it just started to feel like a commercial being aired too often, not that I'm complaining, mind."

"Oh, I'd be complaining, same as that," Danny said, deadpan.

"His assistant sent me a bottle of champagne and flowers for Sara."

"Ach, so they mean business!" Danny said, impressed. "All that, before they even know if you're going to do more than one episode? Which might not even be seen?"

"Mad, isn't it."

"But you're moving out there with no surety of the future either, are ye?"

I shrugged. "Sara and I thought, you know, this place is too small for a couple, but otherwise living together isn't as bad as we thought—"

"—except for the dog—"

"Except for the dog, but we're both getting better about that. We're mad for each other, Danny, we want to live together for real—"

"Ach, that's great, big man."

"So it means we need to move anyhow, so why not move to the

place where it all happens?" I was oversimplifying, it's true. We didn't really need to move all the way to Los Angeles as yet, but the idea seemed kind of exotic. Sara was game for adventure, and I loved her for that.

Danny shook his head in wonder. "Wee Sara suggested you move in with her to fool the U.S. government. I think you're the one got fooled, mate. All you did was kiss her, and now look."

"I'm a very lucky bloke," I said reverentially. "Did I tell you we're driving cross-country?"

Again his eyes got big. "Are you *mad*? Not in the wee MINI *Cooper*? With the *dog*?"

"Well, we're shipping some stuff, it doesn't all have to fit in the MINI with us. We're getting a furnished flat to start with, and then if the series is picked up, we'll look for something to really call home. And if it doesn't, well, then maybe we'll just hop back in the car and drive back. This way we'll get to see America, plus we'll have a car when we get out there."

"That'll be a grand adventure, then. And where will you go along the way, so? Mount Rushmore?"

"Too far north."

"Texas? You'll go through Texas, surely?"

I nodded.

Danny looked delighted for me—and probably jealous.

"Always wanted to see Texas. And Graceland?" His eyes were wide. "I've always had a yen to see it."

"Obviously Graceland," I said.

"And the Grand Canyon?" he asked.

"Of course."

"You know, all of County Donegal would fit *inside* the Grand Canyon."

"Well, maybe they should dump it in, waste of fuckin' space in Ireland." I grinned.

Danny shook his head, almost tearing up. "Always wanted to see the Grand Canyon," he said. "Where else? Do you know your route yet?"

I rolled my eyes. "Her Ladyship has planned out the *entire* trip. I'll show you." I picked up a wire-bound notebook from the coffee table and opened it to a random page and held it out to Danny.

It took him a moment to digest the enormity of Sara's project. "Show don't tell" is the actor's mantra, so here's an example. The page I'd opened to was titled "ST. LOUIS, MISSOURI" and read:

THIS MORNING, DEPARTING FROM:
Columbus, OH (sunrise 6:20 am)

DRIVING FOR:
9 hours including <u>all</u> stops (418 miles)

EXERCISE:
Waggin' Tails Bark Park, 10450 E. 63rd St, Lawrence, IN 46236

LUNCH STOP:
Indianapolis, North College Ave. area (Yats?)

AFTERNOON EXERCISE:
Silverlake Park Nature Trail, Highland IL 62249

ST. LOUIS:
2199 FOREST AVE (sunset 8 pm, sunrise 6 am)

TOMORROW, DEPARTING TO:
TULSA, OK (6 hours, 380 miles)

DETAILS: We'll be staying with Candace and Michael, they have a Jack Russell named Dixie and a fenced yard for Cody, plus they have an urban farm with chickens, so we can have fresh eggs for breakfast. There's an Italian restaurant down the block and the St. Louis Arch is 6.9 miles away if we want to go in the morning before we head to Tulsa.

Danny pursed his lips, humbled and awed.

"The whole thing's like this," I said, and added, because I couldn't help myself: "Because of the dog."

Any further conversation on that topic was stifled by the sound of the outer door opening. The dog leapt toward the door, her tail wagging madly, her body almost hopping. Could it be . . . might it be . . . possibly? Maybe? Yes! Sara was home! How *astounding*!

As if she hadn't spent a perfectly companionable evening with myself and Danny, Cody began to fling herself in anticlockwise circles, making a stifled whining noise as if barely restraining herself from bursting into song, as if she'd been abandoned for months and was desperate for human contact.

"Hello, sweetie," Sara hummed to her, the moment she was in the door. She knelt down to be eye level with the dog, who was desperately relieved Sara had entered. "Hello hello hello, my darling." Of course, a brief tarty-dog pose as Sara stood again, and then much pushing of the dog's nose against Sara's legs as if Cody was trying to clear the smell of Irish Males out of her olfactory system.

"Hi, love," Sara said to me once Cody had been mollified. "Danny! Hello there!" She put her bag on the counter, grinned at him, and gave him a big hug. Somewhat shyly, he reciprocated.

Then, and only then, did I get a little love. She moved around the counter into the kitchen area, and held her arms open a moment, gazing at me, then stepped closer and wrapped them around me. That felt, as always, magic. I hugged her back and decided that it really wasn't such a big deal that she was organizing all the spontaneity out of our entire cross-country adventure.

"How are you, Sara?" asked Danny.

"Oh, you know, we're sort of all over the place here," she said, smiling. "Thanks for helping Rory out today."

"So you're leaving your job at the museum, then, Sara?"

"My manager said I could take a three-month leave to sort of study at another museum," she said. "Till we know more."

"She's sent electronic flocks of her résumé to museums around L.A. County," I said. "Already had some nibbles. Somebody will want her. She's a great catch." To demonstrate, I caught her around the waist and pulled her to me from behind.

She turned to me as I released her. "Somebody *does* want me," she said. "Well, maybe." She bit her lower lip, and oh that grin of hers was always so adorable. "I heard from the *Getty*. They want to interview me in person."

"Fantastic!" I said. I felt a certain relief. Knowing she had something worthwhile to do out there would make me feel less guilty for taking her so far away from all of her people. I gave her a big fat kiss, and patted the nearer stool for her to sit on. "Tell us about it."

"It's a new position they're creating," she continued, beaming. She folded one leg under herself as she always did when she sat on the stools. "Sort of like what I do now, but I'd be setting the job up and training somebody to actually do it. And while I'm there, I would be learning about some programs they have, and bringing those ideas back to Boston to try to incorporate them. I'll tell you more about it later, probably not interesting for Danny." She flashed him a knowing smile, then turned back to me. "The one thing that's important, though, is that the in-person interview window is nearly over, so . . ." She grimaced. "I . . . need to get to Los Angeles earlier than you do."

"Okay," I said uncertainly.

"The only date they're willing to see me is . . . the twenty-seventh."

It took me a moment. "That's the day after we leave here," I said. "That's before we're even due in New York."

"Before *you're* even due in New York," she corrected. "You're going to drop me off at Logan and I'll fly to L.A., and then . . ." She let it hang in the air.

"And then after your interview, you'll fly to New York and I'll pick you up there," I finished, anticipating.

She grimaced and shook her head. "There's another complication. I was having the final conversation with the landlord, and somehow it turned out that when we said we had a dog, he thought we said we didn't have a dog. Dogs aren't allowed."

"In the place we just signed a *lease* for?" I said. Cody, as if sensing this conversation was about her, looked very alert and trotted over to push her nose against Sara's leg.

"Well, he released us from that because of the misunderstanding. He was really very sweet about it."

"What, so we have nowhere to *live*?" I said. My incredulity attracted Cody's interest. She left off nosing Sara and started to nose me, but I gestured her off me.

"Maybe I should be going now," said Danny.

"I'll find a place," said the ever-efficient Sara. "I have a couple of college friends out there, I can stay with them and look for something. So it's sort of a blessing that I have to go out there anyhow, so I can find us housing." She gave me a compassionately disappointed look. "I'm sorry, sweetheart, but you've got to drive across on your own." Pause. "With Cody, I mean."

There was a pause as we looked at each other.

"Okay, big man, I'm away now," said Danny with a nervous laugh. "Have to be hitting the road."

I know we were both perfectly pleasant to him as he exited but I'm not really sure how, because it seems to me we just kept staring at each other until we were alone.

"You're joking," I said.

"I'll join you en route as soon as I've gotten the housing sorted out. Maybe I can meet you in Flagstaff so we can at least do the Grand Canyon together."

"Amazing," I said. I took a moment to absorb the disappointment. "Well, I can make lemonade out of lemons. You won't mind if I chuck all that hysterical overplanning out the window, will you? I'd rather wing it."

"No," said Sara. "That route has all the dog-friendly places—"

"Oh, for fuck's sake!" I shouted toward the ceiling. "Everything is always about the fucking dog!"

The fucking dog, excited by my excitement, jumped up and

rested her front paws on my leg. I pushed her off. Undisturbed, she trotted into the living room and found a bone to chew on, on her bed.

"I am uprooting *my entire life* as a show of good faith," said Sara. "We don't actually *need* to be moving to Los Angeles yet. So if I need to know that you're someplace where the dog can get exercise, can't you give me that?"

"But you're missing the point," I said. "Of course I'd give you that, I'd give you whatever you needed, I adore you and I'm grateful for all of it, but we *wouldn't need* that hysterical level of order if it wasn't for the dog."

"Actually," Sara said fiercely, "we *really* wouldn't need it if we weren't going to Los Angeles to *start* with. I married you so you could do a series that was supposed to shoot in *Boston*. If I'm willing to accommodate you by moving to Los Angeles, can't you be willing to accommodate the dog?"

"Nobody has to accommodate anybody," I retorted. "You don't *have* to come to Los Angeles. I never *said* you had to come to Los Angeles. You could have renewed your lease and stayed here. We could call the L.A. bloke back and I could take that place on my own."

"No, you can't, we can't live on separate coasts," Sara said impatiently.

"We can do whatever we want!" I retorted. "We're grown-ups!"

"We're married," Sara countered sharply.

"We're married grown-ups! It's the twenty-first century. We can define the rules of our marriage for ourselves, for fuck's sake."

"For the next two years, we have to be a seamless couple and behave exactly the way the U.S. government thinks a married

couple should behave. We can't be living on separate coasts because you don't want to accommodate my dog. If you're going to
Los Angeles, I'm going with you."

"Don't accuse me of forcing you to move to Los Angeles!"

"I'm not—"

"You say you're not, but actually you are, you're saying you have
to give up everything you care about because you're doing me a
favor, meaning I am totally beholden to you! Don't play that guilt
card on me!"

THIS WAS THE beginning of a period I'd just as soon skip details
of. Moving is never fun to live through, and therefore not much
fun to read about, is it? We survived it without *too* much drama.

The single thing we both agreed about during that run was
that Cody and I would keep our arboretum routine going—Sara
wanted it for Cody to have regularity, and I wanted it for me to
have sanity. Sara had lots of good-bye parties that I was sure were
designed to make me feel guilty for taking her away from her
people.

Near the end of all the planning and stress and disruption, my
actual green card—the thing for which all previous things had
happened, except that first kiss—finally arrived in the mail. We
hardly even noticed it.

Chapter 15

Finally the day arrived. April 26. The day of Shakespeare's christening, and also of his death. So, a good day for transitions, especially for theater people.

All the plans had been laid and were ready to hatch. All the arguments had been argued and either resolved or definitively shelved. Sara's college friends were waiting for her late-night arrival in Los Angeles, where she had an interview and five apartment-seeking dates over the next two days. Boxes had been shipped. The decisions about the dog's lifestyle (not ours, mind you, but the dog's) had been made. Sara had given me stunningly detailed directions, as if she did not trust me to drive to the grocery store, let alone across the continent.

Sara had created a travel pack that would share the backseat with Cody and her dog bed: water, clothes, toilet paper, first-aid gear, a flashlight, a compass, motor oil, dog food, an extra leash, poop bags, a cell-phone charger for the car, matches, an umbrella, a water dispenser for Cody, and then in the front seat there was a GPS into which Sara programmed every lodging and restaurant the dog and I would be patronizing. To placate her I bought a smartphone with navigational apps as backups.

The dog and I would be spending our final night in the Boston area in Danny's living room. But for the final few hours of the day itself, there was the dilemma of what to do with the dog during our awkward last hours of cleanup. Sara fretted that as soon as Cody saw her dog bed go into the car, she would get stressed out, and we couldn't have that, now could we? So she wanted to remove Cody from the premises for a few hours while we packed the car and did the final clean. Only we couldn't think where to put her, as Danny and all our other friends would be working.

Then I'd thought of Jay.

"One of my arboretum friends could take her."

"Who, the kid from Bay State Caffeine?"

"No, this guy's forty-something, he lives right by the arboretum. We were in his house—" and then I realized where *that* explanation would lead, and shut up very rapidly.

She gave me a curious look. "Why would you have taken Cody to his house?"

"He's a friend of mine who I knew from before, he just moved to the area and we ran into each other at the arboretum and one day it was freezing out, so he invited me in for a cuppa."

"You've never mentioned that."

I shrugged, relying on my acting chops to summon the appearance of nonchalance. "I forgot. Didn't seem especially noteworthy. Anyhow I see him almost every day along with Alto and the mom with the two little boys and others. They can all vouch for him He's sound and he loves dogs, had one himself that died recently, and Cody loves him."

Sara frowned thoughtfully. "Let me think about it. We could just put her in a kennel for a few hours, too. Although I distrust most kennels."

"KENNELS ARE AWFUL," said Jay, when I broached him about the possibility the next day. "I had a friend whose dog contracted some rare disease in a kennel and died. Don't subject Cody to a kennel. I'd be delighted to take her."

"AND YOU REALLY know him? And trust him?" Sara was giving me the third degree about it.

"Yes! Yes, I do. I really wouldn't suggest him if I had the slightest doubt—he's sound! Do you think I would do anything to endanger Cody? Knowing the hell I'd be in with you if I did? I've been to his house. You want me to describe it for you?"

"And he likes dogs."

"Yes," I said, with such absolute confidence that it convinced her.

"It's only for a few hours anyhow," she said to reassure herself. "All right."

So, late morning of the twenty-sixth, Cody jumped into the car to stay close to her dog bed, giving us both suspicious looks. The suspicious looks had actually been going on all week. She knew something big was up, and she was not happy.

"Want to come?" I offered Sara.

Sara, her hair adorably tied with a green bandanna, shook her head, and rubbed her slightly grimy forehead with her slightly grimy forearm to avoid touching her bleach-covered rubber gloves to her face. "But tell him thank you, and let's get him a bottle of wine or something. Do you know what he likes?"

"Scotch, I think," I said. "I'll grab something on the way."

"All right." She kissed me. (She had already indulged in endless permutations of "Good-bye, my best friend, the most important creature in my life, my one and only, the best puppy in the whole wide world, I'll miss you more than anything" with the dog.) Then she went back inside.

I drove to Blanchard's for the Dewar's and then realized I had no idea how to actually *drive* to Jay's, only how to walk there from the far side of the arboretum. So we had a few false starts but eventually figured it out. I'm a big advocate of intuitive driving. (As if any other kind would work in Boston, anyhow.)

I parked in his driveway behind a white Lexus SUV, got out, and rang the bell. Cody sat politely on the porch beside me.

Jay, humming Leonard Cohen's "Hallelujah" to himself (like he always did) came to the door in his long black coat, welcomed me, welcomed Cody, rubbed her head, and invited me to tea.

"Thanks, I better pass," I said. "We're trying to get the last little bit done before her plane at six."

"I understand," said Jay, with a slightly melancholy smile. "But I must say I'm disappointed. I'd have liked to say a proper good-bye before we part ways forever."

I chuckled. "It might not be *forever,* now," I said, blushing with pleasure but playing the self-deferential card with total sincerity. "The whole thing could tank and we could find ourselves back here in six months hanging out with you in the arboretum."

He gave me a knowing look. "I don't think so. I have a feeling."

"Well . . . I'm hopeful but I'm superstitious, so I don't even know how to respond to that."

"I've rendered an Irishman speechless," said Jay. "That's got to be bragging rights for something." He glanced beyond us at the car. "So that's your chariot for this historic sojourn?"

" 'Tis," I said. "Seems a bit daft."

"My father had a MINI when I was a kid," he said, looking vaguely wistful (which to be fair is sort of how he always looked).

"Mine, too! I learned to drive in one."

"May I take a look?"

"Of course," I said with a gesture. Jay left his stoop, came down to the car, and began to walk around it, studying it nostalgically.

"Practically made of tinfoil, aren't they?" he said, kneeling down and testing the thickness of the wheel well. "Amazing."

"Oh, here's a little thank-you, by the way," I said, remembering, and brandishing the scotch.

He smiled, rose, and took the bottle, holding it up as if toasting with it. "That was very sweet and entirely unnecessary," he said. "I shall raise a glass to you when first I open it." (Do you see what I mean about how he'd have made a grand ruined baron?)

He looked down at the dog. She had been staring up at the two of us, watching our exchange intensely as if trying to learn English.

"Hello, Cody," he said, with a smile.

Instant collapse to tarty-dog position. Jay reached all the way down from his great height and rubbed her belly, humming "Hallelujah" softly. Cody shimmied back and forth, like one of those fortune-telling fish you hold on your palm. He rubbed her some more. Her tail thumped the ground.

"We are going to have fun," he said to her.

"Made for each other," I said cheerily. I was so glad to know she was in good hands, and especially chuffed that I could take credit for it.

"Absolutely," said Jay. "Get on back to your bride and finish the cleanup. So you'll be by, when, four or five hours?"

"Hopefully no more than three," I said.

"No rush," he said comfortably.

We exchanged phone numbers. It's funny we'd never done that, but we were so used to seeing each other regularly. Then we shook hands and I headed back to Sara's apartment.

Sara had stopped for lunch and I joined her before gearing up for the last little bit. We put some great Trad tunes on her iPad and danced around the apartment with the mop and broom for a couple hours. It was fun. Then we turned the music off to spend our last few moments of work in Zen-like quiet.

Sara swept and I held the dustpan. As is nearly always the case when I let my mind wander, I got a song stuck in my head—an earworm, the Germans call it. It was Leonard Cohen's "Hallelujah," because Jay had been singing it when I'd dropped Cody off. Of course, he sang it almost constantly. I thought he'd just been humming it, but in retrospect, he must have been singing, because one line in particular was stuck in my head.

"Maybe there's a God above," I heard myself mumble. *". . . but all I really learned from love . . . was how to shoot at someone who outdrew you."*

"Oh God, please stop it with that song!" Sara said, setting down the broom against the kitchen counter. "Especially *that* line, it's so creepy."

"It is?" I asked, feeling chastened. I stood up, tapped the dustbin a final time in the garbage bag, and then set the dustpan on one of the chairs.

"Rory, think about it: *All I really learned from love was how to shoot at someone who outdrew you.* That's vengeance justified as self-defense."

"I never really thought about it," I confessed, and reached for the broom, so I could clip the dustpan to the shaft.

"And those lyrics remind me of Jonathan," she said almost to herself.

I froze, and felt the world tilt a bit, and slide.

"Who's Jonathan?" I asked, setting down the dustpan.

"My ex?" she said, as if I should have known this. "The one whose name Lena spits at? He *loved* that song."

"His name was Jonathan? Like, starts-with-a-*J* Jonathan?"

She frowned at me. "Jonathan always starts with a *J*. Sometimes I even called him Jay. You knew that, Rory."

"No, I really don't think I did," I said, fighting off just a bit of panic.

She shrugged. "Why's it matter?"

"Well, it's not like we talked about him much. So . . . right. His name is Jay. Jonathan. And he likes that song. He's not, em, tall and bald by any chance, is he?"

She stared at me for a moment. Then the penny dropped, and her eyes bugged with alarm. "Did you just hand my dog to a tall bald guy named Jay who loves Leonard Cohen's 'Hallelujah'? Especially the line about how failed love leads to *vengeance*?"

" . . . I'm sure there are plenty of people named Jay who like Leonard Cohen—"

She had already grabbed my Manchester United sweatshirt and brandished it at me. "Go and get the dog back. Right now."

"Sara—"

"Now," she said. And then, the worst possible question rose in her mind: "How the hell do you even know him?"

"From the arboretum," I said, feeling miserably like a three-year-old who had been caught in a lie.

"I thought the guy in the park was an old friend of yours. You said he was a dog expert or something."

I felt myself growing pale. I didn't know you could actually feel such a thing. "He's a new friend, and he's really good with dogs, he's really good with Cody—"

"You just handed my dog over to my ex-boyfriend?!" she nearly screamed.

"I admit it's a possibil—"

She hurled my sweatshirt at me. "Go and get her right *fucking* now!"

"I could call him first," I offered meekly, not wanting to make a big deal out of this. Not wanting this to be a big deal. "He gave me his number."

"Really?" she demanded. Not disbelievingly; more of a so-there tone. "Are you sure? Are you sure it's his number? Go on, then. Dial it."

Wishing I were somewhere else, I pulled out my phone, found the number, and pushed call.

"Put it on speaker," she insisted.

I did. It rang. Four times.

Then it went straight to voice mail for a carpet-cleaning company run by a lady from, by the accent, maybe Indonesia.

"This is not happening," one of us said.

She pulled out her phone and frantically, feverishly, began to tap the keyboard screen, muttering numbers to herself. "I can't believe I still remember it," she said. "There." She tapped the final digit, and firmly handed me the phone.

"Me?" I said, alarmed.

I'm not talking to him. *I'm* not the one who gave him Cody!"

I heard the ringing and reflexively brought it to my ear, but felt a sick sensation in my stomach. Whether my Jay answered or not, I had completely fucked this up and no mistake. I mean I had *completely*—

"Hello, Sara," said a horribly familiar voice over the line.

"It's not Sara, it's just Sara's phone," I said awkwardly, dying inside.

"Rory," said Jay, sounding pleased. "Hello. How's the cleaning going?"

"Why did you give me a false number?" I demanded. Sara gave me a long-suffering look, rolling her eyes as if she wanted to wipe the ceiling with her lashes.

"Did I? Must have switched a few digits by mistake. Anyhow, I figured Sara might still know it. I'm so happy she did."

I held the phone out to Sara. Her eyes flashed. "You did this," she hissed. "You fix it. *Now.*"

"Where's Cody?" I asked into the phone.

"Right here," he said pleasantly. "Right where you left her. Right where I saved her life last month."

"I'm coming over there now to get her," I said.

"Mmm . . . Not sure about that," said Jay. "She is my dog."

"She's Sara's dog," I said. "You bought her for Sara. She was a gift for Sara."

"Was she? Does Sara have any material evidence of that?" A sound of paper rustling. "It's my name on the contract with the rescue shelter. Yep, there it is. Happy to show you if you like."

"Why are you doing this?" I demanded.

"Because she's my dog," he said in a reasonable tone.

"I mean really, *why* are you *doing this*?"

"Let's meet for coffee and I'll lay it out for you, Rory."

"I don't have time to meet for coffee—" I protested.

"Meet for *coffee*?" Sara nearly shrieked. "Get my *dog* back!"

"I heard that," said Jay calmly. "Tell Sara hello from me. And explain that Cody is *my* dog. Women are faithless, a man's dog never is. My dog belongs with me."

I could never have imagined Sara looking as she did now. Her skin was splotched red, she was breathing hard and fast, and she had a dreadful expression on her face, as if she were trying to make herself look ugly (although for the record she failed to achieve this goal). "She's registered in my name," Sara said defiantly. "Tell him that. The city of Boston officially knows I'm her owner."

"She's registered in Sara's name," I said obediently into the phone, feeling very stupid.

"I had the registration transferred to my name," Jay said smoothly. "You wouldn't believe how easy it was. You'd think they'd be more diligent about these things. The fact that I have her rabies vaccination number off her collar helped."

"Why are you doing this?" I demanded for the third time.

"She's my dog," he said, in a smooth, reasonable voice. "Sara took her. I've reclaimed her. It's as simple as that. Go on to Los Angeles now and have a wonderful life. Get a new dog. One that you actually think of as *yours*." There was a mechanical sound; I pulled the phone away from my ear and looked at the face. CALL OVER, said a banner.

For a long silent moment, I just stood there.

Then I looked up at Sara, stricken.

"I . . . I don't . . ." I began.

"We're going straight there," said Sara. "Right now. Let's get in the car and go." She snatched the phone from my hand and tapped redial even as she was grabbing her jacket. She tossed the jacket up in the air and then lanced her arm up the sleeve to start to get it on. "Let's *go*," she ordered, and was already out the door. I hurried after her. Her body moved toward the car as her attention moved toward the phone. "I know you're not picking up," she said into it, "but you're not getting away with this, Jonathan. I have a *lot* of questions about how this even *happened,* and I will get to the bottom of it, and I will get my dog back. I'm sure you are *very* pleased with yourself right now, but I would not rest easy if I were you. Call me if you are willing to negotiate."

She hung up and was already halfway in the driver's seat. I had to ball up to fit onto the passenger seat, the well was full.

She didn't recognize the house we drove to; that really was a new purchase. She was too upset and furious to speak to me on the short drive over, which is good because I'd have had no idea how to answer her. "Let's get her back first and we'll discuss it afterward," she said. "And I'm taking her with me on the plane. I can't leave her with you, *obviously*." That was the closest she came to expressing actual anger at me, and it stung like a badly macerated knife.

"I . . . Sara, I swear, I don't . . ."

"Not now," she said grimly.

When we got to the building, the SUV was no longer in the drive, but there was an older-model Subaru Outback in its place. Sara parked behind it, and we both leapt out of the car and dashed to the steps. I began to buzz the buzzer; Sara pounded her fists on the door and then tried the knob. It opened and she bounded up the stairs, steam nearly coming out of her ears.

I followed quickly but meekly, my head still reeling, still getting my breath back from the karmic sucker punch. How could Jonathan be Jay and how could Jay have pulled all that off? Was it just dumb luck or had he shepherded me to this moment from our first encounter? How naive and stupid was I really?

"Excuse me!" Sara said loudly over the sound of vacuuming. As I came up behind her on the stairs, the noise stopped abruptly, and a short, stout, redheaded woman came out of the next room, frowning and dragging an upright vacuum cleaner.

"Can I help you?" asked Marie.

"What are *you* doing here?" I demanded, horrified.

Marie looked at me strangely. "I'm a housecleaner, you know that. I clean for Jay. He asked me to clean this afternoon."

"Where is he?" Sara demanded fiercely.

Marie, a native Bostonian, was not impressed with fierce. "Isn't this your wife?" she said to me, pleasant but confused, pointing at Sara.

"Where is he?" Sara repeated, more fiercely.

Marie shrugged. "Got me. I think he said he was headed out of town for a vacation, didn't he say Peru or something? Do you remember, Rory? Hey, aren't you leaving for California, like, today?"

"Not if we can't find Cody," I said. "Jay has taken Cody."

Marie seemed to think maybe this was *Candid Camera*. "What?" she said, grinning. "That doesn't make any sense. Why would he do that?"

"Have you seen him?" Sara said. Her intensity was finally permeating Marie's hearty indifference.

"Calm down," said Marie firmly. "Not today. Today I was cleaning a house over in Cambridge, so I didn't even get to the park with the kids. Jay asked if I could come by around two. I just got here."

"And he wasn't here?"

"Nope," she said. "I have a key."

Sara huffed with frustration. "I'm going to look around," she said, moving past Marie and into the apartment.

Marie looked at me. "Hey—"

"Something really strange has happened, Marie, and we're trying to figure it out," I said. "He's not answering his phone, he's got Cody, it's complicated."

Marie looked displeased. "Jay? There must be some mistake."

"How well do you know him?" Sara asked, almost accusingly.

Marie shrugged. "Just, you know, like everyone, from the arboretum. He found out I clean houses, he asked me to be his cleaner, that was, I dunno, maybe six months ago. He pays cash, he's neat, he remembers my kids' birthdays, which is sometimes more than my husband does."

"He's taken Cody and run off with her," said Sara.

"That doesn't make sense. There's got to be a misunderstanding," said Marie, with a dismissive wave, but Sara cut her off.

"No, we've talked to him on the phone, he has confirmed that he is not giving the dog back."

"Why?"

"Because he wants to keep her," said Sara, her fuse shortening.

"He can't do that," Marie said in a so-there tone, as if this fact alone would prevent it from happening.

"I agree," said Sara. "So does Rory. But Jonathan—Jay—he doesn't agree. He's going to keep the dog unless we can find him and take her back. Do you have any idea where he is?"

"Does he drive a white SUV?" I asked, so grateful I had something to say.

"Yeah, a Lexus," said Marie, nodding. "It wasn't here when I got here."

"We're going to look around to see if there are clues to where he went," Sara announced. To me: "I bet he left clues. He loves mind-fucks like that. That's why he was singing the Leonard Cohen song. When I was packing up my stuff to leave him, he moped around the house singing *that* verse of *that* song over and over again. I bet he *always* sings that song, that *line,* when you're around him."

"Jesus," I said, realizing.

"So we're just going to look around," Sara told Marie.

"You're kinda putting me in an awkward position here," said Marie.

"How about this," I said to Marie. "You know me, you know that Jay and I know each other, you know I've been in this house at his invitation—"

"How would she know that?" asked Sara.

"Because of the time Cody ate the chocolate cake?" said Marie.

Oh, fuck me, I didn't think this could get any worse.

"What?" Sara gasped.

I gave Marie a pleading look. "Oh, I get it," said Marie, and continued briskly: "Yeah, okay, so Rory can look around, but I don't know you, I'm really sorry, I don't know what your relationship is to Jay—"

"So I'll look around in here and you ask the neighbors when they last saw him," I suggested urgently.

Sara stared at me. "What about Cody eating chocolate cake?"

"I will explain that when we're not running against the clock," I said.

"Oh God," she muttered under her breath, but then ran back down the stairs and outside.

Marie looked at me. "Sorry I mentioned the cake."

I shrugged. "You didn't know she didn't know."

"She's very upset."

"Her ex-boyfriend stole her dog."

Marie's mouth opened very wide. "What? Jay and your wife—"

"I only realized myself a few moments ago."

She was perversely amused. "That's crazy! So he—wait—so he—"

"They bought the dog together and now he's taken it back. I'm supposed to be driving Sara to the airport right now so she can fly to Los Angeles. Please can I just check around and try to get some clue as to where he might have gone?"

"This is *crazy*," said Marie. "I thought he was one of my *normal* clients." She sighed. "Okay, ten minutes, leave everything exactly how you found it and you didn't hear me say that." She pushed the vacuum so that the upright part clicked into place and stood by itself. "I'll help you."

"Really?"

"He's either a sack of shit or he isn't. If he is, I want to help you. If he isn't, he never needs to know this ever happened. I have permission to go through his stuff as his cleaner anyhow."

We found nothing. His place was very neat—"every cleaner's dream," Marie said. He worked only with a laptop. The dock for it was in his study, but the laptop itself was gone, as was the hard drive. If he ever wrote anything on paper (which in my imagination is how he would keep track of everything), the paper was gone, too. There was nothing in the kitchen except kitchen stuff. He was so fastidious about his mail that there was none lying about. I could imagine him and Sara as a couple—Mr. and Mrs. Particular. They must've had filing competitions as foreplay.

See, that's the other part of this I could not get my head around—not just that the dog was gone, not just that I'd been so completely played for a fool, but that *he used to be Sara's lover*. They had lived together. They'd slept and played and ate and *trained Cody* together. They'd made *love*. He was the bloke who'd bullied her out of pursuing her painting career, told her to get a real job. What did she *see* in him?

Or, the question another part of me wanted to ask: Why the hell did she leave him? He was a much better match for her than I was. They were both highly educated and . . . *organized*. They probably came from similar backgrounds. He was about ten years older, but that wasn't so much, and he was charismatic and cultured—now

I noticed the great art in his apartment and wondered if Sara had helped him pick it out . . .

"Jesus, I remember that painting," said her voice just behind me, with uncanny timing, as she came back up the stairs. She was pointing to something that looked like a Sargent knockoff from his Spanish phase. "The neighbors say he threw some bags in the car and drove off before lunch." She sounded like she was about to be sick. Oh Jesus, this was a nightmare. "So," she went on, swallowing her bile and rubbing her hands along her temples briskly. "Here's what has to happen. We have to file a claim of stolen property—"

"He said he changed her registration to his name," I said.

"Well then, I have to contest that," she said. "We have a car full of raggedy old dog stuff that proves she's been living with us. Even if he went out and bought her a bed and toys and stuff, that will all be new. We have her stuff. I have years of photos of her being with me. I can absolutely contest ownership if it comes to that, but first we have to *get* her, so we need the police to be looking for him. Do we know his license-plate number?"

She glanced at Marie, who looked almost affronted.

"No," said Marie. "But it's a white Lexus SUV. If you know that and his name, you can file a report. I guess. Do I look like someone who knows about this stuff?"

"Isn't Alto's dad a cop?" I said.

"I think he's a fireman," said Marie, "but I bet firemen and police are familiar with each other's MOs."

"Great," said Sara. "Rory, call Alto—"

"I don't have his number. But I think he's at work now. I could drive over to Centre Street and ask him."

"All right," said Sara. "Do that. I'm going to call Jay's family and a couple of friends of his that I might still have numbers for and see if I can get any information from them. Thank you," she said to Marie. "Thank you for letting us look around. If you get any leads at all, please let us know."

"I have to get you to Logan," I said, wondering even as the words came out if this was a ridiculous thing to say.

It was. She looked at me as if I'd just shat on the rug. "I'm not leaving Boston until we've found her," she said, clearly appalled she'd even have to say that. "I'll cancel the flight. Right now." She held up her phone, but gave me an urgent, whisking gesture. "Go on, go talk to Alto. I'll meet you over there."

Chapter 16

Two hours later, we finally reconvened, but not at Bay State Caffeine. *James's Gate,* read Sara's text. *I need a drink.*

It was late afternoon, so it was quiet in the pub when I entered, and the only light was from the frosted windows. Sara sat at the bar with a half-finished glass of wine. I ordered a coffee. Somewhere in the frenzy of the day, she had lost her jacket.

"First I called his parents," she began in a low voice, after a kiss of greeting. "They loved me, they didn't want to see me leave him, so that's good and bad. They're in Florida. I asked them about his plans to go to Peru and they didn't know of any, and I checked all flights from Boston to Peru and they're all morning flights, so I think that was a red herring, or at least, he hasn't left yet. They haven't heard from him lately. I told them I had something to give him, and created the impression we've started chatting a bit and are back on friendly terms, so they were happy to offer to let me know if they heard from him. I also called a few mutual friends we're both occasionally in touch with and explained to them what's happened, none of them had any leads, or at least, none of them was willing to confess to any. Two people commented on how attached he was to Cody and how devastated he was to lose 'both his girls in one fell swoop.'" This, with air quotations and rolled eyes.

"I can't believe he's your ex," I said.

"I can't believe you *gave him Cody,*" she said. "We are going to have a very serious conversation about all of that, too, but first we get her back. So: no leads from his people. What about the police?"

I shrugged. "Filing a report is about as useful as throwing a match down a well. I know people who have been mugged and beaten up and gone to the cops, and the cops acted like they were filing a weather report."

"But we *can* file one, right? And describe the car and all that."

"I already did," I said, reveling in the fact that I'd been useful.

"But she's not your dog."

"She's my wife's dog," I said. "That makes her my dog."

Sara's face suddenly crumbled and she started crying. She grabbed me hard around the waist and started sobbing into my shoulder. I hope it doesn't make me a prick to say that pleased me. Finally I was doing something right. I put my arms around her, and rubbed her back slowly.

"It's going to be okay," I said into her ear. "We'll find her. I'll find her. I screwed up but I'm going to make it right. And at least you know he's not going to hurt her."

"I *don't* know that," sobbed Sara. "Medea killed her own children to get back at Jason."

I'd never done *Medea,* so I wasn't sure what she was talking about. So I didn't say anything, just hugged her tighter. In the midst of all the trauma and stress, it was one soft and peaceful moment.

Until she suddenly cried out, and jerked away from me, spastically pulling her light blue, long-sleeved T away from her skin because somehow in the course of our hug, she'd dumped the rest of her burgundy all over it. Her face screwed up as tight as a raisin. She growled between clenched teeth and then nearly exploded with *"Fuck it!"* to the ceiling of the Gate, startling the barman and the few patrons huddled at the other end of the bar. "Sorry," she added quickly, head still upturned, eyes glancing down at worried faces. A few murmurs of sympathy and people returned to their own personal programming.

I was in such a ragged state that to be honest, the first thought that went through my mind was, *Thank God it wasn't me who spilled it.*

"Here," I said, immediately unzipping my Manchester United hoodie and handing it to her. "Go to the restroom, take your shirt off and wear this."

Pressing her eyes to make the tears stop, Sara took the sweatshirt, sniffled, and kissed me on the cheek. "Thanks," she said, and jogged through the swing doors into the restaurant.

THE NEXT TWENTY-FOUR hours, I have to tell you, were a blur of adrenaline, anxiety, waiting, bureaucracy, hope, and fear. Jay never called, and never answered when we tried calling him, no matter what number we called from. Alto's father, as it turned out, worked for EMS—Emergency Medical Services, those folks forever shredding the humming streets of Jamaica Plain with sirens. He was a terrific help, knew the people that we needed to speak with, helped Sara file even more reports than what I'd done—changing licensure of Cody back to her name, for example—and talked to certain people in certain offices about tracking down Jay's car at tollbooths or stoplights. Alto played go-between once he was off his shift and he didn't smoke all evening. There was a lot of to-ing and fro-ing and no time for conversation. Sara and I went to Lena's that evening, where Danny, Steve, and Elliot joined us for a strategy session. I was firmly put through the third degree, having to confess the whole story of the chocolate cake. Sara simply buried her face in her hands, but Lena lit into me a bit, in the unflinchingly direct-but-matter-of-fact manner of a Filipino woman, and I snapped back at her in the hotheaded re-actionary style of an Irish man.

In the end, Sara took the guest bedroom, I took the couch. This was Lena's terse directive, but I got the feeling that it came from Sara, who by that point—following an impromptu dinner that she didn't touch—was so enervated she mostly just wanted to curl up into a ball. A ball that had no room for me.

Early in the morning we were at it again. We called every vet's office and shelter in eastern Massachusetts; every newspaper and radio station, e-mailing photos of Cody to the papers and offering a cash reward for assistance. Marie stalked Peters Hill with flyers, leaving a pile when she had to pick Nick up from preschool. Alto organized some friends (I'd no idea Alto had friends) to stake out Jay's flat, should he or anyone else return to it, and then he himself went to post flyers all over town. The MFA gang did useful stuff involving computers that I didn't really understand—I suppose when you make your living seeking out the provenance of obscure artwork, or (on the other extreme) reaching out to ask wealthy powerful people for assistance, you can transfer these skills into other arenas. Danny put the word out on the street to be looking for a dog of Cody's description and anyone in a white Lexus SUV. So, the point being: it was heartening how seriously everybody took this, and turned out to help.

But nothing came of it.

Sara had her interview in Los Angeles (rescheduled) and I had my meeting in New York. It seemed callous to suggest that either of us pursue these things, and yet sitting around Lena's guest room hoping to get a lead seemed rather pointless, almost masochistic. Somehow—I don't know how I did this, because I'm pretty shoddy at staying calm in stressful circumstances—I convinced Sara she should go out to California in time for her interview, and then fly back. I promised her I'd go to the meeting in Manhattan but then turn around and come back to Boston, too, and we two would absolutely not leave again until we got the dog back. I had to be in L.A. by mid-May, but if need be, I'd just hop a JetBlue flight last minute. Sara, looking terribly haggard, with the buoyancy of a popped balloon, dully agreed to all this, and then immersed herself in seeking the most unattractively timed flight out of Logan.

She found one that left Boston at five A.M. and reached LAX at seven, on the day of her rescheduled interview, which was also the day of my morning meeting in Manhattan. It was some airline that I'd never heard of, which sounded a bit dodgy to me, but she pointed out that I was in no position to judge dodginess.

We were up late at Lena's the night before, or rather she was, scouring online stolen-pets sites. It would have seemed unfeeling of me to sleep while she was doing this, so together we stayed up until nearly one A.M., and then (having slept, again, in different places) we woke up at three thirty so that I could get her to Logan Airport in time for her to get her flight.

The whole drive to Logan we didn't speak, and I kept playing out all possible farewells in my mind. Maybe we'd hug tightly and she'd let me know that everything would be all right in the end between us, no matter what happened to the dog—or maybe I'd even say that to her. Maybe she'd inform me with her efficient firmness that once we had settled all of this, we were to be sundered as a romantic couple but she would at least honor her promise to me to see it through for the green card. There were plenty of variations occupying my mind.

But when we got to Logan, none of them could be enacted, because as she was getting out of the crowded MINI Cooper, she suddenly realized she had been living in my Man United hoodie for the past thirty-six hours, with nothing under it except a sleeveless T-shirt, and she wanted to wear real clothes for the flight. She tore off the sweatshirt, threw it back into the car, and then right there on the pavement opened her small duffel bag to paw through it looking for a decent shirt. The state trooper at the curb (sound track: "Gee, Officer Krupke") would not let me stay to help her—although there was barely any traffic so early in the morning—and so we had a very awkward, rushed good-bye, not so much as a hug, just her glancing up from her strewn clothing on the sidewalk saying, "Thank you, Rory, I love you, drive safely, I'll see you in L.A., let's talk soon," all of it mechanical as she set about to find a shirt in the strange early-morning outdoor fluorescent airport light, shivering in forty-degree weather in a tank top.

I drove away, peering into the rearview mirror so frequently I almost drove into several taxis, and then nearly missed the exit that would take me to New York. It was 4:14 A.M. My meeting in Manhattan was at ten. I was in desperate need of a shave and fresh clothes. Having slept fewer than three hours that night, and no more than five the night before, I was going to be a walking zombie-troglodyte when I went in to meet the suits. I was very glad I'd signed that fifty-page contract, the mutual consent that they were stuck with me unless the show flopped. Of course, they could probably arrange for it to not be a success; Dougie had said it really was all about the backroom politics of the studio. Which meant they couldn't actually fire me for showing up as a troll, but they could pointedly turn their attention toward other projects.

I stopped somewhere on the road to get coffee, which was pure muck, and then barreled my way in the predawn gloom toward New York City, faster than a choirboy running from a priest. If the meeting ran an hour, I'd be back in Boston before sundown. Maybe I'd crash at Danny's. If Lena and I were in the same building alone together, the static electricity between us might set it aflame.

I MADE IT to Manhattan in less than four hours.

Then I was stuck in traffic on the West Side Highway for nearly ninety minutes.

I looked like shite, it's true. I'd been wearing the same clothes for three days running now, I had a beard that was in that dreadful state of more-than-stubble but not yet clearly-beardlike. I probably smelled terrible, that piquant skunklike smell of anxiety-sweat mixed with the corn-chip odor of haven't-managed-to-bathe sweat—but I was too in it, too immersed in my own body ming, to know for certain how badly I reeked. My hair was a moppish disaster, and in the rearview mirror the skin around my eyes looked twenty years older than the rest of me. Most of all, my brain was fried. I rubbed my face, slapped my cheeks a few times, and got out of the car.

As soon as I was standing, my calves and inner thighs immediately went into muscle spasm and I nearly hit the tarmac. I lifted myself up, tried some stretches, leaning against the cold roof of the car. I rested my head briefly on the warm bonnet and wished I had a blanket so I could curl up on it and take a little power nap. But no. I had to go. This meeting was very important although I could not remember why. After a few more stretches reminding me of my questionable balance, I left my key with the handsome, cheerful Jamaican car-park attendant (sound track: no, not Bob Marley, haven't you any imagination? More like a Motown ballad) and began to walk as fast as I could make myself toward midtown. As I walked, I tried to drag my attention away from the calamitous and stressful past few days, and remember who I was becoming and why I was even here: I was a legal resident of the United States of America, the lead in a new television series, a rising star. Right?

Chapter 17

It was mad that here I was, about to walk into a meeting that was the beginning of my new life—and all I wanted was to take a nap and then wake up somewhere else. Dream come true, one in a million, better than *American Idol* without even having to deal with those snarky judges. This was it, I was *it,* the man of the hour. I was embodying every aspect of the American Dream: Immigrant from the gutters makes good! Aspiring actor plucked from obscurity hits the big time! *This* was my life, this was what I had been striving toward—with practice, talent, and experience— for so many years. This was the payoff.

All I could think about was the fucking dog.

I realize that it was about far more than the dog. Here I was, on top of the world, and yet I had also proven myself, beyond all doubt, a proper eejit—irresponsible, duplicitous, gullible, unre- liable, and impotent to fix things. And right now I wasn't even good-looking.

So telling myself, *It's just a dog,* or even, *I'm heading right back to Boston to take care of this* didn't help at all, because neither of those changed the fact I'd fucked up. I'd never felt like such a winner and such a loser at the same time. Somehow being a loser diminished the glory of being a winner, but being a winner didn't at all diminish the humiliation of being a loser. Maybe because I was desperately craving a shower.

And so I didn't strut the way I'd imagined I would, charming the bejaysus out of all I passed, oozing confidence and cockiness. Rather I almost *snuck* through the crowded, harried streets of Manhattan, aware how easily, how effortlessly, something could go wrong and turn my whole world even more topsy-turvy. To be honest, I felt a little paranoid. At least the exhaustion meant I didn't have a lot of energy with which to feed that paranoia.

The auditions and callbacks had been in a sound stage. I'd felt right at home there and had continued to imagine all-things-pilot-related as happening in that space. But this meeting was in midtown, just east of Times Square, near the library, in an ugly glass-and-steel skyscraper the cable network owned. The vibe had about as much in common with a rehearsal room as a proctologist's office. It didn't even have the charming scruff of an old hotel or anything—it was all modern, gratuitously expensive-looking, almost clinical. It made my scruffiness immediately ten times scruffier.

Inside, the air was sterile. One wall had half a dozen TV monitors on it, all playing muted programs—a classic movie on one, starring an adorable dog; nonstop news on another, including something about a dog; a couple of DIY shows (cooking, dog training, carpentry); some dramatic original programming on the sixth and largest, which didn't seem to be about a dog. Across from this, up a couple of stairs, was the reception desk, which looked like the Ritz-Carlton version of a carnival barker's stand.

There were two dolled-up birds with lacquered hair and perfectly made-up faces, wearing sleek headsets strapped to their ears with gizmos that rested on their collarbones and looked, in all honesty, a little bit like dog collars; from the bust down they were hidden behind the stand, but you could tell from the industrious movement of their shoulders that they were busily answering a bank of phones and asking people to hold. They looked like they were having the time of their lives. And why not? They worked for a cable network! It left them plenty of time for personal grooming. I envied them.

I took an uncertain step toward them. Suddenly I couldn't remember the name of my own series. *Private Irish* was the only phrase that came to mind because it was some kind of stupid pun like that, but I really hoped it was not *that* stupid, only I couldn't remember now because I couldn't get the image of the dog out of my mind, and that just choked everything else out. Every moment I was here was a moment I wasn't hunting for the dog. This meeting better damn well be worth it.

There were people crossing efficiently through the lobby, waving identification cards against scanners before entering elevators. Some of these were women who truly looked like they were made of metal with a thick covering of silicon and makeup. Others were men, all in very expensive clothes, even if casual, and all with (it seemed) professional manicures. I did not belong with any of these people. These people all belonged with each other, but I was an outsider, so much so it seemed impossible I was about to be embraced by them.

"Rory!" It was a familiar voice and something inside me almost relaxed. There was Dougie, all the way from Los Angeles—good ol' Dougie, near the bank of elevators, on the other side of the ID scanners.

But same as that, I hardly recognized him. He was wearing an expensive suit, and his hair looked almost as shellacked as the receptionistas'. Was this going to happen to me, too? Would I walk out of here today smelling of Dolce & Gabbana, my mop-top firm as a helmet? "Rory, man, good to see you!" Dougie came past the scanners to me. I hadn't actually seen him in person for a couple of years; he looked a little plumper and yet also a little more toned, as if somebody had airbrushed him. "Dude!" He hugged me—a warm, real hug, which I hadn't been expecting but which I realized I needed. "These guys are so hot for you," he whispered enthusiastically, before releasing the hug. "This is going to be awesome." But then he looked me over, seeing my actual state of havoc. "Hey, guy. Everything all right?"

I'd no clue how to answer that. A simple no was not what he wanted to hear, but to try to give it context seemed absurd: "No, my wife's dog has been kidnapped" would sound awfully bizarre and require further conversation, and I did not want the first conversation here, in the lobby of my brilliant new life, to be about (a) the dog or (b) what a fuckup I was.

So I just stared at him.

"Rory? You okay?" He sounded worried now. "You need a glass of water?"

"I'm just a bit dizzy," I said defensively.

"You want to lie down before the meeting?" A pause. "Do you maybe need . . . a shower? Some freshening up?"

Oh God, so I really did look that bad. There was a shower in an office building? The thought of it almost made my knees buckle with desire. But if I said yes, that would appear to be weakness. Couldn't do that. God, I wish I could remember why we were having this meeting.

Suddenly I wished Cody was there to lean against me. I had grown quite fond of how she leaned against me, even though I never admitted it, and it was really endearing how she leaned against Sara.

If she never again got to lean against Sara, that would be one hundred percent my fault.

"I'm grand," I said, shaking my head a little. I'd be fine. I'd think of something clever to do or say and I'd shake myself out of this, I'd have them all eating out of my hands, I just had to get in front of an audience and I'd be grand.

"Okay," said Dougie, not sounding convinced. "Let's get you signed in, then."

One of the receptionistas printed out a white tag with a very blurry image of me that had been taken by some camera I hadn't noticed, clipped it to a lanyard, and handed it to me. "Have a nice day," she said, to either me or whoever she was simultaneously on the phone with.

The tag let me past the scanners. We took the elevators up about thirty floors, enough for my ears to pop. The farther away we moved from Planet Earth the less comfortable I was. I needed to be on Planet Earth to look for Cody.

The elevators doors opened into a broad, largely empty reception area, flooded with natural light but inorganic in its modern-meets-postmodern look. Despite the casual sprinkling of Emmy Awards along the counter (real-life Emmy Awards!), the message here was definitely "We're really wealthy," not "We make good art." Not that there's anything wrong with that—I'm grand with being adopted by the wealthy. But I would have been so comforted by the presence of a fellow actor, and there didn't seem to be any of those around. What did all these people do? Would it be my responsibility to make sure the show was good enough that they continued to be paid their salaries? God, the pressure. More than I could handle today. I wished I could just call this off and go right back to Boston, but it was an important meeting—although I couldn't remember why it was important. That added to the dreamlike (slightly nightmarish) feeling of being here.

Dougie strode up to the desk, said something to these new receptionistas, and then signaled me to come. I followed him through a glass door into a glass corridor, with glass offices lining either side.

At the end of the corridor was an actual solid wooden door, and we went through this . . . into a room whose opposite wall was glass, and looked out over midtown Manhattan from hundreds of feet up, and I have to tell you, it was breathtaking. Even though half the buildings were ugly as sin, it was *impressive*.

So. Here we were in the room with The Suits—although actually, none of The Suits was wearing a suit (except Dougie). I suppose that's an outdated expression now. Everyone—one woman, the rest men—was dressed in civvies and generally looked like expensive versions of normal people, and much better groomed versions of me. I think I'd expected them all to match, like a Secret Security detail or something, but they were quite the hodgepodge. A few were in blue jeans and turtlenecks, several (including the bloke who had flirted with me back in the sound stage last winter) were dressed all in black, a few were in suit coat and khakis. The Suits were dressing down. But Jesus, not as much as I was.

I was wearing jeans (now very baggy and stained) and a collarless shirt (ditto) and a pair of Docs. And a hobo beard and hobo hair and bleary red eyes and a general air of eau-de-Rory. I looked like a strung-out PBS host contemplating converting to Rastafarianism. I saw every pair of eyes scan me. Each time, there was the briefest hesitation, followed by an indulgent smile. I didn't know if I should trust the indulgent smiles. As I said, I was feeling a bit paranoid.

They were all so fresh, so perky, so positive. They also looked, in some ineffable way, terrifyingly competent. Especially compared to *me*. I couldn't even summon a sound track for them and I *never* had that problem. I was *such* a fish out of water. I bet none of these people had ever trod the boards a day in their life, except Dougie. Dougie now made introductions, including the people I'd met before.

One of them was a production executive who worked for the network, and another was an executive producer who worked for the studio. Then there was an executive producer who was going to be the music supervisor—he looked like someone I could probably have a decent chat with, another time, though. Two others were executive producers because they had come up with the idea for the show and sold it to the network. These two—one was the geekiest bloke in the room, so probably the writer—*almost* felt like theatre people, but not quite. Someone else seemed to be a producer because he was dating the show-runner, the woman, who was the *chief* executive producer, and two others were mere producers, but nobody explained how that was different from the executive producers.

And then two other blokes were co-executive producers.

None of this made any sense to me. I just wanted to accomplish whatever this important meeting was supposed to accomplish, just do my job and then reunite with Sara and Cody. First I had to rescue Cody, though. Did any of these people have a dog? Did they coddle it as much as Sara coddled Cody? Did they argue with their spouses about how the dog was treated? Would any of them have been stupid enough to hand the dog over to the *enemy*?

These were not the thoughts I wanted to be thinking at this should-be moment of triumph. This was enormous, what was happening right here, right now, and in some parallel universe, I was doing it right, and Rory O'Connor was on top of his game and on top of the world and handling it all *brilliantly*.

But meanwhile in this reality, I felt so wan and haggard, and I could feel Dougie's worried gaze on me, but I managed to put up a false front for a bit, smiling and shaking hands and nodding appreciatively, accepting the gushing compliments of all these people who had seen the videos of my audition and callback. I had gleefully ad-libbed my way through half the material and I'm sure they were expecting me to be the same virtuoso of improv now, the prince of charm, but it was almost all I could do to sit up straight and smile placidly. I wished to God I could remember what this meeting was about. No other actors were here, and I saw no signs of a script.

Almost immediately the energy in the room drained to zero, because the guest of honor—me—was a nearly mute black hole.

There was nothing I could do about it. Sometimes your brain just switches to EconoMode, and that was happening now, and the button was stuck. If my getting the gig were even one percent dependent on this moment, I would have lost it. I was the least interesting I have ever been since birth, including all periods of REM sleep. The thought of REM sleep was so seductive now.

I could see them all sneaking glances at one another. They were disappointed. No. It was worse than that. They thought I was on heroin or something!

I had to let them know I was not on heroin. I could not take that rap. Unfortunately, the worst way to convince somebody you're not on drugs is to say, "In case you're wondering, I'm not on drugs." On the few occasions in the past when I'd needed to convince somebody I was not on drugs, it was because I *was* on drugs. I'd no idea how to convince someone of my innocence when I was actually innocent.

"Do you want a drink of water, Rory?" Dougie was asking me for the third time.

" . . . Yes," I said this time.

"Are you all right, Rory?" asked one of the executive producers. There was an almost audible sigh of relief amongst the others, gratitude that somebody had just come on out and called it.

I opened my mouth to talk, then hesitated. I wished I were back in the arboretum, or better yet, the apartment in Sara's arms, or even in my old place or maybe even Dublin or, hell, if we're going for complete regression, possibly my mother's womb. I felt everyone lean cautiously closer to me, as if they were intrigued by my dental work but didn't want to be rude. I wasn't going to be able to fake my way through this.

"I'm sorry," I said, giving in with a heavy sigh. "There's been a family emergency and I'm a little distracted."

That was, unexpectedly, pure gold. Immediately the vibe of the room was bubbly again, this time with ten people eager to show the talent (me) that they cared more about my well-being than any of the others, and could do the most for me.

"What's going on?" asked everyone in several concerned variations. Dougie, having shunted off the water-carrier chore to someone else, was practically holding me up.

I could not imagine how to explain the situation succinctly without my looking very bad. "If you don't mind I'd rather not talk about it," I said.

That pushed me right to the top of the charts. Their attention was suddenly vacuum-sealed to my face. I almost felt suffocated by their assertive compassion.

"I'm sorry," I said. " There's been . . ." No. I couldn't say it. You can't use words like "kidnapping" or "taken hostage" and then refuse to go into detail, and the detail would make it all seem ludicrous. "There's an emerging situation and I don't think I can talk about it." *Not bad, Rory,* I thought, and then went out on a limb and added, not untruthfully albeit somewhat misleadingly, "We're waiting to hear from the police."

The police! *What?* Instant credibility. "What can we do?" asked everyone in several variations.

Suddenly they were putty in my hands. I hadn't wanted that, but it was better than the alternative. "Is anyone hurt? Is anyone dead?" And so on. Which was lovely of them—I don't mean to paint them to be anything but lovely, only I was too overwhelmed to rise to the task of actually deserving their solicitude. What was the best thing to do now? Stop talking and seem mysterious and possibly tragic? Tell them the truth, and appear to be irreparably odd? Take a different route altogether? Mostly I just wanted to get out of there as fast as possible.

"I have to get back to Boston," I said. "I probably should have asked to postpone, I'm terribly sorry—"

I was karmically drenched with a warm loving cascade of assurances that I had done nothing wrong, that I was a terrific team player for coming all the way out here despite the emergency, that they felt awful for having compelled me, and so on—I hardly noticed the specific words, I was aware only that I was getting out quickly, my humiliation undiscovered.

Don't feel too sorry for me, though. Part of me was also furious that I wasn't getting my pat-on-the-head moment, and I wasn't furious at myself, or (at that particular moment) even Jay. I was furious at Sara for not okaying a kennel, back on the day we moved, or better yet, just agreeing to take the dog on the plane. It really was all her fault, it was her fussiness, her coddling the dog, that had led to this bollocks. I was being robbed of my moment, here, and I wanted to be angry at someone else about that robbery. So all in all, I felt like a walking piece of poison, and I was just immensely grateful to get out of there before the poison spread.

"ARE YOU SURE you don't want to talk about it?" Dougie asked a few minutes later, in the most confidential voice possible, as he walked with me through the lobby downstairs. But I suspected whatever I said to him would be conveyed back to all the suits. I shook my head.

"I'll tell you as soon as I can talk about it," I said. "I'm really sorry about this, Dougie, I know you came all the way out here—"

He waved this off. "The agency pays for it. There's a production of *Pinafore* playing off-Broadway and I thought I could take you tonight, but obviously whatever's going on is more important."

I was genuinely touched by this moment of nostalgia. "You have no idea how much I'd love to have done that," I said. "Rain check?"

"I'm only here for two nights, but it's Gilbert and Sullivan— somebody will do it somewhere, someday, and we'll go then."

"Good," I said. "And thanks, mate. I know none of this would be happening without you."

"If I live to be a hundred, no gig is ever going to give me the satisfaction of this one," said Dougie, grinning. "Dude, you so deserve it, and I'm just thrilled to be the conduit."

God, how I wanted to be in a headspace where I could enjoy and believe that!

"Sorry to sound like a dope," I said, "but . . . it's bugging me that I can't even remember why we had to have this meeting. I know it was important, but—"

Dougie looked carefully amused by this. "Not really. You were coming through New York anyhow, and a bunch of the suits were in town anyhow, so we thought we'd just have a quick hello while everyone was in the same place. Not a big deal."

I blinked. I had just exhausted myself and taken time away from the dog hunt, just to show up in a room and do a terrible job of saying hello to a bunch of strangers. One more embarrassing karmic punch in the face. Back in the golden buzz of anticipation, pre-abduction, Dougie must have mentioned this as a casual opportunity and I'd been so high on my impending glory that

I'd seized on it as Significant. How utterly ridiculous of me. I was such a wanker. I'd just given Jay an extra ten hours of getaway time.

"I've got to get back to Boston," I said faintly, "right away."

"Call me later, when you can tell me what's going on," he said. I nodded, gave him a quick hug, and headed out the door.

As soon as I was outside, I called Sara, although I wasn't sure if her plane had landed yet. She answered. "Out of the meeting," I said simply. Didn't expect any kind of chummy response from her, it was all business, it would be all business, until I got the dog back. "How was your flight?"

"Not bad, considering," she said. "How was your meeting?"

"Quick," I said, hoping she'd be too distracted to ask for details.

"How soon can you get back to Boston?"

"I'm heading to the car right now. I'll be back by midafternoon."

"That's great. Someone left a voice mail while I was in flight, I'll call you back if it's relevant. Otherwise, when you get home, check in with the police," she said.

"I know," I said.

"Check in with all the shelters."

"I know."

"Okay," she said. "Talk later, then."

Click.

So *that* went well.

I GOT BACK to the car, and sat inside, feeling the city buzzing all around me, hard and unyielding as a jackhammer. All I wanted to do was collapse onto the steering wheel and take a nap. But I had to get back to Boston, back to Lena's, back to Command Central.

I reached for the ignition.

The phone rang again. Sara.

"Have you left the city yet?"

"We talked seven minutes ago and I hadn't even reached the car park," I said.

"We have a lead."

Thank God! "Really? Tell me! See, I knew something would come through."

"Yeah, it's an amazing bit of luck. I'm going to give you an address. Put it into the GPS and don't stop driving until you get there."

"I might need to pull over somewhere, I'm not safe to drive unless I take a nap."

"Get some coffee."

"If I've got to drive *another* four hours, this is too much tiredness for coffee."

"Please, Rory, this is *very* time-sensitive. I'll call you back as soon as I can, to explain."

"All right." I turned on the plug-in GPS. "Boston?"

"Gardner," Sara said. "North Carolina."

Chapter 18

North Carolina had definitely not been on my route. And it was a long distance away. I'd never get there without food, gas, and a toilet break. But I knew I better get out of the city first.

I couldn't remember Sara—or Jay—ever mentioning North Carolina . . . what the hell was in North Carolina? I listened as the soothing voice of the GPS lady told me how to head south out of the city, and waited for Sara to call back with an explanation. The GPS lady calmly told me the route she had personally selected for me would take nine hours. Ten with traffic. I could drive from Barcelona to Milan in that time—going through four countries and the southern Alps. I had already driven more than five hours today, some of it through rush-hour traffic.

The Lincoln Tunnel spilled the traffic out into the unspeakable ugliness of industrial New Jersey. Except for Newark Airport, featuring a nice tidy fleet of FedEx planes, it was mostly a sci-fi dystopian vista of cement, sprawl, and smoke-belching factories along a twelve-lane highway. The wires of the power grid hovered everywhere. Marsh grass peeked up from the Citgo storage-bin facilities but amidst all the concrete, it didn't look organic; it just looked like mismanagement.

After a few miles, nature started to gain some ground, but only as something nobody had gotten around to paving over yet. I stopped at a Traveler's Aid for the toilet, and to buy some horrible foodlike substances, fuel the car, and get back on the road.

After about half an hour, Sara called back, sounding anxious and excited.

"I have a cousin named Alex Craggs. He's actually my second cousin once removed, my mom had the kind of family that kept tabs on that sort of thing. He's an accountant."

"And I need to know this why?"

"We were great pals, we'd visit each other vacationing when we were growing up. I didn't see him for years, but when Jonathan and I first got together, we decided to take a road trip. Since Alex had moved to North Carolina and I wanted to catch up with him, we decided to make him our destination. Can you hear me?" she asked, sounding either irritated or concerned, I couldn't tell which over the white noise of the MINI going eighty-five.

"Alex Craggs. North Carolina. Cousin. Accountant."

"All right. So. He had gone native. He's even got a little southern accent now."

"Let's cut to the chase, he does the Ku Klux Klan's taxes, doesn't he?"

"It's nothing like that. He and Jonathan hit it off, which was really surprising. I would never have anticipated that."

"It's hard to imagine Jay befriending an accountant," I agreed.

She ignored this. "Anyhow, they got along so well, and Jonathan had started making good money and wanted a vacation home, so he decided to buy a little cabin in Gardner. We stayed there several times, and even took Cody once when she was a puppy. So Alex has met Cody."

"Okay," I said.

"When Jay and I split, Jay stopped going there. I thought he had sold the cabin, so it didn't occur to me to call Alex. But then Alex called this morning, that was the message on my voice mail, and he said, 'Sara, this is strange, I saw Jonathan in the Piggly Wiggly, but he was trying to avoid me. I was just wondering if you knew anything about his coming back here.'"

I felt relief flood through me, and gratitude for this beneficent all-seeing cousin who was going to save my arse. I had no idea what I'd do when I got there, but at least now I had a place to go—complete with in-house ally!

"That's fantastic," I said. "I'll drive straight there. What's a Piggly Wiggly?"

"Supermarket chain. Let me warn you, though, Rory, I can't say he was thrilled to learn about you."

"Why?"

"He didn't know you existed till an hour ago, so he gave me the third degree and I don't know if I sold him on the validity of our marriage."

"Accountants are so anal and proper. It's none of his business," I said.

"It is if we want him to help us."

"You're family! Isn't that enough?"

"Mmm . . ." she said carefully.

"Mmm? What does 'mmm' mean? Why 'mmm'?" Why

couldn't this just be simple? Why couldn't *something* about our circumstances be *simple*?

"Well . . . okay, for starters, *before* he was an accountant, he served in Iraq and Afghanistan, he was in the army, so he's got more of a band-of-brothers kind of loyalty than a conventional sense of family loyalty."

"What do you mean when you say that? You've never seen *Band of Brothers*," I said. "I bet you haven't even seen *Henry V,* which is where the phrase comes from."

"Oh, good, a history lesson," said Sara tersely. "That's one thing you and Alex will have in common. You get all yours from Shakespeare and he gets all of his from Civil War reenactors. I wish I could be there to hear the mash-up. And I did too see *Henry V,* you were the Welsh guy and you were a hoot, and I hadn't even *met* you yet."

"I am appeased."

"My point is, blood is not thicker than water to Alex. He's got a very specific . . . code."

"Like a tax code?" I asked.

"That's not even funny, and I've clearly done a bad job of explaining him."

"Actually, if you're explaining the weird men in your life, I'm much more interested in what you have to say about, eh, *Jonathan*? Because as much as I admit it's my fuckup, it's hard for me to believe I'm *in* this situation."

"I don't know what to tell you, Rory," she said, softening. "He believed he was entitled to have the perfect girlfriend and the perfect dog, and when the girlfriend wised up and escaped, he still felt entitled to the dog."

"But he gave her to you, right? I mean, she is *your dog*? You own her?"

"Of course," Sara said impatiently. "He put a bow on her and everything. But in his universe, he owned *me*—sort of, I don't mean he consciously thought of it that way—so by extension he also owned her. So when I left his universe with *my* dog, he saw that as someone stealing *his* dog, because he couldn't grasp the concept that I existed independently of him."

"I absolutely don't get that," I said.

"That's why it's not worth talking about. I think it's more important you understand what you're getting into with Alex."

The walls around the highway had disappeared, replaced by mostly open land—despite the cranes and bland office buildings and pylons, it had a more comfortable feeling than New England, as if when I breathed, my lungs could freely expand outward, not just up into my collarbone anymore. I had no idea where I was.

"All right," I said. "I'll bite. What am I getting into with Alex?"

"Well . . . he's not really the kind of guy who would approve of a green-card marriage. I mean if it was *just* a green-card marriage. I tried to make it clear to him that we have a real relationship, but he knows the actual getting-married part was just for the green card, so just don't be surprised or defensive if he spends some time sussing you out to make sure he can be certain of your intentions toward me."

"My *intentions*? You're joking," I said.

"I'm not," she said. "And you need his help, so please indulge him. I mean, just be yourself, but really *be* yourself. You're a wonderful man. Let him see that. Show him you've got integrity and you're serious about treating me well."

"Isn't it enough his own government already believes that?"

"He's an accountant. He knows how easily the government can be fooled."

"Funny girl."

"Anyhow, he's expecting you, but he hopes you get there soon because he's postponing his fishing trip for us."

"Smokes his own trout, does he?" I said archly.

"Yes," she said, not noticing the archness. "And herring or something, I forget what they catch down there. Also, just so you know, he's a biker."

"Cyclist, like?"

"No, Harley-Davidsons. He's pretty serious about it."

"Everyone's got their hobbies," I said. "I'll be sure to act impressed."

There was a hesitation, then: "Well, anyhow, he's waiting for you. I'll text you his number when we get off the phone, and just keep me in the loop. Call me as soon as you arrive. Sooner, if you need to."

"Okay," I said. "I think this nightmare will be over soon."

"I hope so," she said, and sounded so fragile for a moment that it melted all my defensive irritation.

I had to get there in one piece, which meant staying awake. Having despaired of finding a diner, let alone a real café, I stopped at a traveler's mini-mall for a Starbucks sandwich on the go with a large coffee, and set off for the slog ahead.

I was on the largely tree-lined New Jersey Turnpike for what felt like light-years. I could see housing estates through the trees. Things were more leafed out here than in Boston. In the arboretum. In the place where I'd met Jay. Jay. For fuck's sake.

How did this all happen? I had to sort this out, it was such a head-wrecker.

He had moved to the area less than a year before I hooked up with Sara—so almost right after she had taken Cody and left him. Was it a coincidence that he'd moved near her, that he'd taken to hanging out in a place where his ex-lover's new husband just *happened* to walk the dog?

No way to know that one, plus: not a good time to think about his being her ex-lover, so: skip to the next point.

The karmic sucker punch, the part that flummoxed me, was that I'd trusted him so completely. His whole abduction plan relied on the fact that I trusted him completely *but also* that I wouldn't want to tell Sara *why* I trusted him—that being that he took care of Cody after the chocolate cake incident. So either the chocolate cake incident was an amazingly convenient coincidence for him . . . or else *he had staged* the chocolate cake incident *in order to* win my trust that way.

Was that possible? He hadn't provided the cake . . . but he had suggested it.

No, Nick had asked for it.

But . . . Nick had asked for it because of the way Jay was talking about chocolate. And the cake was large because Jay had suggested a party.

So, all right then . . . Jay, having prompted Nick to ask for a huge chocolate cake, and being in charge of that cake, had deliberately placed it where Cody could reach it, at a moment when I was distracted.

Yes, that could have happened. He could have staged that scenario, knowing that he could immediately bring Cody to his house and fix the problem. The result being that I would trust him with Cody's well-being, but wouldn't want to mention the event to Sara. He had even made a comment about having recently lost his dog and that he hadn't gotten over it yet.

And come to think of it . . . if I was right about all this . . . he'd suggested the party the day—the hour—the *moment*—he'd realized Cody might be headed to Los Angeles.

Could that possibly be right, though? He could not have known that we'd need a place for Cody to stay for a few hours on that final day. We ourselves didn't know that until a week before. Maybe he'd had a number of plans in place, and we just stumbled along a labyrinthine path to one of them. Maybe if I'd never asked him about her staying with him, he had some *other* scheme, or schemes. If he was that determined to snatch her, then I didn't feel like as much of an eejit. He'd have gotten her somehow, even if he couldn't make me look stupid as part of the plan.

But if he could make his ex's new man look stupid, naturally he would. That was the other part of this that made my world wobble: he was Sara's ex. I could not shake off the creepy feeling this knowledge gave me. Sara had wanted *that*. Sara had been drawn to him, somebody so unlike me that I was—as Lena had even called me to my face—the anti-Jonathan.

How could Sara—*my Sara,* who seemed so perfectly designed by God for my companionship—be drawn to somebody so entirely different from me? She'd gotten something out of that relationship. Whatever it was, she couldn't be getting the same thing out of our relationship. So our relationship was lacking something, and therefore doomed. Unless I could figure out what he offered her that I didn't. I made a mental list.

He had more money than I did. That was all right, I was about to make it big in Hollywood. And even if that fell through, Sara seemed remarkably indifferent to material wealth. I mean, she'd married an unemployed actor, for starters.

He was better educated. Yes, but I could recite Shakespeare as well as Beckett, Joyce, and Synge, and transpose major keys on the fly. And I did know something about art and music and American history from my "guest lecturer" gig at the museum. His education led *to* his work; mine came *from* my work. Surely that was of equal value.

He was more exacting and controlling than I was. That couldn't be it; that was the very thing that drove her away—after bullying her into giving up painting. She liked my impulsive, free-spirited half-arsedness. It was part of my charm.

He was incredibly calm all the time, paternal and fatherly. Well, I was more fun.

He loved Cody more than I did.

Um. Yes. Obviously. No way around that one.

NEAR THE CITY of Baltimore, the urban spread began again. It was a little lusher, broader, and relaxed than up north, but still basically the same stuff. Home Depot. "Business Centers." Huge freight rigs. Pyramidal piles of what would eventually become cement. The Port of Baltimore. A tunnel that looked as if it had been tiled with snakeskin.

I emerged from the tunnel into the actual city—no, *above* it, really, the huge curving highway arcing, looming over water. I was part of the skyline, driving above America, detached from reality, with limited access to all below. This felt somehow symbolic but

I was too tired and frazzled to make out how. After Baltimore, I was returned to ground, where cement walls sprang up on either side of the freeway, to protect me from America, or more likely, the other way around. The sky was grey, inviting drowsiness even going eighty-five. *Drowsy*. What a lovely word. How seductive to just get lost in *drowsy*.

Thank God my phone startled me to alertness. It was Alto. We'd swapped numbers back in Boston while he was helping us hunt down Jay.

"Squire Alto!"

"Just checking in for news."

"Thanks, I appreciate it. We've actually got a lead, he's in North Carolina. I'm driving there now."

"Shit, that's a long way," said Alto, expressing my own sentiments. I explained the situation, asked him to tell Marie and the museum crowd, and gave him Danny's number to keep him in the loop, too. It lifted the despair the littlest bit to know that there were folk back home looking out for us and thinking of me as something other than a wanker.

Of course after the call, my mind wandered back to Jay. Had he bought his place just to be close to Sara? Had it been an if-then sort of thing: maybe he heard she'd moved to Jamaica Plain (how, though?), and figured, *if* she lives in JP, *then* she probably takes the dog to Peters Hill, the place all the dogs go off leash. *If* I buy a house overlooking Peters Hill, *then* I might see her with the dog.

And then—the one thing he could never have anticipated—the dog *but not Sara* starts making regular-as-clockwork appearances. Which is a coup for him, only it happened in a manner that must have insulted every fiber of his being.

First, Sara was willing to hand off the treasured creature to someone who didn't treasure the creature. This made Sara bad and further surely confirmed for Jay that he'd be the better owner, and therefore justified in nabbing Cody. Also, Sara had found romantic happiness so quickly after dumping him—with somebody who was inferior to Jay in every way that mattered to Jay. I was poor, undereducated, unreliable, and foolish. I was dependent on Sara to even have the right to be in America. And Sara wanted me more than him.

So your Mr. Jonathan was a deeply insulted man. I thought I'd be petty enough to find satisfaction in that, but instead it only made me anxious: the more deeply he felt insulted, the further he would go in seeking satisfaction. It only takes a couple of Shakespeare villains to know that about human nature.

Howard County. Montgomery County. Spring came at me in a rush as I hurtled southward. Everything along the road was now a lush, glorious, full-bodied green. After a stretch of raised and crossing highways, the road spilled toward and over water, ushering me into Virginia. I wished I knew my American geography better. How far exactly from Virginia to North Carolina?

Suddenly I missed Ireland something terrible. If this had happened back home, it would have been easy enough to deal with it. I knew people in every county, could set up a network to keep an eye out, and it's a small country, he couldn't hide forever. But nobody in Ireland would be fool enough to get so obsessed about a dog in the first place! That was part of my exasperation: this was such a ridiculously American problem we found ourselves with. In Ireland, we saved our fury for family feuds, or sports competitions, or complaining about the government without actually doing anything about it.

I had definitely reached the fatigue point, where everything looked exactly like everything else. Virginia is proof that you can have beautiful country roads and also plastic shite side by side. Given the choice, the American ethos will still go for plastic shite. But then I remembered all the ghost estates all over Ireland and realized that nobody has cornered the market on plastic shite, or abuse of the environment or resources. Shortsighted ugly greed is common to all cultures. Well, maybe not so much in the Scandinavian countries that despite being, like Ireland, too far north, underpopulated, and alcoholic, had still managed to create the highest standard of living in the world, at least according to Facebook polls that Marie liked to inform us about on Peters Hill.

God, I missed Marie. And little Nick. And Alto. And even the person I'd thought Jay was. In fact, I think I missed him most of all. No, most of all I missed Danny, but at this point even Lena would have been welcome company.

The road was slick but the sky ahead was clearing as I turned onto a smaller highway, just two lanes each direction. There was less urban sprawl now, and incredible lushness everywhere. It had rained here recently and the hardwood trees looked particularly lovely, with the trunks so dark from the wet. The sun was slanting heavily westward. Would I make it to Alex's by nightfall? I had been on the road since four A.M. Except for failing to get a hug from Sara at Logan, and making an utter eejit of myself in midtown Manhattan, I had done nothing today but drive. I hated that steering wheel and that big retro-style dashboard almost as much as I hated Jay.

I was getting very bleary-eyed again. So I can't vouch for this, but I believe the "Welcome to North Carolina" sign went on to say it was "the most military-friendly state." Hang on: North Carolina! What? Here I was in North Carolina! A mere ninety miles or so and finally I'd have arrived at Alex Cragg's. And then I'd get the dog back.

The main thing I noticed about North Carolina compared to all the states above it was the emergence of incredible pine trees—full and robust and enormous, and when I looked down the highway, everything was a mottle of different greens.

"Welcome to Durham, City of Medicine," said a sign as the GPS lady sent me onto a smaller highway. I skirted the city then found myself in suburbia. Except for those amazing looming pine trees, it could have been any suburb in any state or county in New England. How could I have driven so fucking far—farther than it would take to drive across Western Europe—and find myself in the same place I'd left?

Finally, in a suburban cul-de-sac right in front of a nondescript ranch-style house, the GPS lady uttered those six magic words that made me love her: "You have arrived at your destination."

Time to get out of the car at last. Time to meet Alex Craggs. Time to get the dog back.

Chapter 19

To review: I had just driven sixteen hours, stopping in Manhattan long enough to make a bad impression. I hadn't washed in days, or hardly slept, and had eaten very little on the road, none of it healthy. I had three and a half days' growth of beard on my face, I could not remember when I'd last combed my hair, and (a new detail) I had spilled my last cup of coffee, leaving New Zealand–shaped stains on my shirt. I was about to meet a man I didn't know—an accountant–slash–army vet, so probably very disciplined and tidy—and, in my state of dreck, I had to show him I was a respectable bloke. Ha.

I got out of the car and walked up the brick path past a red Ford pickup to the door. I saw no sign of a motorcycle. Maybe he'd moved on to a new hobby. When I rang the doorbell, a volley of high-pitched fierce barking erupted from the other side. Must be terriers? Jack Russells?

I heard a booming male voice calling off the dogs; then various doors opening and closing; the barking continued, muffled, and unhurried footsteps finally approached the door. Alex Craggs paused on the other side and took a moment before opening the door—maybe, like me, preparing his "greeting face."

The door finally opened.

Beaming down at me through the screen door was a muscly and fair-haired bloke, grinning with a jocular smile worthy of a toothpaste advert. He was big—not as tall as Jay, but brawnier. Extremely clean-cut, smooth face and neat short hair, jeans and a button-down shirt opened at the collar. More Accountant than Army Vet. I realized I had been clenching all sorts of muscles because now I felt them all start to relax. This would be grand. We'd have a quick chat and then be off to get the dog. I'd even let her sleep in the same room with me tonight.

"Hello, there, sir," said Alex Craggs, with a hint of some generic southern accent. He stared at me for a moment with glittering-bright green eyes. "You must be my new cousin-in-law. Want to come in?" He pushed opened the screen door. Those eyes—the one physical attribute he shared with Sara—did not leave off staring at me. I suppose he was noticing my strong resemblance to a homeless bum.

"Thanks," I said, and held out my hand as I entered. "I'm Rory. Sorry we're meeting under these strange circumstances."

He shook my hand with a firm grip. Then he grinned, then laughed, then cuffed me on the shoulder. I couldn't tell if it was a gesture of affection or aggression. "Yes, sir, they are strange circumstances, but I'll tell ya, they're not *that* strange," he said in a friendly, comforting voice, and then without a beat immediately went on to say, "Certainly not as strange as Sara going off and marrying an undocumented foreign gentleman without even *telling* anyone about it."

"That happened pretty fast," I said, flustered.

"*I'll* say." He laughed like a friendly but all-powerful sheriff in a comedy western. "My jaw just about dropped to the floor when she told me about you a few hours ago."

I decided not to say the feeling was mutual. His energy was so *big*, I felt almost pinned to the tiled wall of the foyer.

"I understand your marriage had something to do with . . . placating certain governmental agencies." His gaze was piercing and his voice loud, as if he wanted to be overheard by his neighbors. I was clueless how to interpret his tone—it could as easily have been approval for beating the bureaucracy as condemnation for trying to scam Uncle Sam. I should have acknowledged the statement and followed up immediately with a tribute to how madly in love with Sara I was. If I'd done that, the whole evening might have gone so differently. But I could not convince any of my speaking-aloud neurons to fire, which is quite the rarity with me, as you might have heard. I just stared at him, taking in his bigness.

"Well, make yourself at home," he said. He gestured vaguely to the open-plan innards of the house. "You look like you could use a drink."

"I'd love a glass of water, thanks."

"Yes, sir, glass of water coming right up. Have a seat." We crossed the carpeted living room to the kitchen area, and the barking began again behind a door down the hall. Alex ignored it. He gestured toward the kitchen table. Everything about this house was perfectly normal, like what you'd see on a television show depicting normal American suburban life. If a pretty wife and 2.54 healthy kids came around the corner at that moment, I would not have been surprised. His was a Neil Diamond sound track. Played very loud.

The barking dogs finally stopped barking, and after a final irritable scratch at the door, down the darkened hall, they were quiet. Cody never barked.

Alex set down a glass of water on the table. "Want some ice with that?" he asked, reaching for the freezer door of the humming white Frigidaire.

"No thanks," I said. I considered making the frequent European jab about how Americans are obsessed with ice, but thought it would be sounder of me to wait till we knew each other's humor first.

"You Europeans generally find the American obsession with ice a bit peculiar, don't you?" he said, giving me a knowing look. *What?* Okay, that was *weird*. "Have you been in the States long enough to still hold that opinion?"

This was the kind of thing Sara had warned me about. If I acknowledged how long I'd been in America, he'd want to know why I had only now gotten a green card, and then he'd grill me about having been undocumented all those years. I actually forgot about my performance visas for a moment, and felt a flush of anxiety, the way I used to feel in the early days, coming through Immigration at Logan Airport.

"I've been ice-obsessed since childhood," I said. "Had to swear off the stuff for health reasons."

Alex burst into a loud and hearty laugh, far louder and heartier than my quip deserved. "All right, then, sir," he said, still aggressively friendly. He pushed the glass of water in my direction. "You look like you've been through the wringer."

"It's been a rough couple of days," I said.

"Want to acquaint me with the circumstances under which our mutual friend Jonathan ended up in possession of the dog of contention?"

"Oh," I said, "I thought Sara already told you everything."

"Oh, yes, sir, she did," he said. "I'm just seeking verification, want to make sure I've got the whole story straight."

The smile was both entirely genuine and yet also a challenge. I could almost see how he and Jay would have hit it off, according to the principle of opposites attracting. It would have been a mashup of alpha maleness, though. I wasn't a contender in that ring. I relied on peppery impish charm. Peppery impish charm flies right under the alpha male radar.

"Well . . . I first met him in a park in Boston," I said. "I walked Cody every day and there was a group of regulars we got to know. One of them was Jay."

"You're saying that my cousin's ex, who had bought her that very dog and was heartbroken when she took the dog away with her, just *happened* to be one of these regulars?"

That detail had been niggling at me. "Yes," I said. "I don't think it's a coincidence. He had moved to the area recently, and now I wonder if he moved there because he somehow knew it was where Sara and the dog would be."

"Yes, sir, I think you're right about that," said Alex Craggs. He was still talking as if he wanted his neighbors to overhear, but maybe that was just his normal speaking voice. "I happen to know he was aware she had moved to Jamaica Plain because *I'm* the one who told him that, back before I understood how desperate she was to break all ties with him. I didn't realize what a schemer he was, because like a lot of schemers, he's *really* charismatic. I mean, despite myself, I still *like* the guy, even after what he did. But I'm feeling a little bit responsible for what's happened here."

I laughed, pained. "I promise you, you're not to blame. It's all on me."

"No, sir, I am a part of the bigger picture. Not saying that makes me guilty but it sure doesn't mean I'm innocent. Anyhow let's get back to the park."

"I don't really have much else to say," I said, not wanting to get into the chocolate cake incident.

"He somehow won your trust," Alex said meaningfully.

"Yes," I said, realizing I was going to have to get into the chocolate cake incident.

"How?"

I told him about the chocolate cake incident. Including my theory that Jay had orchestrated it.

Alex grimaced, agreeing. "That guy always knows how to get what he wants."

"Sure. So I really appreciate your helping me to get her back."

He grimaced again. "Well, hold on now," he said. "I didn't say I was going to do *that*."

What?

"What?" I said, more calmly than I was thinking it.

"I love Sara, but just because she's my cousin doesn't mean her interests here come first."

"Oh," I said, alarmed. In fairness, she had warned me about that.

"This is not about Sara. This is about Cody. Cody's well-being comes first. Obviously."

Right, so he really was Sara's kinsman, if he put the dog ahead of his own cousin. I nodded agreement but kept my mouth shut.

"And more than that," he continued, enjoying himself, "I need to get up to speed on *you,* my friend. I'm sure you can appreciate that this is all a *lot* to take on, and I need to be informed so I can act with integrity. So. Here's what is going to happen. Earlier today, right after I got off the phone from Sara, I called Jonathan—"

"You *what*?"

"—and told him what he stood accused of, to hear his side of the story."

"You what?" I repeated. "Why? Did you think Sara was *lying* to you?"

He held his hands out in a pacifying way. "No, sir, but a man's got a right to clear his name. Just wanted to hear what he had to say for himself. He told me why he felt entitled to the dog, and explained how he went about getting her. I told him that his modus operandi was clever, but it was also rotten and underhanded. Now that I've heard his side of things, and Sara's, too, I want to make sure I can endorse your being the dog's rescuer."

I was incredulous. "What does that mean?"

He was clearly entertaining himself. He was playing petty tyrant, and found the whole thing hilarious. "You might be a fine man, but at the moment I don't know that, I only have Sara's word and, nothing against Jonathan, or you, but Sara does not always make smart choices when it comes to her men. And let's be honest, now: she married you so you could get a green card, she came clean to me about that. After, what, a *week*? Ten days? So obviously, no offense, but I need to see for myself that you pass muster." A big, knowing, neighborly grin. "If not, I will send you packing, and I've already told Sara as much."

"I'm Sara's husband, that should be enough!" I said. "What needs to happen here is that we go get the dog—and right *now,* before Jay disappears with her again. Why did you tell him I'm here?" I tried to stay cool, but it was fucking aggravating to learn I'd pushed myself hard to get here in stealth only to have my arrival *heralded.* "He's probably left town already, we need to act *now.*"

"No, sir, we're not going anywhere tonight," said Alex pleasantly. "My turf, my rules. I need to suss you out first."

"I just drove fourteen hours to get here for Sara's sake. To fix a problem I freely admit is my fault. How much more do you really need to know about me?"

"As I said, this is about the dog," said Alex, firm but avuncular. "First I need to know if she'd be in good hands with you."

I was almost too tired to suppress the stream of invectives that wanted to come hurling out of my mouth. This was just pure and utter bollocks. "I'm taking her straight to Sara," I said with deliberate calmness.

"Well, we'll see about that," said Alex, cheerily. "No offense, but you haven't really demonstrated to me that you're worth a gnat's gonads yet."

"We've got to get her, now that he knows I'm here!" I said angrily, and stood up. "We've got to get her *now.* He'll disappear again!"

Alex stayed seated and comfortably, almost smugly, said, "Already got that covered. Jonathan gave me his word as a gentleman not to leave town, and to meet us tomorrow at noon at the Club-house to settle matters."

Oh, for fuck's sake. "And you *believed* him?"

"He assured me he understands the consequences of fucking me over and not honoring his word, and he knows what a good shot I am."

That last bit shocked me; I'd forgot he'd been a soldier. "This is *ridiculous*," I said to the ceiling. "Just tell me where he is. I'll go on my own."

"My prospect Plugger is over at Jonathan's cabin right now keeping watch on him, and Jonathan is fine with that."

"Your what?"

"My junior associate. Also I've got my brothers for dozens of miles in every direction on alert. He makes a run for it overnight, he is asking to get his ribs crushed. For starters."

"Your brothers?"

"My biker brothers," said Alex seriously, looking every inch the accountant. (Caveat: the very large accountant.) "So he's not going anywhere. Neither are we. Got it?" His toothpaste-advert smile was almost manic. He was cracking up over this scenario. It was all a joke to him, I was just his amusement for the evening, saving him from a boring night of watching the telly. "Might as well settle in."

I stubbornly stayed standing, but gave up arguing, since it was pointless. Suddenly the cacophony of frenzied yapping began again from behind a closed door down the hall. Alex stood, wandered over to the door, and opened it, his gaze cast downward. I looked as well, expecting scrappy, fiendish-looking little terriers. Instead, two bratwurst-shaped dogs came waddling with feverish speed out the door.

I had not been expecting dachshunds, I admit. They were so quirky and cute, it was hard to reconcile them with the bloke who'd just casually said he'd shoot Jay if he didn't keep his word. These two dachshunds, like most dachshunds, wore slightly concerned expressions. They trotted briskly past Alex as if they had no need of him now that he'd opened the door, and made a beeline for me.

I temporarily, with effort, pushed aside my irritation with Alex. To demonstrate I was a dog person—as that seemed to be part of what he was looking for—I leaned down and offered each of the dachshunds the back of one hand. Their damp noses probed me, and then, having determined that I was a human, they looked up at me, wagged their whiplike tails, and barked approvingly. Cody, of course, would not have barked; she'd have flipped over onto her back and given me a hopeful, submissive look. I felt my diaphragm tense suddenly. I actually *missed* her.

"They're cute," I said, hoping that was an appropriate term.

"Why, thank you," said Alex. He ambled to the kitchen sink and opened a cabinet above it. "All right, then," he said. "Let's the two of us get better acquainted." He took out a lidded mason jar, filled with a cloudy, light brown liquid. I could easily guess what *that* was. So. That's how you proved what kind of man you were: You got plastered. I was Irish, so I knew all about that.

"All right now," said Alex happily. He placed the jar on the table. "And let's get some munchies." He turned to the humming white refrigerator with decorative magnets stuck on, opened it, and took out an oval plate on which was preset a variety of sliced cheeses, all colored variations of what is called "American cheese." (That's because no other nation will claim responsibility for it.)

There were also other snack foods, mostly lots of chopped veggies, and hummus, and a serving of that American oxymoron "jumbo shrimp." After Sara's phone call, Alex must have gone out and shopped especially for my arrival. I felt oddly flattered, and very grateful that I'd soon have real food in my belly. Also: this gesture probably meant that he *wanted* to like me. So the game should be mine to lose.

"There we are," he said, setting the plate on the table. "I believe that should do us for a while." He rubbed his hands together and planted himself in the creaky captain's chair across from me.

Soon as he sat, the dachshunds lost interest in me and scrambled back across the floor to him. They looked up, a matched set, and he patted his broad thighs. In perfect synchronicity they leapt up onto his lap, landing one per thigh. They gazed at him as if for permission and then—again in hilarious unison—flopped onto their sides between his body and the wooden arms of the chair, so that they were cradled, and also cradling him. Granted Cody was bigger, but I couldn't imagine even Sara having her dog on her lap while she was eating.

I looked at the food, grateful for the veggies and hummus. I didn't know about that cheese, though. "Hey there, little cuties," said Alex. He scratched each under its chin, and they both raised their heads to offer their necks. "Let's get you guys taken care of first." He reached over to the most fluorescent of the cheeses, tore the top square in half, then in half again, and offered a quarter of it each to the dogs, who licked their lips like starving orphans, eyes upraised solemnly. "There you go, snuggle bunnies."

For a moment I thought he was speaking a foreign language, saying something that just happened to sound like "snuggle" and "bunnies," because "snuggle bunny" was not the kind of word I'd expect from a big boisterous man like Alex. But there he was, saying "snuggle bunnies." To some dogs. This man was definitely related to Sara. If he was a softy with his dogs, then he was a softy, period. Probably in Iraq he'd had a desk job or something; stupid of me not to realize that sooner.

"All right now," said Alex, looking up. He reached for the moonshine. "Here's a little homemade North Carolina truth serum to get the ball rolling. You're probably not used to drinking out of a jar."

"As a matter of fact," I said, eager to gab my way to charming him, "there was a pub in Dublin called the Diggers, beside a grave-yard, and all the gravediggers would come in on break, for a pint, but then take the glasses back out to the graveyard with them and leave them there, and the pub owner got tired of his glasses always going missing, so he started using jam jars so it wouldn't be so costly, and that became the vessel of choice and now we say we're 'goin' for a jar.'"

I'd said it all in one sentence because I had a feeling he would start talking over me if I didn't. But it made me sound nervous. Then I realized that, in fairness, I *was* a little nervous. The man was waving moonshine under my nose and expecting me to drink it so he could get to know my character—I, who was such an unre-liable character when I got lit. 'Course I was nervous. A bit.

He pulled his chin in, interested in my anecdote. Briefly. "Really? I like that story. We're going to share this jar. Made this batch myself."

"Wow," I said.

"Apple-pie flavored," he added. "With cinnamon."

"Doubly wow," I said. "But, sorry, I don't drink."

If I had said, "I don't breathe oxygen," or "I don't eat solid food," he'd have given me about the same look. This explained why Jay had been agreeable to the arrangement. Jay knew I didn't drink—hadn't I said so in his very home? That wasn't gospel, but still, he knew Alex would measure me in part by how much I could put away.

"An Irishman who refuses to drink with his host?" Alex said with a delighted yet incredulous laugh. "Ha! I gotta tell you, brother, that's just going to raise suspicions here, not relieve them any." He was mightily amused by all of this.

Fuck.

I took a deep breath of both resignation and determination. But as I began to reach out for the jar, Alex pushed it aside. He stared at me for a moment with Sara's intense green, dark-lashed, almond-shaped eyes. It was disorienting to see those eyes in such a different face. God, I missed her. I had to get her dog back safely. "Well, all right, then, sir," he said. "We'll *ease* our way in. You with me?"

I nodded once. I bet Jay had already hightailed it out of town and how the fuck was I ever going to find him now?

"This your first time in the South?" Alex asked.

"Yes."

"Well, welcome. A lot of us are descended from a lot of you. Natural affinity. Which is interesting 'cuz there's actually a lot in common historically, too."

"Is there?"

"Sure," he said. "What you guys call the Troubles over there in Northern Ireland? Just like the Civil War."

"Really?" I said in a neutral voice, pretty certain that was bollocks.

"Oh, yeah. There are those who will tell you that the Civil War was all about slavery, but that's just bullshit."

Oh, fuck.

Chapter 20

No, really," he assured me, when I said nothing. "It's bullshit. I use a simple pop quiz to prove it. I debate this in bars and I've changed a lot of minds."

I decided not to comment yet. This bloke was more complicated than I'd anticipated and I'd better play my cards close to the chest until I understood him better.

"This is how the quiz works. First, I'll throw 'em an easy one, like, what were the dates of the Civil War?'

"Sixteen forty-two to 1651," I said on reflex.

He blinked, then laughed. "Ha! *English* Civil War, right? But you're Irish."

"Born in England."

He nodded. "All right, you get a pass. The correct answer is 1861 to 1865. Which everyone knows, so that makes them feel cocky. And *then* I'll ask: 'True or false: prior to the Civil War, there were slaves in *both* the northern states *and* the southern states. Answer: true. Final question. The North cared *so much* about fighting a war to end slavery that in 1861, the North freed—multiple choice here—*all* of its slaves, *some* of its slaves, or *none* of its slaves."

At this moment, I noticed that the decorative magnets on the refrigerator depicted what looked like the Union Jack or the Saltire of Scotland. Confederate flags. It was the twenty-first century and the bloke had *Confederate flags* on his *refrigerator.*

"The right answer," said Alex, "is: none of the slaves. The North quote-unquote 'went to war over slavery' and felt so strongly about it that they freed *none* of their own slaves!"

"So I s'pose it was about something other than slavery," I said, pulling my gaze away from the magnets. I'd better play *very* close to the chest until I got a feel for him—Sara had not prepared me for a secessionist. "What was it about, then?"

"So glad you asked! On the side of the Confederacy, there are literary references, from soldiers of all ranks, infantrymen to generals, saying that they're going off to fight for independence, for freedom from a northern oppressor. You find very few references to 'I'm fighting to preserve slavery.' That just wasn't *there.* For them it was all about *freedom.* Freedom from *oppression.*"

Except for their slaves, for fuck's sake, I wanted to say. But this bloke was a little alarming now, and I didn't want to engage until I had a better sense of him. So all I said for now was, "But for the *northerners*, it must have been about slavery? I saw *Lincoln—*"

He smirked. "The great myth is that Lincoln was a guy with a mission, but in fact, he stated in his inaugural address, in 1861, that he had no intent of ending slavery! You can Google that, it's right there in the speech."

Well, good for him for evolving, then, I thought. *Good for him, for changing and growing and learning to operate for the greater good and all that.* But aloud, I just said, "Oh."

"See, it was a time when, really, you had two different societies, you had an agricultural South and a more industrial North." He settled his large hands, one to either side of the jar, to represent the North and South. He did it in a way that suggested we were going to be here for a while. "They had grown apart economically and culturally, but they just happened legally to be this group of united states. It was a pretty dysfunctional situation, so the southern states started to secede, and you know what? Nobody in the North gave a shit. They didn't care about maintaining the Union. In fact, they tried to institute a draft up north just to raise an army, and they had draft riots, because nobody wanted to fight. And *that* is how the Civil War became about slavery." He reached for a piece of cheese.

"Sorry?" I said.

"The government in the North needed people to go to war," he said, tearing the cheese in thirds and offering a piece to either dachshund. "To stop the secessionists. But they couldn't find any actual issue that everyone could get behind—except fighting slavery."

Was this some kind of logical-reasoning test? Is *that* how he was going to "suss me out"? "If everyone could get behind that one thing," I said, "doesn't that make it, by definition . . . the thing that they went to war for?"

"You're missing the point," said Alex earnestly. "Slavery was an *excuse,* it wasn't a *cause.* But the winners write the history books and that's why it became 'about' slavery." He used air quotes for "about," a strip of orange cheese flopping between his left thumb and forefinger.

"Ah," I said. So it wasn't a logical-reasoning test, it was what he actually *believed.*

Alex tore the remaining bit of cheese in half and again made an offering to the dachshunds. "And even then," he continued, taking a gulp of moonshine but not, thank God, pushing the jar toward me, "the North never had the passion the South had. Which is why the North got the shit kicked out it for the first three years of the war." He reached for one of the shrimp. Food. Good idea. I began to shovel hummus into my mouth with a celery stick. "Because in terms of the staffing," Alex continued, "when the United States Army split up, the South got all the good officers. They had almost no natural resources but they had a whole bunch of guys willing to fight for their rights, while the North had the resources, but nobody who actually wanted to fight a war."

"That's ironic," I said, "Given that, y'know, they won." What was the polite way to mention that down here, anyhow? Express condolences?

He made an exasperated sound. "The only reason the South didn't win the Civil War is because Lee's right-hand guy, Stonewall Jackson, was killed by friendly fire earlier on. If Stonewall Jackson hadn't been killed, the South would have won the war. See, Gettysburg was an accident. Shouldn't have happened." He was warming to his subject as the drink warmed him. I could not believe how abruptly and intensely he had hijacked the conversation from anything relevant. "The South had been kicking the North's butt. Lee felt they only needed one more victory on northern soil. Then the South would win the war—not as in taking over the North, but just that they'd be allowed to secede and finally throw off their oppressors." Bright green eyes stared intensely into mine. "You're Irish, so you can relate to that part, right?"

I couldn't pretend slavery didn't count for anything, which

meant I couldn't equate the Confederacy with Sinn Fein or 1916 as a way for us to get jolly and pally. I wanted the dog back, but not on those terms. Roddy Doyle had already pegged us as the blacks of Europe, and I wasn't in the humor to hear how we were somehow also the rednecks of Europe. But hard as it was not to say anything, I wasn't going to argue with somebody like this. We'd be at it for hours, and for no reason but to argue. I would let him talk himself out, then have him take me to Cody. "So the battle was an accident?" I asked quickly.

"Right," said Alex, apparently failing to notice I hadn't answered him. "Lee didn't have maps of the area, and got entangled in the battle accidentally and that kind of caused the destruction of his army. *But* the historical thought is that *had* Stonewall Jackson been there, *then* the battle wouldn't have happened as it did, and the South *would* have won the war."

I said nothing. I sensed we were nearing the end of this.

"Now, if that had happened," he continued, "in my humble opinion, it means that we would have had one country that was the northeastern states, another that was the southeastern states, and then a whole bunch of territories out in the West, that would have eventually formed their own country. We might have evolved like Europe, with smaller countries having wars every five years, for hundreds of years, until we came together and made a permanent peace treaty, just like in Europe."

That wasn't exactly how I remembered things from my history classes, but I wasn't going to argue, because that would lead to more shite talk and all I wanted was to get through this part and then get the dog back.

"So in the larger picture," he continued, "it's good that the

North did win the war—not because their way was better, just because the long-term, big-picture alternative would have made us more like Europe, and that would suck, don't you think?"

Not that I'm a big defender of the EU or anything, but maybe he had already forgotten I was Irish? Or maybe he thought Ireland didn't count as part of Europe? No matter, I continued to strategically keep my mouth shut.

"That said," he continued ruefully, "the period of Reconstruction was very painful for the South. So. As I said. Was the Civil War about slavery? No. But at the end of the day, the winners write the history books." He reached for the moonshine and took another large swig.

Then he gave me a meaningful look, and pushed it across the table toward me.

I stared at it. This would be like bungee jumping without the bungee cord. I drew a breath to prepare myself. *It's okay,* I thought, *it's for a very good cause.* I sipped a little bit—it went down smooth as apple cider, and oh, did I feel those wee alcohol molecules right off. Alex grinned at me.

I took a breath, brought the jar to my lips again, tipped my head back, and swallowed.

It burned like a flame all the way down into my gut. It was almost a religious experience.

"Wow," I coughed, coming up for air.

"Yes, sir," said Alex. He looked more pleased with me than he had since he'd started monologuing. "That's the real deal. Didn't know if you could handle it. Glad to see you can."

"Of course," I said.

"Because at first you said you didn't drink at all, so it's interesting to me that you crumbled under peer pressure and just downed it like that. I can't help but wonder what that says about your moral strength."

Taken aback, I felt my mouth drop open, and I deliberately closed it. "Seemed impolite to refuse a local custom," I said, scrambling, praying my smile did not look like I was sucking up to him.

He mulled over this a moment, and then nodded. "Fair enough. Especially given, no offense here, you seem to be the ingratiating type."

I felt myself redden. "Do I?" I said. If my mates could hear anyone ever say that about me! Rory O'Connor, ingratiating? Charming and persuasive, but *ingratiating*? Desperate times called for desperate measures, but still that was an insult. I couldn't believe I had to sit here and take all this bollocks all for the sake of a dog.

"I've been saying some things that don't go over well with most Yanks," Alex was continuing. "I've been saying them *deliberately*. You can argue with me if you want to, y'know."

Did he really think I'd fall for that? Alienate him when I needed his help? Anyhow, what's the point of arguing with somebody so married to his own opinion? Maybe if we had nothing else to do for the evening, but I wanted to get to Step Two: Dog Retrieval. "I'm not a Yank," I said, and gave him a friendly smile. "I have no argument."

He grimaced. "Well, that's disappointing, I have to tell you. You probably think I was just running my mouth off—"

"Oh, no," I said. He ignored me.

"But I told you that this evening was about sussing you out, and that's what I've been doing, and I hate to report it, sir, but I'm not finding much to suss. You're giving me nothing. You're opaque."

"Opaque."

"Yes, sir. I trust transparency a lot more. See, that's what I always liked about Jonathan. He thought my ideas were all wrong, but he liked me for stating them honestly. We'd have some truly awesome debates. We'd get drunk and shout at each other. Don't know that we ever changed each other's mind about anything, but we got the honest measure of each other, and I respect that in a man." He gave me a searching look, a challenging look, a you-are-such-a-loser-Rory look. "Can *you* respect that in a man?"

Oh, fuck me. I'd gotten it exactly backward. And I would never be able to simply outdrink him to make up for it. I was screwed. I felt like a character stuck in a Beckett play. *Try again. Fail again. Fail better.* Well, at least I was getting *that* right.

That moonshine, man. What a lovely buzz. It felt so fucking good, and I suspected now that I would not be feeling good again for a while. Possibly ever.

"Do you understand what I'm saying, Rory?" Alex said, perfectly friendly, like a coach explaining why he had to bench me.

"You're saying you find Jay to be a fine upstanding gentleman and I am full of shite."

"Well, sir, that's awfully harsh if by 'shite' you mean 'shit.' Jonathan's not exactly upstanding, but at least I know what he's made of. He's passionate; he genuinely believes Sara did him wrong and he's just getting his own back. Whether I agree or not isn't the point—the point is I know his position. I'm not saying you're a bad man, don't get me wrong. I'm just saying I don't know that you're a good man because frankly, sir, I'm not seeing any evidence that you're a man at all."

"I drank the moonshine," I said bitterly, almost under my breath.

"Even ladies drink moonshine," he said, light as a breeze. "Unless they declare themselves nondrinkers. In which case they don't drink anything. Which I respect, because they're sticking to their principles. You didn't do that here."

I was almost in tears from the pressure of keeping my cool while feeling the heat of the drink in me. "Are you saying I've flopped? Is that the bottom line? Are you telling me I've failed and you're not going to help me get the dog back?" This last sentence came out furious staccato, like a machine gun.

"I was never going to *help* you get the dog back," said Alex, as if this should somehow be comforting. "I was going to decide if you deserved a shot at helping *yourself* to get the dog back."

"And you're saying I don't," I said, still staccato because I was so close to losing the plot. "You're saying: fuck you, Rory, and to hell with Cousin Sara. Jay keeps the dog, end of story, because I like how he behaves when we get drunk together."

He gave me a surprised look. Remarkably, that might have been the first time I'd cursed in front of him. It helped!

"Well, I'm not passing *definitive* judgment yet," he said. "But I have my doubts."

I took a deep breath and released it as slowly as I could—which wasn't slowly at all—trying to calm myself. "I *have to* get the dog back," I said, trying to sound calm.

"Or else you lose your green card," Alex said, with a sympathetic nod. "I figure that's what this is really about, you have to get her dog back or you lose your work permit."

"It's not that simple!" I snapped, and then pursed my lips hard to keep them from trembling.

Alex shrugged comfortably. "Seems pretty simple to me. Sara would help out anyone, she's a bleeding-heart liberal to beat the band, but the one thing that would piss her off is losing her dog. It's real clear: you get her dog back to her or she goes to the feds and rescinds the green card and your ass gets deported. I get it. How well do you two even know each other, really?"

I stared at him, so enraged I didn't trust myself to speak without murdering him. "We're *married*," I said.

"For a green card," he reminded me, as if it were a private joke between us.

"We're *in love*," I said, feeling the tendons in my neck standing out about a foot.

He shrugged. "If you say so, brother. I can't vouch for that 'cuz you're giving me *nothing* here. I've given you about seventeen chances to show me you have some passion or personality, and from what I can tell, you don't!" He laughed in a no-harm-done sort of way. "You're probably a lovely guy back home, but I don't know you from shinola."

I could feel tears of rage and despair clinging to the roots of my eyelids. I was shaking—could actually see my own body shaking, as if I were something separate and apart from it. Impulsively, I grabbed the moonshine and took another mouthful. I wanted to fall into that fucking jar. "This is like lemonade compared to the *poitín* my uncles used to make back home," I said, which was childish, I admit, but felt good anyhow. I wanted to pay him back for all the insults.

"Good to know," said Alex. "I'd love to go to Ireland sometime and maybe I can look 'em up and drink with them. Or with you, since you're likely to find yourself back there. Perfectly happy to get to actually know you, sometime when you're up for showing me what you're made of."

"You've got me wrong," I said, and rubbed my hands over my face. How lovely it would be if I could just pull the skin off and then reattach it to be somebody else.

"Whatever you say," he said sympathetically.

I looked morosely around the room. I was half locked already and there was no reason not to just fall all the way—at least I could escape myself for a couple hours. Nothing to lose now. I'd failed to demonstrate character. How *fucking ironic* for an actor—failing to show *character*! The room was starting to spin a little, pleasantly, and the buzz of the refrigerator and overhead lights was muffled by a more internal buzz. In the corner, by the hallway leading to the back rooms, were two objects I somehow didn't notice before: a banjo, leaning against the wall. Beside it, a fiddle case, lying open, with a fiddle right inside it. The only thing that felt familiar in the universe right now.

"You play?" I asked.

"Banjo? Since high school," he said. "Part of why I wanted to move to North Carolina. Tommy Jarrell country, man."

"Can I . . ." I was too depressed to even feel I had the right to ask. "I play a little, do you mind—"

He gave me a skeptical look. I realized I had slurred that request into almost a single syllable. I was drunker than I realized— damn, that happened fast. I could tell what he was thinking: *Not only a cad, but can't even hold his liquor.*

Alex picked up each dog in turn, and with a kiss on each nose and a brief lisping apology, set them down beside his chair so he could raise his bulk to standing. He crossed to the banjo and grabbed it round its slender neck. The dogs, apparently used to a certain nocturnal banjo-and-moonshine routine, looked at each other in disappointment and then waddled side by side over to a little dog bed beside the door, climbed in, and lay down, pressing up against each other. In unison, they sighed.

Alex sat and reached for a peg to tune the banjo, gently plucking the first string, which made a plunky sound. "I'm in G," he said. "Or I will be in a moment. I play old time, not bluegrass so much. What's your pleasure?"

"Actually I meant the fiddle," I said, trying to make it more than one syllable, which made me sound so drunk I almost started laughing at my own patheticness.

"Fiddle's new for me," he said. "Still getting the hang of it."

"But. I. Play," I said, carefully. "The. Fiddle. May. I. Play?"

He looked at me a moment and then burst out into one of his alarmingly loud laughs. "Brother, you are *wasted*," he said. "You have the tolerance of a *squirrel*."

I took a breath, paused, and then willed myself to enunciate. "I'd like to play around with the fiddle."

He shrugged. "Suit yourself. Let me get it for you, I don't think you can stand up." He set the banjo on the table, got the fiddle from its case, and offered it to me, with the bow.

"What are we starting with?" he asked, grinning, watching my jerky, uncoordinated moves, amused at the prospect of what a disaster this would be.

"'Sailor's Hornpipe'?" (Everyone knows this tune. It's the most-played hornpipe in history. The moment you hear it, little cartoon sailors start dancing about in your head. Even if you aren't on moonshine.)

I tightened the bow, wishing I were sober, took my time rosining it and tuning to his middle G. A fiddle in my hands, the roughed-amber texture of the rosin and the pressure of the strings, these were all reassuring, but it was an unfamiliar fiddle and I wouldn't have a chance to make friends with it. My only choice here was to go for broke. Oh, boy.

"Let me just try a few scales," I said uncertainly. Starting at high C, I played a very wobbly scale down to middle C, as on-the-edge-of-wrong as a rank beginner. Alex winced, embarrassed for me as I teetered through it. "I suppose I'm pretty drunk," I said ruefully. He nodded, cringed. Looked appalled. At C, I hesitated, then played D again, a little sharp, then pushed up to E—

—and then *flew* into "Flight of the Bumblebee" at a nice clip (if you don't know it, that's the classical piece made up of chromatic scales played so fast it sounds, well, like a bumblebee. Obviously!). This was my favorite old busking trick. I'm no virtuoso, and I only knew about twenty measures, but I'd spent my otherwise misspent youth practicing them until I could almost literally play them in my sleep—and being a good Irish musician, I could *definitely* play them drunk. Not with any artistic finesse, Isaac Stern would be spinning in his grave. But it always did the trick. As it did now.

Alex gaped, astounded. I gave him a sweet smile and closed my eyes. After a dozen or so measures—about where Rimsky-Korsakov starts using all those fucking accidentals—Alex absolutely *hollered* with the laughter, which gave me an excuse to stop playing just as I was running out of notes anyhow. The dogs jumped up and checked in with each other again before looking up at him for directions.

"Sorry?" I said blearily, as if I were too drunk to understand him.

"All righty!" he said, applauding. I took a breath. Maybe this would be okay in the end. "Christ, man, you can do that on *moonshine*? I gotta keep you around a while."

"Alas." I shrugged the same cheerfully complacent shrug he'd been subjecting me to all evening. "I'm already booked."

He looked at me with the sudden possibility of maybe, just maybe, finding me respectable. "So Sara wasn't bullshitting me? You do this stuff for real?"

"Well, they gave me a television show," I said. My God, that quadrant of my life seemed impossibly distant at the moment.

He strummed his fingers across the banjo strings, looking very pleased. "All right, then. Let's see what happens when Redneck meets Paddy."

"Mick, if you please," I said.

"Awesome," he said. "I'll take it off you."

So I started in on "Sailor's Hornpipe," decorating it with trills and grace notes. Alex snorted. "That's sissy playing," he said. He joined in, immediately driving the tempo so hard that I stopped decorating it. "That's better," he approved. "See, here in America we play it for folks to *dance* to."

"Oh, well, now, in Ireland, we play it so it's *good*," I retorted. Again he hollered with approving laughter.

And that was what it took. Now we were mates.

Chapter 21

Two hours and several swigs of moonshine later, we were still playing.

"'Hop High Ladies'!" Alex suggested.

"Don't know it," I said.

He started to play a familiar melody.

"That's 'Miss McLeod's Reel,'" I said scornfully, in a tone I'd never have used earlier. "Learn the fucking name, you ignorant cracker."

He bellowed a dachshund-alarming laugh. "Brother!" he hollered, and faster we played.

He capo'd up to A for a while, for "Old Mother Flanagan," "Red-Haired Boy," and "Old Molly Hare" (which I wanted to play in F, but the bastard was too lazy to retune).

When we were bored with G, we moved to D. Started with "Fisher's Hornpipe," one of my favorites. "Boys of Blue Hill," "Rickett's Hornpipe," "St. Anne's Reel"—it was great crack. It was strange and different playing with an old-time banjo, there was a rough-and-ready, primitive quality to the music, but it was thrilling, with the driving beat to make you want to dance with abandon while you were playing. And, combined with moonshine consumption, it provided an excellent environment in which to breed insults, name-calling, and all kinds of slagging. And Alex was a fantastic musician. Under other circumstances, I'd have played with him until my fingers bled.

But these weren't other circumstances. It was late—so late it was early, and I'd been up twenty-two hours straight—and I was actually here not to have a bromance-jam with Sara's cousin, but to get her dog back as quick as possible. I had to get some decent sleep, which hadn't happened in a couple of days. Alex looked like he could have continued to play without pause for several hours, so I'd have to lull him. You can't lull much with old-time music.

"In honor of southern history," I said, when we paused for another slosh of moonshine, "how about I play you Thomas Jefferson's favorite tune."

He gave me a suspicious look. "What the hell would you know about that?" he asked. "You going to tell me it's 'Irish Spring' or something?" Then he bellowed with laughter.

"I met the celestial Sara Renault when she hired me as a guest lecturer to play at the Boston Museum of Fine Art. I'd go around with the tours and play music that was specific to each era that was represented. Phrygian scales for the Egyptian art, Fauré for this one particular John Singer Sargent. They've got a big Colonial collection, so I played all the tunes popular back then, especially what Jefferson liked because he was a fiddler himself, and as a southerner, clearly had the best taste."

He grinned. "Don't you suck up to me, brother, I'm actually from Chicago."

Without retorting, I began to play the Adagio of Corelli's Sonata no. 1 in D Major. Alex, poised for another foot-stomper, looked briefly taken aback, then tipped his head thoughtfully. "Well," he said, almost grudgingly. "That's beautiful."

"Sit back and enjoy it," I crooned. Really I was a crap violinist, so I was hardly doing it justice, but compared to what we'd been getting up to, it was as if a ballerina was dancing the encore for a hip-hop concert. Alex set down his banjo, sat back, closed his eyes, and, sure enough, was snoring before I'd finished the Adagio. The dachshunds waddled out of their bed to stare at him, then me, dumbfounded.

He snorted himself awake a moment later, shook his head, and looked around bleary-eyed. "All right. I believe it's time for bed," he declared. "I got the guest room made up for you all."

You all?

Seeing the look on my face, he gave me a sly, sleepy grin. "You haven't forgotten that you're here to show me you're a dog lover, right? Well, nobody knows a dog lover better than a dog. My two buddies are going to hang with you overnight. They'll give me a full report in the morning."

AND SO IT came to pass that about six hours later, I awoke with a hangover worse than I'd had the day of the green-card interview, if that was possible, and one small dog spooning up against my back . . . and the other lying across the length of my pillow, pressing his back into the top of my skull. So that when I finally managed to drag my scratchy-dry eyes open, I was looking directly at his skinny tail. When I moved slightly, the tail wagged, smacking the pillow in front of my nose.

"Good morning, tail," I muttered, sounding and feeling very crusty. My tongue was twice its normal size and dry as asbestos.

The door opened. I felt both dachshunds raise their heads and glance over. There was Alex, in the same clothes he'd worn last night, grinning as if he'd never slept, or would ever need to. "Morning, everyone!" he declared. Both dachshunds tensed, preparing to leap toward him on his order.

"I like the look of that," he said. "They approve of you. That's a thumbs-up. C'mon, puppies! Who wants breakfast?"

When they were gone, I pulled myself out of bed and groggily looked around. Sunlight was slanting viciously through some venetian blinds beside the bed, illuminating a nondescript guest room. My memory of getting in here last night (or rather, earlier this morning) was sketchy at best. I was still wearing my clothes from the day before, and moonshine must have spilled somewhere, because something stank of rotten apples.

My bag sat on the carpet across from the bed. I couldn't actually remember bringing it in here. Dying for a glass of water, head throbbing, I clumsily changed into fresh jeans and shirt, and wondered about a shower. Ran the back of my hand across my face— God, I needed a shave. Or to grow a real beard already.

Blearily, I followed the seductive smell of bacon wafting down the hall, and found Alex in a chef's apron, a blond Emeril Lagasse, frying up not only bacon, but eggs and potatoes as well. It all looked, and smelled, heavenly. Possibly even better than that first breakfast at Sara's place last August—because here, the bacon had promise, looked almost like rashers, big and thick. I was going to comment on it, but I was afraid Alex would tell me he'd butchered the hog himself, and that would make it too personal for me to eat it. So I kept my mouth shut except to say, in a froggy tone, "Good morning." If my salivary glands were working, I'd've been drooling.

"Morning to you!" he said cheerfully.

"Water?" I said.

"Ha! You look like you'd do better with some more moonshine. Works for me." He jutted his chin toward something on the counter. "You got a couple of messages."

I poured myself a glass of water, drank it all down, poured a second, and sipped at it. Who would be calling me at seven in the morning, especially since I'd told Alto I was on the case? I picked up the phone and looked at the voice-mail log. Sara's number. Five calls. All last night, when we'd been drinking and playing tunes. "Oh, fuck me," I said aloud. I had gotten sucked into the Alex Craggs vortex and hadn't even remembered to tell her I'd arrived.

"I got three myself," hummed Alex with perfect understanding. "Do yourself a favor and don't listen to them, she really works herself into a lather. Especially at about four A.M."

I closed my eyes and leaned my head against the glass door that led to the backyard. It was wonderfully cool. "Of course I have to listen to them," I said. "I have to call her back." I seemed to recall something about time zones, but I couldn't do the math. "Later. When we're both awake."

"She'll be awake as soon as you call her," Alex joked. When I didn't laugh along with him, he shrugged agreeably and said, "Suit yourself. Meanwhile, you got a dog to win back."

That brought some alertness. I could feel my pulse quicken, pressing against my dehydrated temples. "You going to help me?"

"I'm going to be impartial," he said. "But as an *independent consultant,* I might be in a position to advise you a bit. On the side. Have some breakfast first."

"Let me just listen to these messages," I said. Alex rolled his eyes. As he set an impressive table, I tapped in my password and sat, steeling myself for the onslaught.

First: "Hi, it's me, it's about seven your time. You should be there by now, maybe your phone died? I'm going to call Alex and see if you've arrived."

Second: "Rory, it's about eight your time. Alex isn't answering. Are you all right? Are you there? Is Cody there? What's going on? Call me please."

Third: "Rory, it's me, it's eleven o'clock, I can't believe you haven't called me. Are you dead? Is Cody with you? What's going on? Call me!"

Fourth: "IT'S ONE IN THE MORNING, ARE YOU ASS-HOLES DRUNK? HOW CAN YOU NOT HAVE CALLED ME? I'M WORRIED SICK AND I DON'T KNOW WHAT'S GOING ON! WOULD YOU PLEASE CALL ME WHEN YOU GET THIS?"

I had never heard Sara speak in all-caps before. I felt horrible. And now it was four A.M. where she was, so I couldn't call her. My fuckup-ability seemed to be increasing daily.

And . . . there was one more message.

In this final one, her voice was cracking but her tone was horribly calm. "Rory," she began. "I just called Jonathan, because he was the only one who would answer his phone. His theory is that you are probably drunk out of your mind right now, which further confirms for him what an unfit dog owner you would make. He tells me you two are duking it out for Cody in a few hours. Whatever that means. Please call. Immediately."

The shrieking had been easier to take.

"Well now," said Alex heartily. "Let's eat."

I put the phone on the table and bent my head over it. Fingertips pressed into eyeballs, I said, "This may be the worst I've felt since puberty."

"We'll call her back and tell her everything's going to be fine," said Alex jovially.

I slid one hand away from my face and stared up at him bleakly. "Is it?"

"Hell, yeah!" said Alex. He put down the plate of bacon and picked up my phone. "She's on speed dial, right?"

"It's four in the morning there," I said, reaching up to take the phone. He casually turned back toward the kitchen counter, moving it out of reach. He examined it a moment, figured it out, and called Sara. "Alex, mate," I protested, "she's—"

The other end picked up and there was instant frenzy and upset on the other end. Alex let it continue for about ten seconds before interrupting with, "Sara, ma'am, it's Alex here, not Rory, Rory is far too considerate to call you at four A.M., but I figured you're still on East Coast time and you seemed to want to hear from one of us. How's L.A.?"

More upset on the other end.

"Now calm down, Sara, he's fine, the dog is fine, everything's going to be fine."

She obviously didn't believe him, but in fairness, if our roles were reversed, I'd probably believe him even less.

"No, ma'am," he said, glancing briefly at me and giving me a thumbs-up sign, "I don't think your talking to Rory is the best idea right now, because if you go on like this, you're going to make his balls shrivel right up inside his body and that won't be good for anyone. I just wanted to check in with you because you clearly wanted that, but now you should just go back to sleep and one of us will call you with news as soon as this is sorted out. I absolutely promise you, it's going to be fine."

Pause. Her voice again. I couldn't tell if she believed him now or not. I laid my fevered forehead on the table.

"I'm letting Cody decide," he said into the phone. "I got it all figured out. Hey, why didn't you tell me this guy plays the fiddle? He's not half bad. Go back to sleep." He hung up.

"I need a shower," I said into the table.

"No, you don't," said Alex. "That's the last thing you need. Don't you know anything about dogs? She's going to go with whoever's smellier."

I sat up again. "Then I should slather myself in bacon grease," I said.

He gestured to the plate. "Why do you think I made so much?"

I blinked. "Seriously? That's how I win? With bacon grease?"

Alex laughed. "You don't *win* that way. Jonathan's going to think of doing the same thing. You cancel each other out with the bacon grease. Which means it comes down to something else."

I could not think what. I could not have named the primary colors the way I was feeling.

"There's two things that rule a dog's life," Alex said. I really wanted to hear what he had to say but I couldn't sit through an Alex monologue just now. He sat across from me and pushed a plate of scrambled eggs and potatoes my way. "Eat," he said. "You'll feel better."

"Two things," I echoed him. I reached for my fork. "Tell me, please."

"Smell, as we've established. Bacon grease aside, your smell means more to Cody than his smell does, and brother"—he laughed—"you've got a lot of smell this morning." Serious again. "The second thing is the pack. She will go with the leader of the pack."

"Jay's got that one tied up, he has that calm alpha-male energy. And I don't. I have will-o'-the-wisp energy. And I can't change that. So I'm fucked."

"I wasn't talking alpha male," said Alex. "These potatoes came out *great*. No, my friend, when I say pack, I mean *pack*. Who is Cody's pack? You and Sara."

"That might work if Sara were here," I said. "On my own, I hardly rate as Cody's *pack*."

"Sara is the leader of Cody's pack."

"Sara's not *here*," I repeated, frustrated.

"Cody doesn't know that," Alex said, and winked at me.

Chapter 22

We'd be meeting Jay and Cody at the motorcycle clubhouse at noon, and "settling things." According to Alex, this decision (declared by Alex and imposed upon Jay by Alex and his "brothers") had been a rude surprise for Jay: when Alex first confronted him the day before, Jay had assumed Alex would "see things his way."

"What *is* his way?" I asked as I put the breakfast plates into his dishwasher.

"Oh, the usual," said Alex, which made me wonder what kind of friends he hung out with. "Faithless woman ruined my life, she should at least let me keep my dog."

"But he spent about a year not even *trying* to get the dog back, why did it suddenly become so important to him?"

Alex grinned. "It was always important to him, but he finally acted because *you* showed up, brother."

What an eejit I was, I should have realized: "It's not the dog he wants back. It's *Sara*."

Alex shook his head. "Nah. Or if he does, it's just to punish her for dumping him. He genuinely wants the dog back." He nudged me out of the way, to rearrange some things in the dishwasher. Accountants are fussy that way. "See, he's got this vision of the life he feels he was *entitled* to. Sara ruined the vision by walking out on him, but the one part he feels he can resuscitate is the part where his faithful dog is curled up at his feet every night. He'll never get any of the rest of it back, but he can still have *that*." Satisfied, he smacked the dishwasher door closed.

"Why doesn't he just get another dog?"

"If Cody had died, or run off, he'd do that," Alex said. "But Cody was *stolen*." He clapped his hand on the counter; the dachshunds jumped. "In his eyes, I mean. And when something vital is stolen, what does a man do?" Now he clapped me on the shoulder. "He *gets it back*. You're just the poor chump who showed up and gave him a way to do it. In a weird way he's sort of grateful to you."

I groaned. Alex laughed.

"We have a couple hours. Go back to bed and take a nap."

That was the best suggestion anyone had ever made to me in the history of suggestions (not including Sara's suggestion we get married, but then again that wasn't a suggestion, it was an instruction).

I left a message for Dougie telling him I hadn't fallen into the East River after leaving him, and promising to be in touch for real as soon as possible. I called Sara, apologized, and briefly updated her. Then I slept a deep and blissfully dreamless sleep—without any dogs—and awoke a couple of hours later alone in the guest room. I took a moment to collect myself, then stripped the bed because I try to be a considerate guest even when my host has practically poisoned me with alcohol. I came back out into the living room.

Where I met Alex Craggs, Badass Biker Dude.

From the waist down not much had changed, although I didn't remember the heavy biker boots from last night. His collared shirt had been ditched for a red T-shirt, a black leather vest, wrap-around shades, and a red bandanna tied over his close-cropped hair. The vest had a circular patch on the front; he was turning away from me as I emerged, so I got the full rotational view. The back had the same patch, much larger, and emblazoned around it, the words SOUTHERN RIDERS MC. The patch seemed to show two flags crossed into an *X,* but don't quote me—I was too distracted by LANCER (as he was named on his vest) standing in Alex's living room.

Here's an important detail: it was not at all ridiculous. Despite his beaming grin, he was, frankly, a little scary. And he seemed fine with that. His sound track was *not* Neil Diamond. It was Johnny Rebel.

"Wow," I said, respectfully.

"Exactly," he said. "Let's go."

We went outside and he took his bike out of the garage—it was a great and glorious thing, and if I knew a damn thing about such machines, I could rattle off all kinds of impressive stats, but the information Alex gave me went in one ear, through my still-hungover brain, and out the other ear. As vehicles go, it looked like a large robotic insect that could probably set half the neighborhood on fire.

With him in the vanguard and me following in the puny MINI, we headed off about three miles down the road, to the motorcycle club's clubhouse. Alex's home away from home. (Sound track: Lynyrd Skynyrd.) A neat, white cinder-block building baking in the sun, set back from the road next to a grass-and-dirt parking lot. It was almost perfectly nondescript except for two things.

First: the pair of large flags hanging limp in the hot still air on either side of the door. One was the traditional American flag. The other was the flag of the Confederacy. It still reminded me of a Union Jack, and so despite Alex's suggestions the night before equating the southern and Irish struggles for freedom from oppression, my reaction to the flag was kneejerk rejection. Roddy Doyle was right. We were the blacks of Europe, not the rednecks.

The second feature of the place that kept it from being nondescript were the forty-odd parked motorcycles surrounding it, and forty-odd bikers milling around them. Many of the bikes were marked with the decal of the club, all gleaming bright in the sun and reviving my hangover headache. Most of the bikers—unlike Alex—looked the traditional role of Biker Guy, with ponytails and at least a little facial hair (meaning about as much as me, that morning). They all wore varieties of his regalia: the vest, at least, and usually the red T below it. Jeans, boots, sometimes bandannas. While generally strapping blokes, they were all sizes and shapes, but pretty much only one color and definitely only one gender (and surely only one acknowledged sexual orientation). The place was whiter than a Dublin pub in the 1970s.

Alex rode his bike into the lot and parked it with the rest of the metallic herd. I parked across the country lane from the clubhouse . . . right behind the white Lexus SUV with Massachusetts plates. I punched the passenger seat a couple of times to let off some steam, but that made my head hurt, so I stopped. Took a deep breath. I promised myself not to jump the prick.

Alex summoned me across the road. I got out of the MINI,

sweating bullets. I was half the weight of the average biker, driving a car that had less power than most of their bikes. I left the window down in case the testosterone levels catapulted me back across the road and I needed to dive for shelter. Crossed the lane . . . and there, between a row of bikes and the entrance to the clubhouse, was Cody.

My heart raced, seeing her. "Hey, Cody! Cody girl!" I shouted, my voice cracking in my throat. She turned and saw me. Two things happened to her body at once: first, she began to joyfully rush toward me; second, she began to wag her tail so hard that the sideways action halfway canceled out the forward action, and so she came galumphing toward me with an odd camel-like gait, sweeping the ground behind her with her tail. I ran to her, collapsed to my knees on the packed dirt, threw my arms around her. I'd never squeezed that dog so hard.

She raised her chin, her tongue darting briefly in and out of her mouth with her Little Match Girl kisses, as if sipping some unseen Essence of Rory. I rubbed her ears and her muzzle and her chest and wanted to just pick her up and run away. "Hey, Cody," I said. "Cody! So sorry about all this, girl. Let's go." I stood up. In response to the word and gesture together, she scrambled up to her feet, her attention trained devotedly on my face to see what we were doing next. It's dazzling, what that devoted stare can do when you have spent a few days thinking you'll never see it again. I'd have offered her my liver for dessert if she wanted it, I was that relieved that she was near me. She had never looked so happy to see me, but that was probably just my imagination. I'm sure that pox had been spoiling her rotten.

After our initial moment of joyful reunion, she looked around for Sara. She saw the MINI. Heedless of the lane, she galloped toward it, tail wagging wildly, panting expectantly.

"Cody, wait!" I called in a panic. I heard footsteps start running toward the car from behind me.

Eagerly she jumped up, forelegs grappling at the open window, like a little kid grasping for a treat from the ice-cream man. I ran across the street and opened the door. She scrambled in excitedly, looked around as if expecting Sara was maybe hidden in there, clambered into the back and sniffed at her bed, and then curled up and lay down on it, looking very happy. Seeing her in a familiar place, seeing her where she should have been all along, I released a little cry of relief. Then I took a deep breath to keep from tearing up in front of all the manly men.

I turned back toward the clubhouse. Alex was trotting toward me. Behind him was Jay. It was the first time I'd seen him in person since he'd taken her. He looked ridiculous here in his long black coat, surrounded by all the bikers—and yet somehow the ruined-baron dignity was still intact. Fucker. "Well, there you go," I said, calling out to him across the row of bikes. "Nice try, wanker, we'll just be going now. Thanks for your hospitality, Alex." I turned back to the car to get inside, but Alex had reached me. He casually grabbed me around the shoulders and pivoted me away from the vehicle, as if I were a Bunraku puppet and he was the puppeteer.

"That's not how it works, brother," he said, cheerfully admonishing. "We haven't started yet. We're just balancing the scale here, getting her used to both of you again. You need to start on equal footing so that her choice is not determined by excitement or distraction."

I shrugged him off me. "Why should we start on equal footing? We're not *on* equal footing. We shouldn't be on *any* footing. We shouldn't *be* here. I should be halfway to L.A. with Cody in my car."

"It's actually your *wife's* car," called out Jay. "And, oh yes, your *wife's* dog."

I clenched my fists and jaws and neck and shoulders and it was a miracle I kept myself from sprinting across the road and decking him. "I'll be dug out of you, ya pox bottle!" I threatened. Alex stuck out a large, cautionary arm across my chest to keep me contained. "Someday," I informed Jay. "Just you wait, pal. You are going to scream for mercy while I rip out your fingernails. Then I'll push you off a fucking cliff."

"Your green card's still conditional," Jay said calmly. "Be a good boy."

I had to turn in circles, fists clenched so tight I almost sprained some hand muscles. My entire upper body shook with the rage. I heard Alex say (but he sounded amused), "Jonathan, buddy, don't be an asshole, okay?" He gave me a moment to go through my convulsions, then firmly propelled me back across the road, and called Cody out of the car because I refused to. She came trotting over beside him, looking delighted that two of her favorite people—Rory! Jonathan!—were in the same place! And both smelled of bacon! That dog was having a really great day.

Alex ordered her to sit, and obediently she did so, between Jay and me, in a patch of dirt outside the clubhouse, looking back and forth between us, very happy. Being close to Jay without leveling him took all my willpower.

The sun was bright and the day was beautiful, nature so big and magnificent, and all of us so small and dull in comparison that it was hard to believe we piddling mortals were doing any-thing of consequence. It was just a little disagreement about a dog. No biggie. I'd heard Sara's version, I'd heard Alex's, but now I needed to hear it from ground zero: "Why did you do this?" I demanded.

"Do what, get my dog back?" Jay answered. "An opportunity presented itself. I took it."

"She's not your dog," I insisted.

He gave me a mildly contemptuous look. "Of course she is. Sara forfeited her right to ownership."

"How?"

He gave me a lofty smile. *"The funeral baked meats did coldly furnish forth—"*

"Oh, for fuck's sake, don't quote Shakespeare to an actor," I groaned. "That's *tacky*. Anyhow Hamlet was—"

"Save it for the after-party, guys," Alex said. "We're not here to *chat*. We're here for Cody. So. You may both touch her." We both immediately reached out to put a hand on top of Cody's head. I got there first, and gave Jay a childish, angry look of triumph. He peaceably moved his hand to her muzzle and began to rub along her nose. Cody, blissed out by two of her people patting her at once, flopped into tarty-dog pose.

So we competed to put a hand on her belly first. Again, I won. Jay, looking unperturbed, began to gently rub her face again. I studied his expression. He really loved this dog. Arsehole.

But he really loved her. Maybe not as much as Sara loved her, but more, in truth, than I did. It wasn't as if she'd suffer, spending her life with him instead of with Sara. She'd be grand no matter what happened, as much as I didn't want to admit it and Sara would never believe it. There was no bad outcome for Cody here. Only for me.

"Here's how it works," said Alex, like a presenter on a game show. "You will both rise on my order and walk into the club-house. Jonathan, you'll move to the right of the door; Rory, you'll go to the left. Turn your faces to the wall so the dog cannot read your expressions. I'll bring her in. Neither of you is to call or make any kind of visual or audio sign at all. *At all.* If you try to pull a fast one, the other guy wins immediate possession. We see where she decides to go. Might take her a while. She might get distracted. But we just wait. Got it?"

"That's a thick-stupid way to make a decision," I protested.

"Nice way to talk to someone who made you such an awesome breakfast," said Alex with a grin. "Once she's made her decision, we will all abide by it."

"What does that mean?" I demanded. "If she happens to wander over to Jay, I just go on to Los Angeles and tell Sara to forget about her?"

"As soon as this is over," said Alex, ignoring my question, "Cody and her guy will get in his car and drive away. The other guy will remain here with me and my brothers for four hours. Four hours, got it? At that point, he's free to go, if he doesn't want to party with us any longer, and I take no responsibility for what happens after that as long as you don't fight over her on our turf. This has been entertaining, but my brothers and I don't want a sequel." He whistled suddenly, high and sharp and piercing. Cody leapt to her feet in alarm, showing the whites of her eyes. What happened next was like something out of a movie.

The forty bikers left off whatever they were doing in the parking lot (or in a few cases, within the building), and all began to walk toward us with a wondrously quiet dangerousness. They moved close enough to describe a half circle that began at one exterior corner of the clubhouse, arced out around us, and then cemented itself at the far corner. They looked like a hirsute version of the Rockettes. Most of them did not acknowledge us directly, although a few nodded and several grinned at Cody. Cody stared at them in fascination, wagging her tail slowly. She moved tentatively around the enclosed space. Then, as if swooning from the attention of so many alpha males, she fell back down into her submissive tarty-dog pose, craning her neck a bit to the side to try to see if they had noticed.

When the men had completely settled into place, creating the impression of an impromptu bare-knuckle boxing ring, Alex gestured to them and spoke to the two of us. "Just so you see, gentlemen, I am not fucking around here," he said, with a congenial smile. "Got it?"

Jay nodded calmly. I frowned and ducked my head once in acknowledgment.

"So we're all in agreement this is how it works, gentlemen? Your hands on it, please."

Jay first, we both shook hands with Alex himself. Then Jay languidly extended his hand to me. I grasped it and shook it, avoiding his gaze and clenching my jaws together with all the pressure I wanted to use to break the bones in his fingers. I nearly cracked my molars from the force of it.

What the hell was going to happen after Jay drove away with Cody, and Sara's cousin kept me captive for half a day? How was this going to end in any way besides complete disaster?

"Excellent!" said Alex happily. "And if it helps I want you to know that whoever stays here gets the better deal, in my opinion. We have several kegs and other drinkables waiting inside, Rooster is ready to DJ, and the strippers will be here in an hour."

"I'm sure Rory will enjoy that," said Jay. He gave me an infuriatingly confiding smile. "I won't tell Sara about that last part." I could have vomited with the rage. Maybe I should attack him and just let all forty bikers have a go at me—I would be the avenging Irish angel, liberating them all from their kidneys. Yeah, right.

"So," Alex said, clapping his hands together. "We might be standing around for a while. Does either of you gentlemen need anything before we start? A drink of water? A piss? A cigarette? Speak now if you want anything."

Despite the warm day, I was having hangover-induced chills, which would surely get worse inside, out of the sun. "I want to grab my sweatshirt," I said. Alex nodded and I jogged over to the car, the Arc of Bikers parting for me. Inside the car, I reached in for the sweatshirt. I put it on, and zipped it up as I reemerged. There was a poignant comfort in feeling the fabric against my skin, because Sara had practically been living in this sweatshirt for a day and a half before she got on the plane. In my imagination, her scent, some ineffable Sara-ness, still lingered on it.

I stumbled back across the road—lost my footing, giddy with the sudden relief as I reentered the ring of bikers. I couldn't take credit for doing it deliberately, but I'd just saved my own arse. Nothing in all Dixie screamed "Sara Renault" the way that sweatshirt did. I wasn't going to get Cody back. Only Sara, the leader of the pack, could do that. And I was now wearing her.

I crouched down beside Cody, opposite Jay. Cody's nose immediately started working subtly but madly. She looked around as if trying to trace the path of a passing butterfly.

"What have you got in that sweatshirt?" asked Jay.

"Nothing," I said. I reached for the zipper. "You want to take a look?"

"*I'll* examine it," said Alex. I shrugged out of it and gave it to him. There was a guitar pick in the right-hand pocket, nothing more, except a hundred thousand scent molecules that only Cody and I knew about.

"It's clean," said Alex, and began to hand it back to me.

"Wait a minute," Jay said sharply, and grabbed it from Alex's hands with a jerkiness unlike his usual legato movements. He buried his face in it, breathing in deeply. For a long moment, he did not move, even to breathe out.

When he pulled the sweatshirt away from his face, he looked ashen. He gave me a weary, accusatory look. It was the first time he had ever seemed at all vulnerable.

"This smells like Sara," he said very quietly.

It was an awkward moment. I really wanted to say, *That's right, you wanker!* but in fairness, it's an awful thing to be up close to a bloke when he's having a moment like that. He probably didn't even realize that he remembered Sara's scent—until he did. It was like watching someone's skin get peeled off.

"And *you* smell like *bacon*," said Alex, trying to make light of it.

"Do you concede?" I asked quickly. "You know if you can smell it, the dog can, too."

"Her name is *Cody*," said Jay, in a low purr of disgusted anger.

"I win," I said quietly. "What do you say we just call this farce off?"

Jay shook his head with the sad dignity I remembered from the arboretum. "I'm not *conceding*. We play it through," he said.

It all happened pretty quickly after that.

We went into the clubhouse, a place I don't imagine I would've ever found myself invited into under less extraordinary circumstances. Inside was a whitewashed cinder-block room with a pool table ("regulation size," Alex pointed out) down toward one end, a bar with a refrigerator and all the promised booze along one wall, and a bank of chairs, sofas, and even an old church pew along the other for seating. The walls were covered with frame photo collages of motorcycle rallies, or snapshots of the club members and their birds at barbecues or picnics or parties. One photo montage was large enough to see one of the women clearly—a cheerful, pretty blonde, her arm around a bloke with a club patch that said his name was Elephant. She also wore a patch—PROPERTY OF ELEPHANT. Hanging from the rafters was a wide assortment of brassieres. Alex saw me staring at them.

"Donated by some generous ladies." He grinned.

In the corner hung a large Confederate flag emblazoned with the words *I Ain't Coming Down*. There was a stink of old beer and old sweat accented with the stench of old tobacco, but to be fair, the place was actually neat and clean.

The near half of the room was largely open. I stood to the left, and Jay, looking even more depressed than Leonard Cohen, stood to the right. We both turned our faces to the walls.

Cody was mildly interested in all the unfamiliar scents in the room, taking inventory, and meandered both toward and away from each of us to make sure she wasn't missing any morsels. But most of all, she wanted Sara, and her nose told her exactly where the Sara-est place was. She wandered over to me and sat before me, staring up at me with her big brown eyes, her tail slowly, hopefully, sweeping the floor. I did not dare to move, even to slide my eyes in her direction, lest Jay claim I was breaking the rules. After a moment, wanting my attention, she moved toward me, leaned heavily against my leg and stared up at my face adoringly, her cheek pressing against my knee. It was fucking adorable but I didn't dare acknowledge her.

"I'm calling it," said Alex. "She goes with Rory."

Part Three

Chapter 23

When Alex spoke, four of the bikers entered, and came across toward us. Seeing that Cody was with me, two of the bikers stood in front of Jay, in case he tried to rush me. But he had no intention of doing that. He was playing it cool for now, refusing to acknowledge any of us.

"You fucking prick!" I felt all the tension return to my muscles. The relief of getting Cody back didn't relax me—all I wanted was to smash his face. The other two bikers moved in front of me to make sure I didn't.

Alex stepped up to me immediately and shook his head. "None of that now, Rory," he said, firm but friendly. "This was a gentlemen's arrangement and you are to continue to act like gentlemen. That doesn't only mean that Jonathan's a gracious loser, it also means that you're a gracious winner. So why don't you just take the dog and go."

I pressed up to tiptoes and craned my neck to look over his shoulder so I could see Jay, and opened my mouth to tell him—

"Rory," Alex said curtly. "I don't care if you hate the man. Out

of respect to me and my brothers, you need to leave now, without making a scene."

I took a deep breath, feeling my heart pounding against my sternum, feeling the pulse in my neck, even inside my ears. "All right," I said. "Fair enough, I understand"—although I didn't, really, only that it was a code of conduct that he genuinely believed in. It seemed a lot of bollocks to me because that bastard had it coming to him. "Thanks, Alex." I took another breath to calm myself. "I mean it, mate. Thanks."

I threw one arm around him; he pounded me once on the back, said, "Brother," and stepped back. Then he literally showed me the door.

My hands were shaking as I put the car into drive and pulled away.

Cody was delighted to be back on her bed, surrounded by the smells of familiar things. She sat up, her head brushing the ceiling of the tiny car, and I swear she smiled at me through the rearview mirror. Her head cocked slightly to the side as well, as if to say, *But what have you done with Sara?*

Sara had carefully packed and arranged the backseat—pre–dog nap—so that a water dish designed for travel was wedged in tight between two bags, with a water bottle beside it; I'd filled the dish that morning. She had also planted—in the passenger-side well, within easy reach of the driver's seat—a bag of bully sticks (otherwise known as pizzle sticks, which gives you some idea which part of a bull it's made from). I pulled one out and tossed it back over my shoulder onto her bed, but she was too excited and interested in our new adventure to be bothered to eat it.

After about half a mile, signs of civilization encroached upon the green around me: houses, shacks, a gas station. I could not stop shaking. At an intersection with a McDonald's, I pulled into the car park and cut the motor. I unclenched my hands from the steering wheel and sobbed.

Cody looked over at me and stuck her muzzle against my neck.

"All right, it's all right, girl," I said, getting my breath. "I'm grand. You're grand. Everything's going to be grand." I turned in the seat and put my arms around her, pulling her as tightly as I could against me. She tucked her head down and pressed into me.

"Ah, Cody," I said to her as I released her. I roughly tousled her head. "First things first." I reached for my phone. It wasn't in my pocket.

No, come on, I'd been fucked around enough today.

Brief moment of me frantically clutching at every pocketlike piece of my clothing and the car, until I found the fucking thing down in the console, where I never put it. I hurriedly called Sara.

"Hi—" she began, but I cut her off.

"I've got her! She's here! She's with me! We're on our way to you!"

Silence.

"Sara? Can you hear me? Did you hear what I said? I've got her with me, she's here in the car. She's right here!"

"Really?" Sara asked in the tiniest of voices. She was crying.

"Yes. Yes. I promise. It's over. She's back." I'm no fool, I knew this was the best moment for clemency. "And I'm sorry I was such a fuckup, I'm sorry I was stupid and too trusting and not honest enough, I'm so sorry, I'll be better, but I got her back for you and isn't that what matters? I'm bringing her to you and I'm going to put her right into your beautiful arms."

She hadn't even been listening to me, she was crying-laughing with relief on the other end of the line. "She's okay? Really? Was she happy to see you?"

"Of course she was, she's no fool," I said. "And she knew she'd get to be with you if she was with me, and that's what matters most of all."

"Oh . . ." she was saying, "Oh . . . God . . . thank God . . . thank you . . . I can't even tell you . . ."

"I know," I said, "It's okay. We're grand. We're better than grand. We're going to grab a bite and then I'll run her around a bit and we'll get on the road. If you can give me a heads-up where I should try to get to tonight—"

"Chattanooga," she said, already collecting herself. "I checked. The next best place heading west with a dog-friendly hotel is Chattanooga, I'll call and make a reservation for tonight."

"Do you know how much I love your hyperorganizational impulses?" I said.

"I bet you say that to all the girls whose dogs you lose."

"No," I said, "only to the girls whose dogs I get back."

"Thank you," she said quickly. "Thank you. I didn't mean to sound like a bitch."

"You don't sound like a bitch. I have a bitch right here with me in the car and you don't sound a thing like her."

"I love you," she said. "I'm saying that because you can't see how much I'm smiling."

"I can *feel* it," I said, relieved and grateful. That was the flavor of the day: relieved and grateful. With a plate of deferred vengeance on the side.

"What about Jonathan?"

"Right now he's stuck in a clubhouse full of bikers who are getting drunk and throwing money at strippers."

"What? Oh my God!" She laughed. "That's so Alex."

"He's not allowed to leave for four hours. Alex seems to believe that, given an hour to shrug it off, he'll enjoy himself."

She burst out laughing again. God, it was a great relief and a joy to hear her laugh. "I could kiss Alex for that," she said. "Okay, just head west for Asheville. That's about four hours, and there should be signs, I think you'll hit 40 eventually. By the time you get there, I'll have a place in Chattanooga. Drive safe and give my puppy a big belly rub for me."

"I will, of course, darlin'. Love you," I said. "Hey, how'd your meeting go? Your interview?"

A pause in which I could imagine her nodding. "Pretty well, I think. I'll hear next week. I guess it doesn't make sense for me to fly home now."

"True. The taxi fare to meet me in Chattanooga would break the bank."

"Let me think what to do," she said. "Talk soon. Love you."

After we hung up, I called the newest addition to my speed dial.

"Hey, Rory," said Alto, picking up after one ring.

"I've got her."

"Awesome!" Alto shouted, the happiest I've ever heard—meaning, actually *happy,* like. "I'll tell the crew!"

I grinned. "The crew?" I asked, keeping the grin out of my voice.

"Marie, Lena, Danny. I'm head of communications."

"Alto," I said. "You're the man."

"So to speak," he said. His tone of voice cheered me up. This whole thing was almost worth it just to hear Alto happy. (*Almost*, I said. Not *quite*.)

After I hung up from Alto, I glanced over at the McDonald's. It had a drive-through. I glanced back at Cody. Ah, what the hell. "It's a special day!" I declared. "Want a treat?"

She stared at me, panting a little, happy and vapid. Her eyebrows lifted slightly at the word "treat."

"All right, then," I said. "Don't you dare tell Sara we're doing this."

I pulled up to the speaker, ordered a chicken sandwich for myself. And for Cody, a cheeseburger and chips. (I mean french fries.) At the delivery window, I took the bag, set it down on the passenger seat. "Cheers," I said to the snub-nosed, freckle-faced teenage boy who served me. (Sound track: some kind of squeaky-clean fifties medley. Really.) As I pulled away, I reached in and pitched the whole container of chips over my shoulder, onto the dog bed.

"Have at it, Cody!" I said. In the rearview mirror, I saw her stare in astonishment at the shower of forbidden goodies. She glanced up toward me almost guiltily.

"Okay," I said encouragingly. "It's okay, girl. Good girl!"

Loving me more than God (that's to say, Sara), she nibbled, explored them, and then she went into a frenzy feed, wolfing them down. They were gone in seconds. Whatever that wanker Jay-hole had done to spoil her, I bet she forgot all about it now.

I headed west back into rural territory. The huge pines faded back, and the road opened up—two lanes in each direction, the tarmac laid directly down on Mother Earth, with a broad grass meridian and grass shoulders. It was a spectacular sunny day, the kind people write songs about and remember fondly from their childhood. About a mile past McDonald's, I pulled way over onto the broad grass shoulder of the road. I rolled down Cody's window and opened the sunroof, then gestured her to come up to the passenger seat. We sat there together, man and dog, enjoying our artery-clogging burgers as the sun-warmed field gleamed green beside us. "Well," I said to her as I finished, "that promises some fantastic indigestion sometime soon. Let's stretch our legs."

I got out of the car, went round to the passenger door, and called Cody out away from the road. She glanced around the wide swath of green, taking it in, looked toward the shadows of the pines a hundred paces back from the highway. Then she looked at me, and bowed, and began hopping around in circles as if she had springs on all four paws, studying me for a response.

I cracked up laughing, but also felt my throat constrict. She was safe! She was here! She was cute! "Don't tell Sara I said it, but you're one supercute dog. Let's go!" I took off running toward the pine forest. Cody reared into the air, hopped like a kangaroo, and then began to chase me. Her floppy ears blew back from her face, and the whites of her eyes showed, like she was a crazed Chinese dragon.

I ran as far as the start of the pines but then stopped, the hastily consumed chicken lurching around uncomfortably within. Cody darted past me into the forest. Ten yards in, she stopped abruptly, amazed by the otherworldliness in there—an overwhelming scent of pine, with no undergrowth, little more than russet needles carpeting the springy, shaded earth. She turned slowly in circles, looked round above herself, like a little kid entering a cathedral for the first time. Awed, but not really understanding why. She kept glancing at me in amazement, as if I had built it for her.

"Nice one, hah, Cody?" I said. "Get a good whiff, I don't think they have this in L.A."

With my voice, the spell was broken. She reared up again and dashed ecstatically toward me, wanting to chase me again. I made a face and a raspberry sound—*pthththt*—in her direction, because I'm really mature like that, then I turned and legged it back toward the car.

Only, when I got there, I turned to see she hadn't actually chased me. She'd stopped to eat grass. Like a hungry horse, she was chomping entire mouthfuls of the stuff. Sara once explained why dogs do that. (At some point or other, Sara had explained why dogs do everything.) For an upset stomach, was it? So that was my bad—the fried food must've made her queasy. After a dozen or so chomps, she stopped grazing. She looked up and around, searching for me. She didn't seem as chipper as she had moments earlier.

"Hey, Cody," I called out. "How you doing, pup?"

She gave me an accusatory look, then turned away, as if trying to be discreet, and her torso began to heave. On instinct, I turned away too. A moment later, I heard . . . well, you can guess.

My gorge rose just from the noise. I can handle someone vomiting if I'm drunk, but sober, forget it. I'm useless. It's as bad as dirty nappies or something. And Jesus, how long had I had her back in my care before I'd made her sick? In fairness, her rescue wasn't really my doing. This, however, was. Bollocks! Put a little damper on my giddiness, and that in turn reminded me how hungover and wrecked I still was.

I waited about half a minute, then glanced over my shoulder.

She had finished being sick, and was now trudging back toward me, shaking her head slightly from, I'm sure, the surprise of sudden sickness. When she reached me, she sat, very quietly, and looked up at me with a pleading expression. It made me feel crap, and irresponsible, which further undermined my victorious mood.

"You okay?" I asked.

She kept staring at me. She wanted comforting. My impulse to kneel down beside her was negated by my disgust at the thought of what had just come out of her mouth. "Nothing like a good barf to get over an upset stomach, eh, Cody?" I said with forced heartiness. "Works a charm for me, every time."

She stretched her muzzle yearningly in my direction. On reflex I pulled back a step.

"C'mon. Back in the car with you," I said suddenly, and gestured. She sat back on her haunches. "Back in the car," I repeated, stern. She sighed, disappointed not to have wrangled more affection from me, then obediently climbed up onto the passenger seat, then back onto her bed. She began to lap at the water, and kept drinking until it was gone. I refilled it and she drank another half container. Being sick was thirsty work. I hoped it was enough that she'd purged herself. I wasn't going to find a vet en route.

So finally we were on our way for real. Despite the comedown of the upchuck (so to speak), it was amazing to have another living being in the car with me. I was so aware of her specific personality, something I'd never thought of her, a dog, as having: a personality. But regardless of species, there was *somebody else* in the car with me, and that somebody was *familiar*. And I liked that feeling.

The road remained two lanes in either direction, grass meridian and shoulders, pine forests set back and interspersed with meadows. We drove and drove and drove and drove. And drove. I was feeling the toxic aftereffects of the drinking, which got worse, not better, as the day went on. Cody perked up, but then eventually got bored, circled on her bed, and lay down to nap. I glanced at her in the rearview mirror. In all fairness, she was about the most endearing dog in the world, and seeing her sleeping safely in her bed, knowing I'd helped rescue her and was taking her safely back to Sara . . . there are no words to express how good that made my heart feel. "Love you, Cody," said a man's voice from somewhere in the car, in an affectionate tone.

Jesus, did *I* say that? At least I hadn't called her snuggle bunny. Then I'd have to shoot myself. (Snuggle bunny! For fuck's sake!)

After a few hours the terrain got hilly, then almost mountainous. Cody was bored, but perked up when my phone rang. I'd set it on speaker, cradled in one of the cup holders. "Hello?"

A booming voice filled the car, declaiming, "Rory, brother! Alex here." There was a lot of ambient noise. He must be in the clubhouse. "Just wanted to let you know that I've fulfilled my duty. I kept Jonathan here for four hours as we agreed. Despite the raucous party we threw for him, he just left."

A small andiron smashed into my gut. "Do you know where he was going?"

"Well, he *said* he was just going to hightail it back to Massachusetts, but I believe that about as much as I believe the Republican Party line. I'd guess he's probably coming after you," Alex said cheerily. "Too bad he didn't stay. It's a *great* party. Anyhow: good luck with whatever happens next. Godspeed, brother!"

"Thanks, Alex," I said morosely. "Enjoy the strippers."

He hung up. I groaned. If Jay were chasing after me, I had to keep that four-hour lead. I couldn't *really* bring myself to believe that he'd chase me across the continent for a dog . . . but I still couldn't really bring myself to believe he'd stolen her in the first place.

Almost immediately the phone rang again. Sara, this time. That woman had no off-duty setting.

"Hey, love," I said, answering.

"It's been four hours," she said. "That means Alex just released him."

"Yes, he just called giving me a heads-up," I said in a reassuring voice. Then I realized I didn't actually have anything reassuring to say.

"Jay knows you're headed to Los Angeles."

"Oh, please, he wouldn't be stupid enough to try to follow me when I'm hundreds of miles ahead of him."

"He's not giving up," she said decisively. "He's going to do *something*."

"Well it's a massive country," I said. "I'm a needle in a haystack. If he's got a plan, I'm fucked if I can guess it."

"I wonder if he'll guess you're headed to Chattanooga tonight. Do you think he'll guess that? Maybe you should detour somewhere?"

"Sara. My love. We'll drive ourselves mad that way."

A pause. "You're right. Just get out here as quickly as you can. You know, *safely*, but—"

"I could drive straight through," I said, leaping at the opportunity to extend my superhero status beyond my fabulous Indian cooking and intrepid dog rescuing. "What is it from here, thirty hours? Forty? I can do that."

"There's no need to make yourself miserable. Pace yourself. How's Cody?"

"She's grand," I said. "Happiest dog in the world. She told me to tell you that I'm her god now, and you must thank me for her rescue by letting me undress you whenever I like."

"You don't say."

"She'd also like some lamb chops."

"We'll work on that," Sara said, a smile in her voice. "Call when you take a rest stop and I'll give you the address for the Chattanooga hotel. And I guess I should stay in L.A., not fly back east, but maybe I could still come out and meet you in Flagstaff and we could go to the Grand Canyon. It's so close and everyone says you've got to see it to believe it, and it'd be a great way to celebrate Cody's rescue. I'd like to do something romantic with you."

She wanted to do romantic things with me again!

I stopped on the far side of the city to grab a bite of prefabricated food consisting mostly of starch and fat, and to let the dog stretch her legs again and to take a poo. I looked at a wee map of the American Southeast on my phone, then I called Sara, who gave me the address for the dog-friendly Chattanooga hotel, which I fed into the GPS.

The GPS gave me several route options to Chattanooga. I thought between here and Chattanooga all the roads were essentially the same—just different ways to divert around the Great Smoky Mountains.

Several hours later, I had come to realize that wasn't true. *Bollocks*.

Somehow, I had programmed the GPS to steer me *through* the mountains, rather than around them. While the Great Smoky

Mountains Parkway turned out to be one of the most beautiful roads I've ever driven on in the entire world, it's hard to appreciate much of it when you're a white-knuckled and knackered driver staring at the tarmac right in front of you, anticipating the next curve, which is starting before you've finished the last curve, which you were already on before you finished the curve before that one. I'd take a year of Boston driving over one more hour on the fucking thing, even though I hardly saw another car. Every time we took a sharp curve Cody yawned, which (Sara had told me) might mean she was queasy.

"Please, *please,* don't be sick again, please, I *cannot* deal with that now," I said to her, glancing into the rearview mirror and then immediately focusing my gaze back to the road. Of course the notion of Cody being sick brought Jay to mind and my mind began to regurgitate—excuse the term—all the dread and angry thoughts about him. I wondered what he would do next. No way would he follow me. That would be mad. But what would he do instead, then? Was he simply on his way back to Boston? Hard to believe. So what was it?

After 7,258 more hairpin turns, with the car reeking of bacon and apple-pie moonshine, and the carcasses of eight million dead bugs splattered against the windscreen, the sun started to slant in the west, throwing a tangerine dust in broad stripes across the trees and the road. Despite the foul overstressed state I was now in, despite feeling more hungover than I had earlier that day, I have to admit it was *gorgeous.* I opened the windows to discover the air here smelled like honey. It would have been a lovely drive, if all three of us were here together—me, Sara, and Cody—and Mr. J. Baldy didn't exist.

Finally we approached a major highway, the kind of road I'd intended to be on all along. We were losing the light, and I was driving almost directly into what little light was left, so I could not see details as the urban sprawl crept in again and the sun set pink and beautiful before me. Beautiful through the smear of dead bugs, I mean.

Then I saw, for just the briefest moment, a white Lexus SUV. It snaked up near my right flank, and then fell back. I couldn't see it after that one moment, masked as it became in the glaring headlights behind me. I had not seen the license plate.

It couldn't have been Jay! No way! *Don't be paranoid,* I told myself. I'd played with the dog a bit before getting on the road, I'd been slowed down by the Great Smoky Mountains Parkway, and of course there was a faster way to get to Chattanooga, but he could never have eaten up my *four-hour* lead that quickly . . .

Could he?

No way. No. Mad to even think it.

The GPS guided me to the hotel in the exurb sprawl. I pulled into a parking spot and turned off the ignition. A motion-sensitive light lit up outside, backlighting the windshield smear of dead bugs. I let Cody out on her leash to pee, then made her get back in the car so she wouldn't be underfoot in the lobby. "Hang on, girl," I instructed, "let me get us checked in."

I left the window open a crack, locked the car remotely, and went into the hotel. It was one of those beige, bland chain hotels, no personality whatsoever. The bloke behind the counter was humming along with the piped-in Muzak crap of Kenny G (his sound track). It was quiet, at least. I was *so* grateful to be out of the car and done driving for the day. I was dying for a nice cold ale, ol' hair of the dog to get rid of this brutal hangover. But I firmly decided, no, I just needed plenty of water, a shower, and a good night's sleep.

"How's it going," I said. "Checking in. O'Connor, one night."

Without making eye contact with me, the clerk looked into a computer screen, clicked a few things, read something. His face and expression never changed.

"That's the double suite?" he asked officiously.

"Ye—what? No."

"It looks like an upgraded reservation. Do you need a second key?"

"What? I need a first key," I said, "I just got here."

"Oh," he said, confused but eyes never leaving the screen. "It looks like the rest of your party has already arrived."

Chapter 24

There was a brief pause made out of pure lead. Then I was able to speak.

"Rest of my party? I'm traveling alone."

"Someone has already checked into that room."

"Under what name? Rory O'Connor?"

"Under O'Connor, yes, sir." Finally his eyes glanced up at mine. "Is there a problem?"

"What did he look like? Was he tall? Bald?"

"Sorry, sir, I wasn't on the desk yet."

I couldn't think straight.

"Ok, thanks, I'll be right back, just getting the dog," I said in a stupid voice, and went out to the car.

I couldn't see Cody through the windows. She'd been taken. He'd taken her! Shite!

Frantically I opened the door with the electronic key and hollered, "Cody!" into the car. The motion-detector light was at too high an angle to light the backseat, but I suddenly felt her breath against my cheek and almost collapsed with relief. "Fucking hell,"

I said. "Okay, Cody, okay, good girl." I patted her head and sank my weight back down into the driver's seat.

She, of course, wanted to get out. "Sorry, girl, no, it's not safe," I said, pushing her back. "I'm taking you someplace else."

How could he possibly have gotten here before me? I'd had a *four-hour* lead on him, and Great Smokies Parkway notwithstanding, I drive like a maniac. And anyhow, how could he have known to come to *this hotel*? And more than anything, of course: What was he up to? What the *fuck* was he thinking? What, was he planning to tail me across the continent? *Really?*

I reached for my phone and called Sara to tell her I'd arrived safely. "You know," I continued, trying to sound casual, "we're really making good time here and I'm not tired. What's the next big city we could stay in?"

"Sweetie, we've already paid for the Chattanooga hotel and you need to rest." When I began to protest, she insisted: "You might not think you're tired, but it's been a hell of a few days; as soon as you let yourself relax you'll see how much your body needs sleep."

"He's here," I blurted out. "I need to keep going because he's here. He followed me. And somehow he caught up to me."

"What?" she gasped.

"He's *following* me, Sara. Isn't that mad? He's here, *in the hotel*. He somehow got into my *room*."

"Wow," she said softly. "I guess I should have expected that, but . . . well, anyhow, I didn't."

"So I can't stay here," I pressed. "Obviously."

"Well . . . I guess you could go on to Nashville," she said. "I think that's two hours, maybe two and a half. I'm at my computer, I'll check."

"And that's due west?"

"It's actually a little north, but it's the next city on Highway 40, which is how you'll go, all the way out here."

"And what's the city after Nashville?"

"Memphis, but that's a real schlep. Tennessee is a very long state."

"I'm up for it," I said.

"That's more than twelve hours in the car in one day, and after your drive yesterday, I'm sorry, but that's too much. You'll fall asleep at the wheel and I'll lose both of you."

"I did more than that yesterday," I argued. "I can do it again. And if I can do it twice, she can do it once."

"It will really stress both of you, and there's no need to—"

"As long as I have the energy to drive, it's to our advantage for me to get as far ahead of him as possible."

After a moment, she sighed. "Memphis is too far. You're wired up, and I get that, but trust me, you're not thinking clearly. I'll find a Nashville hotel and text you the address."

"All right," I said, feeling irritable and edgy.

Before I went back onto the highway, I went to fill up the tank, and to scrub—literally scrub, with the scrubby side of a dish sponge Sara had thought to pack for this specific purpose—the bugs off the windshield. While I was stopped, I cantankerously typed in *Tennessee—Memphis* as the next destination on the GPS. Then I started driving.

I didn't know my American geography the way someone traveling cross-country surely ought to. But I knew that Chattanooga, Nashville, and Memphis are all in Tennessee, and so when I saw a sign saying, "Welcome! We're Glad Georgia's on Your Mind," I realized something was wrong.

"Again?! Two GPS fuckups in one day? Fuck fuckfuckfuckfuck FUCK! SHITE!" I shouted, pounding my hand on the dashboard over and over again. Cody jumped.

The fucking GPS assured me I was heading toward Memphis, so I just kept driving into the night. What else could I do? In almost no time at all, the road turned and we reentered Tennessee, which briefly deluded me into thinking I was on the right track after all—until I found myself crossing into *Alabama*. Ala-*fucking*-bama! Gobshite fuck bollocks! Jesus fucking Christ! *Three* GPS accidents in one day? Cody looked frightened of me. I was losing the plot.

I took a deep breath and tried to calm down a little. Okay. Alabama. I knew a few things about Alabama. I knew Hank Williams. I knew Neil Young and Lynyrd Skynyrd's dueling songs about the state. I knew that Mobile, Alabama, was on the *Gulf Coast*. Which proved being in Alabama was a *mistake,* no matter what that useless piece-of-crap shite technology had to say about it. "Look," I said to Cody, staring at me in fright from the passenger seat. "Rory fucked up again. Good man, Rory. That's the way." The thought of having to call Sara made my stomach sour. But at the same time I was stuck, totally lost. With a heavy, resigned sigh, I reached for my phone.

"Hi, love, I was just about to text you the Nashville hotel," she said.

"I'm going to cut to the chase here," I said. "I'm in Alabama."

A pause.

"You're what?"

"I just wanted to get the fuck out of there, Sara, and I ended up in Alabama."

"Umm . . ." she began, which was enough to make me so defensive I could *hear* my blood pressure rising. "Nashville is *north*. Alabama is *south*. How could you possibly end up in Alabama if you were headed for Nashville? That would require some kind of . . . non-Euclidean geography." Then she laughed a little, nervously. I remembered fuck-all about geometry, but I suppose that was intended to be funny. She was trying to avoid an argument. All right, then, so would I. First I took another big breath and let it out slowly.

"I didn't put Nashville in the GPS," I confessed. "I put Memphis."

"Rory!" Sara said, the humor gone. "We agreed you'd go to *Nashville*."

"*You're* the only one who agreed to that, and anyhow, going to Memphis is supposed to take me *through* Nashville."

"Well, obviously it's not doing that," she huffed. Huffy wasn't generally her thing. I wanted the old Diana Spencer–with–a–kindergartner back. It had been ages since I'd seen that side of her. I wondered if I was coming across as especially inept in light of that bollocks of an ex-lover's crafty efficiency. Look at me, failing better and better all the time. Beckett would be proud of his countryman.

I heard a few muffled clicks and taps as she sorted out what I'd done wrong. "All right," she said shortly. "You need to drive west across all of northern Alabama and all of northern Mississippi, and then you'll reenter Tennessee at its southwestern corner, and that's where Memphis is. Please don't forget to feed the dog."

And she hung up. So much for the sweetness of early afternoon. At least I could now be confident that prick was no longer on my tail.

"I'm still lookin' out for you," I said grumpily to Cody. "Lot of thanks I get."

She carefully rolled over on the front seat for a tarty-dog pose, craning her neck to check out my response. She looked ridiculous.

It was hard to see much, now that it was dark, but I'd say if New England were a size-eight shoe, this part of the country was a size 8.5 wide. There was a general broadening—of roads, of car lots, of meridians, of housing estates, of fields—and between long stretches of undeveloped land, clatters of gas stations, convenience stores, towing facilities, storage facilities. I drove for dozens, then scores, then *hundreds* of silent miles, trying not to think about either Jay or Sara. The smell in the car was gank. My early sense of exultation was completely eradicated. I was spooked. So spooked, I simply had to keep myself from thinking.

My phone rang.

"Hi, Rory," said Alto as I picked up. "Just checking in one more time before bed to see how you're doing."

His sound track had definitely changed. No more Janis Ian, now it was Pharrell Williams.

"Squire Alto!" I said, with forced heartiness. "We're on the road, me and Cody. Tennessee. Although tonight it's Mississippi and Alabama." (That all sounded so exotic.)

"That's great," he said. "Everyone's delighted you got her back."

"Actually, you know . . . it might be a bit dodgy still," I said. "Don't tell Lena that. Do me a favor, just give me a bell tomorrow or the next day."

"Will do," said Alto.

Although there wasn't a thing he could have done, it was a good feeling knowing he was looking out for me. Sweet kid.

My phone dinged with a text from Sara, which I read because the road was so straight and empty. *Sorry for tone. Memphis hotel address attached, reservation made. Oklahoma City rez for next night, too. I want to rendezvous at Grand Canyon. Love you xx.*

Instantly my mood improved. See? All I wanted was Sara's love.

IT WAS A warm night, and at least there was enough Bible talk radio for me to practice my southern accents. Maybe I'd get to use them in the series.

The series. Ha!

I had a television series. I felt utterly unplugged from that side of myself. I couldn't even remember, now, what it felt like to be *on-stage*. To reassure myself that I really was an actor, I started quoting, in a southern accent, the "Commodity" speech from *King John*. That's a great speech, by the way, it works really well with a southern accent. Too bad the play is such crap.

Cody tilted her head and stared adoringly at the back of my right ear. Then she poked her nose at it.

"I promise I will feed you in Memphis," I said.

She poked her nose down the back of my shirt. To be safe, I pulled over onto the shoulder of the road and let her out to pee. It was so warm here. There were no cars in sight, not a sound or a light, and that steadied me a little. Maybe that beige clerk in the beige uniform in the beige hotel in Chattanooga had goofed off on the paperwork. Not that I now thought for one moment that prick was on his way back to Boston, never to pursue the dog again. Fat fucking chance. I knew now he meant business. But it occurred to me that I was overreacting a little to the possibility of actual at-hand danger. I took a deep swampy breath and looked into the darkness.

WE FINALLY REENTERED Tennessee sometime after midnight, and then it was pretty quick before we were in Memphis, and met another beige clerk in a beige lobby in a beige hotel—and who was piping through the beige speakers? Kenny G. There was no restaurant or room service. I had eaten almost nothing since the chicken cutlet sandwich, and I was weak with hunger, but nothing was around unless I wanted to eat the dog food.

"Of course she packed plenty for *you*," I said grumpily, once I was settled in the room and dispensing some into Cody's travel bowl. "I, of course, have to fend for myself."

I peeled my reeking clothes inelegantly off me and keeled over onto the bed, shattered, absolutely knackered, staring straight up at the ceiling. This was not going to procure me a meal. Nothing was going to procure me a meal. There would be no meal. I should just get a good night's sleep.

I turned the lights off, got into bed, and drifted off.

Or nearly did. I hadn't brought Cody's bed into the hotel—not having it for one night wasn't going to kill her. The problem was, her choosing a spot. So she sat right by the head of my bed and stared at me. I could feel it even in the dark. I could hear her dog sounds. Then she brought her nose so close to my face that I could feel her breath, and when I opened my eyes, she moved in even closer and touched her nose very gently to mine.

"Leave me alone, Cody," I said.

"Leave me alone, Cody" is apparently canine for "Don't leave me alone, Cody." She knew she had my attention. I heard her tail in the dark brushing across the floor as it wagged. She brought her nose to mine again.

"This is Sara's fault," I informed her. "You're a good dog but this behavior is not acceptable, Cody, and it's entirely Sara's fault."

Fifteen seconds later I realized that no, it was my fault. She wanted water and I'd not given her any.

I got up. Filled her travel dish with water from the sink, and placed it on the floor by the bathroom door. As I got back in bed, I heard more than saw her pounce on the bowl. She drank and drank and drank and drank. I thought that would be the end of it and now she'd go to sleep. But no. She was *so* revived after drinking and seemed to want to let me know, wanted to *thank* me. And started bumping noses and staring at my face so hard I could feel it even with my eyes closed. She rested her head heavily on the side of the bed. "Go to sleep," I said, "I'm knackered." No change. I could still feel her presence. All right, *Jesus.* Lamp on. She was startled by that. I hit the corner of the bed. "Come on, Cody. Up here. On the bed."

She looked disbelievingly between my face and the side of the bed where my hand was. I hit it again. She yawned uncertainly.

"I mean it," I said, sharply. "Just get the fuck up here."

Again, the eyes going back and forth between my face and my hand. Finally, after I was practically banging out a drum roll on the bedding, she leapt gracefully onto the bed, tail high and wagging happily, like she was anticipating the greatest slumber party ever. The movement reminded me, so much, of the night we'd met last August. Ah, well, I'd held out for eight months before giving in. "It's just for tonight, d'y'hear?" I said. "I'm bringing your bed in tomorrow, so make the most of it, little bitch."

She did. As soon as the light was off, before I had even gotten myself fully prone in bed again, Cody had rolled over into tarty-dog pose.

But only for a moment. Then she needed to stretch out on her side as far as possible, so that from the air she would resemble the silhouette of a graceful dog bounding over an unseen hurdle.

But only for a moment. Then she needed to stretch out on her other side and do the same thing, as if evenly sunning herself.

But only for a moment. Then she needed to fluff up the pillows I was not using, and push her body down on top of them so that her hind feet were pushing against my shoulders.

But only for a moment. Then she needed to sleep at the foot of the bed.

But only for a moment. Then she needed to sleep in tarty-dog pose in the middle of the bed.

"Cody, for fuck's sake!" I snapped.

This went on for at least an hour. That includes the period during which I yelled at her and made her get off the bed, but she wouldn't stop bumping my nose, so I put her in the bathroom but then she whined oh-so-softly until it was driving me mental and I couldn't take it any longer, so I let her out and threw pillows onto the floor for her to sleep on. She ignored them and lay on the carpet. Until she wanted to get on the bed again.

I turned off my alarm, and decided I was going to sleep in, so that finally, once on this cursed trip, I could start the day's drive feeling something close to human. I'd only to get to Oklahoma City, after all, and even though that lanky parasitical prick knew I hadn't stopped in Chattanooga, he had no idea I'd pushed on all the way to Memphis.

I hoped.

Chapter 25

I woke with my belly stuck to my back with the hunger. I looked up frowning in the dim light. Cody was hovering over me, staring at me, nose to nose. In what appeared to be the far distance, I saw her tail slowly, tentatively wagging.

"Right," I said. "Right. And we're off."

I took her out for her morning pee, fed her, left her in the room to see about finally getting some grub for myself. This required driving. Memphis—at least this part—was not my kind of town. There is something wrong when you are elated to find an International House of Pancakes as your best chance for a healthy feed.

Got back to the hotel, had a shave and a shower. Barely recognized my face when it was shaved, it'd been so long. I took a long, long shower, maybe twenty minutes, and it made all the difference in the world, letting the warm water soak into my skin, relax my muscles. I breathed in the steam, scrubbed myself down with the washcloth. I had almost forgotten what it felt like to be clean and I was happily reinvigorated. Plus, it was great not to stink. I'd almost forgotten what it felt like not to stink. I balled up my bacon-ized clothes and shoved them into the plastic bag with the shirt that stank of moonshine. My laundry would be ten times more flammable by the time we reached Los Angeles. Maybe we could throw a housewarming party and use my clothes to send off fireworks.

I took the dog for a walk around the narrow band of grass surrounding the hotel. She was almost hysterically in need of proper exercise, though, and there was no place to do that here. I led her back into the room, took off the leash, and then I leapt up onto the bed and bounced on it like a trampoline.

"*Up,* Cody, up!" I ordered as I bounced, patting my thighs. She scrambled up onto the bed and tried to jump up on me. I grabbed her front legs, wrestled her down to the bed, threw the covers over her, and hopped off onto the floor, leaving her to fight her way out.

Covered by the sheets and blankets, she circled blindly to the edge of the bed and tumbled off in a heap on the floor. She started fighting with the sheets, snarling—Cody, snarling! I'd never heard her snarl before!—although her tail, which was clear of the covers, was wagging wildly. She looked like a cheap science-fiction effect. I got such a fit of the giggles. Her head finally popped out from under the blanket—and it was as if she saw me laughing and got embarrassed, because she jumped up, ran to me, and literally slammed me, shedding dog hair all over me.

"Cody! You're getting aggressive!" I said, cracking up. "I needed that, thanks, Cody! Let's do it again!" I got back on the bed and started bouncing. She fell for it a second time. And then a third! My stomach hurt from the laughing. We kept it up until somebody in the next room pounded on the walls.

It was great crack. Most fun I'd ever had with her.

SARA HAD ALREADY sent me the Oklahoma City hotel's address for tonight, and I knew she'd check in once she was up. It was going to be an easy enough driving day, about eight hours with rest stops. And as long as the slog ahead of me was, I took comfort knowing that wanker was way off my trail.

Feeling calmer and more in control of my life, I regretted having missed Nashville. Jamming with Alex had been a blast, actually, and gave me a new appreciation of American music—the original, homegrown stuff—and Tennessee seemed the perfect place to get immersed in a scene. Under other circumstances, I'd have stopped in every little hamlet along the way, sussed out the chance for a few tunes. Ah, well. Anyhow, it didn't really work like that here (like it did in Ireland). Here people flocked to central points—Nashville, Memphis. And even though here I was in Memphis, I could not take time to make the pilgrimages I'd liked to have—Johnny Cash, Willie Nelson. Not my music, in fairness, but I'd pay homage to any really great musical legend, given the chance.

In the car, I asked the GPS lady if she could take me to Oklahoma City without getting me lost. She didn't answer, but I had no choice but trusting her. Somehow she got confused while trying to get on to Highway 55 going out of the city, so I found myself going south when I should have been going north. Bollocks! Please don't start this shite again!

I figured out how to solve the problem faster than the GPS did—which obviously wasn't saying much, given what a shite piece of technology it was—and exited the freeway pronto and then back onto a surface street. The GPS lady finally caught up, chimed in at last, and told me to turn right on a Highway 51. We were in that industrial-urban sprawl you find outside any major city, where you go for car dealerships and self-storage units. Over to the left I saw . . . no way: the Elvis Presley Boulevard Shopping Center?

"That's . . . that's *awful*," I said to Cody. "What do you think, Cody?"

She didn't give a flying fuck, of course.

Beyond the shopping center, bizarrely, I saw some grounded planes—their tail fins and dolphin-slick backs were visible over a high cement wall. I couldn't make any sense of this, until a few hundred yards beyond that, set slightly back from the road and looking like an overwrought marquee for a Greek restaurant, the mother of all Memphis signs:

"GRACELAND."

"No way," I said. "Cody, *look at that*!"

If you've ever so much as heard of the United States of America, you can't drive past Graceland without at least rubbernecking. It may have been mega-tacky (let me clarify: it *is* mega-tacky) but he was the King.

I was on the wrong side of the road, and anyhow I could see no trees in the parking lot and the day was far too warm to leave her in the car. "So once again, Cody," I said. "You're wrecking my buzz. I might as well get used to it, I s'pose. As long as you're around, the story of my life will be that you'll trump me with Sara every time. And it's *Graceland*. Do you understand? Do you understand what you are *depriving* me of, you little—"

Then I saw a white SUV about five cars behind me, and even though I *knew* it couldn't be Jonny Bald-head, a feeling of dread shook me, came out the bottom of my foot as I accelerated right past Mecca.

(By the way: Presley? Good ol' Irish name.)

THE GPS GOT me back on track. We crossed the Mississippi River—an iconic American Thing that was deeply underwhelming, since there was so much industrial hardware making up the bridge that I couldn't see the water. Who built that thing? A bridge with a view is half the reason to have a bridge. In my mind, it should have looked like the Whitefield picture, the one I'd played waltzes in front of for the tours at the museum back in Boston. Maybe these days people liked to jump off it or something, but Jesus, all cars were inoculated against having even visual access to it. What a shame to block a view like that!

On the other side of the Mississippi was the state of Arkansas, all of which I'd need to cross before getting to Oklahoma. After yesterday's drive this would be a breeze. I should make plans to stop for lunch, though. Maybe Little Rock? One of Sara's texts had said I'd be driving right by Little Rock. (I wondered how little. Would I see it?)

The river basin spread out to the west, flat and a lush dark brown. There were lots of broad fields, mostly green, although some still grey-brown from last year's stubble. I tuned the radio to a local station just in time to hear a paranoid anti-immigration rant from a bloke who sounded like he was trying to raise his own blood pressure. He was claiming that ranchers had discovered Islamic prayer rugs on their ranches, which meant obviously the guys calling themselves Juan Valdez were actually Akbar Shah Khomeini.

"Arkansas," I said to Cody. "My kind of state."

But Pink Floyd was on the next station.

"Arkansas," I said to Cody. "It's cool."

She agreed, tongue lolling contentedly out the side of her mouth. Actually, there was something about Arkansas that reminded me of the West Midlands in England, which I knew from early childhood. Maybe it was just the spitting rain that was starting, but also we passed vast fields of soil that was a deep, strange color, almost orange-maroon, a color I'd only ever seen before in Herefordshire. It was much warmer here, though—the dashboard thermometer read seventy-nine.

We passed a "XXX Adult World Open 24 Hours" drive-in, and moments later, a large religious billboard. "Look at that, Cody," I snickered. "Which came first? The Christian or the slag?"

Cody yawned and climbed in back to lie down.

"Cody, you've no sense of humor. Did Jay ever complain about that?" Jay! Wanker! He was too far behind me to even eat my dust! At least, I hoped.

As we approached Little Rock, the traffic got sluggish, and I'd no idea where to look for grub in the city, so although it was lunchtime, I decided to keep driving through to the next town. I pulled over at a station to let Cody out, and refueled. The rain was coming down pretty hard now, but I didn't mind getting wet because it was so wonderfully warm.

We skirted Little Rock amidst a riotous sea of purple clover covering the highway shoulders. When I had the city in my rearview mirror, the sky *exploded* with rain, and a fog welled up with amazing speed—the outside temperature had plummeted about twenty degrees, according to the dashboard. The landscape was rolling into the first swell of some new mountain range, barely visible in the heavy mist. There was a little bit of red rock cropping out of the rise of hills to the right, and in the distance, seen fleetingly, were almost flat-topped ridges. "I wonder where we are. What do you think, Cody?"

"Aux Arc Park," announced a road sign that I could barely read through the bucketing rain.

"Hey!" I said to Cody. "Aux Arc! I know the Ozarks!" There was a Thomas Hart Benton picture about the Ozarks at the Museum of Fine Arts, and I played "Cluck Ol' Hen" in front of it. "Cody, do you know 'Cluck Ol' Hen'? *Cluck ol' hen, cluck and sing, you ain't laid an egg since late last spring*—well, the words are shite but it's a *great* fiddle tune. Sounds just like a barnyard full of clucking hens." I was oddly reassured by finding a familiar reference point in the middle of fucking nowhere. Back at the MFA, the Ozarks had seemed impossibly far away.

Cody yawned.

"Sorry to bore Your Ladyship," I said. The rain was now so loud on the roof I had to shout. "I don't understand what Jay sees in you, frankly, you're dull. Speaking of that wanker, I wonder if he's turned tail and gone home yet. I hope so." No response. "Cody! Hey! Cody!" Instantly she was alert, scrambling eagerly onto the front seat, hopeful for attention, tail wagging cautiously. "You're dull but you're cute," I amended. I reached down and got her a bully stick, chucked it in the back.

The temperature had dropped to fifty.

Before Cody had finished the bully stick, the temperature had dropped to forty-eight. The rain was falling like an enormous shower, impossible amounts of rain—and now it was cold rain.

Suddenly a little musical alarm sounded and an icon blinked to life on the dash above the steering wheel. A tire, with an exclamation mark on top of it.

"No!" I begged the car, smacking the dashboard. "No, don't do this to me! Bollocks! *Bollocks!*" The rain was pelting the car so hard I did not even hear myself say this. I started kicking the floor of the driver's side with the heel of my left foot, and banging on the console with my hand, scaring the dog again. I pulled over onto the shoulder and killed the engine—the sky was dark, the air was dark. It was midafternoon but it looked like twilight, that's how fierce this deluge was. I riffled through the glove compartment for the owner's guide, and checked the index to see what the icon meant.

Flat tire.

"Well, that's wrong," I informed Cody loudly. "It better be fucking wrong, at least." The drop in temperature, combined with the higher altitude, must have meant lower air pressure, which confused the system into thinking the tires were going flat. Or something.

I stared out the window at the cold rain. I didn't want to go out in that. I just *didn't want to*. Enough, already! But I'd feel like a right gobshite if there *was* a tire going flat and it did awful damage to the car. "Stay," I told Cody. "Once I'm too wet to care, I'll let you out to run around a bit."

Sara had preset an umbrella in the little holder on the side of my door. The rain was bucketing down. I was drenched in the microseconds between opening the door and opening the umbrella. Once outside, it was hard not to fumble—

I pressed my hand against the front left tire. It was grand. Why did I even bother doing this? Now I would be saturated and drenched the rest of the way to Oklahoma! I didn't want to put the heat on because that would fog up the inside of the windshield. I had never bothered to figure out the defogger on this stupid car.

I started to get up. A gust of wind and rain slapped my hair into my eyes, the wind caught the umbrella and almost pried it loose; trying to hold on to it, I was pulled sideways and lost my balance. I grabbed for the car, and gripped my hand around the fender for balance.

Inside the fender was something shaped like a small box.

Another gust, and I let go of the umbrella, which went flying away into the squall. I dropped into a squat and grabbed the box. I was already guessing what it was, but I couldn't believe it was really there. It really fucking was. Everything got dialed up a notch, because this sort of thing doesn't happen in normal life:

It was a tracker! It was a fucking *tracking device*. I ripped at it. It was stuck on like a magnet. With blood rising, I yanked it and it came away in my hand.

Chapter 26

W hat the *fuck*?!" I shouted into the rainy air. "This bloke is psycho! Am I in a fucking *movie*? Is this *Breaking* fucking *Bad*?" My face was drenched. Everything was *drenched*.

I looked at the box in my hand. There were some lights, blinking, and other lights, not blinking. All mocking me. This was becoming just . . . surreal. It was mad enough that this bloke had turned out to be Sara's dog-stealing ex, but this was going beyond the pale.

With a rage I hadn't felt since adolescence, I bounced it off the ground. I fucking *danced* on it, cursed at the top of my lungs. In my rage, I reduced it to shards.

I stopped and stared at the ruins, completely spent and soaked to the skin.

Then I thought—and screamed aloud—"What an *eejit*! Why did I *do* that?" I should have left it on the roadside, or put it on some other car at a rest stop, some car going into a completely different direction! Instead I'd *smashed* it to smithereens. Fuck and double fuck! I started shouting again. It was no longer transmitting, so he'd figure out that I'd discovered it. Talk about failing better and better!

But . . . how could that devious bastard have put the tracker on my car? He hadn't been *near* my car—I retraced every moment of the time in North Carolina. He hadn't had a chance.

Maybe it wasn't him at all. Could it have been Alex? When I was drunk? Why, though?

Maybe Sara did it herself. Keep tabs on me since I was too irresponsible to be trusted without oversight. *Oh, for fuck's sake, Rory, ease up,* I thought.

Alto! It was *Alto*! He was a double agent, working for Jay while pretending to be helping us. That little wanker!

And then I remembered: when I dropped Cody off. Back in Boston. Jay had wanted to check out the MINI because he was nostalgic for his father's. I bet that was a lie. Bet his father only ever owned American cars or something. I howled with frustration. And then I got back in the car, bringing gallons of water with me, and called Sara. I expected her to be as hysterical as I was but she seemed relatively calm.

" . . . It actually shouldn't be surprising," she said. I could hardly hear her thorough the din of the rain, so she might have been more hysterical than I was giving her credit for. "Like you said, he put it there before he knew you'd get her back. Meaning he was just trying to track you while *you* were following *him*—so he'd know if you were gaining on him. I have to say one thing for him, when he makes a plan, he *commits,* he's *thorough*."

I brushed away an irrational impulse to see this as a critical comparison of the two of us. "Well, now he's probably been using it to follow me, so what should I do about it?" I said. "I'm headed straight for Oklahoma City; don't you think I should divert, and then I'll have lost him?"

She said something I couldn't make out above the artillery effect of the rain. "What?"

"I said good idea!" she shouted. "I'm checking the route! Where are you?"

"There's a sign ahead for a place called Alma."

A pause. "Okay. Tulsa! Tulsa's about an hour or so northeast of Oklahoma City. You're just about due south of it now. Set the GPS for Tulsa and I'll text you an address for a hotel in a few minutes. Okay? Can you hear me?"

"Okay, thanks," I said.

"Drive safe in that rain!" she said.

I was overwhelmed for a moment with a sense of relief, gratitude, even elation. No matter how lost or freaked out I felt, there was Sara. She was a little rigid, but she was always there, she always had a solution, she always made everything better. And she asked little in return. Except that I embrace her dog. I really was working on that.

The worst of the rain passed, and minutes later, it felt like a scenic drive in Ireland. With the combined help of Sara's advice and the GPS, I changed direction to head north, but could see almost nothing in the mist. Just enough to truly feel as if I were back in the British Isles. Despite the stress of the circumstances, it was nearly comforting. I expected to see a little pub rise out of the fog, where I might duck in for a pot of tea, homemade soup with soda bread and butter.

I kept driving as evening gathered. And then . . . I'm not sure how this happened, but instantly—instantly—there was a city. Tulsa. It came out of nowhere. From the dark wet night to sudden civilization, marked by a Hard Rock Cafe and a casino-resort hotel, brightly lit billboards, and streetlights. It was dazzling. Jarring, but dazzling. A final cloudburst made all the neon signs look like a riot of dancing jewels.

I turned up the GPS volume and let it guide me, first to a petrol station, and then to the hotel. Ah, yes. Welcome to Beige-ville. I walked into the beige lobby with the beige clerk in the beige uniform to get a key to my beige room, which opened onto the car park, which was not, thankfully, beige. The rain had stopped completely but now the cooled wind was whipping around. I let Cody out on a grass swath along the side of the building, but she mostly wanted to keep her nose down to take in all the smells from the rain.

Ten minutes later: moved the car right in front of my room, got Cody and her gear inside with my rucksack, fed her, and was headed into the shower. Turned it on really hot to try to work out the knots in my shoulders and arms and back. I was waterlogged by the time I got out, it was great. Two long showers in one day! Life was improving!

A quarter hour after that, feeling fully human for the first time in nearly a week, I locked the door behind me and went round to the lobby to ask about nearby restaurants. This hotel had none of its own.

As I approached the desk, I saw that one of the beige chairs in the beige lobby looked different from all the others, because there was somebody sitting in it.

Somebody I knew.

Chapter 27

I halted as if I'd walked into a Plexiglas wall.

"Hello, Rory." It was him.

For a moment, I could not think. Of anything. I entirely forgot the English language. "How . . . *what?*" I felt as if a ragged zipper were being pulled up and down, open and close, inside the entire length of my body.

"You want an explanation of how I'm here?"

"Eh. Yes. And *why*. Look—" Since trying to avoid him wasn't helping, I might as well try to engage him directly. Maybe even talk some sense into him. If that were possible. I was calmer than I had been back in North Carolina, so maybe it was possible. Some dozen people milled about between us, waiting to check in. I brushed through them to get closer to him, still gobsmacked.

He shook his head a little. "The *why* should be obvious. I want Cody back. Do you consider me so feckless that one setback would defeat me? Give me a little credit. But I thought you'd be curious how I could find you without the tracker."

I tried to sort out my best move. Cody was in my room. Trying to get her back into the car without his interfering was unlikely, as he now seemed capable of anything. She was safest where she was, but somehow I had to keep him away from her. And he was right: of course I was curious.

"I'm curious," I admitted.

Jay, always happy to know more than the rest of us, nodded. "When the tracking device stopped working, I guessed you'd found it and redirected, and Tulsa seemed the easiest place to go in lieu of Oklahoma City."

"That gets you to Tulsa, but not to this hotel."

He shrugged. "Remember last night in Chattanooga, when you were told somebody had already checked into your hotel room?" I still hadn't sorted that one out. I wasn't going to give him the satisfaction of saying so, but he could read my face. "Right, you do remember. That chain came up first in a search for dog-friendly hotels in Tennessee. So I called all the Chattanooga branches saying I wanted to upgrade the Rory O'Connor reservation until I found the one that actually had the Rory O'Connor reservation."

"But I had a four-hour lead on you, how did you get there before me?" I demanded.

He smiled slyly, the old ruined-baron dignity intact. "I didn't, Rory," he said, in a tone of mock apology. "I was never there."

"But—"

"Everyone has their price," he said. "In this modern age, you can bribe somebody over the phone without ever meeting them. The hotel clerk was going off duty and agreed to log my arrival even though I hadn't arrived."

I blinked, confused. Shook my head. "*Why,* though? Why would you do that?"

"Because I could," said Jay, slowly. "Because I want you to understand who you're dealing with. I'm taking this very seriously, so for your own sake, you should, too."

That was the first moment I realized: this bloke must be a sociopath. Nobody goes to such extremes over a *dog*. Not even Sara would behave as mad as this and I've never met anyone as mad about their dog as Sara. "I do know who I'm dealing with," I said. "I'm dealing with a grown man who is obsessed with somebody else's pet."

"It sounds so tawdry when you put it like that."

"When I *put* it like that? That's what it fucking *is*!"

"You'd think an Irishman would have more reverence for elemental needs," said Jay, as if I'd disappointed him. "For the primal, the romantic. Anyhow, back to the point: once I knew which hotel chain it was, I knew it would be the same chain here. Sara's methodical that way. The trick was guessing Tulsa over any other city. Lucky guess. For all of us. As you'll understand in a moment. You're going to be very glad I found you, Rory."

I stared at him for a moment, not wanting to give him the satisfaction of the obvious question, but finally relenting: "Why? *Why* am I going to be glad you found me?"

Jay smiled and stood up. "I'm starving and I'm sure you are as well. Why don't we get a bite and talk this whole situation over? We're working with a bit of a time crunch, but luckily there's a restaurant within walking distance."

So he was going to be infuriating.

"Let's talk first," I suggested, even though my stomach was growling.

"You need to eat. I need to eat. There's only one restaurant nearby, and I have more money than you, so you might as well let me buy you dinner."

"What's the trick this time?" I asked.

"No trick," he said, a bit too innocently.

I crossed my arms, lowered my voice so the beige people waiting to check in could not snoop on our conversation. "Bollocks," I said. "You *always* have a trick. I've learned that much at least."

"Well, if you need someone to *vouch* for me . . ." He took his phone out of his coat pocket and tapped the screen. The lobby hubbub was quiet enough that I could hear the little whooshing noise as he sent a text, I supposed prewritten. He pocketed the phone and gave me a knowing look. "Just hang on for one minute till that goes through. And then do what you like." His implacable calm—once a panacea—was now his most infuriating quality.

My phone rang. I took it from my hip pocket. Sara.

"Answer it," he suggested, since I was staring at it.

"Hey, love," I said cautiously.

"Go to dinner with him," she said in a low monotone. She sounded as if somebody were holding a gun to her head.

I felt the bottom of my stomach drop about a foot. "What?" I said, my gaze reflexively going to Jay's face. He gave me a Cheshire-cat grin.

"Do what he says. Go to dinner with him. Give him what he wants." And then she added, as if it were an effort, "This isn't your fault."

"What isn't my fault?" I demanded.

"That you'll have to give him Cody."

"*What?*" I said harshly, louder than I'd meant to. The lobby quieted abruptly, as if insulted, and Jay, with the air of a kindergarten teacher, made a keep-it-down motion with his hands. God, how I wanted to punch him.

"He'll explain," Sara said, sounding hoarse. "Give him what he wants. I will not blame you. Call me when it's over." I heard her voice break on the last word, but she hung up before I could respond.

I stared in disbelief at my phone. Then I glared up at Jay.

"Dinner?" he said.

THE HOTEL SQUATTED in a compound of corporate-headquarter-like office buildings. For blocks around, all was toneless glass-and-concrete buildings, now almost entirely devoid of human presence. These were ringed with overfertilized strips of grass that were in turn bounded by cement sidewalks that were probably almost never trod on. We trod on one now, however, in the dusk, the cool wind tugging at us. We were headed to the only restaurant in sight. It was a gaudy Mexican chain, without one single authentic Mexican anywhere near it. But it was pretty busy, with hotel guests, I s'pose.

Inside, it was low-lit but full of bright Mexican knickknacks, sombreros, blankets, and the Disney version of indigenous art. There was loud pop music playing, and a baseball game was silently filling four large screens around the room. These were placed so that it was impossible to sit anywhere and not see one.

A dolled-up blonde wearing a lot of eye makeup and lipstick, and who wanted us to notice her cleavage, led us to a booth and left us with menus and a drinks list. Even the way Jay, in his long, narrow coat, slid into his side of the booth suggested an old-world, old-money grace that belied his actual identity. Everything about this bloke was a smoothly executed fraud. I had no idea who he really was. Or—I was realizing—what he was really capable of.

"An enchilada would hit the spot right now," he said, glancing at the menu.

Despite the ambient noise in the place, our booth seemed to have its own sound buffer; we did not have to yell to hear each other. Which didn't mean I didn't want to yell anyhow, but I refrained.

"Yes, it would," I said. So when the waitress came to the table a few silent moments later, I ordered what Jay was having: chicken enchiladas with a side of mole. He also ordered a margarita on the rocks. God, I'd've killed for a drink, but I ordered a club soda.

"Still recovering from the moonshine?" he asked.

"Very funny. Look, Jay, I know Americans are mad about their pets and all, but this is a bit *too* mad, isn't it? I know you were upset about losing Sara and Cody, and I know you want Cody back—I know all that, right, but why are you following me, *really*? Do you think I'm just going to give her back to you?"

"By the end of this conversation, I'm pretty sure you will," he said. He unfolded his napkin and placed it on his lap.

"No, mate, I'm not," I said. "No offense, but you need *help*. You can't keep following me. It'll drive us both mental. I'll do things we'll both wish I hadn't. So we have to come to an understanding now, tonight, because you *have to* back off." It was the strongest and most decisive I'd felt in over a week. Good. Thank God some of my Roryness was finally coming back.

He shifted his weight to slouch against the bench back. "I will definitely back off after tonight, since Sara has finally agreed that I should have Cody."

"Bollocks."

"Didn't she say so on the phone?"

"She was very upset on the phone. She wouldn't just randomly decide to give you her dog. You said something to scare her into it."

"Hmm," Jay said, as if trying to remember what this might have been. "Probably it was about the rat poison."

And with that, we hit a whole new unbelievable level of insanity.

"What," I said.

"I need my dog back," Jay said, calm as always, but a little more urgent around the eyes. "She is all that's left of the life I should be leading right now."

"So you fed her rat poison. Right, that makes sense."

"The interesting thing about rat poison," said Jay confidingly, leaning in toward me, "or at least, certain kinds of rat poisons, the kind I'm familiar with, is that they take a while to work."

"You haven't been near the dog for a day and a half. You couldn't have poisoned her," I said, feeling a rising certainty that somehow, he had poisoned her. Why the fuck would he poison her when he wanted her back so badly?

He continued calmly, as if I hadn't interjected. "If an animal, let's say a dog, eats rat poison, they don't get sick right away. It takes a while before they're even symptomatic. The way it works is, the poison prevents blood clotting, and so eventually the animal bleeds to death internally. But not right away. It takes a few days."

The booth was bobbing, swaying like a lifeboat on the open sea.

"You poisoned her *again*?" I managed to say.

"Chocolate isn't poison," said Jay in a kindly corrective tone. "I had complete control over that situation. She was never in the slightest danger. This time, there are variables. That's why I was worried when the tracker stopped working. You see how lucky it was that I found you anyhow?"

"You poisoned Cody."

"I think it's only poisoning when it results in death or sickness. Is Cody sick?"

"You're telling me she's about to be sick. And then dead. You're *telling* me that."

"Luckily for us all," said Jay, "there's an antidote."

The booth stopped spinning as I realized this was a mindfuck and not her death sentence.

"Let me guess," I said. "Hydrogen peroxide again? That's so *unoriginal*."

He grimaced. "We're long past hydrogen peroxide. Unless she'd puked it up within an hour, she needs massive doses of vitamin K. Which I have, and you don't."

I stared at him, appalled. "You made her sick on the grounds that only you could make her better? You poisoned her in order to quote-unquote *save* her? *Twice* now? That's *twisted*."

"I neither poisoned her nor saved her with the chocolate cake," he insisted gently. "She would have felt bad for a while, but she'd have gotten over it on her own. That gambit was entirely to win your trust."

"Bollocks," I muttered under my breath.

"Well, it worked," he pointed out. "This is a little different. This time, yes, she *needs* the antidote."

"I can get vitamin K," I said. "I can find a vet and get some."

"In a strange city at eight o'clock at night?"

"There have to be emergency vet services," I said.

"The window is closing. She needs an injection as soon as possible followed by massive oral doses."

"You're full of shite. You never poisoned her. Why the fuck would you poison her? You're bluffing."

He looked briefly affronted by this suggestion. Then he said, all business, "If you think I'm bluffing, then you should *not* give her vitamin K. Because the amount of vitamin K she'd need to save her life if she *has* been poisoned will probably kill her from blood clots if she *hasn't* been poisoned. How about that? And I'm the only one who knows if she's been poisoned or not, so don't make me unhappy."

This was not happening. This was not happening. This was not happening. What kind of . . . "You're bluffing," I said again, now uncertain. "It's all a bluff. She's fine. She doesn't need any vitamin K, so I won't be giving her any, and I won't be giving her to you."

He grimaced, looking sad. "If you want to risk taking that position, I can't force you to believe me, but it will be quite distressing to *all* of us when she dies."

"How could you do that to her?" I said, furiously. "How could you do that to a creature you love? What do you *gain* from it?"

He did not quite meet my look. "Leverage," he said. "If she'd gone with me at the clubhouse, there'd have been no problem. I had hydrogen peroxide waiting in the car, I'd have just made her throw up right away. Then she'd be fine and we'd be on our way back to Boston. In fact, we'd be home by now."

"And what were you planning if she *didn't* pick you?" I demanded.

"Exactly this," he said, gesturing to our booth. "This chat we're having now, which ends with your giving me the dog so I can give her the antidote. Although I hoped you might join me for a drink first." He gave me an invitational look. "Perhaps?"

I scowled.

He shrugged. "Ah, well." And back to business: "Look, I gave Sara the choice. Cody alive or Cody dead. She chose Cody alive."

"This is *mental*."

"She'd rather have Cody alive and not with her than to have Cody dead. I think that's a commendable decision. Solomonic, in fact. In fact it's the *only* good decision she's made in the last year and a half."

"I can find the vitamin K," I said. I could not believe this was happening. "I'll find an emergency vet clinic—right now—" I began to rise. Jay calmly reached out and tugged the sleeve of my sweatshirt, stopping me.

"As you pointed out," he said, "there is the slight possibility that I am bluffing, in which case you'd be murdering Cody." Mock-apologetic smile. "That's the point of this exercise. Sara grasped that faster than you did. It was a difficult choice, but she made it. Give me my dog."

With a shock, I realized I could win this game. But I was so pissed off at him that now I knew I was on top of things, I wanted to play as much as he did. "What if I *don't*?" I said.

"She'll die," he said. "Unless I'm bluffing, but no way to know for sure until it's too late, is there? Assuming I'm not bluffing, she'll die."

I shrugged. "Then what?"

He blinked. He had not been expecting that. Good. "She will die a painful and prolonged death," he said sternly.

"Hmm," I said. "That's a shame. Then what?"

He stared at me, annoyed. "Then she's dead. And her blood is on your hands."

"Not yours? You're the one who poisoned her but you're not responsible for her death?"

"If you'd like to debate the moral quandary, I'd be happy to," said Jay, sounding tense. "But meanwhile she will have *died*."

"Right, let's go back to that part. Cody dies. Then what?"

He stared at me. "Then . . . Cody is dead."

"Right. And then what?" I asked again, ever so fucking politely, cupping my hand around my ear. "Sorry, can't hear you, so much ambient noise in this place."

He was getting angry. "Rory, it's not your choice to make, it's not your dog. Sara has given you instructions to turn Cody over to me. I'm sorry I had to resort to such banal manipulation but neither of you was being reasonable about this."

"All right, listen," I said, ignoring that last preposterous statement. "Here's the thing. Sara's every bit as stubborn as you are, and as long as Cody is alive, she'll try to get Cody back. And so this nonsense will continue—my wife will be obsessed with her ex-lover *as well as* her ex-dog, and that's not a situation I'm interested in."

"Meaning?" said Jay, uncertainty creeping into his voice.

"That frankly, of all possible outcomes, Cody dying is really the thing that's in my best interest. In the big picture. You did something inexcusably horrible. And I'm benefiting from it. So thank you for poisoning her. I owe you one. And since she'll be dead, could you please back the fuck off and stop tailing me across America?"

He stared at me. With alarm.

"You're going to let her die," he said, in a small, disturbed voice.

"No, *you're* going to let her die because you're not going to give me the vitamin K," I said.

"You think I'm joking," he said, repressing anger. "She really will die if you don't do the right thing."

"She really will die if *you* don't do the right thing," I corrected him.

Somehow during this standoff, the food had arrived, and the drinks, too, but neither of us had noticed. "Sara will never forgive you," he warned. That was the thing he was counting on: that I'd do whatever Sara said, even if Sara wasn't thinking clearly. I could sense something inside of him approaching panic. Until that moment I thought he must be bluffing about the rat poison. Now I wasn't sure.

"I can handle Sara," I said. "The only thing I can't handle is being tailed, so you've got to stop, mate, or I am going to hit you with a hammer. Okay? The dog will be dead, so there's no reason to chase me."

Long pause. He was horrified.

"So," I concluded. "Unless there's anything else, I'll head back to my room to get some sleep. Thanks again about the rat poison. Enjoy your margarita and safe travels back to Boston." I pulled a twenty out of my pocket, slapped it on the table with a victorious smile at Jay, turned, and walked out of the restaurant.

Chapter 28

My hands were shaking as I opened the restaurant door. The cold wind pushed me through the dusk, along the sidewalk, back toward the hotel.

My phone rang. That didn't take long—Jay must have called Sara before I was even out of the building. "Sara love," I said into the phone, lighthearted for the first time in days.

"What are you doing, Rory?" she said, nearly frantic. "Go back inside and tell him you'll give her to him."

"Remember back in Boston how I used to feed her fish and chips?" I said.

The briefest pause. "What?"

"Fish and chips."

"You never did that, what does that have to do with anything? What are you doing? Just give her to him."

"Right, I never did that because fried food makes her sick."

"So? Rory, are you listening to me? Go back to Jay!"

"You know what I did in North Carolina, as soon as she was in my car? Eejit that I am, I bought her a whole bag of chips, and she wolfed them down and then she puked her little guts out right away."

Silence. Then the penny dropped, and I heard a gasp. "Really?"

"Same as that," I said, grinning. "According to Jay, if she expelled it within the first hour, she should be fine."

"Oh my God," she said, "I've never been so grateful to you for not listening to me! Did you tell him?"

"No." I laughed. "He's completely freaked out right now."

"But that means he'll keep following you."

"I don't care," I said. "Honestly I don't give a shite what he does. I don't think he'd stop following me now anyhow, the bloke's completely mental, Sara, he's out of control. If he really did poison her, he deserves to stew in it a while. And I'm too wired up now to sleep, I'm going to keep driving for a while. I'll call you in a bit and we'll figure out where I can stop next. Love you." Wow, I could feel the adrenaline coursing through me, and it felt *great*.

I was back in the car park by now, walking in big, determined strides, master of my universe for the first time in days. I unlocked the car remotely and opened the hotel room door.

Cody was waiting for me. I pushed the door inward and immediately she was ready to jump up on me. I pushed her off. She swooned into tarty dog. "Get up," I said. "Cody, get up. Where's your leash? We're going."

I briefly contemplated staying the night to rest, but—although I still needed a bite to eat—I felt better than I had in days, and I wasn't likely to sleep well in a strange room anyhow, so I might as well get more miles behind me. Jay must have been getting worn down as much as me. Even if he insisted on following me, he'd be fading. But he had to be out of tricks now, right? He'd put the tracker on back in Boston, and he'd come up with the rat-poison gambit in North Carolina. Anything else now would require starting from scratch. He seemed like a man who liked his creature comforts, so hopefully, even if he was off-kilter enough to keep pursuing this, he'd go back to Boston first to regroup. We'd be in L.A. by the time he could try anything new. If he had actually fed her rat poison, he'd assume that she was dead. And he'd deserve whatever grief he felt for it.

As I mused on all of this, my hands were working almost of their own accord. I packed up my rucksack, grabbed Cody's food, her bowl . . . I clipped her lead to her collar. She was very excited that something exciting was happening, hopping around the room, straining at the leash, her gaze glued to my face for clues about our exciting new adventure. Her tail, as always, was wagging half the rest of her body. She looked *really* alert. Probably thought food would be involved.

Took me just a few minutes to get out the door. I tossed my backpack onto her bed, signaled her onto the passenger seat, closed her door, moved around to slide into my seat, glanced in my rearview mirror. In the lights of the parking lot I saw Jay, his long straight coat slapping awkwardly against his legs in the wind, walking briskly toward the Lexus, which somehow I hadn't noticed earlier. He got in and started the engine. Oh, for fuck's sake, he was going to keep tailing me. Leave behind whatever he had at the hotel and just drive. The *wanker*! He didn't seem the type to get violent, but it would be really aggravating to have him on my arse. Tulsa was the first city I'd hit that was on Sara's original map, so from here out, I had some idea where I was going—once I got back to Interstate Highway 40, there'd be little opportunity to get away from him.

Car had a full tank. Dog was fed, although sadly I wasn't, but I could probably remedy that soon. I pushed the car to ninety, hopefully it wasn't low on oil. I could probably drive three or four hours before refueling. I glanced over my shoulder to see if he was coming, but there were too many cars, too many headlights, to have a clue. I was pissed off, but resigned, not panicked: if he wanted to follow me, then let him, I'd just have to be on guard.

But I really did not want him to follow me.

I called Sara. "Go ahead and tell him," I said. "You're right, I don't want to give him an actual *reason* to feel justified to follow me."

"I'm on it," she said.

Tulsa ended as abruptly as it had begun, and I was immediately back in rural territory, two lanes in each direction with a grass meridian and intermittent sprawl. The treetops cha-cha'd recklessly in the wind, while a rising full moon looked on as cool and placid and immovable as Jay on his boulder throne back on Peters Hill. Maybe the full moon accounted for his lunacy.

Sara called back. "I should have predicted this," she said, "but he says he thinks you're lying and that Cody's only chance of survival is if he hunts you down and gets her away from you."

I kept myself from screaming while I had Sara on the phone, but I did let rip an irritated, throaty *aaaaarrgh*.

"Sorry. I tried," she said. "Maybe if you'd told him in the restaurant—"

"Well, I didn't," I said sharply. "It's my fault, I get it. Thanks for trying." Heavy sigh. Really pissed with myself and him now. "All right, I'll call again in a bit and you can tell me what we've got for hotel options."

The angled moonlight limited what I could make out, but the

woods here seemed less dense, scrubbier than before, with the horizons a little farther away, and the lanes of each road maybe a handspan wider than before. There were dozens of cars in the few hundred yards behind me; I'd never know if one them was his until he was right on top of me.

"Fuuuuuuuck!" I screamed into the ceiling, so aggravated that my body stiffened straight with early-onset rigor mortis. My arms shook from clenching the wheel and my right foot floored the accelerator. The car whined and then shifted into a higher gear. Cody very tentatively tried to lick my cheek with one of her Little Match Girl kisses.

"Stay away from me!" I barked at her. Startled, she sat down abruptly on the passenger seat, huddling against the back. "Do you know how *insane* my life is right now, Cody?" I demanded. "Do you know *why* it's insane? It's insane because of *you*, Cody. You bring out the *crazy* in people."

I turned on the radio and was surprised to find a classic rock station, which helped me to stop obsessing on what I couldn't see in the rearview mirror. Alto called to check in on behalf of everyone. For simplicity's sake, and because I could not have told him the truth without mocking the very words coming out of my own mouth, I just told him we were grand and all was quiet on the Western Front. I really hoped he'd take his newfound organizational skills and apply them to something more meaningful than a pet abduction.

I'd gotten back on Highway 40, which looked like Highway 40 everywhere else. Of course, judging all of Oklahoma by what was near the federal interstate was like judging Ireland by what was near the Galway Road. Authentic culture lay elsewhere. I passed a sign for Oklahoma City limits, and absolutely nothing changed—I could have been on a freeway in New York State. I drove miles seeing no change at all, just lush acres of frenetically waving treetops, a sickly hue in the road lights. A road sign said that downtown was twenty-one miles away. So different from Tulsa, which had sprung up immediately out of the earth. A few minutes later, I saw a single tall building on the horizon, night-lit, promising that there was in fact a city up ahead. Moments later I zoomed by trailer parks on both sides of the road, well lit and neat, and then the start, very gradually, of urban sprawl.

The phone binged at me. Sara.

"Where are you?" she said anxiously. "I thought you'd call back by now."

"Sorry, I'm sorry," I said, " I was focused on getting on the road—"

"Are you driving now?"

"Yes," I said.

"You'll need to stop to rest—"

"Not right now I don't," I said. "I'm wired. I just want to push on through so I can throw my arms around my sweet girl as soon as possible."

"Your sweet girl wants that, too, but you're on an adrenaline high and you'll crash soon," she said. What a mood wrecker. "So promise me when that happens, you'll pull over onto a service road and nap in the car. If you can do that without his seeing you, maybe he'll pull past you on the road and you'll end up behind him."

"We still on for the Grand Canyon?" I asked.

"Of course," she said. "But let's get you safely to morning first.

If you won't stop in Oklahoma City, then you're heading off into a whole lot of nothing. You'll probably hit Amarillo a little after midnight."

"Fuck that," I said. "I'm up for hours now. What's after that?"

She wasn't happy about this. "If you will please stop for a nap along the way, I think you'll arrive in Albuquerque around dawn. I'll find you a hotel there and you can take a breather, get some proper sleep. There's really no reason for you to push yourself so hard. I know it's probably creepy having him on your tail—"

"It's not *creepy*, it's fucking *irritating* is what it is."

"I get it, it's *unpleasant*," she said. "But don't let that push you beyond what's safe, okay? I'd rather wait a day to see you and know that you'll be in good shape. Are you sure you won't stop in Amarillo?"

"Text me the Albuquerque address and I'll talk to you tomorrow. Love you."

"Please drive safe. Everyone I love is in that car."

Oklahoma City—at least from what I could see, at night—was hardly a city, really, just the one skyscraper and a handful of other tallish buildings. I passed it in a moment and drove on.

I'D ALWAYS HEARD Texas was like another country, and sure enough, as soon as we crossed that border, there were changes. The landscape became *western-looking,* the outline of mini-buttes and canyons-in-training here and there. But more than that, the vegetation immediately shortened and flattened, enough that I could tell the difference even in the moonlight.

We drove by a large stockyard with thousands of head of cattle.

And then a meat processing plant. And then empty silence. A while later, a wind farm, the huge turbines making skeletal silhouettes in the moonlight. Otherwise, nothing. For an hour, easy. Just highway and moonlight and open plain, and too much time to think. About all sorts of things.

Or just the one thing, obsessively.

In the monotonous tension of the nightscape drive, the one fact that now became swelled to take up my entire cranium . . . was that they had been lovers.

I could imagine them on a domestic level, no problem. Could imagine the harmonies and discords, how orderly their place would be, how organized, and highbrow, but then again the tension of two deliberate, strategic thinkers, one always trying to control the other, one always trying to evade control. That was all as clear as the subtext in a Chekhov play. I could even see their bathroom in all its tasteful his-and-her-ness. All of that was some other reality that she had decided to leave, and with me she'd found her other half, not a warped reflection of herself as he had been, but a complementary partner like the Chinese symbol with the two fish. None of that distressed me.

What distressed me, naturally, was the sex.

Because I'm a man. And men are horny little pigs, and tend to think about sex a lot. Especially when we're in a new-ish relationship with a gorgeous bird who really makes us step onto the pitch and try to be our best self. As Sara always did. I'm a gentleman, or try to be, and as I've said, the Irish are a shy race underneath all the bluster, so I've spared you all the times I've thought about sex and Sara in the same beat. But believe me: it's loads. The curve of her hip, the weight of her breast in my cupped hand, the scent of her hair, the place on my leg where her feet pressed against me when we were making love.

And I knew how she made love. Not just with my mind and heart did I know that, I knew it with my body. So imagine me, with my mind and heart and body, stuck all alone together in a car with hundreds of miles of prairie and nothing to do but obsess on how some other man—*that* other man specifically—could know her just as well as I did. With florid detail and abandon, I began to imagine them together, and then stopped myself in disgust, and then started again, with some variation on the theme, seeking some obstacle I could live with, something that kept their intimacy from being as pure as ours—maybe he always took her from behind, or made her keep her eyes closed.

That only made it worse, because then the terror of imagining them happy was replaced by the rage of imagining her bullied and coerced by him, and soon my palms were sweating and I was grinding my teeth and panting and ready to kill the bastard for acts only ever perpetrated between my ears and at my own direction. In my imagination I was beating the crap out of Jay with the glorious knowledge that the greater my violence, the greater my virtue.

I was shaken from this righteous vengeance by the dog, awakened, yawning loudly behind my head from the backseat. I started in surprise. She was uninterested in the vengeance I was wreaking for her owner's sake. She plopped her chin down on my shoulder and sighed, as if to ask when we could change the channel because this moonlit-plains show was getting really dull.

My kneejerk reaction was that of a father when his kid walks in on him while he's watching porn. Really. I was embarrassed, same as that. I was so relieved when she yawned again: she hadn't noticed what I was up to! She hadn't witnessed any of my dirty thoughts. The horrible nasty secrets that actually defined my character, that I was lecherous, and insecure, and jealous, and capable of violence. That I could hate. She had figured out none of this. I'd fooled her. Ha! I was still Rory the Hero, the soundest bloke west of the Atlantic, and she adored me no matter what evil I got up to between my ears. Dogs are pretty good that way.

"Want a treat?" I offered.

'Course she did.

As SARA HAD predicted, I found my eyes getting droopy, so I exited onto the service road, and then the shoulder of the service road, and napped as best I could under the circumstances: I was in a ridiculously small car, so full to the gills that my seat could not recline. The only emergency Sara had not packed for was camping out, so there were no blankets or cushions, and anyhow it was too chilly outside to fall asleep there. But for a few restless hours, with the door locked and Cody sometimes snoring beside me, I was able to get a bit of a kip, full of dreams involving highways or dogs or Jay trying to cop a feel from Sara. Jay either passed by without my knowing it, or had given up the chase—there was no sign of him at all. Eventually the moon was so high and bright, it made it impossible even to doze, so I slapped myself awake and pulled back onto Highway 40. From here to Albuquerque, it would just be an awful, boring nighttime slog.

I saw a sign for Elk City, checked the gauge, and refueled at a small all-night station off the interstate. I got a coffee but all the so-called food was too disgusting to consider eating. Here's good news, though: no sign of Mr. Baldy.

In the moonlight, everything looked like flat-out desert. That had happened so suddenly! Somehow between Tulsa and here, I'd hit the Old West, real Lyle Lovett country, but it had happened after sundown and before the moon was high enough to see by. The wide expanses were now filled with unfamiliar shapes that I imagined to be all the exotic western-sounding plants I associated with the American West: hickory, sage, mesquite, prickly pear, Joshua trees, yucca plants. Not that I'd know any of them on sight, but I liked the names.

Cody turned restlessly on her bed, sighed, sulked, started to eat a bully stick, tossed it dismissively into the seat beside me, thought better of it, worked her way carefully forward to retrieve the bully stick, disappeared into the back again, finished eating it, drank water, sighed tragically again, and then yawned—which might mean she was queasy.

"Don't throw up," I begged.

She was delighted that I was speaking to her again. Immediately she inched forward on her belly, like a mobile Sphinx, and proceeded to try to get my attention by rubbing the side of her head against my upper arm. I could see in my peripheral vision that she was looking up at me endearingly.

"Whatever you want, you're not getting it," I said. I had a sinking feeling that I hadn't fed her lately . . . oh, yes I had, right before my own aborted dinner with Jay. *I* was the one who hadn't eaten.

ON WE DROVE, for hours. We passed Amarillo, where Sara had wanted me to stop, and drove hours more, and finally entered New Mexico. Georgia O'Keeffe territory (a good Irish name, O'Keeffe). For the O'Keeffe collection at the MFA, Sara had pushed me to play Aaron Copland's *Billy the Kid* (Billy the Kid: son of Irish immigrants). But O'Keeffe herself had actually preferred classical, so I'd also played some Bach. I wish I had some Bach to play now, or if not Bach, Van Morrison.

Outside a place called Tucumcari, I saw a station with a sprawling minimart attached and pulled in to refuel. It must have been about four in the morning. Eyes so bloodshot you could've navigated by them. Under the awful fluorescent lights of the canopy, I filled the tank, and went inside to pay the bloke. I could've used the ATM at the pump, but I like to do business with other human beings whenever possible, because I'm personable that way. While I was in there, I used the toilet and grabbed a coffee and some Snickers bars, which were the healthiest things in the place.

Then I came back out into the cool, windy night, wishing I'd thought to buy some face cream.

And there was the white Lexus SUV, stopped right behind the MINI.

Chapter 29

I shoved the Snickers bars into the pocket of my sweatshirt but dropped the coffee in the process, felt a few scalding drops splatter at my ankles as I marched back toward the car.

"Hello there," said Jay, reaching for the nozzle on the pump behind mine. He smiled in a neighborly way, as if we were casual acquaintances who routinely exchanged greetings at this very petrol station. He was wearing a lighter version of his long dark arboretum coat. His sleek bald head was bare.

I looked through the MINI's windows. Cody was still there. She was bored, of course. But the sudden movement of my head outside made her look up. Then she noticed Jay, stood and peered out the back window at him. I could see her tail wagging as she recognized him.

"Hello, Cody," he called, and waved at her.

"What are you doing here?" I said.

He gestured as if it should be obvious. "Getting gas."

"I mean how did you *get* here?"

He repeated the look, more exaggerated. "I drove. I followed you. No tricks this time, I simply tailed you."

"I was ahead of you," I said, aggravated. "I was *way* ahead of you, and then I pulled *over*. For *hours*. Anyhow I told you to back off."

He calmly shook his head. "I'm not backing off while you have my dog. How callow of you to think I would. I was directly behind you most of the time, except when you pulled off onto the service road. Then I waited at the next on-ramp with my lights off. You drove right past me getting back on 40 and I've been tailing you since then. When you stopped for gas in Elk City, I waited on the edge of the parking lot and just kept tailing you. One great thing about a hybrid with a big tank, you hardly ever need to refuel."

"Surprised you didn't break into my car and just *take* her while I was inside," I said angrily, embarrassed I'd been such an easy mark.

He smiled pleasantly enough. "Breaking into somebody's car is against the law. I can manage to get my own dog back without breaking the law."

"She's *not* your dog! You know, Jay, you seemed like a pretty sound bloke back in Boston, but this behavior, man, I tell you, it's *demented*. No offense, but if you were family, I'd be calling a head doctor about you. And that's saying something coming from an Irishman."

"I have not been behaving aboveboard, I confess," said Jay.

I spat out a laugh. "Ha! Understatement!"

He hesitated a moment—a real hesitation, not a pause for effect. Maybe for the first time he was about to say something that wasn't rehearsed. "Rory, I know you can't believe I've gone to such extremes over a dog."

"Again, understatement."

"I'd like to explain why. Straight up. I suggested we do that over coffee back in Boston, and I'd still like to do it now." He gave me an inviting, questioning look, like when he'd wanted me to drink with him in Tulsa.

"If it means you'll stop tailing me, I'm all ears. But I have to take Cody out. No funny business."

"No funny business," he said, holding his hands up as if to demonstrate he was unarmed. "I'll finish gassing up here, and when I join you I'll stay at least five feet away from you both."

"You better," I warned. As if his word meant anything.

The ground around the edges of the paved area was dust. I don't mean dusty, I mean *dust*—you could scoop it up like dirty flour. I opened the car, pocketed the Swiss Army knife Sara had left below the console, and put Cody on her lead. She fairly flew out of the car, and without remembering Jay was there, or bothering to thank me for springing her, began to sniff along the outer edge of the pavement where the canopy light just barely lit things, until she came upon a clump of weeds, where she peed. Then, looking chuffed with herself, she trotted off into the scraggly bushes growing in the dust . . . but stopped suddenly, after three strides, beside an evergreen bush. The ground around it was littered with juniper-looking berries, which I recognized from the design on gin bottles, so I concluded it was a juniper bush.

"Come on," I said, tugging at the lead.

Cody gave me a beseeching stare. She raised one of her front paws like a hunting dog on point, but the rest of her posture was sagging and sad, as if she were suddenly exhausted.

"Cody, what's wrong?" I asked, more irritated than concerned.

"She's got a bur stuck in her paw," said Jay, approaching from the pumps. He stopped well short of us, hands slightly raised to show he was behaving. "In this part of the country there are little burs all over the ground this time of year. Look at her paws, I bet you'll find some stuck into the pads."

I stared at him.

"If you don't want to help her, will you at least allow me to?" he asked, impatiently.

"Your idea of taking care of her is pretty questionable. Rat poison?"

Cody, still beseeching, was looking back and forth between us. She glanced down at her paw, then back at us.

"Just pull the burs out, would you *please,* Rory." If he had sounded contemptuous, I would've felt justified in belting him, but his tone was urgent, like a concerned dad.

I turned back to Cody, knelt down, and examined her foot. The light here was crap, but yes, there was a hard, tiny bur stuck to her paw, and several more buried down between her toes. I began to pull them out. She jerked her nose up several times, as if it hurt but she was trying to be stoic. I released that foot and tugged on the other one. There were half a dozen more burs here. Tiny, but hard and nasty, with points like needles.

"You said you had something to say. Say it."

He took a deep breath, stood straight and regal, plunged his hands into his pockets, and spoke. His tone was the wistful dignity of the king of Peters Hill. "I need my dog back. It's that simple. I've run out of schemes, so I'm just asking you outright—begging, if I must—and I'm sorry for the trouble I've caused by not doing that earlier. This might sound at first like an unreasonable request, but I'm not an idiot, and I wouldn't ask unless I felt there was a reason—a genuine reason—for you to say yes."

"You misjudged, then," I said, pulling at the burs, which wasn't easy because they pricked me in removing them. "No fucking way will I say yes."

"You haven't heard me out yet. I'm not just asking for my own interest. I want to explain why it's best for Cody—and also best for *you*."

I wondered what medication he was forgetting to take. "Gotta hear this, don't we, Cody?" I said to her as I continued to ease the burs out of her paw. "Go ahead, then, mate. Give us your best pitch."

He crossed his arms over his chest, in classic listen-to-me-I'm-an-expert position. "First let me explain why it's best for Cody. Dogs like routine and familiarity. For Cody that means going back to Boston," he said. "Jamaica Plain. Going for her daily walks in the arboretum, the turn of the seasons, the dogs and people she knows on Peters Hill. What the hell kind of life will it be for a New England dog, living in Los Angeles? It would be one thing if you were living in the canyons, or Malibu, but I'm guessing you're just renting an apartment in the Valley or something, right? Do you know how miserably hot it gets in the Valley? And Sara will probably be working someplace new, so Cody will be left all alone in a strange little apartment all day, and then maybe get a quick walk in some playground on the leash. What kind of a life is that? If Sara cared about Cody's well-being, she wouldn't subject her to that."

I wasn't all that interested in the quality of Cody's life (bliss compared to most *people's,* in fairness) but I was struck by how much he'd thought this out and how strongly he felt about it. In my mind, this ridiculous chase had become about Jay wanting to win just for the sake of winning—to me, that was the only sensible explanation for his obsessiveness. But he was genuinely pre-occupied with the dog's well-being. In a way I wasn't. In a way I couldn't even contemplate.

He must have seen something on my face, in my expression, because he took a step closer. "Rory." He lowered his voice. "It's not your fault that your good fortune is so disruptive to Cody, but it *is* disruptive. She's had a very good life with almost no stress. Except for Sara's taking her away from our home, of course. But she's coddled, you know it yourself."

Yes, I did. I would never say it, but I s'pose he could read it in my face, my body language, because he kept right on:

"And that's why it's also better for *you* if she's not with you in L.A. She will not be good at handling stress. If you already find her needy, and you already feel that Sara coddles her, trust me: when you get to L.A., she'll be even needier and Sara will coddle her even more."

That was probably true.

"And you'll resent it and it will cause tension, which Cody will sense, which will make her more clingy, which will make Sara coddle her more, and it will be a vicious cycle that won't be good for any of you."

For somebody who'd never lived with the three of us, he had pretty much nailed the worst-case scenario. I focused on the burs.

"It's a domestic meltdown waiting to happen," he continued, calm and parental, about to offer a wonderful solution. He squatted down to be closer to us. I focused on that final paw. Seven burs. "Unless I take her back to Boston. Sara never needs to know you gave her up willingly. Let her think I tricked you. She already knows I'm capable of that."

"Fuck off," I said.

"I didn't mean that as an insult," he said quickly. "I apologize if it sounded like that. Really. But please consider this. In Boston she'd be in a nice roomy home she's seen before, full of furniture from her early days. She'll spend every day in her park, with her original owner and her friends and her climate and her seasons. So she'll be fine. And so will you. You can get a rescue dog or buy a puppy, you and Sara together, and you can raise it together and then it will be something that bonds you instead of causing strain between you."

I said nothing. I had run out of burs and wished I had something else to focus my attention on. I began to look for burs in her tail. He'd struck such a nerve, although no way would I ever give him the satisfaction of admitting it. Of course I knew Cody would be gone someday, and then Sara and I could get a new dog—together. With ground rules that *I* had a say in. I had imagined that very thing, it's true. Sometimes in moments I'm not proud of, I'd even had flashing fantasies of some painless, quick, inexpensive Mystery Doggie Illness expediting things a bit. And here was Jay offering to do the job, guilt-free. If only he wasn't an utter gobshite.

"I didn't really give her rat poison, Rory," he said gently, as if he were following my thoughts. "Letting her eat the chocolate cake was awful enough."

"Come on, Cody," I said, and stood up. Jay stood, too.

"Please be decent enough to acknowledge that you hear what I'm saying. Your marriage would be so much easier without this particular dog in it."

Yes. It would. Fuck him.

"Come on, Cody, back to the car."

"Let me pet her," he said, hurriedly, urgently. He took an impulsive step toward us. I went rigid and held a warning hand up, and he stepped back, tried to collect himself. "Please, Rory. I just want to be near her a moment. For God's sake, it won't cost you anything to be compassionate."

"I don't think so, Jay." Hate to admit it, but I felt guilty for denying him, he was so . . . plaintive. Now it seemed obvious he would never have given her rat poison—and in fact, somewhat hysterical of Sara to believe he had. Sara's relationship with this dog really did bring out the worst in her, from every possible angle.

He closed his eyes a moment, I swear to God as if he were blinking back tears. "I wish you'd consider this. You're always *accommodating* her, I saw that clearly back in the arboretum. No relationship with a pet should be like that, for you *or* them. You're living with a dog you like just fine, but you *resent*. You'll just end up resenting her more out there. You'd be grateful to be relieved of her, as long as she's in good hands, you just don't want Sara angry at you. We both know that. I'm offering you an out, and you're not taking it."

"Let's go, Cody," I said, tugging the leash toward the car and really wanting to slam Jay's head against the pavement because he was getting through to a part of me that I'd been trying very hard to ignore for months now.

He stepped around in front of me to block my path; I stopped short and glared at him. Quickly, he took a step back. "Five feet," he said, "I'm giving you five feet, like I promised. Look, Rory, I'm not trying to hold her for ransom. I'm not going to sell her on the black market. For God's sake, I just *want my dog back*." I broke eye contact, looked straight at the pavement, so uncomfortable. Like she was his *child* or something. "My measure of contentment is my dog curled up asleep by my chair. *Your* measure of contentment is not having that same dog constantly in your face. The only thing keeping both of us from what we want is Sara getting what *she* wants—even if what Sara wants isn't actually good for Cody. Even if it's not good for your relationship."

"Our relationship is fine."

"It would be better, easier, without this dog," he said with quiet certitude. "If you hand me that leash, Rory, everything changes for the better, for all four of us. I admit you'll have a rough patch with Sara but she'll get over it."

"You should talk! You're the poster child for not getting over the loss of a dog."

"Fair enough. So surely by now you have some understanding of how much this means to me."

The weird thing is, I did. If I'd heard somebody else describe this ludicrous scenario, I'd have laughed it off, but I saw his eyes and I heard his voice, and he was hurting terribly. It wasn't just his ego, or his pride, it really was his heart. Fuck me if I could make sense of it, but even without making sense of it, I could still tell that it was real.

"What do you gain by denying me this?" he asked.

"I avoid breaking my wife's heart."

"Get another dog," he said, taking a step closer to me.

"*You* get another dog," I retorted.

"I could do that," he said. "But then everything I've said about Los Angeles will happen. That's bad for Cody *and* bad for your marriage."

"Sara will just try to get her back," I argued. Jesus, I was *debat-*

ing him . . . that meant some part of me was taking the bastard seriously. "It will be a repeat of what's just happened."

"No, it won't," he said immediately. "Because I'll be as plain-spoken and direct with her as I'm being with you now. I'll explain how it's for Cody's benefit, and after she gets over her hysteria, she'll hear me. She'll take it on board. Not if it comes from you, but if it comes from me."

"Why you?" I scoffed.

"Because I know how to make her feel guilty," he said simply. "I'm something of an expert at it."

I was so shocked by this admission that I couldn't speak, just gaped at him a moment. But he was right about Sara. She would make Cody's happiness a priority over her own because as smart and savvy a woman as she was, Sara was utterly mental when it came to the dog.

But I wasn't.

"Tell you what," I said. "Let's ring Sara right now and talk about this. You seem to be good at convincing her of things. If you can convince her now, the dog's all yours."

His face fell. Not the response he'd wanted from me. "That's not the way to make this work."

"It's the only way to make it work," I said, "Because even if I agree with you one hundred percent, it's not my decision to make. I promised Sara I'd return her dog to her, and I keep my promises to people I love even if I don't always want to. So that's what I'm going to do now. Cody, let's go." I turned my back on him and tugged at her leash until she followed me. Back at the car I opened the door. "Get in the back," I said firmly.

With an accusing look, she climbed back to her bed. I got in myself, then closed the door, took a moment to calm myself. It was stuffy, so I opened the window a little.

Jay approached us slowly and calmly, as if we hadn't just had that conversation. He waved to Cody through the window on the driver's side. She leaned across me to see him better. His sad smile was genuine, and so was her eagerness to see him. Why couldn't she realize he was a wanker? Weren't dogs supposed to have some tribal loyalty? Even if she sensed the upset (Sara once said dogs could smell emotions), Cody had no clue her pack wasn't actually a pack.

"Please, mister, can't I just get out and say hi to my dad?" Cody asked.

Oh, Jesus, for a moment I really thought she'd said that. Her eyes were glued to Jay and her tail was wagging tentatively.

"Fuck off," I said to her.

She looked at me, tail still wagging, hoping maybe she would get a treat with that.

With an aggravated sigh I turned away from her, out the driver-seat window, right at Jay, who was bending over to peer in. His expression had changed from plaintive to stern. "Do you understand how cruel you're being?" he asked in a warning tone. "Cruel and foolish. You're going to ruin everything for all of us. That's unforgivably foolish. You should change your mind, or be prepared to live with regret."

I rolled up my window.

"I'll see you in Alburquerque," Jay said, overenunciating to make sure I understood him with the window closed. And a final warning: *"Change your mind."*

I ignored him. Took a deep breath. Found, from Sara's well-supplied pack, the hand lotion, and used it on my face. Drank water, but not too much. Refilled Cody's water dish. I gave her another bully stick, which she accepted but then tossed down onto her bed in the backseat, climbing back there herself to look wistfully out the back window at Jay, who had moved round to the Lexus. He waved to her again. She looked excitedly at me, still hoping for permission to get back out of the car. I couldn't even remember when she'd last had exercise. Oh, wait . . . it was early this morning. Back in Memphis. No, it was actually after Memphis, right? It was all blurring together. I pulled my seat belt back into position. Jay, seeing the movement, got into the SUV. The wanker was going to tail me all the way to Cali-fucking-fornia. Classic example of the dangers of early retirement.

I wanted to burn rubber and tear out of there, but there was no point in racing away from him into the night. There was only one road. I'm impulsive (as we've seen) and a bit hotheaded (ditto), and I wanted to mess with him—drive in spirals to make him accidentally smash into a wall or something. But the MINI actually had a pretty crap turning radius; its main asset was that it was cute. Frankly, it was imbecilic to be driving it cross-country. We really should have just flown, together, and put the dog in cargo. If Sara had just been willing to do what most pet owners did regularly whenever they traveled, none of this would be happening right now. All of this should have been avoidable. It all came down to Sara coddling the dog. Which she would soon be doing more than ever.

I let out a loud growling sigh of frustration, which brought Cody to the front seat, offering to lick my face. I pushed her away and called Sara even though it was probably midnight where she was.

"Hello?" She sounded as if I'd woken her from a deep slumber.

"Sorry, love, it's me," I said.

"What time is it?" she muttered, then before I could answer, "It's three thirty A.M. here. What's wrong?"

"Oh, crap, sorry, I get confused about the time. I wouldn't be calling except I don't think I should stop in Albuquerque, I want to push on to whatever's next. Flagstaff?"

"*What?*" she said. "Rory, you've been driving nonstop since *Memphis.*"

"I stopped in Tulsa."

"Long enough to squabble with Jay. You've been on the road for nearly twenty hours. Where are you now?"

"Tucumcari," I said, "I think that's finally New Mexico. I stopped for a nap back in Oklahoma. Texas is fucking huge. I should have known this would be a bad idea when Connecticut seemed so big."

She sighed. "Just stay in Albuquerque. Please? Get some sleep. Sleep all day and all night before you drive to Flagstaff. You need the rest."

"He's still tailing me," I said. "I'm at a gas station and he's behind me. Five feet away, like. He's not giving up."

"Oh," she said unhappily. "Oh, boy."

"If I stop in Albuquerque, he'll just get a room in the same hotel, and I won't be able to relax because I'll be so pissed off about his being there."

"How will Flagstaff be any better?"

"You're meeting me there, remember? We're going to the Grand Canyon together. I want to be back with you as soon as possible. And so does Cody. I think we three should have some quality time together." For fuck's sake, that sounded so forced and pathetic I expected her to guess what Jay had just been doing to my head.

"Oh," she said affectionately, touched. "But, sweetie, if you're going to be in Flagstaff by the middle of the day, I can't get myself there in time."

"Please just text me the address of a Flagstaff hotel in case I feel up to making the drive."

A pause. "All right. But if you're driving that far, try to find a way to give Cody some exercise."

"Do you not understand what I'm saying?" I said. "He's literally right behind me. I have to keep going. I need exercise as badly as the dog does, but neither of us is getting it. She'll just have to deal with it. Jesus."

"You sound like you need to eat," she said. "You're a little cranky."

"Sara!" I never shouted at her, and I shocked myself. "This isn't a game. He's *serious*. He's dead set on getting her. It's like convoying with Ahab."

"There's nothing he can do as long you have her," Sara said. "He won't do anything violent, he would consider that beneath him. I'll send you the address and let's just keep each other in the loop, okay? Love you."

I finally drove out of the station. Jay followed me. Cody was staring out the window at the dark plains, exactly the same way she'd be staring at them if she were now in Jay's car headed back east. I *hated* myself for wondering if I'd made the wrong decision here, but to be honest, I wondered briefly—but with great intensity—if I'd made the wrong decision.

Chapter 30

I drove on into the night. Behind me, tragic and irritating, and gazed at by the fucking dog out the back window, was Jay. No sense trying to outrun him; that would just make him feel important.

I ate the Snickers bars as I drove and immediately felt even more disgusted with myself. Even Cadbury's—for all the awful childhood associations I had with it—was better than this shite. Drove on for miles and miles more, Jay on my arse, through unchanging, vast, moonlit expanses. The highway went dead straight, and I was on a bit of a height, so I could see it bang on to the horizon, toward the massive full moon. For miles ahead there was nothing at all along Interstate 40. Eventually, a flurry of billboards announced the Flying C Ranch (whatever that was), which, when we finally passed it, looked like a giant gas station. It was surrounded by such a density of juniper bushes that the flat-topped hills beyond seemed forested.

The grey light of dawn was creeping up my backside as relentlessly as Jay, making the world uglier and colorless. We passed Clines Corners (whatever that was), then back to high plains and junipers. My arse was killing me—had been for a while, but I'd been too stressed and distracted to notice the discomfort. Cody sighed, and spent about an hour moving back and forth between the front seat and the back, forever staring at my face for hints about what might come next. I found it a terrible irritant. If she were currently in Jay's car, his whole fucking soul would have welled with love for her while she did that.

CLOSER TO ALBUQUERQUE, Interstate 40 spilled down over one final vast, pale plain. Far ahead rose a lumpy line of mountains, like the worked side of a key. It was a cloudy dawn, but the light kissed the eastern slopes and they were . . . gorgeous. It was the first time anything had looked gorgeous in days. I rolled the window down to let in cold fresh air. Cody leapt to her feet and stuck her nose toward the window, no matter that meant blocking my view. I pushed her away and raised the window again. She sneezed all over me. It was disgusting, as dog sneezes go. Except for the pause in Tulsa and the service-road catnap, I had driven nonstop for a thousand miles, and eaten nothing but three Snickers bars. I don't think I've ever felt so wretched in my life—which is saying something, given my old party days.

Here at last was Albuquerque. Behind me was Jay.

I couldn't stop here. I couldn't risk listening to him anymore. I had to keep going literally into Sara's arms.

Somewhere, the sunlight had changed. It was probably Arkansas or Oklahoma, but who can say, Arkansas had been rainy and I'd driven Oklahoma in the dark. It was a searing light now, the kind of light that triggered the instinct to seek shade, even though it wasn't hot yet.

We skirted Albuquerque. There were no tall buildings, and the mountains rose up around it regally, so that the city was insignificant compared to the landscape, and that was comforting.

Then everything grew flat again. Dullsville.

Sara sent a text with a hotel address, but it wasn't in Flagstaff. *Tusayan,* she wrote. *Closer to GC. Enjoy it for the both of us xx.* I pouted. What was the point of the Grand Canyon if I was going by myself? Or worse yet, saddled with Sara's dog. Especially while Jay trailed along behind us, sighing tragically.

After a good long while of nothing else, I passed the Route 66 Casino, rising up to the south of the highway, random and gratuitous and causing the obvious song to start percolating in my brain stem. Cody was getting more uncomfortable, stressed and bored. She was very dusty from the stop with the burs. She put her nose down by my elbow on the armrest, and covered it with both of her paws trying to scratch her own face, looking as if she were playing peekaboo with some invisible creature under the dash. Sara had included Benadryl in the overly thorough Cody-As-Surrogate-Child bag, complete with half a page worth of instructions (these boiled down to: *Give Cody 2 Benadryl*) but I hadn't thought to give it to her. Jay would have, of course.

We drove on. Then *suddenly*—and really, it was *sudden,* or else maybe I'd fallen asleep at the wheel—as suddenly as Tulsa had sprung up earlier, there were mesas and buttes and canyons and valleys and cliffs and arroyos and lots of other things I didn't know the names of. As if some John Wayne movie had erupted in Technicolor out of the earth and exploded all over. There were little adobe huts and abandoned old shacks and houses all along the way, too. They were, even by the standards of the rurals in Ireland, very picturesque. *This* was the Old West I had envisioned! For a moment I was alert and completely charmed, sloughing off Jay and even Cody, as my Inner Child and Inner Émigré cavorted together through a wonderland of weirdness.

However, as delightful as it was to encounter, I was now so fried and so hungry, and the Old West went on for so long, I got tired of it. So did Cody, who had occasionally raised herself to look around, and finding nothing but more of the same sights and smells (mainly dried earth, secondly dried manure), would sigh, or yawn, then stare at me beseechingly.

"Stop *staring* at me," I said, which come to think of it was something I had said to her at least once a day from almost the very beginning of our relationship.

The car claimed the temperature was only fifty-nine, hard to believe given the bleaching intensity of the sunlight. A slow-moving freight train stretched on for so long, I lost sight of it behind an enormous trailer park, which had appeared almost as suddenly as the interesting landscape—thousands of homes that evolved, farther west, into dingy tract housing.

Whatever township that had been, we were out of it again quickly and into the same open, empty, cooked-salmon rock that now lined the roadway. My phone rang. Danny, this time. God how I wished he was in the seat beside me, or better yet, that I was meeting him in person at the Plough.

"Ach! Big man! The stories I'm hearing from your man Alto!" he said. "You're in the Wild West, yeah? Oklahoma, is it? Is it like cowboys and Indians?"

"I'm done with Oklahoma," I said. "I'm in . . . Arizona or New Mexico, I always get those two mixed up. New Mexico."

"How's it?"

"It's big and dry and empty and dusty."

"Sounds great. Except for the dusty part. How's Sara? How's the wee dog?"

"Sara's in Los Angeles and the dog is dusty but fine."

"You missed a great game, man, they *killed* Liverpool."

"I'm shattered, Danny. I haven't really slept since I can't remember when."

Danny chuckled. "It's crazy, like. That man's mental. Where is he now?"

"Oh," I said, making sure to sound offhand. "He's in my rearview mirror."

"He's not!" gasped Danny. "He's *following* you?"

"He is," I said.

"That's fucking mad! He's chasing you over a wee dog now?"

"He is."

"It's like your own reality show for the telly!"

"I've already *got* a show for the telly," I said. That almost felt like a lie.

"Yeah, fuck that, this one's more interesting," said Danny.

"Piss off," I said. As much as I wanted his company, I didn't have the energy to even hold a conversation. "I've gotta go drive off a cliff now in my Batmobile. Later."

There were billboards for a place advertising opals and agates and gold. Also, moccasins, casinos, Dairy Queens, hotels, and fast food. Soon, increasingly urgent billboards for turquoise. Plus there were now rows of cliff faces to the right, a series of them too indistinct to count, like waves, smaller swells backed by larger ones. I rounded a slight bend in the road to see that they continued on out of sight in the haze.

The sun rose higher, shrinking the car's shadow. The temperature was still cool outside despite the bright blaring sun. This made more sense when we passed a sign announcing the Continental Divide, meaning we were higher than I'd realized. The landscape to the north got pretty impressive. "This is it! We're in Grand Canyon territory!" I announced triumphantly to Cody.

A few miles later, it all got dull again.

But finally, as we approached the small city of Flagstaff, there was respite from the oppressive openness: for the first time in at least twelve hours of driving, there were *real trees*. Pine trees. Not like those great ol' North Carolina pines, but still, their presence changed everything. Seeing familiar bits of nature lifted my spirits, and Cody, smelling the shift away from pure open plains, yawned and rested her chin on my shoulder, nestling her head against mine. Jesus, it was good to know the end was nearly in sight.

The GPS steered me away from the city, onto a two-lane road through a massive ponderosa-pine forest, and then up onto high plains. It looked almost exactly like what I'd been driving through for many hours—sage, scrub, junipers, baked red earth. But it *felt* different, because I knew I was nearing the end. And of course, I knew I was nearing the Graceland of the natural world: the Grand Canyon. This time, I'd actually get to see something. A straight shot up 64 took us into Tusuyan. The hotel was smack off the road.

Jay was still right behind me. If he followed me into the hotel, no good would come of it—I'd either give him the dog or give him a bruising. I began to pull into the hotel car park when suddenly a squeal of tires made me jump. I looked back into my rearview mirror.

Jay was suddenly pulling past me. That damn Lexus SUV sped off up the road and out of sight. Disappeared.

Jay was gone. Gone!

What?

Victory! The wanker had finally called it off!

But why?

Chapter 31

For the first time since I'd got the dog back, I wasn't looking over my shoulder for the man who'd stolen her, and a thousand little muscles in my body all relaxed at once. I took an enormous breath, and let it out, and felt wobbly. I doubted he had *really* given up, but at least he'd left us alone in peace for now, and that was a relief.

Too tired almost to function, I drove into the hotel parking lot. Then I put Cody on the lead and brought her into the lobby with me so that I could deposit her in the room before I did anything else.

It was a large, tacky, pseudo-western-ranch sort of a place, but infinitely nicer than the other hotels where I had stopped. Not beige, for starters; more salmon-orange, like the soil. There was a uniformed bloke who offered to help me with the luggage, an offer I accepted once I'd locked Cody in the room.

It was midday. I was once again filthy, hungry, and exhausted; Cody was filthy, hungry, and restless. An awful combo. I took her out to a designated yard to poo, then put her back in the room, grabbed an actual meal in the hotel's restaurant (awful decor, but the food was deadly, especially the fried potatoes, and God, what those southwesterners can do with cheese), came back up to the room, closed the curtain, and passed out on the bed, which was firm, clean, and not a driver's seat. No amount of Cody's attempts to get my attention was going to work this time. I was out like a light.

IN THE HARD, dense, foggy sleep I'd fallen into, I heard my phone make occasional noises. Couldn't tell if these were part of a dream or not. Then a horrible alarmlike noise that was definitely a dream, and I struggled like a drowning man back toward wakefulness to avoid it, but drowned again before I could get there.

FOR A WHILE there was dreamless silence and dark.

Then a new dream began, so indistinguishable from reality I thought maybe it was real. Sara's voice murmured in my ear, and I felt her fingers on my face. I blinked my eyes open and saw, in the light seeping around the edges of the heavy hotel curtain, those beautiful green eyes gazing into mine. Her hand brushed through my mess of hair.

"Hi, love," she said, with the gentle encouragement of a nurse to a patient coming out of a coma. "How are you?"

In this dream, I threw my arms around her and grabbed her in a bear hug. I was instantly revived, instantly erect, and she was naked and full of lust. So I'll skip the details of the rest of the dream because I am a gentleman, but trust me, it was the most satisfying erotic somnolence of the past century. We were both sweaty, exhausted, delighted, and enthralled with each other by the end of it.

For a while there was more dreamless silence and dark.

Then another dream began, again so indistinguishable from reality I thought it was real. Sara's voice murmured in my ear again, and I felt her fingers on my face. I blinked my eyes open and saw, in the light seeping around the edges of the heavy hotel curtain, those beautiful green eyes gazing into mine. Her hand brushed through my mess of hair.

"Hi, love," she said, with the gentle encouragement of a nurse to a patient coming out of a coma. "How are you now?"

A replay! We were going to get to do it all over again!

Only in this version, when I went to throw my arms around her, they got tangled in the sheets. And I was not instantly revived. I was pretty cotton-brained, actually. Also, she was clothed. That was not how the dream was supposed to go.

"Are you all right, Rory?" she asked, moving her hand to my forehead. "Rory? I was calling and texting, I had the lobby call up here on the phone. I had to show them the credit card I booked the room with to convince them to give me a key."

This was awfully mundane shite for a dream. I liked the first version a lot more.

"Wait a minute," I said in a single slurred syllable. "Is this . . . is this still the dream? Or are you really here?"

Her smile lit up her face and she giggled, the light dancing in her eyes in a way that a dream never could have conveyed. "You're adorable," she said, laughing. "I'm here. I caught a cheap flight on standby and took a shuttle to the hotel."

"You're here!" I pushed myself up to sitting and managed finally to throw my arms around her. Fuck me, that felt good—the cool smoothness of her skin, the smell of her hair, her curves pressing against me, the *reality* of her. "Sara, you're *here*! I'm so glad you're here! Get your clothes off this instant!"

She threw her arms around me and squeezed hard, leaning over me until I was underneath her on the bed. We kissed wildly for a moment or two.

"Something wrong here," I said. "Your clothes are still on. Let's fix that."

She rolled off me, took my hands away from her body, and held them in her own, giving me a regretful smile that implied we were not about to immediately have sex. "I have to give Cody a bath."

"You're fucking kidding me," I said loudly, with a huff, and sat up, propelled by my own incredulity.

She sat up, too. "She's filthy, she's got about a pound of dust on her. She's scratching and chewing—"

"*Jesus,*" I said.

"It will take ten minutes," she said. "And then I can focus more on being with you."

"I just drove that fucking dog across the entire continent, nearly," I said. "I don't even get a thank-you bonk?"

"Of course you do," she said, "As soon as I've washed her."

"Thanks for making it clear who comes first," I said.

"She's in an awful state," Sara said. "It looks like she's been gnawing herself. I thought the Benadryl would have prevented that."

She wasn't trying to trap me but I felt trapped. If I owned up to not drugging Cody, then she'd point out how if I'd just done what I was supposed to do, the dog would be fine right now. If

I pretended I had given the dog the Benadryl, I'd feel a cheat. I was grumpy, and attached to my grumpiness—it was, after all, the first time in a week that it was safe to luxuriate in grumpiness rather than focus on the road ahead—so I decided to silently stay grumpy.

Turned out Sara had tried to wake me, found me not responsive, and so turned her attention to Cody. So I'd slept through their initial reunion, and I was glad to have been spared. She'd been about to wash the dog when I made a noise and she'd come back to the bed. Now Cody—not knowing Sara's cruel, watery intentions—was all over her. I don't anthropomorphize, but, Jesus, it really was like a little lost kid being reunited with its mother. Just ridiculous.

So off they went to the bathroom. I heard the shower and a bit of splashing around, and Sara's voice in an unusually firm tone. I was glad at least that Cody was the one being scolded for a change. It took more than ten minutes, too, for the record. I'd say twenty at least. Long enough for me to cycle through irritation back to gratitude that she was here, in the same room with me. And hopefully soon to be in my arms. At last.

The door to the bathroom finally opened. Cody came leaping out in triumph, spry as a gazelle, hair going every which way, tail wagging madly. She leapt on me, her eyes wide and bright and manic. Chuffed with herself.

A moment later, Sara came out, her clothes motley from being soaked. Her hair was as skewed as her dog's and she was not nearly as effervescent. "I hate doing that," she said, wearily. "And now look at her, she's so happy she survived the torture, she just wants to play."

"You look like you need to take your clothes off," I said helpfully.

She gave me a sly look. "Always looking out for me, aren't you?" she said.

"It's mutual," I said sincerely, and threw her a kiss.

"Well, all right, then," she said, and began to disrobe. She had already cast off a sweater, and now was pulling off a long-sleeved shirt. Cody, distracted from leaping on me by the squiggly movements of the Best Person on Earth, flew away from me and jumped up on Sara as Sara was engaged in her shirt removal.

"Cody!" she said through the shirt, and stumbled sideways. "Down!"

But Cody was not going down. Cody was flying. Cody could not have been higher if she'd just snorted crystal meth. Despite the fact her owner's face could not be seen, Cody bowed to her, asking to play; when Sara didn't respond to this, Cody leapt into the air without changing her position, as if she were on a trampoline, and asked the same of me. "Cody," I said, meaning to calm her, but I s'pose I was smiling too much because off she went around the room: onto the bed, from there to one chair then sailed right over the table to the other chair, then the floor, then she tore across the room to the door, where she did a double anticlockwise circle to turn around, raced back up to the bed, leapt onto the chair, over the table . . . right past Sara, who had finally pulled her shirt off and stood there in a very removable-looking lace bra. That mad dog circled the room half a dozen times, eyes wild like a Chinese dragon's, ignoring even Sara. I egged her on when she lagged: "Go on, Cody! Go on!" She paused on the bed and looked at me, uncertain.

"Go on," I encouraged. "Go on—jump! Jump, Cody!" To Sara: "I didn't know she could jump like that!"

"Oh, yeah," said Sara. "We did agility training when she was little but I stopped it, it seemed so controlling—Jonathan was metaphorically making me jump through hoops and then I was literally making her—"

"Okay, I get it," I said briskly. "She likes to jump."

"And she's had a pretty confined lifestyle the last six months," said Sara. "You think you're the only one who's had to accommodate?"

"Great, let's get into this *now*," I said, "You're telling me that your dog, whom I took out on a long walk every single fucking day, was being *deprived* of a quality doggie lifestyle?"

There was the briefest pause. Then Sara reached for the zipper to her jeans. "How about I keep undressing?" she offered.

"That works," I said quickly.

But—surprise—it was hard to be intimate with a wet dog in the room with us. Our plans of snogging all afternoon were dampened. I found myself thinking of Jay, and how much easier life would be without the dog. We tried shutting her in the bathroom but she pawed and cried piteously, so determined to see her owner. That put a damper on Sara's ardor as much as mine.

The whole situation was crap.

"She won't come into our room in the new apartment, at least," I said.

"Of course not," said Sara, but seemed grudging about it. That actually irritated me more. Cody came over and rested her chin on the bed, looking adoringly at Sara. *What if I had given you to Jay?* I wondered in silence, appalled with myself.

ALTHOUGH I'D SEEN him burn rubber right past me, Sara called down to reception to see if Jay had checked in. When she was told no, she immediately corrected herself, apologetically: "I meant to ask for Leonard Cohen," she said. Leonard Cohen wasn't staying in the hotel either. "That doesn't mean he's given up." She sighed after hanging up. "I'm sure he hasn't given up."

We spent the rest of the afternoon, and the evening, and all night in the room, the three of us. I am a very good and loving man but you have no clue how frustrating it was that Sara was clearly more concerned about Cody's well-being than mine. She was affectionate to me—of course she was. But Cody was not under the slightest psychological stress, she had no clue that all of the past week had been about a bunch of crazed humans obsessed with her whereabouts and well-being. She wasn't the one who'd had to drive through the night, who'd had to live on Snickers bars, who'd been getting guilt-tripped by both Jonathan *and* Sara. *And* Cody, come to mention it. I was the one who needed the TLC— and I'm not saying Sara didn't have any for me, but trust me on this, she couldn't keep her hands off the dog.

On the plus side, she was able to get the dog to lie down and sleep on the floor overnight, which I'd thought was not going to be an option. I thought she'd be all over the bed and Sara would let her be all over the bed. But no, she lay down obediently when told to, and fell contentedly asleep.

Sara smiled at me.

"This is the closest we're going to have to privacy until we're in L.A.," she said, and reached for the buttons of my shirt.

And it was heavenly to be with her, pure pure heaven, really it was . . . but the dog being in the room like that . . . I could not relax into it the way I wished to. It was a frustrating attempt at *amour*.

And although we didn't mention Jay again for the rest of the night, it's not as if he went away. He was literally and figuratively lurking nearby, and we were probably going to have to deal with him again soon. Bastard.

Chapter 32

We decided to get up before dawn to see sunrise at the Canyon. We weren't the only ones doing this, although the hordes of tourists one imagines on a bright sunny afternoon were not yet up and about.

Under a tarmac-tinted sky, we entered the park, and it was still dark when we found a parking area that looped around a lit-up open spot, covered in pine needles from a few, but monumental, pines. We sensed the canyon the way you sense the beach, but we could not see it from where we were. We'd agreed not to leave the dog in the hotel so that Sara wouldn't fuss about how long we'd been gone. Now, as the air lightened from black to slate, we tossed a tennis ball between us for Cody to chase for about twenty minutes, then got back in the car, parked in Lot D near Grand Canyon Village, put Cody on the leash, and walked to the rim.

What can you say about the Grand Canyon? I hope you weren't expecting me to try to *describe* it. Words are wasted—you'd have to make up words, like Mary Poppins does—and every moment brings the next chance for World's Most Amazing Grand Canyon

Photo. It's so gorgeous and mind-bending that your mind loses its memory as soon as it has created one, so the Canyon is constantly making a new impression on you, taking your breath away continually. If you've been there, you know what I'm talking about; if you haven't, you just have to take my word on this: imagine the most dazzling, luminous, awe-inspiring photo you have ever seen of the Grand Canyon. Whatever feeling that evokes in you, make it a hundred times as strong.

That's about halfway to what it's like to be there. It may be the only thing on Planet Earth that can't be overhyped. The place was seductive, like the Sirens in *The Odyssey,* instantly beckoning us to come closer, closer, stay longer, longer. I knew in my bones the Siren call would be just as strong an hour from now, a day from now, a year from now.

"Wow," said Sara softly, after we had stared in silence for a few seconds or just as possibly a few hours.

"Should be nice when it's finished," I said. "Looks like it's still a work in progress—hey!" for she had slapped me. Then she laughed. No sound on earth as lovely as the sound of Sara's laughter.

Cody, cretin that she was, had absolutely no awe of the place. She thought some of the smells were promising, but there weren't enough people around yet for her to suck up to, and Sara kept her on a short leash, which Cody was being uncharacteristically obnoxious about. "Can't we put her back in the car?" I suggested. "You'll have a nicer climb down if you're not concerned about her."

"It's going to get blazing hot in the car as soon as the sun is fully up," said Sara, with the long-suffering good humor of someone married to a moron. "Don't worry, I'm responsible for her now. You're off the hook." She put her arm around me, which was always delightful, and gave me a kiss. "Thank you for taking good care of her. Did I say that? I don't know if I said that, Rory, and I'm sorry if I didn't. You've been fantastic." She kissed me again. God, that felt good. Better than it had in weeks.

There's a kind of quiet in the Canyon, at least there was that morning. The space was so vast, sound got sucked up into it, or was carried away by subtle layers of the breeze, or something. It was indifferent to us puny humans, and after the week that had been in it, its indifference was a big relief.

We waited for the early-morning shuttle that would take us to the South Kaibab trailhead. Guess who had marked down what time the bus was coming, and then calculated backward to make sure we'd have time to exercise the dog before the hike? That's right, it wasn't me. God, it was great to have her back.

But when we disembarked near the trailhead, left behind in a big billow of diesel fumes from the bus as our sundry fellow hikers headed straight for the trail . . . guess what the one thing was that she had overlooked in all her planning?

Dogs aren't allowed on the South Kaibab Trail! Ha!

To which news Sara—the most upstanding person I have ever known—said resolutely, "Screw that. We've *earned* the right to bring her with us."

"*I* have earned the right to do something *without* her, actually," I said before I could stop myself. I tried to make it sound humorous. But it was such a loaded topic between us, with so much baggage. Whatever cheerful sound track was playing in the background of this little moment, the record player suddenly lost power and the music melted to a stop, in that drably comic way you can't re-create with digital. She gave me a look.

"There's no place to leave her, Rory," she chastised me. "She's got to come with us or we can't go."

"It's always about the fucking dog," I said under my breath.

"What do you want me to do?" she asked. "Make a suggestion. I'm open to suggestions."

"The fact that I'd even have to make a suggestion further demonstrates that it's all about the dog," I said. Cody, sensing she was the center of attention, started to wag her tail, her eyes darting about from Sara's face to hand to other hand to face, briefly to my face, then Sara's hand again. She was looking for the cue that meant either "time to pull a tarty dog" or "look, a treat!"

Sara held her arms out and shrugged. "What do you want me to do?" she said.

"I want you to admit that it's always about the dog!" I said.

"It's not like I do that on purpose," she said. "And in case you've forgotten, it has to be about the dog because when people aren't paying attention, the dog gets *kidnapped*."

I exploded. "Would you *fucking* get over that already?" I snapped. "I redeemed myself. I drove all the fucking way to North Carolina, I started at four in the morning, I was up for twenty-two hours straight with the worst hangover of my life when I didn't even want to be drinking, I *got the dog back,* I brought her safely—"

"Rory, let's not—"

"No, you listen to me! Do you know what my *fucking* week has been like? All because you won't put the dog in cargo like a normal pet! I drove from North Carolina all the fucking way to the Grand Canyon with one night's rest and that psycho Jay on my tail—"

There was a relenting, almost apologetic look on her face. "Yes, I—"

"No, you don't know. If you knew you wouldn't have insisted on getting up in the middle of the night to come someplace, *with the dog,* that's a *totally* stupid place to be coming with the dog." Angry at myself for ruining what had been a really lovely morning, I shut my mouth and bit my upper lip to keep from continuing.

"You're right," Sara said, after a pause. "You are right, and I'm sorry." Pause. "Do you want some time alone? You have had no time alone all week. Maybe you just need a little solitude."

"Yeah, so you can go off with your *dog,*" I said bitterly. "And leave your *husband* behind." Hating myself even more. And knowing she was right: a moment of absolute solitude, with no responsibility or obligation, would be such a gift. But accepting that gift from someone you've just snapped at . . . that's uncomfortable. So I did not respond right away, just stood there sulking and hating myself for sulking and resenting the dog for being the reason I was sulking.

There were few hikers here, and the handful who'd exited the bus with us had thankfully started off down the trailhead before I'd begun my rant. There would be no further ones for twenty minutes. So at least we were alone for this ugly moment.

Cody had stopped studying Sara and was now making a nuisance of herself wanting to smell everything, especially the mules that were corralled between the bus stop and the trailhead. Even

I could smell the mules. I slipped off my backpack, which had all the water, and handed it to Sara. "Go on," I said gruffly. "Go have some time with your dog." It was barely after dawn, and yet the sun already felt thirsty-making. Sara kissed me until pulled away by Cody, who was straining at the leash to go find mules. They disappeared down a curving path to the trailhead, and my attention went back to the Canyon.

It was an amazing moment to feel free as a bird and light as one of its tail feathers.

The initial peek here was even more gobsmacking. I'm not generally one to wax in manner mystical, but that place makes you so aware of how vast creation is. I could easily have taken every mile of road I'd driven to get here, draped all of it across the bottom of the Canyon, and not even noticed it. The general palette of the Canyon is red-orange-pink, but there's hues from white to purple-brown throughout it, and it being only the second of May (or thereabouts), the vegetation was all still bright green and leafy, and the contrast against warm earth was *gorgeous*. Too bad the Impressionists never got so far west, they'd have wet their pants with the excitement. And here we were, ruining the moment, because of the dog.

I stayed there studying the beauty long enough to feel my temper cool. Then I started after them, ruing what was sure to be an awkward reunion. To the right of the path leading to the trailhead was the small paddock full of the mules Cody had wanted to meet.

The trail right from the top was a steep descent that hugged the nearly vertical wall of the canyon in a series of switchbacks. It was all so steep and so stacked that I had an almost perfect bird's-eye view of some people's heads. The effect made me a little light-headed.

What made me more light-headed was realizing that the short dark-haired person and the tall bald person staring each other down at a hairpin turn were my wife and her ex-lover.

Chapter 33

I don't know how he had managed it. But I was no longer surprised.

It was the first time I'd seen them in physical proximity. Sara had Cody on a supershort leash right beside her. Cody was sitting obediently, but also straining her head toward Jay. Jay was higher on the trail and his presence prevented Sara from pushing past him to come back up. The only other hikers were several levels down. Sara seemed very stiff and constricted, as if wrapped in Sellotape. Her eyes looked enormous and were locked on Jay's face.

Irrational fear gripped me: What if she went back to him? He had such a commanding presence, he was handsomer than I, by far, and richer, and clearly cleverer. They knew each other well. They liked the same artwork. They never argued about the importance of the dog—who, I have to say, was sitting there looking back and forth between them with nothing short of pure bliss on her face. She was with her two original people. There was some intense emotional *something* going on, which meant hormones were firing, which gave her lots of interesting things to smell and pay attention to. What could be better than that?

I almost shouted out, but then thought I'd done enough damage this morning with my shouting, so clamped my mouth shut and listened instead. The voices came floating up with unexpected clarity.

" . . . done nothing at all to wrong you," Sara was saying woodenly. "Leave him out of this."

"He's even worse than you are," said Jay mildly. "You never understood the harm you were doing. He does—yet he's still doing it. That's cruel. I have no qualms about this. You're just collateral damage."

My body, without instructions from me, began storming down the limestone trail toward them. It was tricky footwork, and I lost sight and sound of them along one stretch and then another, as they were three full sections down the trail. My gait was ungainly, awkward, because of the steep angle. I rounded the third hairpin and came back into view of them, tottering down the incline, my toes jamming into the toe box of my Doc Martens. Sara met my gaze with a strange, involuntary gesture, jutting her chin out. Jay paused in whatever he was saying and turned to look up at me. He was, for the first time in our acquaintanceship, without a jacket. My choices at that moment were to stop resisting gravity and hurl myself into him, or else to check my speed sharply. I wanted to do the first, of course, but I'm not a total eejit, so I went for the second.

"Ah," said Jay. "Welcome, Rory. We were just having a little reality check."

"I would like to join my husband now," said Sara carefully, almost mechanically. "Please let me pass."

"Of course I will," said Jay, an indulgent kindergarten teacher. "Just a moment, though, I need Rory for this part, since it's going to have an impact on the rest of his life."

"What is?" I asked just as Sara said, pleadingly, "Don't ask."

"You've been on my mind," said Jay. "How disappointing it is when someone has the opportunity to do the right thing, and elects not to do it."

"The only right thing to do here is for you to leave my wife alone and get the fuck out of here," I said.

"I don't have to get the fuck out of a public park," Jay said. "And I'm not in any way molesting your wife."

"You're bothering her," I said angrily. "Your very existence bothers her."

"If my *existence* bothers her, then it really doesn't matter where I *am*, does it? She's going to be bothered. So I think I'll just stay here."

"Then we're not staying here. Come on, Sara," I said, gesturing and turning to go back up the trail.

"May I continue what I was saying?"

"No," I said. "She's sick of listening to you."

"Mm," said Jay. "Hearing the truth can be hard sometimes." He turned his attention back to Sara. "I could have forgiven you. You never really understood your faults. If you'd just realized, and apologized, I'd have taken you back."

"Stop it!" I said. Sara stood quietly with eyes averted and shoulders slightly stooped. I realized, with a sick feeling: this was their

dance. This was how he'd treated her; this is how she'd taken it. It wasn't the Sara I knew. But it was the Sara Jay knew, and that's why he was doing this. What he really wanted, all along, was to take the dog *from Sara*—from *this* Sara, the one who had betrayed him.

"I never wanted you to take me back," said Sara with a nervous tinge to her voice that was utterly unlike her—as if she were afraid of saying the wrong thing and somehow losing. As if she were walking on eggshells. But at the same time, busting out to speak. "And you've never had the right to take Cody from me. You brought her home unannounced and said I had to train her for you because you were too busy, and when I said, 'Why should I train your dog?' you put a bow on her collar and said, 'All right, she's your dog, now train her.' And I did. And I did a great job. And if I'm the one she's around all day, of course she was going to listen to me more than to you, she *knew* me better. *I* was the one making the effort. *I* was the one bonding with her."

"There you go again," Jay said sadly. "Giving yourself so much credit."

"Stop insulting my wife!" I shouted.

"When you're dealing with someone who never admits her faults, it takes effort to make her really appraise herself. She's just a self-aggrandizing pathetic narcissistic masochistic victim," said Jay blithely. I realized too late that he was stringing unflattering phrases together just to upset me. I only realized this was his goal as he succeeded at it—as I grabbed his shoulder, spun him around to face me, and landed the most satisfying punch of my life squarely on the left side of his face—I hit him right in the sweet spot.

"Rory, *no!*" shouted Sara as my fist landed.

It felt *fucking great*. I wanted to do it again.

Jay winced, cringed, brought his hands to his face . . . and then stood up straighter and smiled lazily at me with a twinkle in his unhurt eye.

"Thank you," he said. "That'll do perfectly."

"Oh, *Rory,*" Sara moaned, so intensely that Cody tried to jump up on her. Sara pushed her down with morose aggravation, distracted. Cody, who of course assumed this was about her, groveled slightly, too leery of the steep drop so close at hand to just fall into tarty dog.

Jay reached into his pants pocket with his free hand and pulled out his cell phone. He pressed call for what was obviously a preset number. "This'll just be a moment," he said.

I gave him a dumbstruck look.

"I need to call the ranger station to tell them I've been assaulted by an Irish male driving a MINI Cooper with Massachusetts plates, who just stole my dog. The Irishman only has a conditional green card, so I think he's going back to Ireland. Unless he wants to give me my dog, of course, in which case, I don't need to make the call."

Sara, in a rage, grabbed the phone out of his hand and flung it over the hairpin turn and into the Canyon. She took in a deep lungful of air and was about to start screaming at him, when the worst thing in the world—really the absolute worst thing in the world—happened:

Cody, instinctively responding to Mom Throwing Something, chased the phone right over the edge of the cliff.

Her leash jerked out of Sara's stunned hold and flew out behind

her, and she disappeared from view before Sara could begin to
scream. We heard a screech and a whimper from below, instantly
drowned out by Sara's hysterical cry.

The next few events happened very fast: Sara, also acting on
instinct, actually tried to jump over the edge to get to Cody. I
grabbed her, shoved her away—right into Jay's arms, actually—
and went after Cody myself. Rather than diving headfirst, which
I swear is how Sara was about to do it, I went feetfirst, but it was
frightening all the same because I had no idea what, if anything,
was below.

I slid down a vertical slope, creating billows of pale dust that
kept me from clearly seeing all the scree and boulders and roots as
I approached them.

There were tiny precarious outcroppings sticking out from the
canyon wall—roots, stones, eroding ledges. Cody had miracu-
lously fallen, or scrambled, onto one such ledge, and looked like a
mountain goat, all four feet taking up an area of less than a square
foot, the leash dangling below. She was horribly upset, making
Chewbacca-like protests. The whites of her eyes were enormous
even through the dust. I landed on an outstretched tree root, a less
reliable perch than hers, about five or six feet to her left, shudder-
ing with fright until I realized it was strong enough to hold me.
But I had to literally hug myself to the canyon wall to keep from
toppling over and plunging farther down. Some ten feet below us
both was another ledge, larger, sticking out maybe five feet and
twice that in length, hardly a safe place to fall to.

Cody turned on her tiny ledge and saw me. Right away she
squatted awkwardly in preparation to hop across a distance I
knew she couldn't span.

"Cody, stay!" I said, pushing myself against the canyon wall. "Calm down. Stay, girl, good girl!" She was making desperate little mewling sounds the like of which I'd never heard before, and trying to figure out how to get close to me. Thank God she was still with us, but how was I going to get her back up to Sara?

In a new shower of scree and pebbles, Jay lumbered down on her far side, landing on a rocky outcropping, closer to her than I was. Had his, like mine, been a blind leap—was it pure luck that he hadn't just now thrown himself to his own demise? Jesus, *nothing* stopped that fucker!

Cody, seeing him, began to complain to him as well. He took a moment to get his footing, recover, register the three of us in a row like that. On reflex he held out one arm toward Cody as if calling her.

"Don't do it," I said as she looked at him pleadingly for help, yelping. She was getting hysterical.

He wobbled on his perch. "Cody," he said urgently. It wasn't malevolent, just instinctual but stupid. "Come here, girl."

"Don't!" I shouted. "Cody, don't!"

She almost jumped toward Jay, but hearing the intensity of my voice, stopped herself, looked over her shoulder, and started trying to arrange her feet on the tiny outcrop so that she could turn and jump toward me instead. She was losing control of her footing, as if the ledge was covered with lard.

"Stop! Stay! Cody, don't!" I shouted. I risked letting go of the wall with one hand, holding the flat of my palm toward her. She yipped and whined more intensely, panting, anxious, terrified—but above all, wanting to please. She was trying to figure out what her humans wanted so she could please us.

"She's a strong jumper, she can reach me," Jay insisted.

"No, she fucking can't," I said. "Don't risk it."

"Cody! Good girl! Come here, girl!" said Jay, leaning over more, patting his thigh.

I couldn't let him summon her to jump; she'd never make it. But if I kept shouting over him, she would get so hysterical she'd try to turn around and jump toward me, who was farther away, and that was even worse.

"Come, Cody! Good girl! Come here! I'll catch you, girl!" He was barely audible over her frantic shrieks.

I saw her draw her weight back on her haunches as she prepared to spring toward him. Without thinking, I did likewise. I leapt half a heartbeat before she did and I landed on her small foothold as she was departing it. The moment she was airborne it was clear she wasn't going to make it. Jay, realizing this, look shocked, then mortified.

I threw my weight forward after her, and wrapped my arms around her as I reached her. We were a foot short of Jay's ledge. So once I had her firmly in my grasp, we did the only thing we could do next. We fell.

It was a slithering, nasty, bumpy fall to the larger ledge below, and I felt something crack inside me as I landed. Cody was hysterical, struggling against my grip as if against an ocean whirlpool, yelping piteously. I lay there, winded and pained, and tried cooing to her softly until she realized we were both alive and still. We took up most of the ledge—inches ahead, above, and below, endless Canyon air opened up all around us. "Good girl," I croaked, releasing my grip enough to stroke her head. She still scrambled to get away, but I held on. I rubbed her ear vigorously, and that got through to her. She looked at me, made wary eye contact, and finally stopped struggling.

"Good girl," I repeatedly voicelessly, and smiled. "Good girl. You're okay now. Let's get you back up to Sara."

"Is she all right?" Jay called down, in a shaken voice.

"She's fine," I called back. He heaved a sigh.

I squeezed her against me and kissed her between the eyes. She struggled a little again, but without the frantic fear of a moment earlier; now it was more like a child trying to avoid the affections of an elderly auntie. I loved that dog so intensely in that moment; I had not known I could love her so much. I was responsible for her being alive. This time I'd gotten it right. If the story was always going to be about the dog, at least I was the hero.

Very gingerly, arms still round her, I started to rise. Everything hurt. I tried to take a deep breath and everything hurt more. I flexed the fingers of each hand in turn while holding Cody with the other. My hands were scratched and abraded but undamaged. Except the right-hand knuckles hurt from smashing Jay in the face, but that was a *good* hurt.

Because I moved so carefully and slowly, Cody calmed, paid attention, adopted a somber attitude. I released her but kept the leash short, got to my feet successfully, and looked up. Looked right past Jay—I hardly registered his presence now. Above him was Sara, looking down anxiously from the hairpin corner of the trail. Had she been screaming the whole time, and I simply hadn't heard it? I moved cautiously to the other end of the ledge, underneath the tree root I'd been on, as far away from Jay as possible.

Above, Sara shifted her position on the trail so that she was exactly above me. I pointed up the cliff. Sara waved. "See, Cody? There's Sara. Go to Sara."

"Cody, come!" cried Sara nervously. I unclipped her lead, to prevent it catching on anything. She scrambled up the slope as I put my hands under her backside and pushed her. I felt as if my ribs were going to implode into my heart.

Delighted by the apparent ease she'd started with, Cody scampered up, but as soon as she was above my reach, she began to backslide and scrambled desperately. This sent a rubble of dirt straight into my face. I blinked painfully and turned away, listening to her yelping, and to Sara's calls for her to come.

After a moment I could see again. I looked up to find dog and owner a few feet away from being reunited. A soft sob escaped me, I admit it. They were gorgeous together.

And then I realized that Jay had climbed, not back up to the trail after Cody, but down here onto the ledge with me.

"So it's over, Jay," I said.

"It is for you," he said. And shoved me.

Chapter 34

I grabbed his shirt at the shoulders and pulled my weight straight down. On reflex, to keep from toppling over with me, he squatted back and down very fast, to get his arse as far back from the edge as possible. I was still attached to his shirt, so now I hovered over him, and as he fell into a squatting position, I shoved him onto his back. His one good eye widened, startled, now that I suddenly had the upper hand.

Before he could collect himself, I straddled him and sat heavily on his stomach—took the air right out of him. He grasped upward at my shirt, so I let go his shoulders and grabbed his wrists, lifted each of my knees in turn, and pulled his arms under them so the point of my knee rested just above his elbow. He grunted with pain at the pressure on his biceps. Now my hands were free and I wanted to smash the other side of his face, but I stopped myself.

For a moment we glared at each other in the morning sunlight. The cracked rib made me feel about to vomit. He had a fantastic shiner and his nose looked all wrong. I was so exhausted, and so angry, and so victorious, all at once.

"Right," I said. "Listen to me. This ends here. I am going to get up off you, and climb back up to the trail, and leave here with Sara and Cody. *You* will get up, and climb back up to the trail, and get in your car, and drive back to Boston. We will never hear from you again. Right?"

"No," he said in a strained voice, trying to get his breath back. "You'll regret this."

"Jay!" I said, grabbing for his face in frustration, but stopping myself. "We're on a fucking *cliff*. I've got you *immobilized* here. I knock your gobshite head around a bit, you're so fucked up, you go right off the edge. It's thousands of feet down. Whoever goes over the edge here *dies*."

"I'm glad you're aware of that," he said. He bent his right leg and, with a convulsive move, bucked me up off his right hip enough to pull his right arm out from under my knee. Immediately he swung his freed arm up and used the impetus of his movement—taking me completely by surprise, I wouldn't have thought he knew even a half-arsed grappling move—to drive himself over on top of me, straddling me, his weight right on my fuckinghellarseholegob-shite ribs. Almost fainting from the pain, I reached up to claw at his face, but his arms were longer than mine, and I couldn't get near him. He grabbed my hands and pushed them up over my head—another near blackout from pain—then pinned them to the dirt with one of his.

His free hand he placed around my neck and tightened it a bit.

"Are you fucking *mad*?" I shouted, my voice strained.

"Make amends," he ordered. "You saw my hurt, and you chose not to help me, even though you gained nothing by depriving me. That's a senseless, selfish cruelty. *Make amends*."

"I don't need to make amends for trying to save my wife's dog.

Take your fucking hand off my throat! We're not killing each other over a dog." That seemed insufficient. "We're not killing each other at *all,*" I clarified furiously.

"If that's your answer, you've only yourself to blame for this." He began to squeeze and I felt panic because—like *that*—he cut off my breath completely. "I can do this," he said steadily, softly—more to himself than to me. "I can do this." I saw that old melancholic gaze on his face as the edges of my vision started blurring out.

With the intensity of a jackhammer I desperately jerked one knee up and against his lower back, which shoved him forward over me, and he had to release my throat so he could put a hand down to steady himself. I took a huge painful inhale.

In that moment between his releasing me and his reaching ground, I twisted all my weight and energy to my left—toward the edge—and pulled him over with me so that we were side by side, my face at his chest—but only for a beat.

Because then the lip of the ledge began to crumble under his weight.

He clutched wildly at me while I clutched wildly at him. I caught his wrists and planted my body totally flat on the dirt. He swung like a clumsy pendulum down along the vertical cliff face—his only attachment to the ledge was my hands on his wrists. Within seconds, either his weight would pull me down with him or I'd somehow yank him back up to safety—where he'd go at me again.

"Oh *Jesus,*" I said, horrified.

There was a third option: I could just let go of him. He would fall, and I would not. We both realized it at the same moment, and looked right at each other, directly face-to-face now. It wasn't even a choice, really. We both looked down at our hands as his, slippery with sweat, began to slip slowly through mine. We looked back up at each other.

Our shared horror and disbelief made time slow way down. He was falling, we both knew it, and neither of us could stop it happening. We both could feel I wasn't holding tight enough. But even if I squeezed tighter, his weight would drag me over, and unless I released him, we would both plummet.

"If you're the least bit decent this will haunt you every moment for the rest of your life," he said, trembling.

"No fucking way," I said. I let go one of his hands. A true mortal fear, like I've never seen before on anybody, tightened his face. He wanted to die with dignity but it wasn't going to happen.

Instantly with my free hand I grabbed under his arm, under his shoulder, around his back, my body spread flat on the ground to hold me stable, only my shoulders, arms, and head over the edge. I released his other wrist and wrapped my other arm around him, too, at the same moment that I torqued my body, jerking hands, shoulders, torso up and over to try to roll him over me. Every muscle in my body clenched against the pain. Utterly disoriented, I heard myself scream, thinking I was falling as everything went white. A great and terrible weight was pulling at me, like a ship being heaved up onto a beach during a storm—

. . . and then suddenly there was no weight. My arm muscles and back muscles spasmed and then released, vision returned, and I saw blue, blue sky—sky everywhere and reddish dust. I was lying flat on my back drenched in sweat, ribs blazing with agony. Lying beside me, snug against the cliff, gasping for breath, was Jay.

He took a huge breath in, released it. I tried to, too, but it hurt like hell. For a moment we just lay there staring at the enormous, brightening sky, and breathing.

"Now you *can't* haunt me," I declared. "So for fuck's sake, leave me alone."

I was so winded and dazed by pain, he could have easily rolled me right off the edge. He didn't. A pause. "All right," he said. "I guess we're even."

"Even?" I echoed, incredulous. "I just saved your fucking *life*. Get some *perspective*."

"I have," he said. "Just like they say, your life flashes in front of you. I saw so clearly what's mattered most."

"About time," I said.

"It was Cody," he said. "What she represents, I mean."

I considered pushing him off the cliff.

"Never seen it clearer," he said, with his philosophical melancholy, still staring at the sky. "But there's a price to pay for everything. The price of my life is losing her. I get that."

Thank God! "Look at it this way," I suggested. "You should have died just now. You didn't. No way I should have been able to haul you back up here. But I did. You just got a new life. A fresh start. So you're not really losing anything, because you're starting from zero."

He closed his eyes and laughed, but it was a brief, pained laugh. "That's a pathetic attempt at sympathy. I'll manage my own loss, thank you."

"But you admit it's loss?" I said. "You let go? You accept she's mine?"

He looked startled. Truly startled. He looked at me with his one good eye, and considered me as if he hadn't seen me before.

"Yours?" He smiled the saddest smile I've ever seen, all the sads of Leonard Cohen and Samuel Beckett rolled up together—with a little smugness just to oil it up. "You've never called her that before. At least my loss has been for something."

I slapped my hands up to my face and shouted briefly into them. "If this fight wasn't over, I would punch you in the face," I said.

Chapter 35

I don't know what exactly Sara told the park rangers, but they seemed to believe it was all just a family scuffle. Which in a way, I suppose it was. We were tended to in a ranger station—Jay's face, my ribs. My memory of getting there is fuzzy, due to the excellent quick-acting painkillers they gave me. Sara, with Cody, hovered just at the door, not willing to come close to Jay, not wanting to be far from me.

"You can come in, you know," I said. "I think he's been deactivated."

"Hallelujah," Sara said drily. But she went outside anyhow, to call Alto and Marie and Lena and all them, and let them know about our little rollicking adventure.

Jay was staring into space with his good eye, an ice pack strapped over the damaged mess of his face. He wasn't really in the room. He was completely empty. I felt compassion for him, which I hadn't before. He was no danger now. He'd given it his best shot and failed brilliantly, far better than I would ever fail at anything. Probably not much use in pointing that out to him, though.

For my ribs, the ranger medic gave me the lovely meds, which were starting to work without really working—meaning I felt warm and fuzzy except for my rib cage, which still hurt like hell. He advised me to see a doctor and asked me to sign a bunch of papers, so, for the first time ever, I got to use my green card to prove that I was really me.

"That signature will be worth a lot of money one day," I told the medic bloke. (His sound track was "Astral Weeks," but actually that might have been the meds talking.) "If I were you, I'd make a copy and save the original. You can sell it and send your kids to college."

"Oh yeah?" he said, with a sweetly goofy grin. "That's cool." Nice kid, he'll probably be the surgeon general in a couple of decades.

A few minutes later, I'd been discharged from his services. I joined Sara and Cody in the shade of a tree near the parking lot. "Hey," I said to Sara.

"Hey," Sara said to me. Then she burst into tears and reached out to grab me.

"Ribs," I said quickly.

"Sorry, right," she said, and released me, reluctantly, sniffling.

"You all right?"

"Yeah. You?"

"I'm grand," I said. "Sorry about arguing."

"Me, too," she said. Pause. "Do you think we're clear of him finally?"

"Definitely," I said. "He's a Tragic Hero now. It's a much better fit for him than Vengeful Victim."

She nodded. "I think that's probably what he wanted all along."

"Good thing I came along to show him how to do it, then. How's Cody?"

"The medic checked her out and said she seems fine, although we should take her to a vet in L.A. for a real checkup. But she's not scratched up or limping or acting strange, her breathing and heart rate are normal." She smiled sheepishly. "She's more resilient than her owner."

"Bet most pets are."

"The medic also said you shouldn't try the climbing trails while you're doped up on the painkillers, but we can still do the Rim Trail if you're up for it," she said. "It's paved and fairly level, not too exciting but great views, I hear."

"Of course I'm up for it," I said. "How often do I get to see the Grand Canyon with the most beautiful bird in the world on my arm?"

I just loved her smile. "While they were tending you, I asked around and there's a place I can put Cody for a couple of hours, so we can just have time for the two of us. You're right, we could really use that."

I widened my eyes at her in mock amazement. "But you don't *trust* kennels."

She smiled sheepishly. "I'm adaptable. Clearly there are some things worse than kennels. This place has been vetted by the Park Service, it's not cheap but it's safe, and as long as you don't think Jonathan would try to—"

"He won't," I assured her. "Pretty confident about that. The Tragic Hero thing will keep him busy for a while."

"So if you want to grab yourself a coffee at the restaurant, I'll drive her over to the kennel—why are you smiling like that?"

What a wonderful woman. "Ah, don't bother," I said, as off-hand as I could manage it. "I suppose she can stay with us."

She looked pleased, but also cautious. "I'm okay with it, Rory," she said. "I wouldn't suggest it if I didn't feel *really* comfortable about it, given how our morning's been."

"I appreciate that," I said. "But . . . now, don't hold me to this, but . . . she's kinda grown on me. I'd feel like I were missing an elbow or something, without her staring at me."

"I thought you found that annoying."

"Well, I do," I said. "But, you know, if she wants to stare at my handsome face that much, who am I to deprive her?" I winked at Sara. "Just don't tell her mom that, or I'll never hear the end of it."

"I never met her mom," said Sara promptly. "I'm just her owner."

"Yeah, right, we'll see how long that lasts," I said, rolling my eyes.

Cody, assuming—as always—that we were talking about her, bumped against my leg, tail wagging, and looked up, trying to give me her Little Match Girl kisses.

"You!" I said, reaching down to grab her by the scruff of her neck and shake her. Her tail wagged harder. "I've got you under my skin, Cody. Don't you be taking advantage, now!"

I tousled her head roughly and released her. She looked happily between Sara and me, head bobbing a little as if she were getting ready to jump up on one of us.

"Let's go, Cody," said Sara, and turned toward the Rim Trail. I took a step to be beside her.

"Hang on," I said. "You're the newbie here. Cody and I are the pros at adventuring. You better walk behind us and let us blaze the trail for you."

She gave me the Princess Diana look, which I hadn't seen in weeks, and which I loved. "You're my favorite adventurer," she said. "I'd follow you anywhere."

"All right, then," I said. "A stroll along the Grand Canyon with my girls." We took hands. Cody pulled ahead on her leash, sniffing excitedly at everything, and then turning round to check in with us in case we'd sniffed it, too. As I said, it's too beautiful to describe that place in words. But Sara's smile was the most beautiful thing there, and her smile was like honey spread over a bit of crunchy, buttered toast, offered with a perfect mug of tea. It was like that every time she smiled. Still is.

In fairness, it wasn't a bad way to end a hectic week, and it's a pretty good way to end a story. Which is good, because I have to end this story now, and finish tuning the fiddle before they call for quiet on the set. Today we wrap principal shooting for the first season. What can I say? It's been amazing. I'm giddy, elated, content all rolled into one. Waiting to hear what happens next.

Sara found us a great little rental off Mulholland. Her temporary gig at the Getty has ended, and she's hanging out with Cody in Coldwater Canyon Park in the gorgeous sunshine, painting her heart out and teaching watercolor classes. It's not the arboretum, but it's pretty sweet all the same.

Cody thinks so, too. Just ask her.

Acknowledgments

For general assistance, advice, guidance, and love, I am joyfully indebted to:

Kathy Cain, for early enthusiasm and the unforgettable reassurance that "the Irish use the word 'fuck' as if it were a comma." My favorite official Irishman, Billy Meleady, without whom this book would not be possible—or necessary! The Gorgeous Group—Kate Feiffer, Laura Roosevelt, Cathy Walthers, Melissa Hackney, and Jamie Stringfellow—for responding at all the right spots in all the right ways, when this was still in utero. Brian Caspe, Eowyn Mader, and my ever-wonderful attorney Marc H. Glick for being my hearty "early readers." My fantastic agent, Liz Darhansoff, and equally fantastic editor, Jennifer Brehl, for their continued faith in me, especially in supporting and standing by as I shifted gears. In an age obsessed with "branding" you have chosen to let me un-brand myself and that's a biggie.

For the "radical hospitality" of providing me a space and opportunity to create during an otherwise very chaotic time,

Hedgebrook Retreat is the nonpareil of writing residencies. If I wrote their name seventeen times here, it would not be enough to express my gratitude. But they are not the only ones who opened a door and provided a desk to work at. For that I must also warmly thank Deb Dobkin & Tim Bernett, Lynne Adams & George Fifield, Dick Davenport & Derry Woodhouse, and Louisa Williams & Chris Brooks. Much of the best work done on this book was done in your guest rooms, porches, and at your kitchen tables.

A shout-out to the "real" Alex Craggs, a British writer who participated in an auction for Authors for Philippines, Red Cross Typhoon Haiyan Appeal . . . and won the right to have a character named after him. (I believe he thought he would get to be a feudal lord; he was a great sport about the change of genre.) Douglas Finn, in exchange for holding my Luddite hand through the terror of computer work, is similarly responsible for naming Dougie Martin.

For individuals generously offering their time and expertise (I take full responsibility for all errors):

"Podunk Plenipotentiary" Mark Judson; my cousin Johannes Jerez Van Osten; Masters of the Industry Chris Parnell at Sony, Steve Breimer, Rich Green, and of course Marc H. Glick again; Mim Douglas, the ethical housecleaner; fight choreographer Scott Barrow; fiddler Jay Ansill; Dr. Michelle Jasny, veterinarian; Cindy Kane and Wayne Ranney, who know the Grand Canyon far better than I do; and Beverly Conklin and Linda Apple at the Boston Museum of Fine Arts.

A special thanks, I suppose, to the USCIS and Department of

Homeland Security for our (relatively mild) matriculation into the immigration process.

And finally, to Anna Yukevich, who innocently prompted my newly minted husband to protest for the first time ever: "She's not my dog, she's my wife's dog." I suspected right away there was a book in that.

About the author

About the book

Insights,
Interviews
& More . . .

Read on

Meet Nicole Galland

Lynne Adams Fifield

NICOLE GALLAND's five previous novels are *The Fool's Tale*; *Revenge of the Rose*; *Crossed*; *I, Iago*; and *Godiva*. She writes a cheeky etiquette column for the *Martha's Vineyard Times*. She is married to actor Billy Meleady and owns Leuco, a dog of splendid qualities.

www.nicolegalland.com
Friend her on Facebook:
  /nicolegalland
Follow her on Twitter:
  @nicolegalland

The Kibbles of Truth Behind *Stepdog*

MY HISTORICAL FICTION is autobiographical in a very private, metaphorical way that only I can see (at least I hope so). *Stepdog* is obviously different. I've never worked at a museum, but I really did marry an Irish actor-friend right after falling in love, because he really did need a green card for a work opportunity. It was my idea—we didn't tell anyone until we had to—we didn't even live together at first and when we did, my dog on the bed really was the first moment of tension between us.

So all of that's true, as are sundry other items. But most of it is fiction, because when you write a novel, you're not only allowed to make things up, you are, in fact, *expected* to. The middle bit is all invented. (For starters, my dog was never kidnapped.)

Then there's the road trip across America, from eastern Massachusetts to Los Angeles. In real life, we took the trip that Rory and Sara (well, mostly Sara) planned but could not execute. One MINI Cooper, two adult humans, one fifty-pound dog, lots of stuff. I did not know then that I would write this book (although I had a feeling it was on its way), but I knew a good research opportunity when I saw it. Billy—bless him!—did almost all of the driving . . . as I sat in the passenger seat, laptop open, staring out the window and touch-typing what I saw, hours on end, for the better part of two weeks. ▶

The Kibbles of Truth Behind *Stepdog*
(*continued*)

"Near Quantico, cascades of wild wisteria over a period of about a mile, riotously, joyously strangling the trees they grow up, distracting us from their destructive powers by being both exotic and dainty at the same time."

"Wild dogwoods here and there in the woods, pretty little exclamation marks in the green calligraphy of the woods."

"Rain sprays up from the pavement, the windshield wipers make a high-toned sigh, like they have coal-miners lung."

"Chattanooga feels like a Berkshire city with its corsets loosened."

The eighty pages of notes are often stream-of-consciousness, sometimes maddeningly vague, sometimes absurdly specific. I went on and on about the degree to which different species of trees had leafed out in which states. I obsessed on the color of the clover on the side of the road, the color of the soil, the color of the pavement, the colors used for traffic-hazard signs in different states. I transcribed evangelical radio shows, diligently tracked the temperature and humidity, marked how the road dividers were spaced and what the license plates of each state looked like. (I also noted, in rather ridiculous detail, *everything* about my dog's behavior in the car.) I did not know how I would ever use this information, but I was sure it would be useful somewhere.

And lo, it came to pass.

—Nicole Galland ᘓ

Rory's Road Trip Playlist

I HAVE A TENDENCY to ascribe songs to people, and I've been asked to do the same for the places on my road trip. So I said I'd give it a little go. Not even pretending this is comprehensive (or proportional), so don't start chucking things at me please. Thanks.

—Rory O'Connor

"America" (Neil Diamond)—Obviously I had to get my arse to America before I could travel across it. This song chokes me up, and in fairness, the man has a unique voice, one of a kind.

"New England" (Jonathan Richman and the Modern Lovers)—The whole region is so small, it can be summed up in one song. This is that song. I always smile and chuckle when I hear it, and I'm always happy to be in this part of the country.

"New York City" (T. Rex)—Bet you thought I was going to say Sinatra or Billy Joel. In Ireland, Marc Bolan's band was *huge*. Died too young, poor fella. He wrote some classics.

"Jersey Girl" (Tom Waits)—My girl is not a Jersey Girl, but she's all I could think about when I was in Jersey.

"Delaware" (Perry Como)—As soon as I hear or read the name, this song pops into my head. And I am a sucker for bad puns. And I remember my aunties and ▶

Rory's Road Trip Playlist *(continued)*

uncles singing and dancing to it when I was growing up in Dublin.

"What's New in Baltimore?" (Frank Zappa)—Perfectly captures my fractured, agitated mood as I was driving through Maryland. No offense, Maryland, it's not your fault I was in the state I was in. So to speak.

"The Lees of Old Virginia" (*1776*)— I was in a production of *1776,* and this song is an earworm. Corny as hell but so very catchy.

"Adagio of Sonata #1 in D Major" (Corelli)—This was Thomas Jefferson's favorite piece, and seeing as how I associate it with Jefferson, and Jefferson with Virginia, this piece = Virginia.

"Tempie Roll Down Your Bangs" (Tommy Jarrell)—Nothing says North Carolina like some kick-ass Appalachian music.

"Oh Carolina" (the Shaggy version)— It's not about the state, but it's great crack!

"The Tennessee Waltz" (The Chieftains featuring Tom Jones)—Lovely song. Plus the lyrics boil down to: "Someone I trusted stole my female companion right out from under my nose." Enough said.

"Chattanooga Choo Choo" (Glenn Miller Orchestra)—You can't *see* the word *Chattanooga* without this song getting stuck in your head.

"Head's in Georgia" (J. J. Cale and Eric Clapton)—Because my head *was* in Georgia while my feet *were* California-bound.

"Georgia on My Mind" (Ray Charles)—It was right there on the "Welcome" sign!

"Alabama" (Neil Young) and "Sweet Home Alabama" (Lynyrd Skynyrd)—Work it out, lads. I'm staying out of it.

"M.i.s.s.i.s.s.i.p.p.i." (Ella Fitzgerald)—How could I pass up a chance to include Ella on a playlist?

"That's How I Got to Memphis" (Tom T. Hall)—That is pretty much exactly how I got to Memphis.

"Arkansas Traveler" (the Pine Tree String Band version)—It's about being in Arkansas, and traveling, and playing the fiddle, and rain bucketing down, so it's a bit of a shoo-in.

"A Little Past Little Rock" (Lee Ann Womack)—She's driving in the wrong direction, but she knows how to describe an unhappy road trip. And what a voice.

"Oklahoma!" (Rodgers & Hammerstein)—I starred in the show, I played Curly.

Rory's Road Trip Playlist *(continued)*

"Pretty Boy Floyd" (Woody Guthrie)— He was the Robin Hood of Oklahoma. I always had a soft spot for rebels.

"Rollin' By" (Lyle Lovett)—If you've ever driven through Texas, you know why this is *the* song about driving through Texas.

"*Breaking Bad* Main Title Theme" (Dave Porter)—This perfectly captures what it feels like to drive through New Mexico.

"Willin' " (Little Feat)—Classic rock song about somebody driving through Arizona. Although, he had drugs, and I didn't.

"Take It Easy" (Eagles)—It's a good song for Arizona. *"Don't let the sound of your own wheels drive you crazy."* Need I say more?

"Home" (Edward Sharpe and the Magnetic Zeroes)—Because it's true, home is wherever I'm with her.

Scan the below QR code to be linked to the *Stepdog* Road Trip playlist on Spotify! ∿

Chicken Tikka Masala Recipe

Rory nicked this recipe from Nicole Cabot.*

Serves 4 hungry adults

Ingredients
2 Tbsp. coconut oil
8 boneless skinless chicken thighs, cut into 1½-inch cubes
1 large yellow onion, diced
1 Tbsp. olive oil
4 cloves garlic, minced
1 Tbsp. fresh ginger, minced
2 Tbsp. Garam Masala
1 tsp. turmeric powder
½ tsp. ground cardamom
1 tsp. cumin
1 Tbsp. sweet paprika
2 tsp. salt
1 tsp. cinnamon
1 tsp. ground black pepper
¼ tsp. cayenne pepper, or to taste
1 small can tomato paste
1½ cups whole milk plain yogurt plus extra ½ cup for garnish
2 bay leaves
1 cup full-fat coconut milk (or cream)
Juice of half a lemon
Chopped cilantro for garnish

Directions:
1. Heat the coconut oil in large cast iron or other heavy skillet until ▶

*Nicole Cabot is a private chef living on Martha's Vineyard, where she also teaches school kids about gardens, farms, and food.

Chicken Tikka Masala Recipe *(continued)*

shimmering. Add chicken in batches to brown. Set aside.

2. Add onion and olive oil to the skillet and cook on low heat 3–4 minutes until softened. Add garlic and ginger. Cook for 1 minute. Add all ground spices and cook 30 seconds on medium heat. Turn off heat.

3. Return chicken to pan. Coat with spices. Add tomato paste and yogurt and coat the chicken. Pour everything into a heavy, covered baking dish or Crock-Pot. Add bay leaves. Cook in a crock pot for 3 hours on low, or in oven at 300°F for 1 hour and 30 minutes. Check that temperature of chicken reaches 165°F.

4. Stir in the coconut milk or cream and lemon juice until warmed through. Adjust salt and pepper to taste. Serve with basmati rice, naan bread, extra yogurt and chopped cilantro. ◝

Have You Read?
More by Nicole Galland

I, IAGO

I, Iago is an ingenious, brilliantly crafted novel that allows one of literature's greatest villains—the deceitful schemer Iago from Shakespeare's immortal tragedy, *Othello*—to take center stage in order to reveal his "true" motivations.

From earliest childhood, the precocious boy called Iago had inconvenient tendencies toward honesty—a failing that made him an embarrassment to his family and an outcast in the corrupt culture of glittering Renaissance Venice. Embracing military life as an antidote to the frippery of Venetian society, Iago won the love of the beautiful Emilia and the regard of Venice's revered General Othello. After years of abuse and rejection, Iago was poised to achieve everything he had ever fought for and dreamed of. . . .

But a cascade of unexpected deceptions propels him on a catastrophic quest for righteous vengeance, contorting his moral compass until he has betrayed his closest friends and family and has sealed his own fate as one of the most notorious villains of all time.

Inspired by William Shakespeare's classic tragedy, *Othello*—a timeless

tale of friendship and treachery, love
and jealousy—Galland's *I, Iago* sheds
fascinating new light on a complex soul,
and on the conditions and fateful events
that helped to create a monster.

GODIVA

Godiva is a crafty retelling of the legend
of Lady Godiva.

According to legend, Lady Godiva
lifted the unfair taxation of her people
by her husband, Leofric, Earl of Mercia,
by riding through the streets of Coventry
wearing only a smile. It's a story that's
kept tongues wagging for nearly a
thousand years. But what would drive
a lady of the court to take off everything
and risk her reputation, her life, even
her wardrobe—all for a few peasants'
pennies?

In this daringly original, charmingly
twisted take on an oft-imagined tale,
Nicole Galland exposes a provocative
view of Godiva not only in the flesh, but
in all her glory. With history exonerating
her dear husband, Godiva, helped along
by her steadfast companion the abbess
Edgiva, defies the tyranny of a new
royal villain. Never before has Countess
Godiva's ride into infamy—and into
an unexpected adventure of romance,
deceit, and naked intrigue—been told
quite like this.

Wales, 1198. A time of treachery, passion, and uncertainty. Maelgwyn ap Cadwallon struggles to protect his small kingdom from foes outside and inside his borders. Pressured into a marriage of political convenience, he weds the headstrong young Isabel Mortimer, niece of his powerful English nemesis. Gwirion, the king's oldest and oddest friend, has a particular reason to hate Mortimer, and immediately employs his royally sanctioned mischief to disquiet the new queen.

Through strength of character, Isabel wins her husband's grudging respect, but finds the Welsh court backward and barbaric—especially Gwirion, against whom she engages in a relentless battle of wills. When Gwirion and Isabel's mutual animosity is abruptly transformed, the king finds himself as threatened by loved ones as he is threatened by the many enemies who menace his crown.

A masterful debut by a gifted storyteller, *The Fool's Tale* combines vivid historical fiction, compelling political intrigue, and passionate romance to create an intimate drama of three individuals bound—and undone—by love and loyalty.

REVENGE OF THE ROSE

An impoverished, idealistic young knight in rural Burgundy, Willem of Dole, greets with astonishment his summons to the court of Konrad, Holy Roman Emperor, whose realm spans half of Europe. Immediately overwhelmed by court affairs, Willem submits to the relentless tutelage of Konrad's minstrel—the mischievous, mysterious Jouglet. With Jouglet's help, Willem quickly rises in the emperor's esteem . . .

. . . But when Willem's sister Lienor becomes a prospect for the role of empress, the sudden elevation of two sibling "nobodies" causes panic in a royal court fueled by gossip, secrets, treachery, and lies. Three desperate men in Konrad's inner circle frantically vie to control the game of politics, yet Jouglet the minstrel is somehow always one step ahead of them.

Astutely reimagining the lush, conniving heart of thirteenth-century Europe's greatest empire, *Revenge of the Rose* is a novel rich in irony and wit that revels in the politics, passions, and peccadilloes of the medieval court.

In the year 1202, thousands of Crusaders gather in Venice, preparing to embark for Jerusalem to free the Holy City from Muslim rule. Among them is an irreverent British vagabond who has literally lost his way, rescued from damnation by a pious German knight. Despite the vagabond's objections, they set sail with dedicated companions and a beautiful, mysterious Arab "princess."

But the divine light guiding this "righteous" campaign soon darkens as the mission sinks ever deeper into disgrace, moral turpitude, and almost farcical catastrophe. As Catholics murder Catholics in the Adriatic port city of Zara, tragic events are set in motion that will ultimately lead to the shocking and shameful fall of Constantinople.

Impeccably researched and beautifully told, Nicole Galland's *Crossed* is a sly tale of the disastrous Fourth Crusade—and of the hopeful, brave, and driven people who were trapped by a corrupt cause and a furious battle that were beyond their comprehension or control.

Discover great authors, exclusive offers, and more at hc.com.